I0757256

Gulchekhra-Begim Makhmudova

FLASK OF CRYSTAL HOOKAH – I

or Sacrament of Treasures of Emir Bukhara

London 2025

Published by Hertfordshire Press Ltd © 2025
e-mail: publisher@hertfordshirepress.com
www.hertfordshirepress.com

FLASK OF CRYSTAL HOOKAH – I
or Sacrament of Treasures of Emir Bukhara

by Gulchekhra–Begim Makhmudova ©

English

Edited by Francesca Mepham
Robert Douglas Sim, Daniel Akhmed
Design by Alexandra Rey

*British Library Catalogue in Publication Data
A catalogue record for this book is available from the British Library
Library of Congress in Publication Data
A catalogue record for this book has been requested*

ISBN: 978-1-913356-90-3

*Dedicated to my parents - Matluba and SaidJalol
who have taught us – their children, grandchildrens
and great-grandchildrens in their lifetime
to show Love and Kindness…*

Dear Reader

I would like to present you with a story that may well have happened to you, your friends or your ancestors.

The Flask of the Crystal Hookah or the Sacrament of the Treasures of Emir Bukhara is an oriental adventure that shows the historical roots underlying the modern situation of Eastern women. It is a clash of good and evil, love and hate, friendship and betrayal, with elements of oriental mysticism and magic overlaid with the profound philosophical sayings of the ancient Sufis.

Through the prism of the Crystal Flask of Hookah and the mist of fruit scent, there are, behind the curtain, fragile female destinies, their faithful love redolent of kindness and self-sacrifice. It is especially important that a wise person expresses this thought, stepping from one century to another and encapsulating the beginning of the third century. That wise person is the last wife of the last Emir of Bukhara.

Many things in these pages may appear to you to be unbelievable or at least not entirely historically accurate. But there is no evidence that these things didn't happen. And that means that it was so - believe it or not...

Gulchekhra-Begim Makhmudova

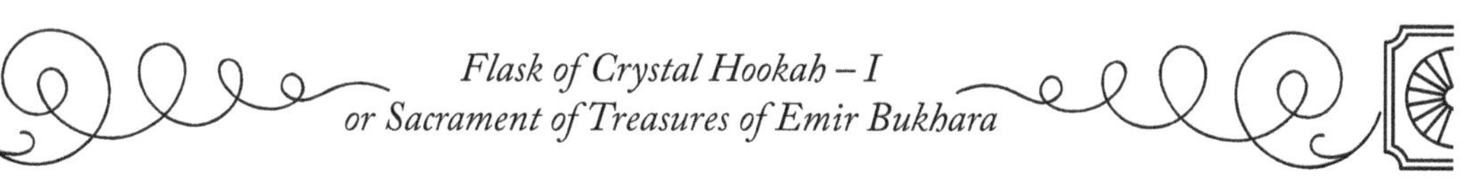

The scent which emanates from older people amazes and excites. Their faces are different, with the wrinkles around their eyes, as they talk about fate and trials. They have a manner of talking that is calm and confident. Their appearance is pleasing and wise.

In Uzbekistan, we say that where older people live, there also is Heaven; and angels live there. The scent that comes from them is thus paradisiacal.

The Holy Quran says that scent is food for the enlightenment of the spirit..

Our soul is astral, filled with scents, and it leads to success and prosperity. It enables self-realization and illuminates the path to perfection and knowledge of the truth.

In the East, scent has always played a leading role in ceremonies. This is the case even in Zoroastrianism, where the deity of Fire and the Sun is worshipped and where fires of fragrant herbs are kindled, creating an atmosphere of freshness and an airy lightness.

All ancient rituals in churches and mosques were accompanied and sanctified by frankincense.

The ancient monetary units at the crossroads of the Great Silk Road were ambergris and musk, expensive saffron and vanilla spices; and today they are the heart of the perfume industry. The ancient monetary units at the crossroads of the Great Silk Road were ambergris and musk, expensive saffron and vanilla spices and today they are the heart of the perfume industry.

Antiquity always keeps its scent. The cities of Bukhara and Samarkand, and the equally splendid cities of Babylon and Athens, are up to the present day fragrant with fabulous scent, saturated with the Power of the Spirit and Romantic Love, the scents of fearless warlords and wise oriental beauties.

The Fabulous East. Uzbekistan and the Sacred Oasis. This is a land where the heroic spirit of Princess Tamiriz still lives. It's the land where ancient Sogdiana and Bactria accepted Alexander the Great. It's the land where the Great Amir Timur, the Conqueror of the World, lived and ruled. Those who followed him are treasured by the great Uzbek land, a Sacred Oasis. They include the famous scientist, Ulugbek, and the ruler of India, Shah Jahan, who built the Miracle of the World, the Taj Mahal, in honour of his beloved Arjuman-Begim. There are many other real and fabulous stories and legends about poets and philosophers.

All the echoes and the spirit of these ancient stories are heard through the fragrant mist of the miraculous Flask of the Crystal Hookah.

The quiet twilight hides the deep wrinkles of a woman whose shining eyes retain their beauty and attractiveness.

A white cambric shawl with lace embroidery covers her head and shoulders. On the table nearby there is an old crystal hookah, over which a fragrant stream of vapour rises with a thin thread.

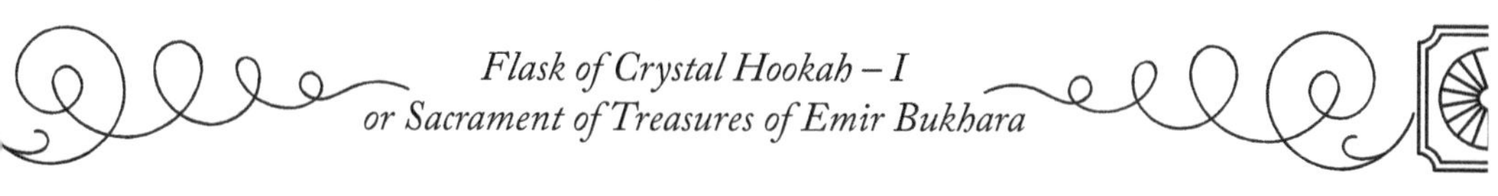

Firuz-begim's eyes are open but her gaze is fixed somewhere in the distance.

On her lap is an album with photographs, her left hand habitually counting her beads. Through the prism of the Crystal Hookah, as each bead falls, her voice quietly chants the poetry of Rudaki:

> *Without evil look at the universe,*
> *With the look of reason, kindness, love.*
> *Life is the sea; and from your good deeds*
> *Build a ship and sail over the waves.*

Despite her advanced years, Firuz-begim can be proud of her memory, and, looking at the photo, she effortlessly recalls the events that she has witnessed.

She loves this, in the evening silence, tucking in her favourite hookah (from which she has never been parted) to sit down more comfortably, take down an album with photos and go back in time with all its worries, difficulties and experiences.

Once again, as if from the outside, to look at her life and at the life of those close to her and once again rejoice with them or feel sad.

Her memory, like beads which hold moments of experience, unfolds before her pictures of a long and - despite everything – happy life.

Shahlo, her beloved granddaughter, happy, in white, leaves the registry office with her husband. They are both bent over the stroller where sits their daughter Sitora, trying to figure out the tricky baby babbles.

Later, trouble happened with her granddaughter, and now she is sitting next to her in the hospital ward, trying to bring this dearest soul back to life.

She felt joy and pride, contrary to all the doctors and their predictions.

Her memories were interrupted by someone's quick steps. A little boy of three years entered the room and went up to Firuz-begim.

"Well, I see that you're awake again. I'll need to complain to mom."

"I do not want to sleep. I want a fairy tale."

"Ah, a fairy tale for you? Who do you want me to tell you about? Again, about the princess?" The boy nodded quickly. "Ah no, come on about the prince - it's a fairy tale which came true. So, believe it or not, once upon a time…"

1

A Bukhara saying goes: "Across the world, Light descends from Heaven and only in Bukhara does Light ascend from the Earth". Truly, a Sacred Oasis.

Bukhoroi-Sharif or Sacred Bukhara. A city as old as Babylon and Athens. It is the city where the great scientist Avicenna or Abu Ali Ibn Sina (980-1037) was born and where Muhammad Al-Bukhari (810-870) and the founder of the Sufi Order, Bahauddin Naqshbandi (1317-1389) also were born, disseminating their philosophical treatises there.

It is the city that inspired the poet and philosopher Omar Khayyam (1076-1092) to write fundamental treatises on mathematics and astronomy, on the basis of which the Ruler of the Timurid power and the great scientist Timur Ulugbek Guragan (1394-1449) created the Starry Sky Catalog – the Gurgan Zij and Gurgan astronomical tables - which were a guide to astronomy in all European observatories.

At the very beginning of the twentieth century, in the ancient city of Bukhara, on one of the shady streets, away from city noise, a small house stands that belongs to Shukhrat, the master, famous throughout Bukhara. It's already evening. He's sitting at the table and sculpting something from clay. His wife approaches and watches with curiosity her husband working, her hands floury from newly preparing the dough for the bread.

"What are you doing?" she asks with interest, looking at her husband's efforts. "A present for Firuz-begim," replies Shuhrat. "It's her birthday tomorrow." "What will it look like?"

"I want to sculpt an animal for her, the like of which she has never seen."

"You'll scare our child! Better make a vase with patterns and she'll beglad."

"No, I won't make it scary. I will definitely make it kind."

At this moment, the door to the room opens slightly and the mischievous face of their daughter Firuz-begim peeps out.

"I've heard everything! You are making a present, and he will be kind!"

"Oh, prankster!" Mom jokingly waved her hand in her direction. "What kind of a gift will it be if you already know everything about it? I will ask your father to do something else."

"No need for anything else!" protested Firuz-begim, entering the room. "I have already forgotten everything about the gift."

"Oh, you're a tricky one," smiled Shuhrat, turning towards his daughter.

Suddenly there was a knock at the door. Shuhrat and his wife looked at each other.

"Who could it be?" Shuhrat went to open the door - and at that moment some people burst into the house. Roughly pushing Shukhrat and his wife aside, they grabbed Firuz-begim and disappeared just as quickly as they had appeared. Shukhrat was still on the floor and his eyes looked madly around the room. His wife was sitting apathetically on the floor and moving her lips, as if saying something. Shuhrat came up to her and tried to lift her off the floor but she did not want to get up.

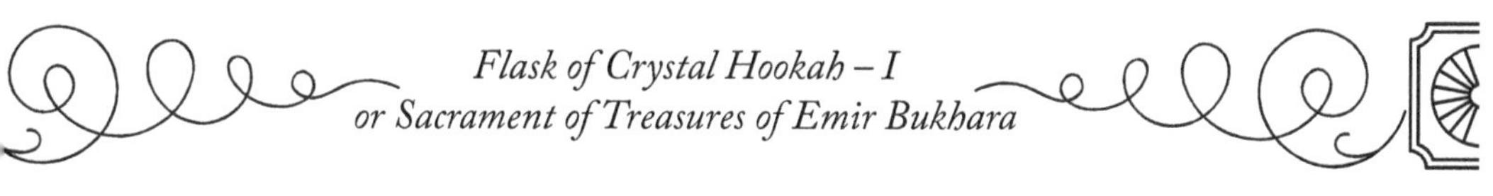

"No, I won't move," she said as she removed Shuhrat's hand, "unless you finish making the present." She passed her hands over his face and white stripes of flour remained on it. "What will I say to our girl? She's standing behind the door, waiting, right?" The woman smiled and looked inquiringly at Shuhrat. "She's a japer - all the time she makes something up."

"She is not there," Shukhrat said with difficulty, not taking his eyes off his smiling wife. He began to realize that the irreparable had happened but did not want to believe it until he had to.

"Of course, she loves hiding," his wife continued in the same steady and calm voice. "Do not scold her when she comes."

"I won't," Shukhrat whispered. He sank to the floor next to his wife, who continued to smile, clasping his head in his hands and groaned in his grief and powerlessness.

2

Several years have passed. Firuz-begim is taking a walk through a magnificent garden, where there are many outlandish flowers that she had never seen before. She is walking from flower to flower and talking to them.

She turned to the rose. "I know you. You are untouchable, you can sting so much that, oh-oh!" Coming up to another flower, she said: "Who are you? How beautiful and grand you are!" She carefully touched the petals with her fingers. "And you even have a tendril!" She leaned over the flower and sniffed it. Her face immediately assumed a disappointed expression: "But you don't smell at all! How pathetic! Why is that? So beautiful - but close your eyes and you can no longer be found. With the other one, when my eyes are closed my nose will lead me to it."

From the window of the garden house, Emir of Bukhara Alimkhan is quietly keeping his eye on Firuz-begim from behind the curtains, with his mother standing next to him.

"Oh, what can I find?" the girl exclaimed, then thoughtfully rubbed her nose with her finger:

"Close your eyes and you'll pass by.

Breathe through your nose – and you'll find a miracle!"

"Come out!" she clapped her hands. Then she closed her eyes and began to follow her nose in different directions, taking one careful step and then another. At first, she opened one eye and then the other and then looked around. "There are too many of you here!"

This scene made Alimkhan smile.

"Well, what did I tell you?" His mother looked inquiringly at him. At this time, one of the older members of the harem ran into the garden.

"Why are you talking to them?" she said whimsically. "To them you need this!" She plucked one flower and stuck it in her ear.

"Oh!" Firuz-begim gasped. "Why did you pick it? It's alive!"

"It was alive and now it's mine," the girl answered defiantly. "Now our lord will choose me!"

Firuz-begim thought for a moment.

"If he did not choose you without a flower, why would he choose a dead flower?" she asked seriously.

"Fool!" the girl shouted. "What do you understand at all?" She angrily grabbed the flower from her ear, threw it to the ground and stamped on it with her foot. "Never mind, we will teach you!" She turned and went into the house.

Alimkhan frowned and said to the eunuch who was standing behind them, "Give this rotter an exemplary penalty and kick her out of the palace. Now let her please the vagrants."

"It will be done, my lord." The eunuch bowed low and backed out of the room.

Firuz-begim ran over and picked up the flower from the ground, straightened it, went to the flowerbed and stuck it into the ground.

"I know that you will no longer grow and will no longer be so beautiful. But perhaps, among friends, it will be easier for you to die. Sorry, I have to go." She rose and went into the house.

3

Alimkhan's mother Eshonoy-begim was remarkable for her rare wit and she was a strong-willed woman who over the years of her residence in the palace had learned all the intricacies of palace life and strictly controlled everything through her servants. Thus, nothing could impede her son in his rule.

She did not intervene directly in government affairs but her advice was helpful. From time to time, Alimkhan consulted her.

Now, sitting with his mother in an open summerhouse in the fragrant garden, he decided to ask her opinion. Taking a ripe peach from the dish, he began to slowly peel it and at the same time spoke in an offhand manner.

"You know, I can't get this girl out of my head."

"Which one?" The woman looked inquiringly at her son, although she immediately understood about whom Alimkhan was talking. "Firuz-begim?"

"Yes. She has something special."

"You're right, my son," she answered after a short pause. "She is quite different from other girls. I have been watching her closely since she got to the palace, and -" She hesitated, thinking something over.

"What?"

"In my opinion, she deserves better than simply being a harem toy."

"Why do you think so?" Alimkhan looked carefully at his mother, as if scrutinising his own thoughts.

"When she sees an expensive thing, she admires not the splendour nor the price but the work of the master who made it - the interweaving of patterns and the accuracy of lines.

She talks to things that she likes, like they are living things, and she does it so seriously and with such faith that sometimes it seems to me that she hears how these things respond to her.

This girl is constantly trying to learn something: composing, drawing or sculpting, and does not lie on pillows like other girls. I tell you - she is special."

"You want to say that she could become my wife?" He looked inquiringly at his mother.

"I will not advise my son to do anything that is bad," she answered her son with a direct look,. "I have seen a lot in my life."

"Who are her parents?

"She is from a well-known but impoverished Seyyid clan."

"Good. I'm not asking how she got to the palace yet." He played with his beard. "Let it be so. I want her to have the best education and upbringing. Hire a governess for her, a Frenchwoman, and let the governess constantly be with Firuz-begim. And we'll see." He got up to leave. "I have to go - affairs are waiting..."

"Find a French governess here in Bukhara?" His mother looked at Alimkhan in surprise.

"You're right," Alimkhan thought. "I'm going to St. Petersburg and I will solve this issue there."

He looked at the unpeeled peach, put it on the dish, wiped his hands with a napkin and left. His mother followed him with her eyes.

4

Through the mist of the Crystal Hookah, the stories of the lives of relatives and friends of Firuz-begim emerge. How difficult it is to put everything into a single string of forever-related inhabitants of Bukhara and any eastern city with ancient roots and fairy tales!

Firuz-begim's life is long, passing from one century to another. At times it is impossible to identify her age in years. And it is impossible to be sure of the reality of the story – whether that's the truth or a fairytale.

Again, through the mist of a crystal hookah, memories arise - or the vision of already tangled imagined sequences of events from the life of Firuz-begim.

At the end of the 1980s in Tashkent, a young graduate student called Shahlo is working on a dissertation on ancient eastern ornamental studies. She is married and has a little daughter, Sitora.

She does the bulk of the work at the Fundamental Library, working with historical materials. Now she is sitting at a table on which there is a large stack of books.

She opens one of the books, finds the page she needs, takes out a pencil and begins to sketch an elaborate ornament on a piece of paper.

A taxi stops in front of the library and a man of about thirty emerges from it. From his appearance, one can see that he is a foreigner.

He pays the driver and goes inside the library. He has already been here once, and now confidently set off in the right direction.

He goes to the front desk, takes out a folded sheet from his inner pocket, unfolds it and fills out the form sheets. Having finished this, he hands the girl the completed forms.

"Please look at these books. I've already ordered them a couple of days ago, so they should be somewhere nearby."

The girl smiled at the visitor, took the forms and ran her eyes over them. "All right, I'll see. Wait a moment, please."

The girl leaves, and Christian sits down and looks around the hall. There are only a few people around.

Everyone is absorbed in reading or writing. One girl catches his attention, in front of her an impressive stack of books on the table.

She also writes something, occasionally leafing through and glancing inside an open book. She has such a look of concentration that Christian smiles involuntarily.

He is distracted from his observations by the female librarian, who arrives at the little table at which he is sitting and hands him a thin book.

"Here you are. Unfortunately, that's all I could find."

Christian is taken aback. He picks up the book, turns it over, and then looks at the girl in bewilderment.

"How is that? Where are the others? I worked with them last time." "I don't know. Probably someone who came before you took them."

"What, all my books? How so? I can't lose a whole day's work just like that! But who took them?"

"I don't know. I've just taken over from my colleague - her child got sick. Go through the hall and look for who has them. Maybe you could persuade them to share.”

“Yes, perhaps. There are no other options anyway. One cannot work with all the books at once. Thanks for the advice.”

Christian again looked around the hall and started to make his way round about it, paying attention only to the big stacks of books. When he came to the table at which Shahlo was sitting, he immediately recognized the top book in the stack. It was with this book that he had worked last time. The girl turned out to be the one whom he had noticed at the very beginning.

“Ah, now we have the - ” He twisted his fingers, searching for the right word, and then said in syllables, “Saboteur. Do you have such a word?”

Shahlo raised her head and looked in surprise at Christian.

“There is such a word but what do I have to do with it?”

“You took all my books,” Christian pointed to the stack on the table. “And I just have this.” He showed Shahlo the thin volume.

“Your books?”

Realizing that he he had spoken in haste, Christian was embarrassed.

“Excuse me, I wanted to say - those books that interest me.”

“Now you want to suggest that I should give them to you and go for a walk, right?”

It was said with such genuine surprise that Christian couldn't help smiling.

“No, no. Of course, not. But perhaps as long as you are working with this one,” - he pointed at the open book - “I could leaf through another one?” Christian jabbed a finger at the stack.

After a moment of thought, Shahlo said, looking cunningly at Christian:

“Well, if you give me your word that you will not leave with this book or will not tear out pages from it -".

Christian immediately pretended to look insulted.

"Do I really look like...," he hesitated, choosing the right word, "A vandal? Why not? If I look like a saboteur, then - " Christian raised his hand in protest.

"Don't be so vindictive - it doesn't suit you. Well, are we in agreement? By the way, my name is Christian, Christian Raboli. I am from France."

"Yes? Very nice. All right, agreed, Monsieur Raboli. Take it."

"Thanks."

Christian carefully removed the bottom book from the stack, sat down at the table and began to leaf through it. Then he looked up at Shahlo.

"You know, this is a little strange."

Shahlo looked up from the book and looked at Christian.

"What, exactly?"

"All this. You."

He pointed to the books.

"Do you want to say that I am incompatible with this? You think a fashion magazine or a romantic novel would suit me better?"

"No, I didn't mean it. It's just a little strange like this, unexpectedly, to find here one..." He hesitated. "No, uni...," he hesitated again, tapped his forehead while muttering "Merde".

Seeing his difficulties, Shahlo decided to tease him.

"Unicorn?"

Christian jokingly shook a finger:

"I know that I have some problems with the language. No, I wanted to say... well, as it is called, when two are one and the same - " He shook his finger at his temple. Shahlo laughed. "Ah, a same-mind person - here it is."

"You wanted to say 'like-minded'?"

"I wanted to say that in the Russian language there are many oddities. So, what connects you with these publications?"

"Well, I'm here because I'm writing a dissertation. That is my topic. What is your interest in these books?"

"You will be surprised. The fashion business and perfume."

"Really? Indeed - a non-standard combination. And what's the connection?"

"I am interested in ancient oriental patterns, ornaments that could be used on fabrics for new models. All this should have the right scent. Here is my assignment from the company. Can't mutual interest arise between us?"

Shahlo raised her eyebrows expressively, showing the ring on her finger. Christian immediately hurried to correct himself.

"Sorry, you are in a hurry with conclusions. Business. Only business." He showed his own ring.

"Well then, if I can help you with something, then I will certainly help. Only, so far, I have no idea what my help could be."

"That's wonderful! We will discuss the details later. But you did not tell me your name. Or should I just call you "girl"?"

"Shahlo. My name is Shahlo."

"Here we are now on an equal footing. Then what about the work?" Shahlo nodded in agreement and each returned to their own book.

Christian is sitting at the desk of his hotel room and looking through the papers that he collected during his stay in Tashkent. Putting aside the last one, he leaned back in his chair and grimaced with displeasure.

"Everything is there, and yet something is missing. But what?" He took the last sheet again, turned it over and put it aside again.

"It's dry, it's cold. The spark is not enough, that's what. And Shahlo does not call." As if in response to his thought, the phone rang. Christian went up to the nightstand where the telephone stood and picked up the phone.

"Hello!"

There was a familiar voice in the receiver.

"Hello, Christian. This is Shahlo."

"Ah, Shahlo. You do not have to introduce yourself - I would still recognize your voice. In addition, I am not popular with women in your city, so I didn't expect anyone else to be calling."

"Don't be shy, Christian. I am calling to let you know that I've finished the work that you asked me to do and I can show you it. When will you be free?"

"I was free from the very moment you called and I can't wait to see what you have done. It seems like I am experiencing a creative blank and I need some fresh ideas. Could you drive up to the hotel now?"

"Drive up, no, but come up, yes. I'm not very far from you, so I can come in about ten minutes."

"Wonderful. I'll go down to the hall to wait for you..."

Shahlo went to the hotel and entered, looking around the hall. From the table at the far end, Christian immediately rose and hurried to meet her.

"Good to see you, Shahlo. You are very welcome. Will we have a seat?" "Hello again, Christian. Of course."

Christian walked Shahlo to the table and waited for her to sit. Then he himself sat down.

Shahlo took the papers from the folder and handed them to Christian.

"That's what you asked, Christian. Alas, I am not an expert in your business, so try not to laugh too loudly."

"Come on, come on - let me have a look!"

He took the pages and began to carefully examine them. One of them held his attention longer and then he looked curiously at Shahlo.

"Interesting. Tell me, Shahlo, where did you get this?" "What, exactly?"

"Here it is." Christian showed her the page that had caught his attention.

"Ah, this one. I wrote it myself. Something came over me. But it's just my fantasy, based on the ancient eastern ornaments of Bactria and Sogdiana, I've recently been working on this period."

"You call this fantasy?"

"Christian, I said that I am not an expert."

"You don't understand, Shahlo. This is a godsend - it can be used - " He stopped, turning something over in his mind. "Well, of course! For the collection of the Lacroix company - and Karl Lagerfeld is working with it. Ah, what a pity..."

"What are you sorry for, Christian?"

"I'm so sorry that I am leaving the day after tomorrow. We could properly work on this idea. But never mind. Tell me, Shahlo, what are you doing now?"

"I am writing a thesis. I've already told you."

"Yes, of course. And then? What are you going to do after you finish?"

"Then? I don't know, I haven't decided yet. This is a very difficult question for me. But why are you asking?"

"But you are not going to spend your whole life in archives and libraries, poking around in papers and admiring what someone once did before you?"

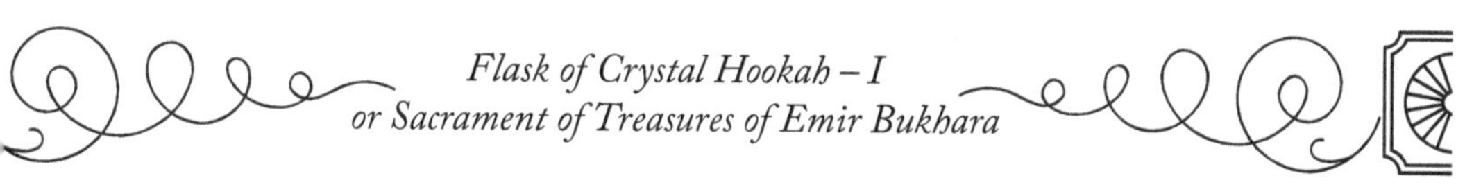

"I agree, the prospect is not the most tempting, but I don't understand what you are driving at."

"I'll try to explain. Why be caught up with strangers if you can create your own work, unlike anything else, and let others admire it. You simply must realize your abilities."

"You're blindsiding me, Christian."

"Oh, sorry," Christian muttered, looked at his feet. "I'm always doing it."

Shahlo smiled.

"No, it was just an expression. I very often ask myself what I want. Where is the most important thing that is mine, for my whole life? I haven't been able to answer these questions up to now. It makes me anxious and affects my wellbeing. I even envy my friend a little, who from childhood knew that she would be a doctor. She became one, and she has no doubts and inconstancy in this regard."

"What you are talking about, Shahlo, is the destiny of extraordinary personalities. You just haven't matured yet. But I want to give you some impetus. What would you say if I offered you the opportunity to co-operate in the field I'm devoted to?"

"Are you kidding, Christian? I don't understand what you mean at all."

"I'm absolutely serious. You don't have to understand anything. You just have to feel it. Believe my intuition."

"I don't know, Christian. You understand that this is a very unexpected proposal. Should I give an answer right now?"

"Not at all. You can come back to this in a month or six months or a year down the line. But -" Christian looked slyly at Shahlo.

"Not at the end of your life."

He took the pamphlet and read:

> *Do not spare your efforts*
> *Until you are very old.*
> *Only on the young branches, after all,*
> *Are there fruits without wormholes.*

"I like it! It's good fortune that it fell into my hands. And here's another:

> *Passes the flow of our days*
> *And only deeds remain.*
> *A flower lives just a short century:*
> *The memory remains...*

To speed up this process, I will call you regularly and - yes, nag you."

"Good, Christian, you may nag. There is only one request."

"What?"

"Not very often, because besides me, there is also my husband, and -"

"You don't need to continue. I get it." He gave the pages back to Shahlo. "Before that, work on your idea if you don't want me to steal it. Honestly - something very, very original may come out of this. Have I persuaded you?"

"Fine, I'll try."

5

Six months have passed. Shahlo has almost forgotten about that conversation with Christian, but, in fact, she is not up to it. She and her husband had decided that it was time to have another baby but this pregnancy had been a real test for her. Everything had somehow gone wrong. Carrying any weight could cause pain or cramps and this plagued her the most. During her last visit to the doctor, she only shook her head in dismay:

"I do not know what to say. In my practice, this is the first case of this kind. I do not think that we have reason to fear for your child, but your condition bothers me. Try to reduce your workload to a minimum and come to see me in a couple of weeks."

"Okay, doctor, I'll try."

Today, she was unwell again. Sitting in a chair, she stroked her round belly.

"What do you dislike, little one? I can't lie or sit 24 hours a day and do nothing. Who will look after your dad and sister?"

Her husband, Kadyr, entered the room, looked at his wife, and his face took on a worried expression.

"The little hooligan is again giving mom no rest?"

"Yes, a little. I am trying to persuade him." She again ran her hand over her belly.

"Let's put him on a cultural programme. What do you think of going to the theatre in the evening? They say that you need to get used to this from the very beginning."

"Let's try. I haven't been inside a theatre for about three hundred years."

"I can't believe it, old woman. You look pretty decent for your age."

"Thanks for the compliment." Shahlo grinned. "I will look at it someday."

"I don't mind. It's just another three hundred years further on."

"By all means. I will make sure I live to that age. But you were going to the sauna with your friends, weren't you?"

"Well, we won't go there till the evening. I'll be back at four o'clock. You and I will have a little lunch and then go to the theatre.

"Good. I agree."

A horn sounded from the street. Kadyr went to the window and pushed the curtain to one side.

"Ah, the guys are here. I'll go and you get ready slowly."

Kadyr kissed Shahlo on the cheek and hurried down to his friends.

Shahlo looked into the room where her daughter Sitora was busy with toys. She saw her mom and jumped to her feet.

"Mom, let's play! I've thought of a great game! You'll be my daughter and I'll be your mother and I will teach you how to cook pies. Would you like to play?"

"No, mommy." Shahlo smiled. "Your daughter will now go to the kitchen and will cook dinner herself and then you will come, try it, and tell me whether I cooked it correctly or not. All right?"

"All right," Sitora said in a businesslike manner. "I will come and check soon."

"I will wait," Shahlo answered, smiled at her daughter again, and went into the kitchen to cook dinner.

An unpleasant sensation inside her did not pass but she decided not to give in to the temptation to lie down for a short while and wait out another attack.

It was also necessary to prepare for a trip to the theatre and this was more difficult than to cook something.

Having put the food to be cooked in a pan, she took the cheese from a bag that Kadyr had left in the kitchen, found a knife and tried to cut it in half with one hand. But, she did not succeed. Then she took the knife in both hands and leaned on it. Such an effort turned out to be excessive for her, and she felt something tear inside her. She clutched at her stomach with her hand and sank into a chair. Her head was spinning and something sticky flowed down her leg. She put her hand there and looked. It was blood. Sitora came running at the sound of the knife falling and saw that her mother had blood all across her hand. She stared at her mother in dismay.

"Mom, did you cut yourself?"

"No, daughter. Something is not good with me. Can you make a phone call?"

"Of course, I can. But to whom?"

"Dial 03 and tell the ambulance to come. Say mom is bad. Do it quickly." Sitora ran out of the kitchen and ran to the phone. Picking it up, she dialed the number. On the other end of the line, they picked up the phone.

"Ambulance."

"Come quickly, mom is bad."

"What happened to your mom?"

"She is sick, she has blood on her hand."

"Girl, if your mother cut herself, let her bandage her hand, or let her answer the phone herself."

"She cannot, she is ill, and dad has not yet come home. Come, please."

"Where do you live?"

Sitora told the address. The attendant wrote it down, asked for their phone number, and then said:

"Well, tell your mom that the ambulance is leaving. Wait."

The call ended. Sitora laid it back down and ran into the kitchen. Shahlo was pale, sitting with her hands pressed to her stomach and being afraid to move.

"Called?"

"Yes, mommy. They said - wait."

"Good - good girl. Bring me a towel and call Aunt Lola. Let her come to us. Can you?"

"I can."

She quickly brought Shahlo a towel and again ran to call.

6

At the same time, Kadyr and his friends were leaving the steam room. All were red, hot and sweaty but their faces expressed pleasure. They sat at the table. Kadyr took a bottle with a beautiful label from a bag standing near the wall and put it on the table.

"All right! The excess fat was lost and it is time to compensate for the loss," he said, rubbing his palms together. "As the song says: 'And a snack on a tubercle.'"

Utkur supported him, a short bald man with a moustache.

"We can hold out with such a snack until morning."

Kadyr's second friend, a healthy-looking man called Hamza, did not object.

"Well, and we will. We have nowhere to get to and the wives are in the know. Let them get bored without us."

Kadyr immediately objected to his friend's words:

"Ah, no, you'll have to continue here without me. We have a cultural event planned for today."

Utkur made a surprised face.

"And isn't this a cultural event too?"

Kadyr grinned.

"Here - cultural and recreational. There - cultural and family. Do you see the difference?" He opened the bottle and poured it into separate glasses. Utkur lifted his glass and looked through it.

"Not yet. But soon, it seems, I will feel it."

Hamza decided to speed up the process and raised his glass.

"Why are you making a toast with the first glass?"

Utkur immediately responded: "Kadyr has been promoted and we should toast this."

However, Kadyr did not like this statement. "No, we'll drink the second one for that. But the first is for the addition to my family."

"No objections!"

Everyone drank.

"When will you become a dad for the second time?"

"We plan to do it in four months."

"Will we arrange a party to wet the baby's head?" Hamza asked.

"You're asking?" Kadyr answered. "A big one!"

"In my opinion, this should be planned." Utkur poured out the next glasses and looked inquiringly at his friends.

"And the promotion?" Hamza intervened again.

"Ah, yes, I almost forgot. We need to make a list, otherwise we'll get lost."

"No lists." Kadyr looked at the clock next to him. "I have a maximum of an hour and then I disappear."

"We will succeed. So - to the light of journalism!"

Everyone clinked their glasses together, drank and busily began to look for a suitable snack.

After the sauna, Kadyr, pleased with the meeting he had had with his friends, drove home. Although he did not particularly like the theatre, he was ready to make a small sacrifice for his wife. At the same moment, Lola, one of Shahlo's closest friends, was already at their place. She escorted the ambulance, reassured the weeping Sitora and went outside to wait for Kadyr.

Kadyr got out of the taxi and went to the house. He saw Lola and waved his hand. "Hi! Why are you outside? Come on, let's go in, Shahlo will be glad."

"Kadyr." Lola pressed her hands to her chest. "Please don't worry but Shahlo was taken away."

"What do you mean taken away? Where to?"

"To the hospital. She became ill. Sitora called me and I rushed here. The ambulance left here about ten minutes ago. I have been waiting for you."

"Then why are we standing here? Let's move!" "And Sitora? Shall we take her to Firuz-begim?"

"No time! We'll take her with us. I'll get the car and you dress her. Only be quick! Ah, damn it! I'm drunk! We'll get there by taxi." He looked quickly around. The taxi in which he had arrived had not yet managed to leave. The driver had got out of the car and was wiping the windshield. "Come on, Lola, come on!"

An ambulance rushes along the street with the siren blaring, driving up to the door of the emergency department of the Central Hospital. Shahlo is carried out of the car and quickly taken to the operating room. She is unconscious. Doctors and staff scurry around her. The doctor who is trying to help Shahlo shakes his head resolutely.

"We can't stop the bleeding. We'll have to operate."

The assistant asked uncertainly, "What about the baby?"

"It's her or the child. Do you have a third option? I can't see one. Clamp here. How's the pressure?"

"It's falling, doctor," said the nurse who was monitoring the pressure. "The pulse is weak."

"Injection, quickly!"

When the operation was over, the doctor moved away from the

table, pulling his mask off his face.

"Seems we were just in time. A little longer and it could have been a different story. Please take her to the ward." He nodded to the assistant. "Watch her condition. Any change - call me immediately." He took off his rubber gloves and left the operating room. Seeing the doctor, Kadyr rushed to him.

"Doctor, how is she? Will she be all right?"

"I hope so. She lost a lot of blood - we just made it in time. Now we just have to wait. She has a healthy heart and that's good."

"She was pregnant, you know?"

"Yes, she was I'm sorry."

"Wait, what does that mean ? Sorry? Kadyr looked at the doctor in dismay. "You mean to say that ..."

"I mean to say that we had no choice. She could have died, along with the child. We did everything we could to save her. Sorry - I have to go."

He went down the hall. Kadyr called to him.

"Can I see her?"

"Later, she's still anesthetized. I'll let you know..."

Shahlo is lying on the bed in the ward - she has not yet regained consciousness. A nurse who is on duty beside her, noticing her hand stir, runs for the doctor to report it. She gently knocks on the study door, opens the door and looks inside. The doctor is sitting at the table, writing. Hearing the knock and the door opening, he looks up from his papers:

"Well? What is it?"

The nurse enters the office.

"It looks like she is coming round. Can take a look at her?"

"Is she definitely coming round?"

"Yes."

"In that case, I'll definitely have a look at her. Let's go."

They entered the room where Shahlo was lying. Her eyes were open and she was trying to say something. The doctor went to the bed and leaned over her.

"Can you hear me?"

"Yes ..."

"How do you feel?"

"As in a daze ... Everything is floating ..."

"This is because of anaesthesia, it will pass."

"What ... happened to me?"

"You cannot talk much - you are still very weak. Regain a bit more of your strength and then I will answer all your questions. All right?"

"No. Why the blood?"

"You must not worry either. Obey my advice. The most important thing is that you are alive and everything else can follow on afterwards. Now you need to gain strength - get stronger."

"No ... I don't know ... Was there an operation?"

"Don't worry about all that. Don't think about it." The doctor felt her pulse and turned to her sister. "She needs to calm down - give her an injection."

"The child ..." Shahlo whispered.

"What?" Again the doctor leaned towards her.

"My child ..."

The doctor short-temperedly asked the nurse:

"Why are you messing about?"

"It's ... not?" Shahlo whispered again.

"I told you - you should not worry. Now we will give you an injection and you will sleep a little."

Shahlo stiffened and tried to rise.

"He is not there?"

"Lie down. Don't get up - you are not allowed."

He spoke vehemently to the nurse:

"Do it quick, her pulse is off the scale."

Shahlo closed her eyes, lay back on the pillow and fell silent.

"What did you inject her with?"

"A sedative.". Fearful, the nurse stammered, "As you said."

"It wouldn't work that fast..." He felt the pulse again and then lifted Shahlo's eyelid. "Oh hell..."

"What's happened, doctor?"

"Seems to be a coma... Damn!" He struck his knee hard. "Ask Professor Khashimov to come here."

The nurse ran out of the ward. Kadyr, who was sitting in the corridor, looked fearfully after her, then rushed to the door of the ward. He opened the door but the doctor blocked his path.

"I'm afraid it's better for you to stay outside right now. I told you that I would call for you when I could. Please don't stand in the doorway - let the professor in."

Kadyr took a step back, not taking his eyes off the bed on which Shahlo was lying motionless. Professor Khashimov entered the room and closed the door.

7

Extremely alarmed and not knowing what to do now, Kadyr went to a tearful Lola.

"Maybe you could explain something to me? You are a doctor too, aren't you?"

"I don't know." Lola shook her head, wiping her eyes. "I have heard about Professor Khashimov. He is a first-class specialist. He will figure everything out ..."

"He might figure it out, but what about me? What should I think? Or am I not supposed to know what is going on with my wife?"

"Kadyr, do not shout at me, please! I know no more or less than you. I am worried about Shahlo."

"Sorry, Lola, I'm just nervous. Listen, talk to the professor. He will not talk to me but he will to you. Please?"

"Okay, I will try."

When the professor left the Shahlo's ward and went down the corridor, Lola rushed after him.

"Excuse me, professor, can I talk to you?"

"About what?

"You just visited my friend ..."

"I see. Let's go to my room." They went upstairs and entered the professor's room. "Have a seat. I'm listening."

"Shahlo is my closest friend - we have been friends since childhood. What's wrong with her? The doctor wasn't letting anyone into her room and then they called you. I am scared. Her husband is really distraught."

"You're asking what's wrong with her." He took off his glasses, took a handkerchief from his pocket and wiped them.

"What is your area of work?"

"I'm a medic. An obstetrician."

"A medic. I see . Then you should be familiar with the word "coma"." "Ah!" A frightened Lola looked at the professor.

"There you have it, indeed. Ah." He massaged his tired eyes. "Of course, this is not the end. The brain is working, the organs are functioning, but -" He spread his palms: "Consciousness is turned off. Why am I telling you this. You have learned about it."

"Yes. Will this persist for a lengthy period?"

"Good question. A week, a month, a year - or tomorrow. Are you happy with this answer?"

"Sorry. I understand. There's nothing that can be done?"

"The body has turned on its defence mechanism. Do you know how to disable it?"

"No, professor, I don't know."

"That's a pity, my colleague. You could win the Nobel Prize. I don't know either. All I can advise is to be patient and wait. Someone from among those closest to her should be with her all the time. You must talk to her as if she hears you. You must try to reach out to her consciousness, so that there will be an impetus from within to find a way out of this crisis. I have no other solutions."

"Will that help?"

"I do not know. Patience and hope are all I can say."

"Yes, of course, I understand." Thank you. Sorry for disturbing you -" She suddenly burst into tears.

"But this is no good." He got up from the table, went to Lola and held her shoulders. "I'm not sure where it says that a doctor should cry."

"Sorry, but she's my friend –"

"It's good that she has a friend like you. You can help her but not with tears. This tool will not work here."

"I will help. I will certainly help."

"So we are in agreement. Explain everything to her family as a doctor."

"I'll do everything. Thank you."

Lola said goodbye and left the office. Kadyr was sitting in the corridor, clasping his head in his hands.

8

Zarina, another close friend of Shahlo's, lives with her husband, Alibek, in Moscow, where he has an internship in Dubna. They have a little son, Sherzod. Today is a day off and therefore Alibek is at home with his family. While he's shaving in the bathroom, Zarina is feeding the child. One more time, she brings the spoon up to Sherzod's mouth:

"One more so that you'll be as big as your dad."

The child obediently opens his mouth. At that moment, the telephone rings. By the frequency of the rings, one can guess that the call is a long-distance one.

The boy also turns his head towards the ringing phone. Zarina puts a spoon on the saucer and puts it away so that Sherzod, as usual, can't get hold of it.

"Someone is calling us, somebody far away. Sit, like a good boy. Now mommy will talk and then we'll eat again, right?"

She answers the phone:

"Hello?"

There is a familiar voice in the receiver. It is Lola.

"Zarina? It's so good that I caught you!"

"Oh hello! How are you? Is everything all right at home?"

"Nothing is all right! We are in trouble!" Lola sobs. "Shahlo ..."

"What - Shahlo? What's wrong with her? Tell me..."

"Shahlo's at the hospital. In a coma."

"What?"

Alibek came out of the bathroom and looked at his wife in surprise.

"How did that happen?"

"A sudden problem - bleeding. She has lost her child. Can you come?"

"Oh my God, that's awful! Come? Yes, of course I can! I'll get on the next flight! Don't leave her - you're a doctor!"

"I'll be by her side. Please come."

"Yes, yes, don't worry. Kisses."

She hung up and sat down on a chair. Alibek came up.

"Has something happened at home?"

"Shahlo's in trouble. I need to fly to Tashkent."

"Of course, of course, dear," Alibek fussed. "I'll take care of the ticket right now!"

It sounded a little false, but Zarina did not notice it.

"What bad luck! She wanted this baby so much." She went up to Sherzod. "Let's eat, little one, and then sleep. Mom needs to get ready."

"Maybe we should bring her to Moscow? To see a doctor? I can arrange it."

"Where would we take her? She's in a coma."

"Yes, indeed. Poor Shahlo." Alibek went up to the telephone and dialed a number. "Hello? I need a ticket to Tashkent for the next flight. Tomorrow morning?" He looked inquiringly at Zarina, who nodded. "Good. Can I give you the details?"

Three weeks have passed but nothing has changed in Shahlo's condition. She is still in a coma. The doctors haven't said anything definite but simply advise her family to be patient. Her relatives take turns to be with her. Today, her grandmother, Firuz-begim, sits near her bed. She is the only one who unflinchingly believes that her granddaughter will cope with her illness and return to her former life. She tries to convey the power of her conviction to Shahlo by talking to her. Now she is once again trying to awaken the consciousness of her beloved granddaughter.

"I know you hear me. The doctors say it's useless to talk to you while you are in this condition. What do they understand? What do they know about you?"

As if through a dark curtain, separate memories break into Shahlo's mind ...

Three girls, Shahlo, Lola and Zarina are playing together in the yard. They're sitting around a low table on which dolls, all sorts of rags, children's doll accessories and a doll are laid out. Lola has a toy stethoscope around her neck and she's listening to the doll's chest. Then she takes a toy syringe and tries to give the doll an injection. Zarina looks at her in surprise.

"Is your doll sick?"

"She's got a sore throat from ice-cream. If you have a sore throat, I will give you an injection. Do you want that? And when I grow up, I will treat you all."

Zarina immediately grabs her bottom and takes a step back.

"Nothing hurts me. You think of everything but dolls don't eat ice cream. Here, look - I made a cake." She shows them some sand moulded into a solid pile. "Let her eat it."

"She can't, her tummy hurts." Shahlo gasped.

"If she has a tummy ache, then she will soon have a baby."

"What nonsense are you saying?!" Lola indignantly objected.

"It's not nonsense. My mother also had a tummy ache, and then I appeared."

During the conversation, she had been shredding the bottom of her doll's dress with a pair of small scissors. After the last sentence, she put down the scissors, brought the doll to her nose and took a sniff. Zarina stared at her in surprise.

"Why are you sniffing at her?"

"All girls should smell good. My grandmother has such perfumes - " she didn't finish as grandmother's voice was heard.

"Girls, come and eat. Samsa is ready. Quickly - wash your hands."

The girls looked at each other, threw down their toys and rushed to the tap to wash their hands.

"...Only I know what kind of person you are," continued Firuz-begim. "You are strong and stubborn. You may not be able to see where you're going but you'll still go on, stumbling and falling. That's your temperament. You haven't reached it yet. Can you hear me?"

Through the fragmentary memories the angry voice of her grandmother breaks through to Shahlo.

...Shahlo and Zarina are sitting at a table in an outdoor cafe, eating cakes. Lola comes up to their table in a hurry. She is noticeably pregnant.

"You're always late," Zarina scolded her. "Do you have longer lectures than the rest?"

"Sorry, girls, I had to consult a professor. Are you demolishing the desserts again? Be careful - you will get fat and even I won't be able to help you."

"Oh, look! What a luminary of medicine that has arisen in our country! By the way, these" (pointing at the cakes) "were made by me. You can evaluate it from a medical point of view. Although no, you're already fat," she added sarcastically. "Does your tummy hurt?"

"No, it doesn't hurt." She reached out to the plate with the cakes. "Give it to me, you're very greedy." She took one of the cakes, ate some of it and rolled her eyes. "Yes – you're giving in to temptation. Here, medicine is powerless."

Taking another bite, she looked at Shahlo.

"You're kind of pale today. When was the last time you were examined?"

"Here we go, Shahina, run away!" Zarina came to the rescue of her friend. "Now our Lola will prescribe a set of injections for you and an enema for a natural complexion."

"That won't work," Shahlo responded calmly. "I'm impervious to those comments." She took another cake and said, "We'd better think about what name we'll give to the firstborn."

"Come on, girls," Lola said, embarrassed. "You're chattering too much."

"You'll continue to show everyone how strong you are." Firuz-begim took Shahlo's lifeless hand. "Don't dare to pretend that you don't care and you don't need us any more, you silly girl!"

Tears flowed down the grandmother's cheeks.

Grandma is busy in the kitchen. With a doll in her hands, Shahlo enters her grandmother's room and looks at the perfume flask on the table for a long time. She looks at the door, goes to the table, takes the flask, opens it and sprinkles some of then contents on the doll. Then, after a little thought, she looks at the bottle, checks how much is left and sprinkles some on herself. Almost nothing remains in the flask. At that moment, grandmother enters.

"There you are – I've been looking for you everywhere!" She

sniffs. "What's that smell?"

She notices the flask that, with no time to return it to the table, Shahlo's still holding, picks it up and looks at the tiny amount of liquid that's left at the bottom of the container.

"What have you done? Your grandfather gave me this perfume! I treasure it and you poured it all over your doll?" She's almost crying with anger. "That's it! You deserve a punishment! I won't bake your beloved samsa again!"

She put the flask on the table and left quickly, shaking her head. Shahlo bowed her head and walked slowly into the yard. There she sat down on a high chair and watched sorrowfully as her grandmother pottered around the table, muttering to herself. When her grandmother sat down and seemed to be thinking, Shahlo carefully approached her.

"Granny - ", she said softly, but the old woman just waved her hand. Shahlo came closer, took her grandmother's hand and spoke quickly so that the old lady couldn't interrupt her. "Granny - please don't be angry with me. I didn't know. I'm still little. But when I grow up soon, I will give you a lot of perfume!"

"How much is that?" Firuz-begim made an angry face, but there was already warmth in her eyes.

"A whole box!" Then she inclined her head thoughtfully. "No, a whole carful - a whole car!"

"And a little cart?" smiled the elderly woman, in whom these arguments drove away the last vestiges of resentment.

Shahlo, as if imagining how much it would be including the cart, adjusted the scarf on her head.

"Yes - and a cart too. Will you bake samsa?"

"Of course, my dear."

Firuz-begim wiped away her tears and continued to speak.

"I will never bake your beloved samsa for you any more - "

She remembered how, once, little Shahlo, after the episode with the perfume, had approached her with a guilty look and had taken her hand. At that moment, she felt Shahlo's finger tremble slightly in her hand. Startled, her attention switched abruptly back to the present. She found herself calling for help, at first quietly and then with her voice rising to a shout:

"Doctor! Doctor! In here!"

"What's happening? Are you okay?"

"Doctor, I felt - "

"What did you feel?"

"Her finger moved! She's coming round!"

The doctor examined Shahlo carefully, checking the monitors, and looked at at the tearful grandmother.

"I'm sorry but you are very tired. You've been sitting beside her for a second night. I am very sorry but it looks like it's just been your mind playing tricks. You see, the devices don't show any change - they don't lie."

"I may be old but I haven't gone out of my mind yet. I don't care about your "devices". What can they feel? Warmth? Soul? Pain? Nothing. They're just blinking and ticking - "

"Alright, alright, calm down. Let me check her again."

He took Shahlo's hand and began to check her pulse simply in order to placate the grandmother, looked at the appliances standing by the bed, and shrugged, barely noticeably. Then he reached out to lift Shahlo's eyelid and stood with his hand extended because the eyelid trembled, very slightly. He shook his head and looked dumb-founded at the grandmother. She excitedly grabbed his hands.

"Did you see something? Did you?"

The doctor, without saying a word, only nodded his head and

then started walking around the room, nervously flexing his hands and glancing at Shahlo. Then he quickly left the room.

"Well, that's good, my girl," said Firuz-begim, not hiding her tears. With her eyes fixed on Shahlo's face, she began to stroke the latter's hand. "Enough sleep. You have so many things to accomplish."

Shahlo's eyelids fluttered again and then her eyes opened very slowly.

"Samsa -" she whispered, barely audible.

Grandma leaned close to her lips.

"What? Repeat, baby - you know that I'm old and deaf."

"I want samsa ..."

"You will, you will have your samsa! I'll bake you a whole wagonload of samsa!"

A faint smile appeared on Shahlo's lips, and she whispered again:

"And a small cart..."

"And the cart too, you are my smart girl!"

Those close to her who were in the hospital on that day squeeze into the room with the doctor, and Shahlo looks around at them.

A month has passed. Shahlo is slowly but surely recovering. Strength and mental stability return to her, although she is not able to forget about the loss of a child. Lola and Zarina, who had come from Moscow, often come to see her, sit with her and try to encourage her in every way so that she does not feel lonely.

Today, they had decided that they should visit again and cheer up their friend.

Lola enters the hospital, walks along the corridor, greets the nurses and walks into Shahlo's ward. Shahlo is lying on the bed with her eyes closed. The door opens cautiously and Lola looks into the room. Shahlo opens her eyes.

"Don't be shy. Come in."

"I thought you were sleeping."

"All I do is sleep. I am tired of it. Tired of lying here."

"Of course, tired, but it's necessary. It's too soon for you to get up. First, you need to get stronger. You lost so much blood walking in the clouds."

"I didn't just lose blood. And I didn't really like the clouds."

"I beg you not to talk about it, okay? You mustn't worry, you know." "Okay, I won't. Have you been working?"

"Yes. I changed and came straight to you."

"You shouldn't tire yourself out. You could have had a rest and then come. It's not like I'm going anywhere."

"I still have time to relax after. Aziz helps me a lot. Have you already taken your medicine?"

"Not yet - it's really unpleasant. It's a real effort every time."

"Anyway, it doesn't matter whether it's unpleasant or not. Make one more effort." She poured medicine into a spoon and brought it up to Shahlo's mouth. "Come on, take it."

At that moment, the door opened and Zarina flew into the room with a bag in her hands.

"Again you're forcing something into her! I don't suppose you would take that kind of thing. But poisoning a poor girl – no problem. Look what they've brought her to: thin, pale, barely able to speak." She came up to Shahlo and kissed her. "Forget this poison. I brought you this - you'll lick your fingers."

"That's what a general specialist means," smiled Shahlo. "One medicine for all occasions. Desserts."

"The doctor will see what you're up to! He won't let you into the ward!" Lola was indignant. "You'll break her entire regime."

"He'll let me in - he'll beg me to come more often."

"Exactly. Don't you know her? She'll get him so hooked on her baking that he'll cry when I leave. The culinary sadist. By the way, one piece of advice. Change your perfume."

"Well, that's it," Zarina spread her hands. "She's started to lecture me so that means things are getting better. A real sign. Why should I change it?"

"Indeed," Lola supported her friend. "A very good smell. I like it."

"It's a little harsh for you. You're a sweet woman. Your style is oriental and your scent is vanilla, ambergris, musk. As soon as I get out of here, I'll choose something a bit more exotic for you. After all, in the Koran it is written: "Scent is food, awakening the soul." Verstehen? Understand?"

Lola froze in amazement. Zarina spread her hands in dismay. She was scared. Lately, Shahlo had begun to speak in different foreign languages, not just her native Uzbek and Russian.

Shahlo understood that an extraordinary thing was happening to her and she hugged her friends tightly.

"Girls, it seems to me that we are the best and what a blessing that I have you, honestly."

"Yeah, you're very lucky to have us. Isn't that the case, Lola?"

The friends laughed carelessly and cheerfully.

9

After the departure of Zarina to Tashkent, her husband Alibek began to live a man's life, free from responsibility, and, since he was a great lover, he missed no opportunity to meet someone.

It wasn't that he didn't like Zarina but she had become a familiar and everyday part of his life, and this pushed him towards seeking adventure.

As always, he came to the park before work, put a bag with some cookies next to him, took an abstract from the folder and began to leaf through it, from time to time taking cookies out of the bag and putting them in his mouth.

A dog barking distracted him from this activity. He looked up and saw a girl walking along the path, and next to her a little dog was revolving, barking and begging for something.

"Leave me alone, I said! I have nothing!" She took a few steps, but the little dog ran forward again and began to yelp. "Go away!"

She came up to the bench on which Alibek was sitting. At that moment, the dog tried to grab her heel. "O-oh, what are you doing?" She quickly sat on the bench and raised her legs. "Why are you attaching yourself to me? Where is your owner?"

"Either dogs love you," Alibek began the conversation, "or you smell like meat."

"I don't know how I smell, but I can't get past it. It even tried to bite by my heel."

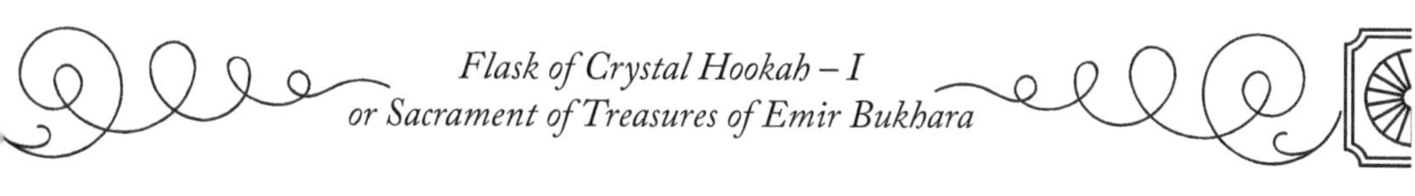

"How long can you sit with your legs up?"

"I don't know - as long as I can."

"You have to be saved from this monster, otherwise I will take you a half a day to unbend yourself again. Hey, you, monster! Come on, come here!" He tapped the package. The dog looked at him, went to his feet and barked.

"Could you say "please". Okay." He took a cookie out of the bag. "Take it and go away as far as you can." He handed the cookie to the dog. The latter grabbed it and sped off. "The dog's taken it to its owner, who probably has nothing to eat. That's all - you can lower your unbitten legs."

"Thank God, they were already starting to go numb."

"Take it." Alibek handed the bag to the girl. "Just don't run away as fast as it's done."

"I won't." She took the cookies. "Oh, almond. My favorite. What if it comes back?" The girl looked in the direction of where the dog had run away.

"So not to have feed it the rest, I propose to disappear from here as quickly as possible. What's your name?"

"Marina."

"Great. If you are in no hurry, I suggest taking a walk. You will have the opportunity to walk with your favourite cookies, and I will drive away dogs, cats and other animals from you, which must be a bonus for you. Do you like the plan?"

"Not for very long. I only have an hour of free time - I still need to go to the library."

"Well, great! You will be surprised, but I also need to go to the library. To return this," pointing to the abstract, "and take some rubbish instead of sleeping pills."

"Let's go."

10

A year has passed. Shahlo returns to work on her dissertation, but she gets no satisfaction from it.

While she was in the hospital, she had thought a lot about what Christian had told her before leaving, and was more and more inclined to think that she should try her hand in a new field. Moreover, from time to time he reminded her about himself and insisted on his proposal.

She decided to call Christian, but first to talk about it with her husband. She did not want to cause unnecessary tension in their relationship, especially since recently Kadyr had somehow begun to drift apart from her.

Shahlo entered the study where Kadyr was working on another article, walked up behind him and put her arms around his shoulders.

"Are you writing a new article?"

"Yes. Our archaeologists dug up something and no one can understand what it is and where it came from."

"Maybe aliens left it?"

"That would be quite nice. Can you imagine what a sensation that would be?"

"I can imagine. You're very lucky indeed."

"If only it was not another canard. Why aren't you going

to sleep?" "For some reason, I don't want to. My head is full of thoughts."

"What kind of thoughts do we have?"

"Somehow I feel insecure. Look at you. You do your favorite thing, everything works out for you, and your soul is calm. And me?"

"And you?"

"What am I doing? What do I spend my life on?"

"Why do you say that? You have a family, a house. You're writing a thesis. What is there that is bad?"

"Well, suppose I finish writing my thesis – what then?" "Then, if there is time and you want it enough, you'll write a PhD."

"Let's say I spend a few more years and become a doctor of philosophy. So what? What is the use of that? For me, you and the rest?"

"You are turning into a heretic. I will be very happy to say: my wife is a doctor of art history. Doesn't that sound great?"

"You are pleased, but what about me? What should I spend my life doing? Just so you can boast about your doctor wife? I can't do this - it's not for me."

"I don't understand you." Kadyr became a little annoyed. "Until now, you liked your work, and you never complained. Everything worked out for you, and suddenly such a change of mood - you don't want to do this. Then what do you want?"

"I don't know. I don't know - but not this. I want to try something else. I also thought a lot about this in the hospital. Before leaving, Christian offered me cooperation, and I keep thinking about this."

"Ah! So this is who is stirring up trouble," Kadyr said venomously. "Our Parisian friend."

"Come on! You're not really jealous, are you?"

"Oh, if there's a reason. What does he offer? Why on earth is he interfering in your life?"

"He has nothing to do with it. I had these doubts long before I met him. He suggests that I should test myself in the development of models and design."

"Are you going to turn into a dressmaker?" Kadyr did not miss the chance to make a cutting comment. "That is still not enough! Tailor Doctor!"

"Don't simplify it! What does being a dressmaker have to do with it? It is about independent creativity - but I feel that I can do it. Is it bad?"

"Whether it's bad or not bad, I don't like this initiative. Impulsive actions like these will only land us in trouble." Kadyr did not try to hide his irritation. "You want to drop everything that you've achieved because of some nonsense?"

"What have I achieved?" Shahlo asked in a tired voice. "Can I, like you, be proud of something?"

"It's very difficult to argue with you as you only listen to yourself. So what did you decide to do?"

"I want to call him and make a deal. I have ideas, and it would be nice to discuss them. Do you want to see what I came up with?"

"No, it's not interesting for me. And you can see that I have an urgent job. Let's postpone this conversation until things are better. Go and relax, and I'll work a little more."

"All right, go on working."

Shahlo kissed him on his cheek and left. Kadyr took up his pen again, but after a few seconds irritably threw it away.

"'She doesn't like it' - look at her! She wants dressmaking courses. And what about this French guy?. I don't know - "

The next morning they hardly talked, and it was clear that Kadyr had been very hurt by their conversation the day before.

His wife was trying to show her independence, but he could not stand it.

After her husband had left, Shahlo cleaned the table, put things in order in the kitchen and sat down to deal with her own thoughts. There were not many pleasant ones.

She faced a difficult dilemma. Either she fully accepted the position of her husband, and then she could safely put an end to all her attempts to get out of this useless and needless vanity. This, first and foremost, poisoned her life.

Or she could go against him and prove that she was capable of something more useful than what she had done so far.

Once again, scrolling through the memory of her conversation with her husband yesterday, she made a decision.

Pulling out her notebook from a drawer, she took a business card out from under the cover, the one which Christian had left for her before departing. Twisting it in her fingers for a while, as if wondering what she would say to him, she decisively sits down and dials the number.

A female voice was heard answering, apparently a secretary:

"Monsieur Raboli's office. Hello."

"Good afternoon. May I speak with Monsieur Christian?"

"I'm sorry, but at the moment he is busy, he has a visitor. Could you call him back a little later?"

"What time?"

"I think he will be free in about half an hour."

At that moment, the office door opened and a dandyish young man with feminine manners stepped out.

"Just a second - it looks like he's just become free."

Before leaving the waiting room, the guy turned around and sent a secretive kiss to the secretary. In response, she smiled cloyingly, and with her right hand made an expressive gesture under the table.

"I will tell him. How should I introduce you?"

"Say that this is Madame Shahlo from Tashkent." "Sorry, where?"

"From Tash-kent." Shahlo uttered the name in syllables and smiled, imagining the secretary's difficulties.

"Just a second. Hold the line, please."

She presses a button. Christian picks up the phone in his office. "Yes, Julie."

"A certain Madame Shahlo from Tash-kent is calling you. Shall I put her through?

"Yes. Straight away, please."

"Hello, I'm connecting you now to Monsieur Raboli Christian." Julie hung up, picked up a directory of firms from a shelf and flipped through the pages, trying to find Tashkent. Failing, she shrugged and put the directory in place. "Christian?"

"Yes, yes, it's me. I'm awfully glad to hear your voice, Shahlo. So the conversation I had with you wasn't in vain."

"Well, first of all, hello, Christian."

"Oh, I'm sorry, Shahlo. Of course, hello."

"Yes, I have really been thinking a lot about our conversation and decided to accept your offer."

"But that's wonderful! Only, for some reason, I do not hear the inspiration in your voice. Is anything wrong?"

"No, everything is alright, just a little tired. So, what is required of me, Christian?" "All your undisclosed talent. We discussed one idea recently, and once again I thought about you. Let's do this."

Having finished the conversation with Shahlo, Christian called the secretary into the office.

"Julie, arrange a meeting with Madame Lange and prepare the documents for tomorrow's meeting with the Italians."

"Good. By the way. Is Tash-kent a New Brand?" Christian pretended to be indignant:

"Well! You can't be that uneducated, Julie! This is a very ancient city. I'll have to give you a geography exam."

"If you want to fire a poor girl, just say. There's no need to come up with nasty pretexts."

"Off you go, poor girl! I'll think about it - "

11

Marina, a new acquaintance of Alibek, with whom he has long maintained an intimate relationship, arrived at his house.

She went to the door of Alibek's apartment, opened it, went inside, hung up a cloak and a handbag, and passed into the room.

She turned on the TV and sat down in an armchair. After about five minutes she got up, turned off the TV and began to walk around the room, rubbing her fingers nervously.

She has something to say today to Alibek, but she doesn't know how to say it. She goes to the mirror, looks at herself and begins to speak as if Alibek was there.

"Alibek, I have something important to tell you. I'm pregnant. No, not that - Alibek, dear, do not be upset, but we are going to have a child. Don't be upset. No, that won't work. Alibek..." Her phone began ringing. While she was thinking whether to pick up the phone or not, the answering machine went off and a woman's voice rang out in the room. Marina froze.

"Alibek, my love, it's me. It's very difficult to catch you at home - you work too much. Don't forget about your health. I haven't heard your voice for a long-time and I miss you. I want to remind you that the day after tomorrow our Sherzod will turn two. He will be very happy if you call and wish him a happy birthday. I kiss you and wait for your arrival. Bye, honey..."

The phone turned off, and Marina froze in the middle of the

room, looking at the phone and covering her mouth with her hand.

Then she slowly sat down on the floor, staring with blank eyes at a point in the corner of the room. Having regained her senses, she rose, looked around the room, went to the door, took the cloak and handbag, left the apartment and slammed the door behind her.

The keys were left on the shelf in the hallway.

After some time, Alibek entered the entrance of his apartment block with a package in his hands. Having taken the lift to his floor, he opened the door to the apartment and entered. He put a shopping bag with food for dinner on a shelf. He shouted from the hallway:

"Are you here or not?"

Alibek took off his raincoat, hung it on a hook and then noticed the keys were lying on the shelf.

"Ok - here. But why does nobody meet me with joyful cries?" The silence in the apartment puzzled him a little. He took the bag and the flowers, entered the room and put everything on the table.

"Where are you?" Not receiving an answer, he walked around the apartment, peering into all the rooms, and holding the flowers in his hand. "Ready or not, here I come…"

Not finding Marina anywhere, Alibek, with a displeased look on his face, returns to the living room. Laying the flowers down near the phone, he walks around the room.

"Where have you gone?" He went to the table and began to take out the items from the bag and then immediately pushed them away with his hand. "She is out walking somewhere, and I have to hang out in the kitchen after work? Well, no way!"

Alibek turned on the TV, sat down in an armchair, and at that moment the phone rang.

"Now she apologizes that she came out and forgot the keys." Alibek answers his phone. "Yes! You made a mistake with the number."

Alibek hung up the phone. Then he pressed the answering machine button. His wife's voice resonated from the speaker. After hearing the message to the end, he frowned.

"Hell, couldn't you have called yesterday or tomorrow?" He nervously walked around the room.

"Did she call while she was here? Of course!" He mimicked Zarina. "Alibek, my love. The other one immediately went into hysterics and ran away. So what?" Alibek looked at his watch. "Maybe she's already arrived. Well, I will have to get out of this."

He picked up the phone, dialled the number once, twice, three times.

Only short beeps were heard in response. Hanging up the phone, he stood for a while, biting his lips in anger and assessing the situation.

Without thinking of anything, he grabbed the bouquet and threw it into the corner as hard as he could.

12

Although six months had passed since that ill-fated conversation between Shahlo and her husband, their relationship had not only not improved, but, on the contrary, had become increasingly tense.

Shahlo plunged headlong into her new job, and Kadyr could not become reconciled with the fact that something in their home was not going as he wanted, and he was no longer the complete master of the situation.

This hurt his pride, and now even an insignificant reason was enough for him to break loose and once again express his dissatisfaction.

As ill luck would have it, today Shahlo had received a letter from Christian, but was yet to open it, and put it on the windowsill in the kitchen. Having prepared dinner and laid the table, she called her husband.

"Kadyr, everything is ready, come and have dinner."

Kadyr came to the kitchen; his attitude was as always very dissatisfied. He sat at the table and began to eat. Shahlo took the letter from the windowsill, opened it and began to read. Kadyr squinted at his wife.

"Won't you have dinner with me?"

"No, I'm not hungry. I feel a little unwell." She went back to the letter again.

"When you are unwell, you have to lie in bed," Kadyr muttered.

"I said a little bit. But if I bother you, I can go to another room."

"Why are we talking about bothering or not bothering?" flared up Kadyr. "If you don't want to have dinner with me, then you can talk to me."

"About what?"

This started to make Kadyr very angry.

"How should I know? What do wives talk to their husbands about?"

"About different things." Shahlo shrugged. "About children, about common interests, general plans. And then about common problems."

"We have nothing in common? Do you mean that?"

"I don't understand why you are angry." Shahlo tried to calm her husband. "So far, we have shared your affairs, your plans, your career. With mine, though, somehow you were not very interested. Just womanish nonsense - nothing to discuss. Has something changed? Doesn't that suit you any more?"

"No, it doesn't. You are my wife, and I have the right to know who is writing to you and what he is writing about."

"Ah, I see. Well, you could simply have askeed. This is a letter from Christian, if you remember him."

"Your Paris admirer is back?"

"Not an admirer but just a good person, and we have a common work interest. I have never made a secret of this. Why does this annoy you?"

"What does he want from you this time?"

"He is inviting me to a fashion show in Paris. In a month. He wants me to develop several models in the national style. I'm just working on them now."

"And you, of course, want to go, right?"

"If I finish everything on time, then yes."

"Aren't you interested in my opinion?" Kadyr almost shouted. "Don't I have the right to decide anything in this house?"

"Do you mean the right to allow or not to allow me to go - do what I love, or something else?"

"What does it matter? I'm your husband!"

"Great, Kadyr, great." Shahlo sadly shook her head. "Why do you not understand?"

"I understand everything perfectly."

"Wait, listen, please. You and I have never talked about this topic, and it's maybe a waste of time. It's about work, about a matter in which I can apply all that I know and am able to do. In which I can realize myself, to which I am drawn and which is now part of my life.

But you want to have the right to cross out all this just because you don't like it, because you can't bear the name 'Christian'? Sorry, but I'm afraid you don't have that right."

Kadyr suddenly pushed his food away and got up abruptly from the table.

"I see. Soon I will have no rights at all. Do what you want, only then don't complain." He hurried out of the kitchen, slamming the door behind him.

"You don't understand anything," Shahlo whispered bitterly. "To complain to whom?"

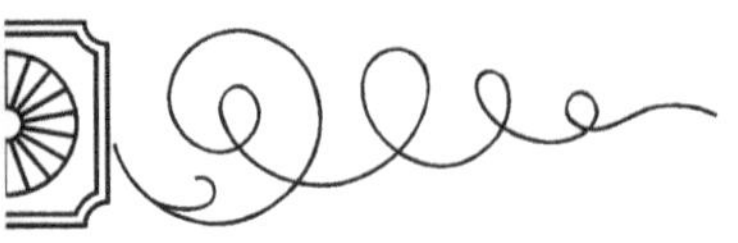

13

Tashkent. The start of the nineties. Shahlo's friend Lola and her husband Aziz had long dreamed of buying a small house, and now they have the chance to do it. Aziz has come to a place known to all, where various people gather to get acquainted with the broker, who has been recommended. Aziz walked up to the table, at which a bald man in glasses sat and was reading something.

"Excuse me, are you Mikhail Semenovich?" The man looked at him over his glasses.

"Well, let's put it this way: I am one of many Mikhal Semenoviches." He smiled.

– "Which one do you need?"

"The one who deals with apartments," Aziz smiled too.

"In apartments, young man?" The broker raised his finger. "Housekeepers are engaged in apartments and I am engaged in real estate."

"Well, I meant exactly that." Aziz was embarrassed.

"Then it's me. What question do you have for me?"

"I would like to buy a house. I have already spoken on this subject with one person. His name is Garik."

"Ah, Garik. I know, a lively young man. But rather inexperienced. What did he tell you?"

"He said that it was not his area and so sent me to you. He said you can do anything."

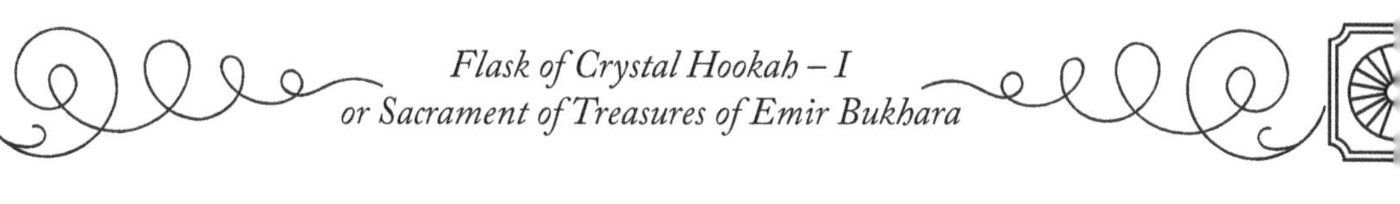

"Ah!" The broker sighed with mock sorrow. "He lied, of course. If I could, I would not be sitting at a table like this in a place like this. Be that as it may, I can do something. Have a seat, young man. What is your name?"

"Aziz."

"Well, wonderful. Now let's attack your problem from all directions..."

As always, once a month, the friends gather in a restaurant to discuss their women's affairs.

"Beauty," Zarina reached out. "Maybe I should order one more ice-cream?" "

You've already eaten a double portion," Lola said indignantly. "More?" "Where, where? Yes there. I love ice cream."

"Also desserts, cakes, cream and all that," teased her friend Zarina. "It's amazing how you aren't three times the size."

"You must be able to but I do better."

"We know, we know. You would open your coffee house - there will be no end of visitors."

"And so what? I've been thinking about this for a long time. You'll see, you yourself will be standing in line. It will be called - hmmm, let me think." She paused.

"Be Free from Healthy Food," Shahlo quipped.

"What kind of person are you? You try to spoil everything. No, you'll be on my blacklist. Never set foot near me."

"Come on. Will you let me come in as your old friend?"

"No, only in turn, like all normal people. By the way, there will soon be a housewarming party. I am going to prepare a lot of things for you."

"What housewarming?" surprised Shahlo.

"Here she is," Zarina pointed to Lola. "Soon she will become a landlord. She and Aziz are buying a house."

"Seriously? You kept that quiet!"

"It's too early to invite people." Lola was embarrassed. "So many problems still need to be solved: the apartment, money, and the design. Although it's not very expensive – but still."

"Indeed, inexpensive. Then you will spend the same amount on repairs."

"No, a very decent house. There is a courtyard, and a workshop. Exactly what Aziz wanted."

"Then why did you ask so little for all this? Something is wrong here. I hope you won't get involved in something."

"What can they get into?" put in Zarina. "People are urgently leaving, they need to sell faster. Aziz was just lucky with a broker."

"I don't know. I don't know." said Shahlo uncertainly. "When do you process the documents?"

" Everything must be completed by the twenty-fifth."

"Another three weeks. You know that when you seal the deal, be sure to let me know. I want to be there, just in case. It will be ok to have another one, right? Then, you never know what may happen."

"Well, why are you scaring her?" said Zarina. "She's fed up with her troubles.

Everything will be OK. I'll get a cat."

"What cat?" Lola asked in surprise.

"So that it can be the first to enter the house. That is an omen."

"With whom?"

"Just the cat. With who else?"

"Ah, I'll take it and give it to the owners. You'll owe a piece of sausage."

"So you also fell in love with a sausage?"

"No, not for me. For the cat - for its work."

"Is everything okay with the money?" Shahlo asked. "Do you have enough?" "We counted with Aziz, that should be enough."

"Look, if it's not - we will help." She looked at Zarina. "So, boss?"

"You're asking? It goes without saying! How can it be happen without us?"

"Thanks, girls," Lola said.

"Not at all," Shahlo looked at the clock. "Well, girls, will we run up?"

At this moment, Shahlo turned her attention to the girl at the next table, who was smacking her little daughter who had spilled a glass of juice on the table. The girl began to cry and her mother began to pull at her daughter's sleeve so that she would not cry.

She showed the girl her hands, smeared with paint, and offered to wash the table, and at the same time her hands. The girl nodded her head and Shahlo made a sign to the waiter, who was standing at a distance and watching the scene.

He understood what was required of him and also joined the game. Looking at Shahlo's hands, the waiter pretended to grab his head and complain that he didn't have enough water and soap to wash such dirty hands.

The girl stopped crying and smiled, then extended her arms and showed how clean they were. The girl's mother watched them perplexedly, then pounced on both of them.

"Are you from the circus or from the asylum? What are you doing getting in to my business?"

Shahlo ignored these questions and continued to make the child laugh. Then the woman roughly grabbed the girl by the hand

and dragged her away.

The little girl cried again, and Shahlo could not stand it.

"Even children in an orphanage are not treated this way. Are you the mother of this girl? Why have you given birth only to hate your own child so much? Have you forgotten that you need to raise children in love, that you need to be their friend, and not an overseer who has the right to hit a child. To show your strength and power over a helpless creature - one who will not be able to hit back. Creatures like you disgust me!"

Now Shahlo was crying, and her friends began to calm her down, casting angry glances toward the woman.

The woman was running away, dragging the child behind her and repeating: "She's mad, mad, daughter, don't listen to her! I love you very much, you hear, I love you." The child stopped crying, and, it seems, already believed her mother...

After meeting with her friends, Shahlo went to her grandmother's. This elderly woman had an amazing ability to foresee the changes that could occur in the lives of people close to her. Very often this manifested itself in her dreams, and everyone listened to what she was saying. Shahlo entered the courtyard, walked over to her grandmother and kissed her.

"Hello, Grandma. How are you feeling? Yesterday you didn't look very well." "Never mind. My arms and legs work and that means everything's good."

"As far as I remember you, they always work for you and are never idle. And the head, too - you read and read ..."

Shahlo began to sort through the books on the table.

"That is true. These books are my teacher-friends, their wisdom heals souls, gives peace and calmness, their thoughts are divine messages. Listen. She lifted Jami's book:

> *Do good so that with love*
> *Good will find you*
> *Evil do not ever do*
> *So that it doesn't find you.*

Shahlo smiled and in her turn said:

> *To gain recognition*
> *And the honour to earn*
> *Do not do the deed*
> *That to harm may lead*

"Ah, Nazir Khosrov… I am glad that you also love his Rubaiyat.

But at night I slept badly – anxiously, somehow. I had a strange dream. Are your friends all right?"

"Yes, nobody's complaining. But what kind of dream?"

"Just nonsense."

"No, tell me. I am curious. You'll not dream nonsense."

"Well, ok. Here it is. Your girlfriend and her husband come home. They come up to the front door but they can't open it. They can't find the right key. They try so many but none of them work. It's as if the house has become a stranger and won't let anyone in. They stand there and don't know what to do."

"Ok, you had a dream. I just don't know what to say. Were you sitting with the hookah for a long time in the evening?"

"I was. How can I be without that?"

"In the dream, which of the friends was it? Do you remember?"

"I only saw it from the back. But it looks like Lola. Don't listen to me."

"No, I have long been convinced that there's a good reason for

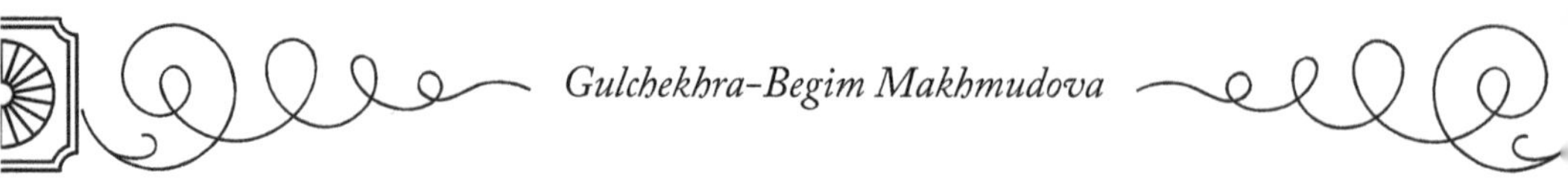

why you dream about something. You are like a guardian angel.

"What are you talking about? Angels have wings, but I, apart from rheumatism, have nothing to find."

"Angels are also different," Shahlo laughed. "With wings, and with rheumatism. So do not argue. Let's drink some tea and talk."

"Today you are in charge, aren't you?"

"How else can it be?"

"Well then, come on - look after your angel."

14

Shahlo has just flown home from the Paris Fashion Festival.

Loaded with gift bags, she opens the door and enters the apartment. She frowns at the unpleasant smell in the hallway, and then calls:

"Kadyr, I've arrived ... are you home?"

Without waiting for an answer, she undressed, went into the living room with packages. A mess reigned everywhere, there were scattered things all around .

"Well - like a child. Honestly." She shook her head. "You can't leave him for a week. Of course, there is no time to clean up after himself. My vacation seems to be over." She sighed.

Then she packed up the scattered things, ran a finger along the polished surface, and shook her head again. Throwing things in the closet, she went to the kitchen.

What she saw there made her freeze in the doorway: a full sink of unwashed dishes, dirty plates on a table with leftover food. She looked in the refrigerator - it was empty.

At that moment, the sound of a key inserted into the door was heard. Shahlo went out into the corridor. Finally, the door opened and Kadyr entered. He was obviously tipsy, his tie astray. He saw Shahlo.

"You're back?"

"I am back."

"Why didn't you warn me?"

"I wanted to make a surprise. In my opinion, we both succeeded."

"What are you talking about?" Kadyr went up to her to hug her. But Shahlo pulled back a little.

"Sorry, there's a smell of alcohol on you."

This was enough for Kadyr to lose his temper.

"My wife drove away and no-one knows where and to whom. She abandoned her house and her husband."

"You know perfectly well where and why I went. And that doesn't mean abandoning my house and my husband."

"What does that mean? Why do I have to live in such a pigsty?" Kadyr waved his hand in the direction of the kitchen.

"This "pigsty", to use your word, you made yourself, not me. You don't have to take out your annoyance on me. Or do you consider it beneath your dignity to get your own meals and tidy up properly?"

"The wife should look after the husband. I am not a cook or a dishwasher."

"And me?" Shahlo was indignant. "Who am I, do you think? Don't you care about how I live and what I might be striving for? Or do you see me as a kind of accessory that's only here to make sure you're comfortable and happy?"

She came up to him and took his hand.

"Kadyr, what is the matter with you? I can't understand you. The Kadyr I married seems to be disappearing. Explain to me if there's something I don't understand."

"No need." He took her hand away. "You understand everything perfectly well. You want a beautiful life with international travel. Of course you do. There are so many new impressions and acquaintances. And you can forget about your husband."

"What are you talking about? If I had forgotten about you, I would not rush home and run around the shops in search of a gift for your daughter and for you in order to see the joy on your faces. But instead of that..."

"I don't give a damn about your present and I'll manage without it. You've already made sure of that. That's it. I'm tired and want to sleep." He turned and left.

Shahlo stood for several seconds, head down, then went to the kitchen, to the sink with the dirty dishes, leaned on it with both hands and froze, looking bewildered.

15

The urgency with which the Kanaki family - Svetlana and her young husband George wanted to sell their house and leave for Greece, was explained quite simply.

In a month, Svetlana's son Alex was supposed to be released from prison. He might interfere with the deal and they didn't want to share it with him at all. In order to make the deal, they needed a reliable person such as the real-estate broker Mikhail Semenovich, whom they had invited to their home and asked him to help.

Mikhail Semenovich listened to them with an expressionless face, then said:

"Well, in general, the job's clear to me. You want to sell a house and I have to find a buyer and get my commission. But..." He raised a finger.

"What?" Svetlana asked curiously.

"I am somewhat confused by the amount."

"The cost of the house or your commission?" Svetlana asked.

"Actually, dear Svetlana," Mikhail Semenovich answered, "These are the same things. I could easily have found a buyer for this amount or even double it."

"You miss an important point. You have to sell quickly," said George.

"Within a month."

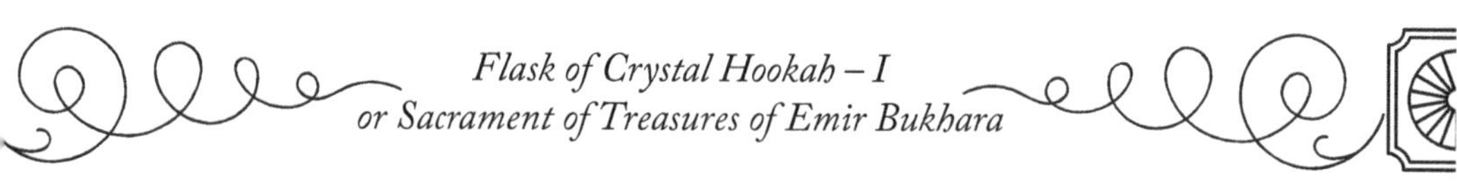

Mikhail Semenovich looked carefully at Svetlana and squinted slightly.

"What about a month and a week?"

George reacted harshly. "This issue is not to be discussed. A month."

"That's amusing." Mikhail Semenovich again looked carefully at those around him. "My father always told me to never play blind. And he was absolutely right – although, on one occasion, I didn't listen to him. Ok, my friends, can you shed a little more light? What will happen in a month?"

Svetlana hesitated, then looked at her husband. He nodded his head.

"In a month, someone may or may not appear on the scene," Svetlana said. "Someone who won't like this option."

Mikhail Semenovich drummed his fingers on the table, thinking.

"I see. You want him not to like it," he grinned, "after your, so to speak - " He moved the first two fingers of his right hand quickly across the table, like a pair of running legs. "However, this doesn't concern me and it's completely useless to me to know it." "That's right." George nodded his head. "As for your commission, if you can put the amount of the sale up a bit you'll get it."

"Yes, that's clear. A deal. I think I understand why we have such a modest amount. If I can put it like this, the buyer shouldn't be someone in business, so to speak, someone who will quickly solve this problem, but one of the common folk. Do I understand my job correctly?"

"It's nice to work with you, Mikhail Semenovich," said Svetlana, flattering him. "We say the first word and you complete the sentence. You should dance on the "Field of Miracles".

"Away." Mikhail Semenovich contemptuously grimaced, "To go so far for some kind of tattered vacuum cleaner? So, I have it. I don't swim in shallow water. Well then. I seem to have a suitable option. I'll work with them a little and in ten days, perhaps, I'll bring you to the bride. Will this suit you?"

"Completely."

"Then, perhaps, that's all." He got up from the table and picked up his briefcase from the floor.

"All the best, I'll call you."

The day came to certify the documents and Shahlo insisted on being present. Something bothered her, and she did not want her friend to be fooled. Therefore, along with Lola and Aziz, she drove up by car to the Kanakis's home. They walked into the house, and Lola introduced those present.

"Hello. This is my friend Shahlo. This is Svetlana and her husband George." They both greeted Shahlo. Svetlana and Shahlo at the same time exchanged glances.

"Have a seat," Svetlana led them to the table. "We invited a public notary and he should arrive soon. In the meantime, if you want, let's look at the documents again so that we don't miss anything."

She took the folder, opened it and began to lay documents on the table. Shahlo took them one at a time and carefully scanned them.

"Here is the warrant for ownership of the house," began Svetlana. "A copy. This is a plan of the site and its copy."

"All copies are notarized," George added.

"Yes, of course," Svetlana confirmed. "This is a contract of sale . In the envelope, all receipts for payment of services for the last year. There are no debts, so you don't need to worry. I think that's everything. George, have I missed anything?"

"No. You always had a special attitude to pieces of paper."

"It must be difficult to leave a house like this?" Shahlo asked. "You've lived here for a long time."

"Of course.I 'm sorry," Svetlana sighed. "But there's too much to do and we can't take it with us."

"Yeah. In my opinion, my friends are very lucky. I think if you were not in such a hurry, then the price for such a house would be much higher."

Alas, that was circumstances. Sometimes, in order not to lose more, you have to sacrifice something." At that moment, there was a knock on the door.

"This is probably the notary."

Svetlana went to the door and opened it. On the threshold, a short man was standing with a briefcase in his hand.

"Come in - we are waiting for you. Everyone is here."

The man came in and introduced himself:

"Hello. Grigoryan Artyom Avanesovich, the first notary office." He sat down at the table, reached into his jacket pocket. "Here are my documents, for those with whom I am not familiar. Well, since both sides are present, let's get started with the deal."

When all the formalities were observed, the friends said good-bye to the owners, got into the car and drove away. Lola and Aziz were clearly in a good mood.

"Did you see the extension?" Aziz turned to Shahlo. "I'll build a really great workshop there! If something breaks, bring it to me and I'll fix it right away!"

"Finally, we will have our own house," Lola added, "The children will have plenty of space. You see," she said, turning to Shahlo, "everything went fine. But you were worried."

"Yeah, I suppose, I was worried for nothing," Shahlo agreed. "Only…" "Only what?" Lola said, some concern in her voice.

"I don't understand but they were somehow tense. They look calm and friendly but in the eyes… Ah, well, it's just my nerves playing up. Never mind. I'm very happy for you. Don't forget to invite me to the housewarming."

"Of course we won't forget!" Aziz promised enthusiastically.

"I'll take you at your word," Shahlo smiled.

Two weeks passed. Again Firuz-begim's dream proved to be prophetic. Kanaki's son, Alex, was released from prison and immediately moved into the house that Lola and Aziz had bought. They had major problems. The first to know about this from a completely shocked Lola was Zarina. She immediately rushed to Shahlo. She was sitting in a room and looking over the materials that Christian had sent. A flustered Zarina dashed into the room.

"I don't believe it! People have no conscience! They received the money and vanished without a trace. Loziz arrived at home, and there was some bandit walking around who said: "Get out! This is my house." Where are they going to go now? They've handed over all their money!"

"Stop, stop," Shahlo begged her friend. "Sit down and be calm. I absolutely did not understand a word."

"What is there to understand?" Zarina jumped up again from the chair. "I said -" "Stop," Shahlo interrupted her friend again. "Can you sit down and not jump back and forth? It's making me dizzy. Now try calmly explain to me who came where, which bandit is walking around and who is Loziz? I am hearing about him for the first time."

"Well, Loziz is elementary. I crossed our Lolita with Aziz, for short." "Well, that's clear," Shahlo grinned. "Keep going."

"They bought a house. All the documents were issued, money was handed over and the owners moved out. While our couple was arranging their move, the owners' son came out of prison and took over the house. They arrived and he was celebrating with his friends there. And he sent them away. The deal, he said, was illegal, they had no right without me, and so on. In short, he says, you can run around the courts if you have nothing to do, but it's better not to anger me."

"I see! What a carry-on! So, what now?"

"What now?" Zarina exploded. "Nothing! Our couple turned and left. They could not start a fight with this gang. They went to the police - they were told to go to the court. They went to court - the claim was not accepted. Look, they say, for the owners. I've come just from them and immediately to you. We must help our friend out."

"Of course we must." Shahlo agreed. "Where did the owners move to?"

"Who knows! The son, if he knows, won't say. It seems to be somewhere abroad."

"Well, we'll find out. It's not such a big problem. But how to get them there…"

"Yeah …"

"Okay, let's not jump too far ahead. You help them to get settled somewhere for a while, and I will search for our scammers. Then we'll think about what to do next. Is that clear?"

"Of course. Then I'll go?"

"Yeah, go ahead with what you have to do." By the time Zarina had reached the door and was about to leave, Shahlo called her.

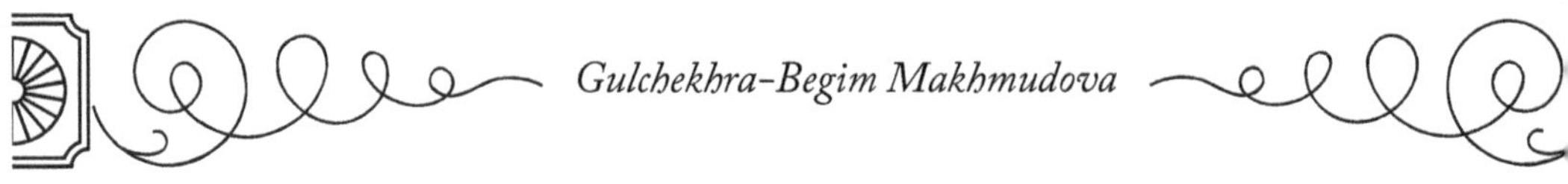

"By the way, my friend, what's our shortened name with Kadyr? KaSha?"

"Oh, you - " Zarina laughed, waved her hand and ran away.

"Loziz ...How did that come into her mind?"

16

After talking with Zarina, Shahlo immediately set to work, and a few days later she already knew in which direction the Kanakis, the swindlers, had left.

Now the most important thing remained - to find an opportunity to influence them from a distance so that justice would be restored.

First of all, Shahlo decided to call Christian, because she remembered how he had once talked about his friend from Greece, and it was there that the Kanakis had fled.

She dialled Christian's home number. Christian's wife, Jacqueline, picked up the phone.

"Hello."

"Good evening, Jacqueline, this is Shahlo."

"Oh, Shahlo! Hello. How are you doing?"

"I'm fine, thanks. Is Christian free? I have one small question for him."

"He's not only busy but also trying to take the phone from me. Shall I give it to him or be tormented?"

"Better give it to him, otherwise he will start brawling."

"Oh, he can. Take it, brawler."

Christian took the phone his wife was holding out.

"Hello, Shahlo. You women cannot be left on your own for a long time. You immediately begin to bother defenceless old us. I want to make you happy right away and tell you that your latest offers have been accepted. So, you can start working."

"Good evening, Christian. Thank you for the good news, but I ventured to disturb you on another matter. I need your help."

"I am at your service. What should I do? Should I send you a piece of the Eiffel Tower?"

"No," smiled Shahlo, "Thanks for the offer, but I have nowhere to put it. Do you remember, you once said that you have friends in Greece?"

"Of course, I remember. Do you have any business there?"

"I don't, but my friend has big problems, and those who created them have gone there. Contacting official channels will take too long and is likely to be futile. I remembered your words."

"I do not see any difficulties. I will call my friend, he will call you, and everything will be alright."

"Can he really help?"

"Who? Janis?" - Christian was genuinely surprised. "Well, if he can't, then I don't know ... Can I give him your details?"

"If that doesn't bother you."

"Not at all. Consider that he has already contacted you."

"Thank you, Christian, you've helped me a lot! Say goodbye to Jacqueline from me. All the best."

"Goodbye, Shahlo. I look forward to hearing from you." He put the phone down and with a mock threat looked at his wife: "So, madam, who's the brawler here?"

17

Christian's friend Janis was a major shipowner, and a couple of weeks later, the matter of Shahlo's trip to Greece, to her great surprise, was solved. Before leaving, she decided to call in the hospital where Lola was working and to reassure her friend. Lola went to Shahlo's lobby. Her appearance was tired, and there were rings under her eyes. Shahlo went to her.

"Hello, friend. I'm here for you."

"Hello, Shahlo." They kissed and sat down.

"You don't look well, which doesn't surprise me." Shahlo said. "Is it all too much?"

"When everything is alright and I'm in a good mood, then work doesn't exhaust me. I'm used to it. But..." She waved her hand. "I'm nervous. Aziz is twitching. You understand what kind of situation we're in, and we can't see any light at the end of the tunnel. Nothing's going right."

"I just came to you to talk about this. It seems to me that you will soon see a ray of light. We found your, um - I don't even know what to call them."

"Impossible! Where are they?"

"They have settled in Greece."

"Where?" Despair sounded in Lola's voice.

"In Greece," Shahlo repeated. "So far away?"

"We will deal with them there."

"To go to Greece? But you understand that neither I nor Aziz will be able to go there."

"You don't have to. I will go."

"You?" Lola's surprise knew no bounds. "Are you going to go to Greece?" "I am, I am."

The sage will call that one as friend,
Who in misfortune hours
Was his friend

"But what a chore! But what about money? What about tickets? What can you do with them alone?"

"Firstly, everything has already been settled, and I will not have any trouble with either money or tickets. And secondly, I will not be there alone. I think that I will not have to do anything."

"Will anyone help you there? But who?" It was evident that a spark of hope appeared in Lola's eyes.

"One very influential person," Shahlo emphasized the word "very."

"Your friend?"

"No, this is a friend of my French friend. He said that we should not worry about anything. So chin up, my friend. We will still enjoy your housewarming party."

"I don't know what to believe and what to hope for," Lola cried. "I'm so tired.

My children."

"You should rejoice, but you are crying. Is there a handkerchief?"

"There is." Lola took a handkerchief out of her pocket and handed it to Shahlo. "Here it is."

"Why do I need it? Wipe your tears and calm down."

"But what about Kadyr? Will he let you go?" Lola wiped away

her tears.

"Kadyr?" Shahlo frowned. "Would Aziz let you go if you went to help me?"

"Are you asking? Yes, he would push me into the plane himself."

"So Kadyr should let me go. Although I'm not sure about pushing me into the plane."

"Scolding, right?"

"Do not bother yourself. Come on, dash off to your babies. Say hello to Aziz from me."

"Sure, I'll tell him. Have a good trip there and, most importantly, back. Thank you."

"You'll thank me later." Shahlo hugged her friend emotionally. "I'll call from there and tell you how everything went. That's all." She kissed Lola on the cheek. "I'm off. Bye."

Having finished all the formalities, Shahlo arrived at the airport, where there was already a small plane sent by Janis to take her to Athens.

Shahlo walked to the registration desk. Her documents were checked, and the escort took her to the airfield.

When Shahlo had moved away from the counter, the inspectors looked after her.

"Wow, what a privileged lady. A plane was brought just for her."

"Who is she?", one of them said, puzzled.

"I have no idea."

"Well, live a century and be surprised for a century."

Shahlo and the escort had reached the tarmac.

"The others are already on the plane?" Shahlo asked. "Am I the last one?"

"Which others?" the girl asked.

"I'm talking about the passengers. Who else flies on airplanes?"

"This is a private flight. You are the only passenger."

"What – me alone?" In response to her surprise, the girl smiled.

"I don't think you will be bored. Personally, I would love to swap places with you."

They approached the plane. The female cabin attendant was already coming down the ramp.

"Here is your plane and have a great flight." She gave Shahlo's documents to the cabin attendant and left. The cabin attendant looked at Shahlo's documents and returned them to her.

"Good afternoon, madam. Welcome aboard. We are glad that you are flying with us."

"Are you really glad?" Shahlo smiled. This remark confused the cabin attendant.

"That's the way to meet guests." She led Shahlo into the salon and pointed to a seat.

"Take your seat. We will take off soon. After take-off, I will serve you at the table, and you can choose your own dish or drink. Here's the menu." She pointed to the table.

The cabin attendant went out. Shahlo settled in an armchair and then, being curious, she took the menu and opened it. Surprise was expressed on her face. She put the menu on the table. "Crazy. Some kind of a flying restaurant."

She comfortably settled herself in an armchair, leaned back and closed her eyes. The engines started and then the plane moved smoothly, accelerated and gently lifted off the ground.

Soon after take-off, Shahlo ate, drank some wine to relax, and decided to take a nap. But the tension that had accumulated lately had not receded.

In her memory, as if in a kaleidoscope, there were snatches of events, unpleasant conversations with Kadyr; and then for some reason she saw her grandmother who escorted her to the plane and by the steps told her not to be afraid of anything and everything would be fine. The plane shuddered heavily and Shahlo woke up and shook her head.

"Did I doze off?" she thought. Pushing aside the window curtain, she looked out.

The whole sky was covered in a dense veil, lit here and there by flashes of lightning. One flashed very close by and the plane shook heavily again. And then again. Shahlo clutched the chair and panic began to overwhelm her.

"Lord, what's happening?" She muttered, startled. "What have I done so that I need to be tested like this?"

The plane was shaken again and again. The flight attendant looked into the salon. "Are you all right?"

"Me?" Shahlo tried to hide her fear. "Yes - but what about the plane?" "It's all fine. It's just that we unexpectedly flew into a thunderstorm front."

"Unexpectedly?"

"Yes. It was supposed to pass by but for some reason it shifted and we are almost in the centre. So there will be some turbulence. But don't let that worry you."

"Wow – it does a little. Can the lightning strike us?"

"Theoretically - yes. In practice, this happens very rarely."

"I hope we don't add to the total of those extremely rare cases. Do you have an extra parachute?" Shahlo tried to appear cheerful but it was clear that she was very scared. The flight attendant smiled.

"On civilian aircraft, they are not provided. The rules."

"Stupid rules, don't you think?"

"Why? Imagine that at the first sign of trouble people start grabbing parachutes and falling out of the plane like cucumbers. How would we collect them and deliver them to those who have come to meet them?"

"Iron logic. It is much easier to gather them in one place."

At this moment, the plane shook especially hard, the lights went out for a second and the plane tipped slightly. Shahlo turned pale.

"What was that? Are we falling?"

"I – I - will ask."

She went out, and Shahlo wrapped her arms around herself and closed her eyes. Once again, a picture of her grandmother escorting her and saying the words "Don't be

afraid" came into her mind.

"I will not be afraid, grandmother," Shahlo whispered, "I will not be afraid."

I know that you won't leave me, you can protect me, so I won't be afraid. Everything will be fine." She opened her eyes, and the flight attendant was standing in the cabin and looking at her in surprise. "We haven't crashed yet?"

"A very minor piece of damage – nothing to worry about Would you like anything?"

"Nothing on the menu."

"What exactly?"

"Valerian."

"I have that. Personal supplies. You won't believe it but sometimes it scares me too. Just don't tell anyone."

"I won't breathe a word."

18

Greece, Athens. An airport.

The plane stopped and the steps were lowered. Shahlo began slowly to go down, clinging tightly to the handrails. She was shaking a little. A man left a car and headed for the steps. He held out his hand, and Shahlo stumbled down the last two steps, leaning on it.

"Hello Madam Shahlo."

"No, I'm not Shahlo," she said.

Janis looked at her bewildered.

"Oh, you're not?"

"I am what is left of her.

And you are Janis? Hello. It's the first time I realized that having solid ground under my feet is so wonderful."

"I was told that up there," he said as he glanced up at the sky, "you were shaken a little."

"A little?" she shook her head. "Whoever said that has a very poor vocabulary."

They approached the car, a long black limousine, and Janis opened the door.

"This thing doesn't fly, so feel calm."

"Thank you – that's very helpful."

They got in, and the car started. Front and rear guards were escorting them. "Now we will go to the hotel, and then, if you want, a little cultural programme. Tomorrow is our holiday, and I would like to show you the evening holiday city. What do you think of it?"

"Honestly?"

"Sure."

"I risk offending you, Janis, but, to be honest, I think of it with a slight shudder. After such a flight, my biggest desire is to make myself look respectable again and fall on something immobile if it's possible. Also, there's the time difference. Have I upset you?"

"Honestly?"

"I count on reciprocity."

"Then yes. But I am a very understanding person, so everything is postponed until tomorrow."

"The hotel too?" She grinned.

"No, we will probably remain here. In the morning, I will pick you up, and we will settle the affairs of your friend. After that, well, the rest."

"You said that tomorrow is a holiday, didn't you?"

"There are no holidays for important matters. You're not worried to be taking part in this?"

"No."

"Well, fine. Here is your hotel..."

The car stopped in front of the hotel entrance, Janis got out, opened the door and helped Shahlo get out of the car...

Morning. Exactly at the appointed time, making herself look respectable as much as possible after a difficult flight, Shahlo went downstairs from the hotel room where Janis had brought her in the evening, went through the hall and departed.

What she saw puzzled her: by the front of the hotel a row of several machines were located, near which guys in black shirts were standing. Each one had a weapon on his belt.

Janis got out of the middle car and headed for her. He came up and kissed her hand.

"Good morning, Madame Shahlo. Today you look even more charming than yesterday."

"Good morning ..." she hesitated, not knowing how to address him.

Janis noticed her difficulties and smiled.

"Do not bother, just – Janis."

"... Janis, and thanks for the compliment. Although, after yesterday's torture in mid-air, it's not very difficult." Shahlo nodded slightly towards the escort.

"Tell me, are we going to storm the fortress? I left my machine gun in the room."

"Well, of course not!" Janis could not help smiling, "A simple friendly visit, and nothing more."

"Really?"

"Yes. But you, combined with a machine gun, is, pardon me, just nonsense. Well, are we going?"

They came to the car, Janis opened the door, waited for Shahlo to sit down, and he sat in the front seat. The procession started off. Shahlo glanced out of the window, watching with pleasure the unfamiliar life of an unfamiliar city. Then she turned to Janis:

"One question. What if they are not at home?"

"They were called and asked not to leave, so do not worry and just enjoy the views of the ancient city."

"I can imagine," Shahlo grimaced, "what kind of call it was."

Janis smiled but said nothing. After a while Shahlo again asked: "What if they do not want to sign the documents?"

"It is possible. They have a wide choice. Do you want to bet on this?"

"Bet? I would like to know what will happen if I lose."

"Well, in this case, I will ask you to go with me on a wonderful sea cruise on my yacht. A mild, warm breeze, the emerald waves, fruits, peace, and lots of sun."

"Impressive. What if I win?"

"Well, then, I'll just have to agree to your offer to go on a wonderful sea cruise on my yacht. And so on."

"Really a great choice," Shahlo laughed. "To make a bet with you is a pleasure, Janis. I don't even feel like asking what choice they have to whom we are going."

"I can satisfy your natural female curiosity. Either they say goodbye to the house that they have here or they restore justice to those to whom they have injured. In my opinion, they will do the right thing."

"You are a dangerous man, Janis. I even got goosebumps when you said that." "Nonsense. It's just that I can't tolerate people who deliberately play dirty tricks around me. But for the rest," he said, as he turned to Shahlo and kindly smiled, "I am a good friend and a very kind person. I hope you are not going to do a dirty trick on me?"

"That's an interesting option," Shahlo smiled. "I'll think about it."

At that moment, the procession stopped.

"Here we are." Janis opened his door. "Shahlo, I do not think that it will be a great pleasure for you to attend this boring procedure. Am I right?"

"Absolutely. I'd rather look at the surroundings." "Great. It will not take much time."

Janis got out of the car and helped Shahlo get out. Some of his people had already gone up to the house. Janis smiled encouragingly at Shahlo and went to the house. A man with a suitcase, apparently a notary, followed him. The procession was completed by several more men. Everyone disappeared into the house and Shahlo turned her eyes to the windows. At one of them, she saw Svetlana. She also looked in her direction. She recognized Shahlo and her mouth opened with surprise. Shahlo grinned.

"It looks like they did not expect to see us."

She turned away, leaned on the car and began to look at the sea in the distance. The stunning, peaceful landscapes that she saw calmed her and made her forget about all the unpleasant moments.

She looked at the sea and yachts and thought how good it was - to get rid of daily problems for a while, not to bang her head against the wall, but just to look at the sea.

Fifteen minutes later, the whole procession in the same order returned to the cars. Janis and Shahlo got into the car and Janis handed Shahlo the documents in a transparent folder.

"That's all your friends need. You can call and reassure them."

"Sure, today." She drew attention to the check, which was lying on top of the documents. "What is this?"

"This is their apology for the inconvenience."

Shahlo looked at the figure and muttered in an undertone:

"I hope they have something left to buy the food for dinner."

Janis heard her muttering and turned to her:

"Yes, and even for breakfast. You don't need to worry about it."

"Thank you very much, Janis," Shahlo shook her head. "I don't even know how to thank you."

"Do not bother yourself with nonsense. Now we have a city tour. I guarantee you will see a lot of interesting things. By the way, do not forget about the cruise."

"Do I have time to think?"

"I begin to think that this is your favourite pastime." Janis smiled slyly and looked at his watch. "But I can stand the suspense for about five minutes."

Janis invited Shahlo to board his yacht in a few days. The time came and they put to sea.

The sea was calm and only light ripples ran across the surface. A warm breeze played gently over Shahlo's face, who comfortably settled in a deck chair on the upper deck. Next to her was a table with fruit. Janis came up and held out a glass of juice.

"Your vitamins, Madame."

"Thank you, Janis." She took the glass and sipped.

Janis settled in a deck chair opposite, took dates from a vase, but, having thought a little, threw them overboard and looked carefully at Shahlo. She was a little embarrassed by this gaze, although she did not show it, and decided to break the silence.

"Tell me honestly, Janis, why are you messing with me? Holiday, entertainment - and now here is the yacht."

"I said that I like to help people who are in trouble."

" But, it was not me who suffered."

"What do you mean?"

Janis was perplexed "Your eyes?"

This answer surprised Shahlo. "What is wrong with them? Red?"

"A woman who has everything in order has no such eyes."

"An interesting observation." Shahlo did not know what else to say in order to divert the topic.

"Am I wrong?"

"With your abilities, Janis," Shahlo shrugged, "You could have filled this yacht with women with healthy and burning eyes, and

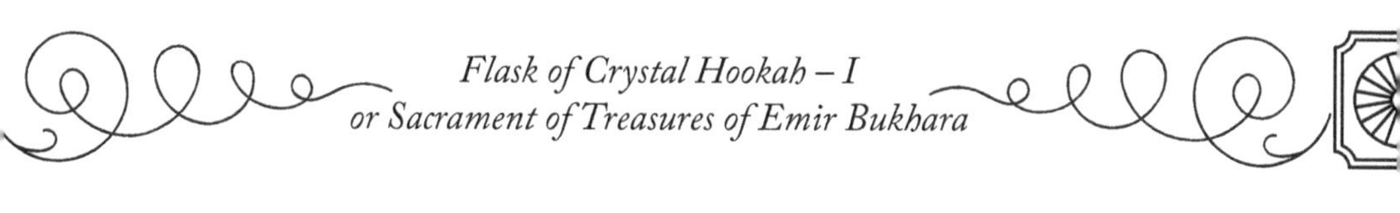

you would not have to treat anyone and complicate your leisure time. Isn't that it?"

"First, you cleverly evaded a direct answer, and that already says something. And second," his voice becoming serious, "I did not think that I was giving the impression of a cheap don Juan. I don't need that at all."

"What do you want, Janis? Why me?" She got up and went to the side.

Janis went to her and stood next to her.

"I need you to at least temporarily drop your carapace of a strong and unbending fighter and be just a woman, a charming woman."

Shahlo turned to face him to object, but Janis gently took her by the shoulders:

"I also need you to tell me about yourself: what pleases you, what disturbs you, what kind of burden you keep to yourself. I want to know everything about you."

"What do you want to know, Janis?" Now Shahlo's voice was tired, and somehow all the brunt of the experience lately fell upon her, and she wanted to throw out all this pain . "That I lost my second child?" Her eyes became wet. "That I have travelled beyond the limits of this life and miraculously got out of there? That my family life is crumbling like a house of cards? Do you want to know this? Why do you need this?" She burst into tears and buried her face in Janis's shoulder.

"Well, well, everything is fine, everything is fine." Janis gently stroked her hair. "You see how simple it is? Reprimanded, and immediately it became easier."

Instead of answering, Shahlo just nodded her head.

"That's why," Janis continued, as kept on stroking her hair, "women live longer than us. We don't know how to do that. Forgive me for bringing you to such a state."

"You are a monster, Janis," Shahlo sobbed.

"Yes," said Janis with mock pride, "I am like that." He moved Shahlo away from him a little and looked at her tear-stained face. "Amazing! Even tears suit you."

" I got your shirt dirty." "Alas, it was the last one."

"You are also a liar," Shahlo smiled.

"Yes, a little," Janis agreed with her. "I think it's time for you to freshen up. Do

do you want to swim? Look, what wonderful water."

"You want to feed the sharks?" Shahlo gradually came to her senses.

"Well," he scratched his chin, "That would be too common-place. In addition, they have a day off today."

"Actually, I don't mind." Shahlo looked at the water. "But somehow I did not think about a swimsuit."

"I don't see the problem," Janis answered right away. "You -" He glanced past Shahlo. She raised her hand in protest.

"Just don't try to say that I am, combined with a swimsuit, also nonsense."

"You didn't finish listening," Janis laughed. "I wanted to say that you will find everything you need in your cabin."

Shahlo once again looked at the sea.

"Are you really sure that..." she depicted a swimming fish.

"They were called and warned."

"I thought so," Shahlo smiled maliciously and went down to the ladder. Janis added:

"In addition, they do not touch bony people."

Shahlo turned around and in mock indignation opened her

mouth:

"You -" she breathed, but Janis laughed and immediately raised both hands, indicating that he was giving up.

"Ah." Shahlo waved her hand hopelessly and began to descend.

Janis watched her, with tenderness and grief.

When Shahlo disappeared, his face contorted in pain and he bent over, pressing his hand to his right side. With difficulty, he sank into a deckchair and took a tablet out of his pocket and swallowed, leaning back and closing his eyes.

Shahlo had a wonderful day.

Bathing in clear water and Janis's unobtrusive attentiveness to her beneficially influenced her mood.

In the evening, when it was time to have dinner, they sat down at a table set luxuriously in the cabin. Janis pushed a graceful dish with a delicacy towards Shahlo.

"Here, try this. You'll like it."

"Oh no, I can't. I've already tried more than necessary. I do not want to become attractive to your toothed pets."

"You, it turns out, are vindictive," Janis grinned.

"Well, alright. Just this one."

He took a crystal decanter and poured a little into Shahlo's glass. "I bet you've never tried this one."

"Well, no," Shahlo shook her head. "To argue with you is a thankless task. You always seem to win. What is this?" she pointed to the decanter.

"Metaxa. Does this tell you anything?"

"Well, yes. I was once treated to this."

"You were treated to a semi-finished product, I assure you. But this is nectar." he said, tapping the decanter with his fingernail. I think that once it was drunk by the gods on Olympus."

Shahlo sipped the drink and shook her head.

"Perhaps you are right, Janis. I don't know what about the gods, but - " She sipped her drink again and put the glass on the table. "However, the only thing you've been doing the whole evening is treating me but you haven't eaten or drunk anything.

For a man, this is a little strange." She looked seriously at Janis. "I always feel your attentive look on me, no matter what I do. You seem to be studying me. For some reason your eyes are sad, even when you are joking. Have I caused you any problems?"

"Well, of course not." objected Janis. "I really like to look after you, and I enjoy seeing how you courageously fight with everything that I push onto you. I am not very hungry so don't let this bother you."

"Is that all?" Shahlo looked more closely at Janis. "You answered only the first half of the question, and not the most important one. That's not fair. From me you sought complete frankness. I am starting to regret that."

"Not that," Janis interrupted her, "there is no need to regret anything, I beg you. Everything is fine. The problem is not created by you but by me. But I can't solve it without you. In general, I would like…" He turned the glass on his desk in his fingers, then looked up at Shahlo. "I would like you to stay with me."

Shahlo intuitively felt the seriousness of the moment and decided to defend herself from it.

"I don't have much choice, Janis, do I? I can't swim to the shore."

"I'm not talking about that," Janis grimaced. "You understood me but then you try to slam your shell shut. I would like you to be with me tomorrow and in a month and - until the end."

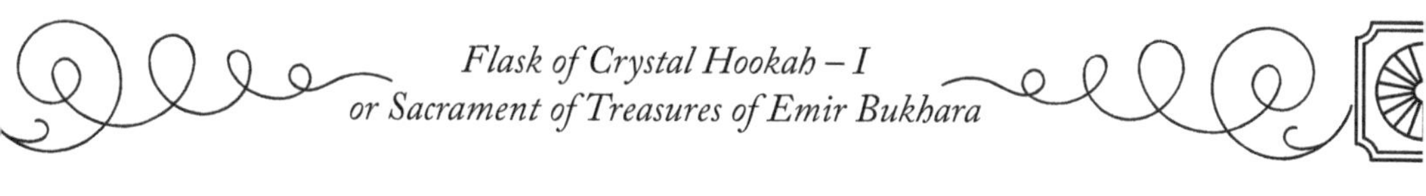

Shahlo got up and walked slowly through the cabin. Then she got up and turned to Janis.

"In what capacity, Janis? Lovers, concubines, friends?"

"Why are you like this, Shahlo? I have given you no reason to think that about yourself. There is also the status of a wife, which you haven't mentioned."

"I am remembering. I am, by the way, married - and you know that."

"Yes, unfortunately, I know. But … if you wanted …" He stopped and shook his head, as if driving away the thought that had settled there. "Sorry, Shahlo. I should not have started this conversation, it was my mistake."

Janis got up from the table and went to stand by the lamp. There was an awkward pause.

Shahlo also got up, went up to him and laid a hand on his shoulder. Janis turned his head and pressed his lips to her hand.

"You have nothing to apologize for, Janis, and, believe me, I appreciate your frankness. I feel good with you, I feel really good and calm and you are so reliable. This is worth a lot, and I thank you for that. But what you have offered me is too serious. I also want to be honest with you. I'm not ready for this, believe me."

"I understand," Janis replied, and Shahlo felt with pain the anguish in his voice.

"I don't know how appropriate it is to resort to the wisdom of oriental poetry,

Janis, but listen:

> *Don't build your temple of love*
> *Carelessly on the sand.*
> *Reliable is that temple*
> *That is built forever.*

There was a short pause, then Shahlo touched Janis's shoulder gently.

"Have I disappointed you?"

Janis turned to face her:

"I would be disappointed if I heard something else. I assumed such an answer. But you know the bad habit of drowning people." He took her face in his palm. "But this does not mean a final and irrevocable "no", does it?"

"You are very stubborn, Janis. Has anyone told you that?" Shahlo tried to get away from the answer.

"That is not an answer."

There was a pause, Janis stared in Shahlo's eyes, trying to read the sentence.

Shahlo also looked at him, and said quietly:

"No ... It doesn't mean ... But ..."

Janis did not let her finish as he interrupted her with a kiss.

19

A luxurious procession accompanied by armed guards of Afghan mercenaries is approaching the gates of Bukhara.

"You dreamed to see the ancient and mysterious East with your own eyes - it is in front of you," Alimkhan said and waved his hand around.

"Oh yeah!"

His companion, a young beautiful woman with a fashionable hat on her head and with a veil that half covered her face, once again brought a lace handkerchief to her nose. This was the famous actress from St. Petersburg, Anna Gallon, who watched with admiration as the fierce guards opened the carved gates.

"This is really impressive!

However," Anna sneezed again. "This dust is killing me. I have the feeling that I haven't tasted water for a month."

"What can you do, my dear Anna," Alimkhan responded, grinning. "If there are advantages, then there must be downsides too. This is called dialectics. I can't run a railway directly to the porch of my palace and turn the ancient city into a railway station."

"Of course, that would be unreasonable on your part."

"But I hope that after the pool with crystal-clear water you will forget about such minor troubles as dust."

"Oh, for that I would give everything I have!" exclaimed Anna.

Alimkhan smiled slightly and stroked his beard.

"But you still have to do it..."

20

A week after her arrival, Alimkhan and Anna, as usual, went out after a delicious breakfast for a walk through the magnificent garden.

Looking at his companion, Alimkhan remarked:

"You are becoming bored right before my eyes, dear Anna. You no longer admire these marvelous plants." He waved his hand in front of him. "The paradise birds singing in the evenings do not sweeten you. I suspect that my company has already bored you."

"What are you saying, dear, dear Khan!" Anna objected with energy. "Can the company of an oriental wizard, whose desires are fulfilled by a wave of fingers, bore me!"

"Do I need to take this as a compliment?" "And more than just a compliment. But ..."

"Here it is! I thought that there would definitely be some kind of but."

"I will try to explain. Here, in your magnificent palace, I live as in paradise, in some kind of oriental tale, and this is impossible not to delight me. But judge for yourself: if you read the same fairy tale every day, it fades a little. Do you understand what I want to say?"

"I think, I understand. You need a different fairy tale and you do not have enough new sensations and impressions, right?"

"Yes, yes!" Anna exclaimed. "After all, your palace is only part of the world which is new to me."

"Do you want me to let you go outside? I think you will not really like it if some fanatics start tearing you apart just because the visit of a European beauty does not fit with their canons."

"May God save us!" Anna shuddered as she said it. "But something is going on outside your palace that we could look at, isn't it?"

"Do you mean something that draws a large crowd of people such as a Mark or a carnival? Alas, the only sight of this kind is the trial of criminals."

"I agree!", Anna said without hesitation.

"Really?" Alimkhan looked skeptically at Anna. "Okay, you will have a new experience. But I must warn you: this sight is not for the faint of heart."

"I can control myself, I'm an actress."

"But you are also a woman, dear Anna."

Anna touched his hand and smiled slyly.

"Have I given any reason to doubt this?"

Alimkhan also smiled back.

"It's hard to argue with you, Anna. But remember - I warned you."

21

At this early hour, the square in front of the palace was gradually filling up with people. In the center of the square, a platform had already been installedon which a fierce-looking executioner was standing.

Alimkhan and two guards appeared on the upper balcony of the palace. One of them was Iskander, his personal guard, a tall, stately man with a strong-willed, courageous face. Hidden power could be seen in his posture. Alimkhan addressed him:

"Bring her, but let her stand behind. If she moves or even squeaks, immediately take her away from the balcony."

"Yes, my lord." He bowed and left the balcony. His place was immediately taken by another tall guard.

In the female half of the palace, girls were dressing Anna up and draping fabric around her so that it was impossible to recognize a European woman behind the apparel.

Having finished their work, they brought her a mirror in which she tried to recognize herself. But apart from her eyes, there was nothing to tell that she was a visitor from St. Petersburg. There was a knock at the door and everyone rose from their seats and led Anna to the door. Anna went out and Iskander silently showed her the direction in which she should go.

A herald appeared in the square with a catapult in his hands and from behind the guards dragged a half-naked man who, in

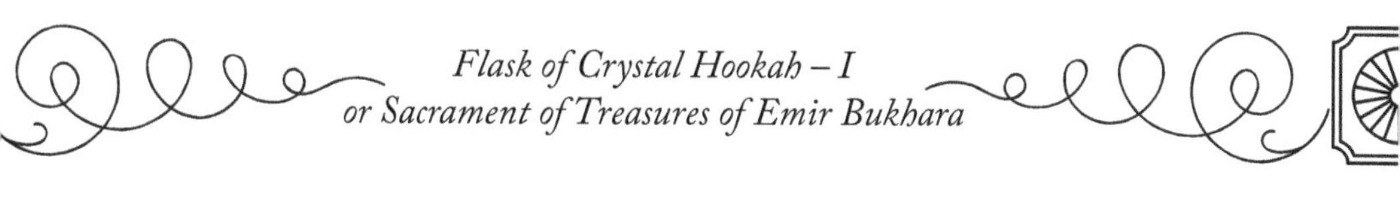

horror, was babbling and looking around. The crowd started hooting. The victim was brought to the platform, pushed down onto a bench and tied there. While Anna was climbing the stairs to the balcony, he had almost finished reading the sentence:

"To tear out his tongue for impious speeches and cut off his head."

At this moment, Anna climbed onto the balcony and began to watch what was happening in the narrow gap between Alimkhan and the guard. She saw a man tied and looking questioningly at Iskander. He was standing with a straight face. When the executioner took out a knife, sparkling in the sun, horror appeared in her eyes.

The executioner made several quick movements with a knife, then the bloodied tongue of the victim appeared in his hand, which he raised above his head so that the crowd could see it. Anna swayed and began to fall. Iskander grabbed her and carried her inside. Alimkhan sensed what was happening behind him and grimaced with displeasure. Then he raised his hand and made a sign with his fingers. The executioner raised the axe and brought it down on the victim's neck. There was a murmur in the crowd...

22

The luxurious room in which Anna and Alimkhan were resting was a sanctuary. Anna's looked exhausted. She absentmindedly went to a vase of flowers and began to fumble with a petal.

"Yet I do not understand" Alimkhan said dryly. "Why did you decide so suddenly to leave me, dear Anna? After all, were you going to stay with me for another month?" While speaking, he was carefully watching her movements and expressions. "Has something happened?"

"What are you saying? What can happen in this blessed place?" Anna tried to smile, rather unconvincingly.

"I'm not leaving you but my idleness. I'm tired of it, and you know my nature, dear Alimkhan. I can't live without a theatre, without a stage, without an audience, I live for it. If I don't see this all for a long time, I begin to languish. Do you really want me to fade before your very eyes in the prime of life?" Anna coquettishly shrugged her shoulders, but Alimkhan noticed that this was done with an effort.

"The Petersburg public will not forgive me for that," said Alimkhan. "However, I think that you are hiding the real reason for your decision."

Anna tensed but tried to look surprised.

"Then what is it?"

"Maybe you were overwhelmed so much by what you saw from

the balcony and you decided that -"

"Oh, please!" The woman pressed trembling fingers to her temples. "No need to remind me of that. This is already in the past and, believe me, it has nothing to do with my desire to leave."

"So I was wrong." Alimkhan got up from his chair. "I respect your decision and will order the train to be ready tomorrow morning." He went to Anna and took her hand.

"But I have one small request for you."

"Oh sure!" Anna readily responded.

"Please do not tell anyone about the bloodthirstiness of the eastern savages. It will be unpleasant for me."

Alimkhan said this in a very gentle tone but what Anna read in his eyes made her feel colder.

"Now I have to go. State affairs await me." He kissed Anna's hand, turned and left the room.

When Alimkhan had left, Anna rushed to the table, poured a glass of water with trembling hands and drank. Then she sat down exhausted in a chair, repeating: "Tomorrow morning! Tomorrow morning!"

On the same day, a messenger from Alimkhan went to the door of an inconspicuous house and knocked quietly. Inside the window, the curtain moved.

Shahob recognized the messenger and went to the door. He opened it slightly so that the messenger could not see him. The messenger slipped a bundle into the gap and left, looking around.

Shahob picked up the bundle from the floor, closed the door and went into the room. Unwrapping the bundle, he saw an oblong box and a folded sheet of paper. Shahob unfolded the sheet. There were only a few words: "Hand to Gallon. In Tashkent." An intri-

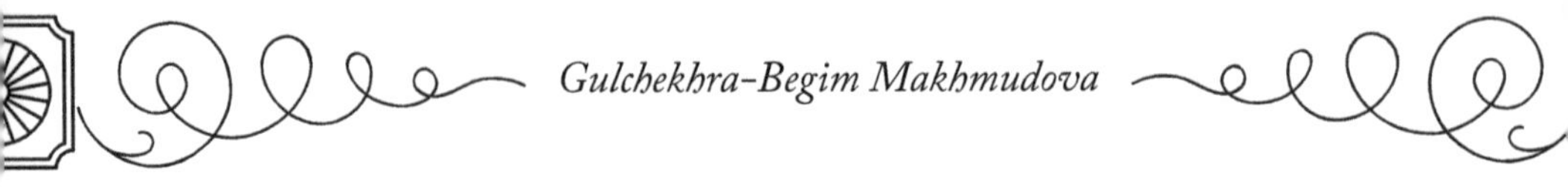

cate message stood at the bottom of the sheet. It was the personal sign of Alimkhan.

This meant that he had immediately to go to Tashkent to fulfil the order of Alimkhan - Emir of Bukhara.

23

The following morning, the carriage in which Anna was sitting pulled up to the train station. Iskander helped Anna to come out of the carriage and escorted her to the train. The last sleepless night had affected her and she was looking exhausted. The guards carried her luggage into the carriage. Then they brought out a large chest and lifted it into the carriage too.

"What is it?" Anna asked Iskander in surprise.

"These are gifts for you from the Emir. He wishes you a happy journey." He handed Anna the key of the chest.

"Ah, thank you, this is very kind of him, be sure to convey my thanks to him." But it was said without much admiration in her voice and Iskander mentally noted this.

"Thank you for your help, Iskander."

Iskander bowed his head and pressed his hands to his chest.

"I wish you good luck, madam."

"I also wish you good luck, Iskander." She leaned on his hand to climb the step into the car, and added quietly so that the guards would not hear, looking Iskander in the eyes:

"Don't get too close to the Emir - it's dangerous."

Iskander looked at Anna. His face showed no emotion and he only slightly narrowed his eyes. Then he nodded his head slightly, making it clear that he understood her hint.

"Farewell, madam."

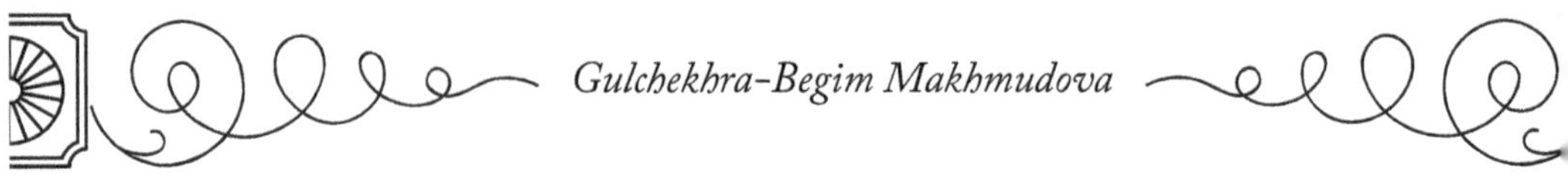

A few minutes later there was a metallic sound, and the train started off slowly. Anna made a light farewell gesture and went into the carriage. Iskander watched the departing train, then turned to the guard and made a sharp wave of his hand: "We return."

Anna went into the car, sat by the window, but immediately drew the curtain so as not to see the landscape passing by. She leant back wearily. A servant girl fapproached her.

"Does Madame wish anything?"

"To forget everything," Anna answered mechanically - but when she saw the girl's surprised face, she corrected herself. "Make me a bed, nothing more. Although, no - bring me a glass of wine."

"Good, madam." The maid made a curtsy and stepped out of the compartment. When the girl had left, Anna slowly pulled off her gloves and threw them on

the table. Then, just as slowly, she began to unfasten the buttons of her blouse.

24

In Tashkent, a carriage was already waiting at the station, which took Anna to the hotel. She had time to relax a bit and recover, but it was not the rest of which she dreamed.

At the hotel, a crowd of fans was waiting for her, among which were a group of officers of the Russian army. One of them ran to the carriage and opened the door. A plump manager was bustling around, who from time to time shouted at the excessively zealous admirers:

"Gentlemen, let her go out! Gentlemen, you can't do that!"

This reception excited Anna. It was her familiar world, and she immediately forgot about all her troubles. Coquettishly straightening her hanging curl and smiling joyfully, she left the carriage. Flowers immediately flew and shouts were heard:

"Viva to incomparable Anna!"

The officers shouted together:

"Viva! Benefit! Benefit! Today is the benefit!"

Anna imploringly pressed her hands to her chest:

"Gentlemen! I am happy to see you but take pity on the poor woman! I'm tired, I'm covered in dust. I can't act right here in the street and like this!"

A brave captain jumped up to the carriage and, dashingly twisting his moustache, exclaimed:

"We love you no matter what!"

There was an approving laugh in the crowd.

"Captain!" Anna jokingly shook her finger. "You are a prankster! If I complain about you, they will call you to a duel immediately."

"I am ready to kill anyone who disagrees with me. Viva Anna!" he cried out.

"Viva!" They all screamed in elation.

"No no!" exclaimed Anna, obviously experiencing the pleasure of the reception. "Let's do without unnecessary victims. But give me a little rest from the road. Then ..." She made an expressive pause. "So let it be - a benefit performance!" The crowd applauded violently. Shahob, sent by Alimkhan, suddenly appeared.

"Madame Gallon!" he said respectfully. "Accept this small gift from my lord, a great admirer of your talent.

"Who is he, this lord of yours?" Anna asked with interest, accepting flowers and a bundle.

"Oh, he prefers to remain incognito." Shahob bowed slightly and disappeared in the crowd.

"He chose the right way!" the captain said after him. "Otherwise, he would have to deal with me!"

"Gentlemen, do not quarrel over trifles," Anna intervened and began to leave the carriage, leaning on the hand extended by the officer.

"Lord officers!" the captain addressed them. "Help take Madame Gallon's luggage to the room, as the porters here do not inspire confidence."

Someone from the crowd shouted:

"Do not forget the horse and the coachman!"

There was laughter in the crowd. Anna, surrounded by officers carrying her boxes, cardboard boxes with hats and a chest, entered the hotel.

Anna went up to her room. The maids began to fuss, unpacking her boxes, hanging clothes and putting her hats in a closet. Anna looked out the window and saw that the crowd was still standing at the entrance. The officers, seeing her in the window, saluted her with sabres taken from their sheath. She smiled and waved her hand.

"As children, by golly!"

"Madame," the maid turned to her, "Should we take things out of the chest?" "No, you shouldn't," Anna answered, "I will myself. Thanks, you can go now. Ask for dinner to be brought to my room."

The maids left the room. Anna went up to the chest and pulled the key out of her pocket that Iskander had given her. Female curiosity prevailed over recent unpleasant memories. She inserted the key, turned it and lifted the lid. After going through the things that were there, she chose one, went to the large mirror and put it on herself.

"Oh, yes! For the benefit, it will be perfect!"

Then her gaze fell on the bundle that Shahob gave her. She took it in her hands, turned it, then began to unwrap it. Inside there was an elongated case of carved wood.

"It seems that we are waiting for a surprise from Mr. Incognito. Well, let's see."

She slowly opened the case cover. What she saw terrified her. The case slipped out of her hands and fell to the floor. She clutched her throat with her hands, struggling to take a breath of air. Losing consciousness, she tried to unfasten the collar of her blouse, but her fingers did not obey. Unconscious, Anna fell to the floor. In the case, which was lying close to her, there was a human tongue covered with dried blood clots.

A waiter with a tray came to the door of Anna's room and knocked.

"Madame Gallon!"

Without waiting for an answer, he knocked again.

"Madame Anna, your dinner."

Again he did not hear any answer. Hesitating in front of the door, he grabbed the handle, carefully opened the door and looked inside. When he saw lying Anna on the floor, he shouted down the corridor:

"A doctor! Quickly! Call a doctor! Madame Gallon is bad!"

An old man with a small suitcase in his hand, accompanied by a manager and frightened maids, hurried to Anna's room.

The manager opened the door and let the doctor go forward. The latter entered, looked around and bent over Anna. He took a stethoscope from his bag and listened to her breathing and then felt her pulse. He got up from his knees and shrugged.

"Well, gentlemen," he said. "My help is not needed. Madame Gallon is having symptoms that do not concern me. She's simply pregnant."

"How so!" the manager exclaimed. "After all, just..." He did not finish the sentence and stopped."

The doctor took off his pince-nez and rubbed it.

"What is so surprising here? Sometimes it happens. One, and ..." He spread his hands. "It's okay, ammonia to the nose and everything is in order."

"Oh my God! What will happen then?" the manager was agitated, twisting and untwisting the fingers.

"What happens in such cases?" the doctor replied, putting on a pince-nez. "Here comes a child."

He picked up his bag from the floor and repeated again:

"The usual story."

"But why?" the manager did not let up. "There must be a reason?" "But I can't tell you another reason, my dear, I don't know."

The doctor headed to the exit of the room. At that moment, one of the maids screamed heart-rendingly and also fainted. The doctor rushed to her and saw the contents of the case. He drew back and had to grasp the manager.

"Call the police. I think I've found one more reason," he said, gesturing at the case.

25

The house was finally returned to Lola and Aziz and the whole family moved into it. Their joy knew no bounds.

Alex, the son of Kanaki, was evicted, and he was forced to live wherever he could.

Spite against his mother and her new husband could not find a way - they were out of reach for him and he decided to vent it against the new owners of the house.

In order to take revenge and not be caught (he was not going to return to prison), he had to substitute someone in his place.

The choice fell on his old friend, Lika. This girl had left him when she found out about his criminal dealings, even before he went to prison.

He found out that now she lived alone in an apartment and that she had an old car. Alex calculated that if she disappeared, he would be able to take advantage of all this without incurring suspicion on himself. He went up to the right floor and rang the doorbell.

Not expecting any surprises, Lika opened it and saw Alex on the threshold. She was dumbfounded.

"You?!"

"You didn't expect me?"

"Why did you come?"

"I missed you," Alex grinned, "and so I decided to visit you.

Would you like some coffee?"

"Sorry, I have no time for coffee. Go away!" She tried to close the door, but Alex put his foot in the opening.

"Why are we so inhospitable today? Rude - trying to slam the door in my face. Not good. Very uncivilized."

"What do you want?" He forced the door open, went into the apartment and closed it behind him.

"Sit, relax, chat. Then you will help me a little and you and I will peacefully part forever."

"I'm not going to help you. I have my life, you have yours. Go away, please!" Lika began to panic.

"Again, you're rude," Alex closed the door with a key and put it in his pocket. "Get this straight, while I'm here, you have no life of your own. You will do what I say. Go to the kitchen and make coffee. If you try to resist, I will punish you." Alex went up to her.

"Don't you dare touch me," Lika stepped back. "I will scream."

"Don't be afraid, I won't drag you to bed." He looked at her, "Although I should. I'm not in the right mood for that. Will you be a smart girl or will we run into trouble?"

"Screw you." Lika realized that she could not do anything and so went to the kitchen, opened a drawer and took out a knife. Alex went after her and stood in the doorway.

"I hear familiar sounds. But with a knife, be careful. You can accidentally cut yourself."

"There's no need to be careful with cutting a sausage."

"Well, well, play the master. Only do not pretend to be Nikita, okay?" he turned and, went into the living room, flopped into an armchair and took a glass vial from his pocket. Lika sat, still holding the knife in her hand.

"Beast…What kind of beast are you?"

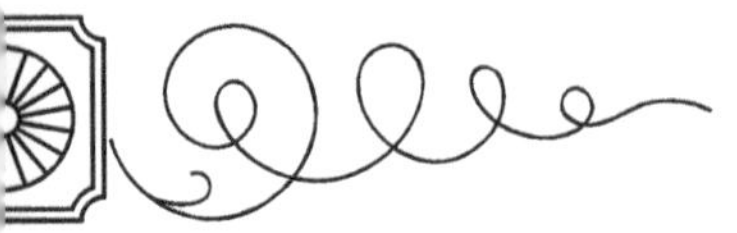

26

Alibek left for Moscow on a regular business trip.

After visiting one of the suburban facilities with a group of Western experts, he went back to Moscow in a special bus together with them.

Due to an accident, a traffic jam formed at one of the intersections. Alibek was looking out of the window. Near one of the shop windows in front of the bus, a woman was standing sideways on, wiping with a handkerchief the face of a boy who was standing in front of her.

Something in her profile was familiar to Alibek.

The woman turned and Alibek recognized her.

It was Marina, with whom he had lost contact several years ago. She bent down to tie the untied lace of the boy. The boy looked towards Alibek. Alibek began to knock on the glass, make signs with his hands, pointing to Marina. The boy laughed and began to pull at Marina.

"Mom, look, look, what a funny man."

"Where?"

"There, on the bus."

Marina looked in the direction the child was pointing and saw Alibek waving from the window. She recognized him and her face changed.

Leaving the lace, she grabbed the boy in her arms.

"This is a circus. Let's go faster, otherwise we'll be late. Grandma is waiting." She straightened up and, not looking in the direction of Alibek, quickly went down the street. Alibek jumped up and made his way to the driver.

"Listen, open the door. I need to get out urgently ."

"You're crazy? I'll lose my license. You see?" He pointed to the traffic cop who was standing near the bus. "Just give him a reason."

"I need to catch a friend," Alibek pleaded. "I will get out discreetly."

"You have to catch your friend, and I need to feed my family," the driver said desperately. "Here, he is already making a gesture."

The traffic cop began to indicate with his baton that the bus should move on. The driver put the vehicle into gear and the bus moved off.

"I'll drive to the intersection and then you can get out." The bus drove about fifty meters and stopped. "Now you can get off. Will you catch us up?"

"No." Alibek looked at the open door. "It's too late."

The driver closed the door and pressed the accelerator. Alibek shrugged and resumed his seat. His mood was ruined.

27

When night fell, Alex made Lika take him to the house of Aziz to carry out his plan. With the headlights turned off, her car slowly drove into the alley.

"Stop here," Alex commanded. Lika stopped the car, trembling. "Turn off the engine. Now quietly open the door and get out. Do not close the door."

"I won't go anywhere," Lika grabbed the wheel.

"You will go. Do not make me angry," Alex threatened, "Otherwise you will get into trouble."

"What are you up to?" Lika asked fearfully.

"Nothing," Alex answered with an unpleasant grin. "Just want to scare them a little before we quickly vanish. After that you will be free. Come on, move." They both got out, Alex took out a bag from the car, in which something quietly tinkled. "Come along - help." He pushed Lika forward.

They carefully approached the extension of the house in which Aziz lived. Alex took a piece of metal from his pocket and quickly opened the padlock. He put the lock on the ground and carefully opened the door.

"Come here," he ordered again. "I need a light."

He let Lika go forward, giving her a small flashlight, and went in on his own, putting his bag down at the entrance and closing the door.

"The light is on." Lika turned on the flashlight and shone the beam around the room. The faint light highlighted tools, planks and garden tools. There was a big vice on the floor. Alex muttered angrily: "Already a mess. Bastard. You can break your legs. Wait - light over here."

Alex went to the place where the ray of light fell and chose a thick timber. "That's what the doctor ordered." He went to the door. "That's it, turn it off." Alex opened the door and carefully looked out. "Sit here and don't look out. I will come soon."

He went out and closed the door behind him. Out of fear, Lika's legs weakened, and she sank down against the wall. Her hand came across the bag Alex had left.

She smelled a faint smell of petrol. Lika turned on her flashlight and illuminated the interior of his bag. Two large bottles were there, with rags sticking out of their necks. The smell of petrol wafted up from them.

She did not have to guess what Alex had in mind and the thought frightened her even more. She turned off the flashlight, got up and carefully peered out the door. She saw that Alex had already approached the door of the house and attached a timber to it to block the exit.

"Ah, evil, pure evil..." Lika whispered. She already understood what Alex had in mind and that he wouldn't leave her to tell the tale. Fear and anger gave her strength, and she began frantically to think how she could get herself out of this trap.

She closed the door and, with the torch guiding her, quickly went to where she had seen the garden tools. Moving swiftly, she pulled out a small shovel and, turning off the flashlight, stood behind the door. Cautious steps were heard. The door opened and Lika saw the silhouette of Alex as he entered.

"Where are you?" Lika did not respond and this angered Alex. "Ah, you've decided to play hide and seek with me, trash? Well, let's play."

A knife clicked in his hand. He took a step forward, and at that moment Lika brought down the shovel with all her strength upon his head. There was the sound of a falling body and a choking gasp that faded to silence.

Lika closed the door and turned on the flashlight. Alex had fallen on a vice, with a long pointed piece of metal, left by Aziz in the vice, protruding from his back. It was all over.

"Oh, my God!" Lika burst out. She turned off the flashlight and leaned against the door. She was trapped like a character in a terrifying story and now she must somehow escape. She noticed that it affected her in a strange way. Fear passed, and instead some sort of detachment came, as if she were controlling events from outside of the action.

"Easy, easy," she whispered. "I didn't see it, so I wasn't here. If I was not here, then my footprints wouldn't be here either." She turned on the flashlight again. A pool of blood was creeping out from under Alex; he was no longer dangerous to her. "I did not touch anything except this." She was still holding the shovel in her hand. "And handles." She took out a handkerchief and rubbed it, holding the shovel with her other hand. She turned off the flashlight, put it in her pocket, and without removing the handkerchief from the handle, she opened the door and slipped out, grabbing a shovel.

"I'll throw it away somewhere along the way." She gave herself commands. Lika closed the door and was about to leave, but stopped. "No, don't take it with you." She wiped the handle and leaned the shovel against the door. "Now, into the car and home."

She took a couple of steps and looked back at the house. The timber still blocked the front door. It was necessary to remove it. She did not want to go there but she made an effort and went along the wall. She removed the timber and put it in the bushes on the way to the car. She got into the car and carefully closed the doors.

These last actions were seen by an elderly man who had risen from his bed to take medicine for the pain that tormented him and had gone to the window to take a breath of fresh air.

Lika did not see him. She started the car and carefully, without putting on the headlights, drove it slowly out onto the road.

19

The elderly man tossed and turned in bed. The chest pain tormented him. He lowered his legs from the bed and pushed his feet into slippers. He turned on the lamp that was on the table next to the bed. The clock showed the beginning of the fourth night.

"When will it end?" he grumbled, clutching his hand to the sore spot. Then he took a pack of tablets from the table, squeezed one out and put it in his mouth. He wanted to drink it, but there was no water in the glass.

"I forgot to pour it again." He got up and shuffled into the kitchen. Without turning the light on, he took the kettle from the cooker and poured some water into a glass from which he took a few sips. Then he went to the window to breathe in the fresh night air. Opposite the window was the house into which his new neighbor, Aziz, had moved with his wife and children. Suddenly he saw a girl cautiously slipping out of the extension, holding something in her hand. It was a shovel.

"What have things come to?" he grumbled. "Girls steal shovels at night. Does he have an antique one?" He wanted to open the window and shout, but changed his mind. He wondered what would happen next. The girl was about to leave, but returned and leaned the shovel against the door.

"Ah, her conscience has started to torture her?" he contentedly grunted.

Then the girl went along the wall to the door of Aziz's house, removed the timber that held it and threw it into the bushes on the other side of the road. After that, she went to the car, the silhouette of which he noticed thirty meters away, got into it and drove away. He waited a little if anyone else would come out of the extension, but no one appeared. The pain subsided, and he went to the bedroom to try to sleep.

Lika drove up to her house and as she began to get out of the car, she felt nauseous. Her head was spinning and everything swam before her eyes.

In order not to fall, she grabbed the door with her hands. Her legs gave way. Realizing that she was not able to get into her apartment now, Lika sank down on the seat with difficulty, gasping for the night air.

An ambulance drove out of a neighboring yard and, passing by, its headlights illuminated Lika. "Slow down," Sergey, a young doctor, requested from the back. "She seems to be feeling bad."

"Probably drink or drugs," the driver said, but stopped the car.

"Do you have another reason?" Sergey went out and went to Lika. She did not react at all to his appearance. He touched her. "What is the matter with you?"

"Sick...headache." Lika forced herself with difficulty to focus on the present moment and then looked up at him. "Who are you?"

"I am a doctor. That's our ambulance. We were passing by. Is something hurting you? Heart?"

"No, weakness... Probably food poisoning."

"Do you want me to take you to the hospital," Sergey suggested. "We can examine you there, if you want?"

"No, I want to go home." She made an attempt to get up but immediately sank into the seat. Her legs were like jelly.

"Where do you live?" Sergey asked.

"On the third floor..." Lika looked up at the building.

"Well, you can't crawl up to the third floor in your condition," Sergey concluded. "Ok - I'll take you and tend to you at home."

"Why?" Lika weakly objected.

"Then," Sergey said, "I won't have to rush here again when you call in half an hour. Or when your neighbours call, when they find you crawling up the stairs." He turned to the driver. "Wait for me. If they call from the control room, say that here is another patient." He held out his hand to Lika. "Come on, I will help you get up. Lean on me."

Lika got up with his help and leaned against him.

"Give me the keys - I will lock your car." Sergey took her keys and closed the door. "Now let's go slowly and try not to fall."

They went up to the third floor and went into the apartment. Sergey put Lika on the couch. He felt her pulse.

"A little sped up, but within the norms. I need to listen to you." He took out a stethoscope, "Unfasten these buttons."

"No." Lika clasped her arms around herself.

"Why did you grab your chest?" Sergey asked teasingly. "I need to listen to your heart and make sure that your condition is not connected with it, that's all."

Lika unfastened the top button.

"Another one. Please."

He listened to her. Lika was again in a fever.

"Your heart is normal. Everything sounds good. Your trembling is from nerves," Sergey observed. "It's been something that has really affected you. You need to calm down and sleep well. I will give you an injection and it will immediately become easier for you.

"No injection," protested Lika.

"Again no! Why is everyone so fond of arguing with doctors? Like in kindergarten, honestly." He took out a syringe and ampoules.

"Where will you do it?" Lika asked plaintively.

"Well, there are two options actually: either into a vein, or in -" his eyes looked at a muscle. Which one would you like?"

"Neither. I 'm scared of injection into a vein."

"Then there is only one option. Lie down and do not twitch. At work, I am a doctor, which means an asexual creature." He wiped the injection site. "And thus harmless."

He made the injection.

"Ow!" Lika exclaimed.

"Well, almost painless." He covered Lika with a blanket. "You'll be grateful in a couple of minutes."

Sergey sat down at the table, took a piece of paper from his pocket and wrote something down.

"Here is the number of our dispatcher. If you need my help, ask Sergey to contact you. What's your phone?"

"Red," Lika responded resentfully.

"It is clear," Sergey grunted contentedly. "That means you feel better. Is the number the same color?"

Lika told him the number. Sergey wrote it down, put everything in a suitcase and stood up.

"You may not accompany me. I will close the door. Have a rest." He headed for the door.

"Thank you," Lika said after him, rubbing the injection spot.

"You are welcome." Sergey smiled and closed the door behind him.

28

Early in the morning, Aziz left the house, did a few arm waves to disperse the
blood.

He looked at the sky - the day promised to be good.

The children were still sleeping and in an hour Lola was supposed to come from duty. Aziz decided to finish the work that he had begun yesterday but had not had time to finish.

"We need to do some work until Lola returns." He went to the extension and saw a shovel leaning against the door. Santa Claus has brought us a present?" Aziz came closer, picked up a shovel, turned it and found a familiar mark on it. "Interesting," he muttered, puzzled. "The blade is mine."

Then he noticed that the annex door was not locked and the lock was on the floor. "So," he added grouchily. "But this is already not good."

He carefully opened the door and listened. It was quiet inside.

Holding the shovel in his hand, he carefully squeezed through the door and took a step along the wall to turn on the light. His foot touched an object that, tinkling, fell to the floor. He felt for the light switch with his hand and turned it on.

What he saw dumbfounded him. A man was lying face down on the vice, a large pool of blood beneath him. Something gurgled beneath Aziz's feet — petrol had flowed out of a fallen bag in a trickle. A shovel was half-clutched in his hand.

"What on earth is this?" he whispered, and wiped sweat from his forehead with a trembling hand. Then, when he saw the petrol under his feet, he picked up the bag and set it against the wall.

He wanted to come closer to the corpse, but the sight of a pool of blood repulsed this desire. The sight and the thick smell of petrol made him dizzy, and he backed away from the extension. He took a few deep breaths to overcome the impending nausea.

Then he slowly went to the house, restraining himself so as not to run from the terrible sight with all his might. He took the door handle, looked back at the extension.

"The police ... must ..."

Entering the house, Aziz went to the phone and picked up the phone. It was possible to dial 02 only on the second attempt – his finger would not obey. There was a male voice on the end.

"The attendant is listening."

"Is that the police?"

"Yes, it's the police. Tell me what happened?"

"I have a man here. He is lying down."

"So what?"

"D-dead, it seems."

"It seems - or actually dead?" the attendant asked.

"I don't know..." Aziz's voice trembled. "A large pool of blood is everywhere..."

"Tell me the address. Do not touch anything and do not go anywhere until the police arrive. Wait."

"Where will I go? But my children are sleeping." Aziz looked at the receiver and put it on the hook. He sank heavily into a chair and looked towards their room. Then for some reason he repeated "The children are sleeping..."

Having eagerly drunk cold water to calm himself down a little, Aziz left the house to wait for the police to arrive. A man came out of a neighbouring house with a hose and began to water his little garden and the stretch of road in front of the house. He turned to Aziz. "Good morning. No sleep."

"Ah, what a sleep." Aziz waved an anxious hand.

"Well, then come back later," the neighbour suggested, "and we will play chess. Today I'll definitely put a mat for you."

"It seems one has already been put out." Aziz waved his hand again.

"What's wrong with you?" The neighbour was surprised. "Today, you're not like yourself. Something happened?"

"Better you do not ask. I don't understand myself. Well, here they are."

A car drove up to Aziz's house and stopped. Three ones got out of the car and one of them approached Aziz. The neighbour threw the hose down and looked in surprise at them. "Captain Kasymov," said one, introducing himself. "Hello. Did you call the police?"

"I did."

"Where is the man you spoke of?"

"There." Aziz nodded towards the extension.

"Have you touched anything?"

"No." Aziz shook his head.

"Well, let's see what you have there..." Kasymov went to the door that stood ajar and looked inside. "Why does it smell like petrol?"

"When I went in, I tripped over something." Aziz began to feel anxious, "Petrol began to pour out of it and I stood it up."

"You said you haven't touched anything?" Kasymov said suspiciously.

"From when I called you, I haven't touched anything. But petrol was pouring out -"

"Okay, we'll figure it out." He waved his hand, summoning the others who stood by the car. They came up. "Ok. You can make a start."

"Will we call for the dog?" one of the men asked.

"Why the dog? The floor is covered in petrol in there. All that happen will be that the dog will find the closest petrol station. But you can order up the hearse. Work, and I'll talk to the owner for now.

"What's happened?" Aziz's neighbour gave up his watering and came up to the group.

"Nothing significant," Kasymov said. "You're a neighbour?"

"Yes, my house is close." He jabbed a finger in the direction of his house.

"Go to your place for a while. I'll come back to you later." He turned to Aziz and said, "Can we talk in your house?"

"Yes. Except the children are still sleeping."

At that moment, the door of the house opened and two sleepy faces appeared.

"Dad!" the boy called.

"It seems they are no longer sleeping." Kasymov nodded toward the children. "Go to your room," Aziz told the children, "I'll be right there. Ok, let's go to the house..."

Aziz and the captain entered the house and sat at the table in the kitchen.

"Would you like some tea?" suggested Aziz.

"I will not refuse. In the meantime," the captain said, taking out a notebook, "I need you to answer some questions.

"I don't know anything," said Aziz.

"We'll talk about what you know. Tell me, in order, what happened before your call to the police."

"Well, I got up early to finish one job before my wife arrived." Aziz began.

"Where is she?" the captain asked immediately.

"On duty. She is a doctor. Must be about to come home."

"That's clear." He wrote something in the notebook.

"The children were still sleeping. I went to the workshop. I saw a shovel at the door."

"Shovel?" the captain was surprised.

"Yes. Someone had leant it against the door of the workshop. I took it and looked at it. It turned out to be mine.

"So, someone took it from your workshop, carried it out and leaned it against the door?"

"So it seems," Aziz agreed.

"It's nonsensical," Kasymov said, puzzled. "Ok, let's continue." He wrote "shovel" in the notebook and put a question mark after it.

"I found out that there was no lock on the door. It was lying on the ground."

"You didn't touch it?"

"No. I opened the door quietly. I entered, turned on the light and saw ... this. I immediately went and called you. That's all. Oh and about the petrol – but I've already told you about that."

"Did you touch the body?" Kasymov asked.

"No, of course not!" Aziz answered hastily.

"Who is he? You don't know?" The captain asked the next question.

"Of course I don't know. I don't understand why he had to climb into my workshop. There is nothing to take."

"So, for some reason it was necessary."

At that moment Lola, who had returned from work, rushed into the house.

"Aziz! What's happened? Where are the children?"

"Calm down, calm down. The children are at home and they're all right. Me too. Go for a while and later we'll talk."

Lola quickly went to the children.

Kasymov made a couple of notes in a notebook, pulled out a blank sheet and wrote something.

"So, for today that's all and tomorrow I will be waiting for you at the station at 11 o'clock. Here's the address. It will be necessary to make a statement about what you've told me today. Maybe you'll recall some other details. Bye."

The captain left the house and went out to his specialist colleagues.

"There should be an interesting shovel somewhere," he said. It is necessary to take prints and issue a warrant. You'll call the owner."

"Already taken away," one of the experts said. "We will finish soon, but our Charons are late for some reason."

"They will come." Kasymov waved his hand. "Poke around further, and I will walk to the neighbours."

After completing all the formalities and the body of the deceased having been transported away, the whole group got into the car and went to the department.

"Well, gentlemen," Kasymov began, "Will we share our findings?"

"Fingerprints were taken from everything that could be related to the incident: the lock, the shovel, the bag, and so on. We will find out exactly who and how many people participated in this when we deal with the prints. There are no obvious signs of a fight. No fight, in fact. But here's the curious thing: the door handle on the inside is completely clean."

"No trace?" Kasymov was surprised.

"Not at all. Obviously wiped," the expert confirmed. "But why, and why it alone, I don't understand."

"What about the petrol?"

"Judging by the wicks in the necks of the bottles, they were going somewhere, or to someone, to be dropped and cause a large explosion," the expert said. "But this is definitely not from the workshop. The scale is not the same."

"What about you?" The captain turned to the second specialist.

"At the moment, I can say that he was lying there for three to four hours. Apparently he was struck with our shovel. The blow was not very strong, the wound on his head was small but he might flake out for a while. As a result, we have two options for development." The specialist bent one finger, "Either he, falling, successfully landed on this skewer like a kebab, or he was pushed there after the blow. I will say more precisely after the examination. In any case, it wasn't something he did voluntarily."

"Clearly." The captain looked out of the window. "So, in your opinion, he was going to set fire to something, or someone, and besides him there was someone else whom this option did not suit at all. Not much is known about them. Did you find anything interesting in his pockets?"

"He had no documents. Just something like a lock pick. Actually, there is still a small bottle of medicine, and the remains of white powder at the bottom. Perhaps he sniffed it. After checking I will know for certain."

"I wonder if they walked here or drove up?" Kasymov looked

at the specialists.

"If there wasn't the successfully spilled petrol and the neighbour, the waterer, maybe we would find something. That's all." the specialist shrugged.

"A strange story." The captain thought. "A shovel, petrol, a wiped handle...

Something does not fit together. Well, what we have, we have. Not the first time..."

28

A few days after the incident, Captain Kasymov came to the authorities with a report.

He knocked and opened the door:

"May I?"

"Come in, sit down," Colonel Kayumov said. Kasymov sat down and opened a folder with papers. "What's the report on cases?"

"First," Kasymov began, "there are the currency traders. We finished the case and it is possible to refer it to the court. In the store robbery, there is already a detainee, and they are being interviewed. We will finish that soon. Second, the killing of Kanaki. I want to ask for a warrant to arrest the owner of the house."

"The grounds?"

"Everything points to him. There are fingerprints everywhere and they belong only to him and the victim. There are no traces of anyone else."

"Or no traces of anyone else have been found?" Kayumov looked at him questioningly. "These are different things."

"Sorry, we didn't find any traces of anyone else," the captain corrected himself.

"So, the scenario of an outsider whose traces you did not find you completely reject?" "No," said Kasymov quickly. "As a possible option, it remains, but so far it has not been confirmed."

"And the motive?"

The captain shrugged. "The motive is classic." Umarov had a lawsuit with Kanaki over this house. The latter was evicted as a result, while Umarov and his family moved in. Kanaki came to take revenge, to burn everything, and Umarov -Intentionally or unintentionally - this is another matter for the court. He does not have an alibi: the children were sleeping, his wife was on duty."

"What about the neighbours?" asked Kayumov.

"No one saw or heard anything. It was night, everyone was asleep."

"But isn't everything too smooth and easy?" asked the colonel. "Why kill him? He could just have called the police."

"He probably wasn't going to kill him," the captain suggested. "Stunned him with a shovel and Kanaki unfortunately fell on the spike. Then for some reason he came up with this strange story about a shovel, which he discovered in front of the door to the workshop before he entered and saw the corpse."

"Outside?" said Kayumov.

"Exactly. Some kind of stupidity."

"Indeed." Kayumov thought for a moment. "Well, if you are sure that everything fits together and haven't missed anything – get the warrant. Is that all?"

"Yes."

"Ok. Go to work and report on the results."

"Yes, sir." Kasymov folded his papers and left the office.

In Shahlo's apartment, the phone rang. Shahlo walked to the phone and picked it up.

"Yes."

"Shahlo, it's me." Lola's voice.

"Oh, hi, Lola. How are you?"

"Bad." Lola's voice was hollow. "Very bad. Aziz has been arrested."

"What? Arrested?" Shahlo was surprised. "For what?"

"Remember that night - the story?"

"Course I do. I still think with horror what could have happened."

"Well, he is the main suspect and is accused of killing that guy..." Lola could no longer restrain herself and burst into tears.

"He ... didn't kill ... He couldn't ..."

"Of course he didn't kill him," Shahlo hastened to cheer up her friend, "No one doubts that. Please stop crying, you won't help him like that. Now listen to me. Firstly, if you go on duty, bring the children to me. Got it?"

"Yes." - Lola sniffed.

"Further. He needs a lawyer, a good lawyer. I will call Zarina, and we will take it up. Don't think about it."

"Thank you," Lola said, barely restraining herself from sobbing. "What would I do without you?"

"The same thing, only slower. Now the main thing for you is the house and the children. If there is news then I'll call you. Bye, friend, and do not feel shaky.

Everything will be OK. Do you hear?"

"I hear," Lola said. "Goodbye and lots of love."

Aziz was brought into Kasymov's office. Kasymov nodded to the escorting officer and he went out.

"Sit down, Umarov." Kasymov pointed to a chair. Aziz sat down. "Let's talk seriously."

"About what?" Aziz asked tiredly.

"About what happened."

"I've already told you everything I know."

"Do you even understand the seriousness of your situation?"

"I understand, they enlightened me in the cell."

"But I don't understand the reasons for your obstinacy." Kasymov expressed his dissatisfaction with such intransigence. "After all, in this story there is nothing that would indicate your innocence. All the facts speak against you. Notice," Kasymov tapped a folder with documents with his finger, "Facts, not someone's gossip or fantasies."

"I also sometimes drive around with the car for half a day," Aziz objected, "I can't understand why it does not start. But I am also a professional. The reason, it turns out, is a trifle that is always in front of my nose, but for some reason I do not see it."

"No need to compare the deceased with the engine. A dead person won't restart. Nevertheless, the facts are a stubborn thing, and you stubbornly do not want to admit them. Prints are everywhere - only yours and the victim's. That is a fact. You knew Kanaki, who had reason to harm you and your family. Although at our first meeting you said that you did not know the murdered man. This is also a fact. You had every reason to defend yourself against this person."

"I didn't kill him."

"I am almost sure that you had no intention of killing him," said Kasymov, showing understanding of the other's situation. "I am sure that it was legitimate self-defence with an absurd ending. The court will certainly take this into account. So, write a sincere confession, and that will also be in your favor."

"I did not kill him," Aziz said firmly. "I cannot confess to what I did not do. How could I then look my children in the eye?"

"How will you look in their eyes after the trial? The court will deal with the same facts that I have presented to you, and nothing else."

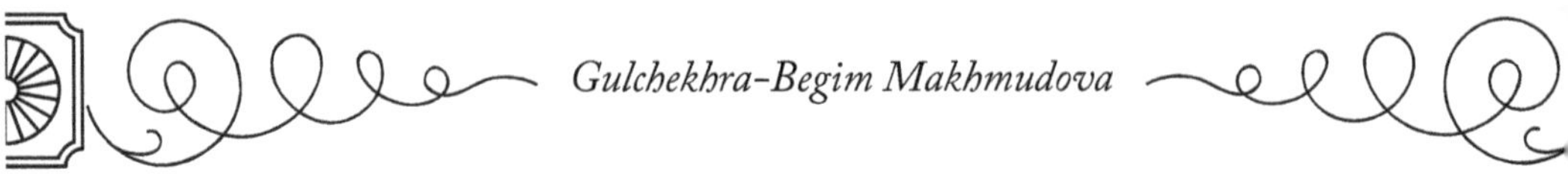

"There hasn't been a trial yet."

"Do you think anything will change before then? You know, Umarov, just from a personal point of view, I would be glad if this happened. But I have no reason for such optimism. You decide." He pressed the call button. The escorting officer entered. "Take away the arrested person." Aziz stood up. "Think Umarov. Think well."

29

Kadyr-bek, the Chief Military Officer of the Emir of Bukhara, entered his house, slammed the door shut, tore his saber from his belt, and angrily threw it into a corner. His wife came running to the noise.

"What happened dear? You'll destroy the whole house!"

"If have to, I'll smash it," he yelled. "I'll smash everything!"

"Alright, alright, calm down and tell me what's happened?"

"Calm down?" Kadyr-bek roared. "This little rootless piece of rubbish got in our way! Emir is going to marry her, which means that all our plans are over! And she still says "Calm down!""

"Are you talking about this Firuz-Begim?"

"About whom else?"

"Are you sure it's not just a rumour? You never know what they say."

"I'm sure, I'm sure - the preparation has already begun." Kadyr-bek threw himself down on the couch and tiredly sank onto the cushions.

"But the wedding isn't tomorrow, is it?" his wife asked meaningfully.

"So what? Can you cancel it?" Kadyr-bek said irritably.

"So we have time."

"Time - for what?"

"To solve this issue for the benefit of ourselves."

"What are you talking about?" Kadyr-bek looked suspiciously at his wife. "Well, you're a military man, just think. Here you go on a campaign with your warriors, an obstacle is in your way, an enemy. What will you do?"

"Of course, I'll join the battle, what else! Could you not ask a sillier question?"

"If there are more of them, and they are stronger, would you run away?"

"I've never run from anyone and I'm not going to start now. I'd go around and hit them in the rear.

"Well, do it!" she said.

When the meaning of his wife's words came to Kadyr-bek, he looked fearfully at his wife, who was quietly watching him.

"You want me to... her..." he said uncertainly.

"Not you, but someone else. For example, some miserable servant."

"Yes, you can imagine," Kadyr-bek hissed at his wife, "What will they do to us if she tells ..."

"She will not say anything, she will not know. Her task is to bring food, but you can always pour something into food, imperceptibly. So, the end. There was an obstacle - and then not any more."

Kadyr-bek jumped up from the cushions and walked around the room.

"It's dangerous, oh so dangerous, but..." he looked at his wife, "It can happen. I do not have a wife, but the top kushbegi. It seems. I know who will help me with this."

A few days later, Kadyr-bek summoned Salimbay, the main supplier for the army of the Emir, to a meeting. They settled down in the garden, and Kadyr-bek carefully watched Salimbay for a while without starting the conversation. Salimbay became noticeably nervous. Then Kadyr-bek began to speak.

"Tell me, Salimbay, are you satisfied with your life? Are you all right?"

Salimbay became worried because he did not like the tone of how Kadyr-bek said it.

His eyes were wide.

"Glory to Allah, everyone is alive, everything is fine," he answered, trying to grasp the meaning of what had been said and to understand where the wind was blowing.

"It's good. You supply my warriors with food, even for various drugs they ask you. Nobody bothers you?"

"Not of course, dear Kushbegi!" Salimbay threw up his hands. "Thanks to you and your support, everything is going well with me, may your days last long."

"So, fine, you say?" Kadyr-bek made a gloomy face, his tone became threatening. "Then tell me, you son of bitch, where do you get this rotten meat, from which my soldiers are turned inside out? What are these drugs from which two of my best warriors have already died?"

Salimbay turned pale and contracted, as his fat body allowed.

"These were not lousy sarbaz," Kadyr-bek continued, "But in all seriousness, what do you think? A cross between a jackal and a toad?" Kadyr-bek menacingly approached Salimbay," If I report to our Emir that you not only rob his treasury, but also poison his soldiers, who are responsible for security, what kind of punishment he will think of for you and all your relatives to the seventh knee?"

Trembling with fear, Salimbay fell to his knees in front of Kadyr-bek and clung to his boots.

"Do not destroy, worthy one, have pity on my children," he cried, and began to bang his head on the ground. "I swear, and may Allah punish me if I do not correct my mistakes. The best meat for your warriors. I will do everything for you. Do not destroy..."

"But will you also resurrect the dead and return them to inconsolable families?"

"It's not my fault, it's all hers, old hag, with her powders."

"What else? What are you talking about?" Kadyr-bek was surprised.

"My wife's mother, the old witch. All day long she conjures her poison ..."

"Okay, stop wailing and beating your head. I will not destroy you. I will not go so far," Kadyr-bek added meaningfully. "But for this you will do one thing for me. And get the money."

Salimbay vividly realized that he would need an important service from him and immediately calmed down.

"I'll do it! I will do anything for you, just order it!"

"Well, then listen," Kadyr-bek said in an undertone, "And remember..."

30

An old maid walked around the palace and in her hands was a dish on which were pieces of something delicious, sprinkled on top with white powder, similar to icing sugar. She carried this dish for Firuz-begim. The maid did not take her eyes off the dish and, struggling with temptation, muttered:

"Oh, Allah! What a smell! Why is so much for her? Anyway, she won't eat it all by herself, and the rest will be given to an unknown person." She looked around. "Never mind, one piece... She won't even notice..."

She looked around again and, making sure that no one was seeing her, quickly grabbed a piece of food from the dish and put it into her mouth in an instant. "Mm, I haven't eaten anything like this in my life..."

However, after a couple of steps, she suddenly stopped, her legs gave way, the tray fell out of her hands, and with horror in her eyes she fell to the floor, clutching her throat with her hands. Then she jerked a couple of times, foam appeared from her mouth, and she lay, silent.

31

Alimkhan was sitting in his study at a table on which documents submitted for his approval were laid out. He took one of the sheets, ran his eyes again, then took the bell and rang it.

A servant entered the study and bowed.

"Call Kadyr-bek to me," Alimkhan ordered.

"He is here and waiting for your permission to enter," the servant answered. "Let him go."

The servant came out, and after a few seconds Kadyr-bek entered the study. Alimkhan motioned him to the opposite chair. Kadyr-bek sat down and it was noticeable that he was worried.

"I read your petition," he pointed with his eyes to the documents, "But I don't quite understand why such a quantity of weapons, and even guns, is needed. Explain."

"May Allah extend your days..." Kadyr-bek began, but Alimkhan interrupted him. "Do not be distracted, appreciate my time."

"My lord, now there is such a difficult situation around. There is a war going on, and I thought that..."

"Yes?" Alimkhan interrupted him again. "And where is the fighting going on?" "But after all, Russia is at war with Germany..."

"Ah, now I understand," Alimkhan said sarcastically. "German troops, bypassing Russia, are moving to Bukhara and our valiant kushbegi is preparing to repulse their attack. Right?"

Kadyr-bek sweated with excitement, wiped his forehead with

a handkerchief.

"No, I didn't mean it."

"Then what?"

"I meant ..." Kadyr-bek began to speak inconsistently, stammering. "Now Russia is not up to us ... A convenient moment for a treaty... It could be..."

"Ah, there it is! Are you interested in big politics, dear Kushbegi? Treaty with Russia, you say. So what? Maybe I ceased to be the master in Bukhara, or is Tsar Nikolai dictating to me how to rule my state? Or do you think that I should ask him for permission to chop off someone's head, for example, yours?"

The tone with which Alimkhan spoke all this caused panic in Kadyr-bek, his hands trembled, and he did not know what to do with them. Seeing his condition and deciding that this was enough for the lesson, Alimkhan added in a conciliatory tone:

"Before deciding to do something, you need to think carefully about what will happen after that. You didn't think about it, dear Kadyr-bek. Did you?

"I didn't think..." Kadyr-bek nodded his head. "Forgive my words, Your Highness..."

"I appreciate your military merits and efforts to strengthen our army, dear Kadyr-bek. The army and our security - that is what your actions should be directed to, and I will take care of the rest. As for weapons ... We will think. You can go now. Kadyr-bek stood up and bowed to the Emir.

"May your days last long, highly esteemed Emir."

Backing away, Kadyr-bek left the study and quickly walked along the corridors of the palace, wiping his face as he walked.

"Damned British!" he muttered softly. "They want me to lose my precious head? Well, I will not!"

Kadyr-bek quickly looked around to see if anyone had heard his murmuring, and rushed to leave the palace.

Alimkhan got up from the table and walked around the study with his hands behind his back.

"A fool imagines himself a great politician. But he can be dangerous. After all, someone threw him this thought? They can throw another one. Yes, my father was right: if you do not want your dog to run around in other people's yards and eat from someone else's hands, keep it on a leash. So, we need to come up with such a leash for him, and my mother will help me with this."

Alimkhan left the study and went to the female half. Walking through the garden, he saw his mother in the arbour embroidering something. Seeing the son coming up, she put off her sewing and looked inquiringly at her son. He came up and greeted her. "I need your help."

"Why else does mother exist, if not for this?"

"You once said that Kadyr-bek has a daughter whom he wants me to marry."

"So he does," the mother agreed.

"We must attach her to the palace and hint to him that his desire could come true. Will you help with this?"

The woman carefully looked at her son, pondering something. Then she asked:

"Is our Kushbergi becoming too independent?"

"No, rather, he's still undergoing that process. Someone will push him to it. And your sagacity can be envied."

"Your father was a good teacher. He also said: "punish not the instrument, but the hand that holds it.""

"I remember his words. So will you act upon them?"

"You may have no doubt, son."

Alimkhan said goodbye to his mother and left. She thought for a while, mechanically fiddling with her sewing, then said:

"Well, then, you need to return the instrument to the hand in which it should be."

32

At this time in the British mission, in the office of Colonel Crosby, head of military intelligence in the East, there was a curious conversation between him and his deputy Major Chambers, whom he had called for a report.

"So, Chambers, enlighten me about our latest achievements. What do we have today?"

"Alas, Colonel," the major answered, "not as much as we would like. A couple of businessmen, military, and so on, trifles. Still, language difficulties, another psychology. Any stranger stands out like a sore thumb. This is not Europe for us."

"That I managed to notice without you, Chambers, so don't expect sympathy from me." He wiped a handkerchief across his forehead, sweating from the heat. "What kind of military man?"

"Kadyr-bek, the chief of artillery and something like a commander in chief. Greedy, stupid. Alimkhan does not trust him and does not allow him to be close to him. So the benefits from him are not very great. The lower kushbegi is the lower one..."

"We have to look, Chambers, to work. We need a man from the immediate environment of the Emir. We must know exactly what is cooked in this particular cuisine, especially in relation to Russia. We absolutely do not need to increase its influence here. I hope you understand that."

"Of course, Mr. Colonel. Now we are working on one very interesting option. This is a certain dervish, Shahob."

"Is the Dervish, in ours, a tramp?" clarified Crosby.

"Oh no, sir, it's not just a tramp. These guys are from the untouchable caste. Everyone sees, everyone knows, they enter everywhere, and at the same time remain as if out of sight."

"What does he have to do with the Emir?"

"Everything, Mr. Colonel. According to rumors, he once saved the life of Alimkhan, and now he is his confidant in all sorts of delicate missions. It costs a lot. "But this is something of worth, Chambers, if only your rumours are true. However, I strongly doubt that you will be able to pick up this fish," Crosby took a pencil and drew some figures on one of the notebook's pages.

"We did not count on it, but pure chance helped." "Chance is not the last thing in our business, Chambers."

"You are absolutely right, Mr. Colonel," Chambers agreed. "However, I will continue. In Tashkent, we have one very valuable employee who has a phenomenal visual memory. Once in the market, he drew attention to one dervish with a birthmark on his earlobe. Overgrown, in a tattered bathrobe. In general, everything is as it should be. What was his surprise when, after some time, the same dervish in a civilian suit, with a cane, entered our office and asked in decent English to arrange. for him to purchase shares of one of our concessions for a very decent amount. Here you have a tramp."

"Are you sure this is the same man?"

"Shahob, Mr. Colonel. There's no chance of a mistake."

"So what?" Crosby grunted. "So what? Is that a crime to share?"

"In Europe - nothing. Here Alimkhan simply orders to chop him into small pieces and feed the dogs to eliminate any doubts about his loyalty."

"It's logical. By the way, where does this type of knowledge from the British come from?" "But this is a mystery," Chambers shrugged. "We are trying to find out, but so far to no avail."

"Do not waste time, it does not matter. In any case, cling to him, and then you will be promoted, I will take care of this.

"Salaries, sir?" Chambers asked with a slight smile.

"Ranks, Chambers, ranks. You do not dream of being a major for the rest of your life?"

33

Several families, including Zarina and Alibek, went on a country outing. Seizing the moment, Zarina sat down beside Alibek, who was sitting on a deck chair and sipping a beer.

"It's great that we got out of town, right?" She decided from afar to start an important conversation. "The air is different, and the mood is different. You will have a little fun. You overwork. Either a business trip, then a meeting."

"You're speaking naggingly," Alibek glanced suspiciously at her. "Are you going to spoil my good mood?"

"Oh, come now! I just want to chat," Zarina put on an innocent look, "Otherwise you have no time."

"What thoughts did fresh air bring you?" Alibek asked incredulously. "Are you really interested or are you pretending to be?"

"Do not wag. I feel like you are bursting to tell me something. Out with it."

"Good. In short, I would like to open my own small restaurant." "What?" Alibek choked on his beer. "To open what?"

"A restaurant. Quite small." She left a small gap between her palms. "Only for true gourmets."

"Can you even imagine this?" Alibek asked in disbelief. "She wants a restaurant."

"Of course, I can imagine. I'm even doing the sums bit by bit."

"Maybe you'll explain first why you need this? You can't sit at home any more?"

"No, I'm tired of sitting at home," said Zarina, "I want to do business. You yourself know what I'm doing well. Sherzod will leave soon, and I will be alone in the house. Do I simply count the walls?"

"If you are bored, get some fish," Alibek offered.

"What should I do with them? All day to watch how they jerk their tails?" "Then learn to knit. Or go to some courses," Alibek did not hide his irritation. "What courses?"

"Any courses you want. Computer, Japanese." "Not interesting to me!" objected Zarina.

"I wonder whether I'll even find my wife at home?" Alibek burst out. "As it is, I rarely see you."

"It is you who disappears at work, not me."

"Ah, don't argue with me," Alibek dismissed his wife. "These are all female fantasies, from boredom. You can fantasize, even make calculations, but when it comes to serious things, you yourself will understand that all this is nonsense."

"But can you even see my sketches when you have time? Maybe then you will be convinced that this is not nonsense and not fantasy."

"Then when there is time, I'll see," Alibek decided at this moment to end the conversation. "In the meantime, do not clog your head and mine with nonsense. Enjoy nature."

At that moment, a voice was heard: "Everything is on the table! The shashlyk is ready!"

"This is a really serious matter. Come along, may our stomachs have fun. He cooks gorgeous shashlyk."

"Okay, if shashlyk, then shashlyk."

Alibek got up and went to the table. Zarina followed him and grunted in an undertone:

"You'll never have seen it... shashlyk-mashlyk..."

34

Lola took the bag and left the house. At that moment, an ambulance drove up to the house of her neighbor, Ahmad-aka. Lola quickly ran to the house. A doctor with a suitcase came out of the ambulance.

"What's happened?" Lola asked. "Our neighbor lives here."

"A call has been received," the doctor answered. "Heart attack."

"Yes, he has a really bad heart," agreed Lola. They both went into the house. "He's probably in the bedroom." Lola pointed to the room. They entered the bedroom and saw an elderly man on the bed, he was breathing heavily. The doctor took a tonometer and a stethoscope from a suitcase. "How are you feeling?"

"Heart, doctor ... is burning," the old man said weakly.

"I am going to listen to you." She took the phonendoscope. "I'll measure the pressure, and we will put you on your feet."

"Don't worry, Ahmad-aka," Lola added. "This is a normal attack, nothing to worry about."

"Ah, Lola ..." the old man looked at her. "It seems that's all... I got myself into a mess ..."

"Don't say that," said Lola. "We'll take you to the hospital, they will fix you there and again you will be like a young man ..."

The doctor measured the pressure and frowned. She began to listen to the heart. Then she took an ampoule, a syringe from a briefcase and began to prepare an injection. Lola caught her concern and looked at her questioningly. She shook her head imperceptibly.

"Now I will give you an injection and it will become easier for you." The doctor turned to Lola. "Meanwhile, call the driver, please, and ask him to bring the stretcher." Lola quickly left the room.

"What, doctor?" the old man whispered, "Really bad?"

"Why bad?" The woman tried to calm the old man. "It happens to be worse, and you still need to go to the hospital."

Lola returned with a driver and an orderly who had a stretcher.

"Take the keys, lock up and call my son ..." whispered the old man.

"Don't worry, Ahmad-aka, I'll do everything. I'll lock up and call. And I'll come to the hospital."

When the old man was put in the ambulance, Lola quietly asked the doctor:

"How is he?"

"I'm afraid it's very bad," the doctor shook her head.

"Will you get him there in time?"

"I hope ..."

... A couple of days later, when Lola was preparing breakfast for her children, the phone rang. Getting up from the table, Lola went to the table on which the phone was standing and picked up the phone:

"Hello."

"Is this Lola Umarova?" A female voice came from the receiver.

"Yes."

"I'm a hospital nurse. Ahmad-aka asks for you."

"Does he feel bad?"

"Very much," said the nurse. "For some reason he wants to see you."

"Yes, of course, I'll be right there." This call alarmed her, she hung up, confusedly smoothed her hair and went to the kitchen where the children were waiting for her. "Son." She turned to the boy. "I urgently need to go to the hospital. You are in charge as the oldest. Look after your sister and do not go anywhere."

"All right, mom ..." The boy was clearly proud of such a task. Lola quickly packed up and ran out of the house. In the street, she saw a neighbour who was taking their car out of the yard and was about to leave. Lola ran to him. "Good morning. Which way are you going?"

"Something happened?" The sight of the troubled Lola alarmed him. "You know, Ahmad-aka is at the hospital and is very bad. I need to go there."

"So what are you waiting for? Sit in quickly. She is still asking where I go. Where it's necessary, we'll go there."

Lola jumped into the car, and the driver immediately pulled away.

The neighbor's car drove up to the hospital. Lola jumped out and ran to the entrance. She quickly climbed the stairs and, out of breath, entered the ward where Ahmad-aka was lying. He was pale, fingers were nervously tugging at the blanket. Lola pulled up a chair and sat down beside him.

"Hello, Ahmad-aka. It's me, Lola. How are you?"

"Sorry." It was evident that the conversation was difficult for him. "You said yesterday ... Aziz was arrested. Forgive an old man... I did not immediately realize.

... He did not do that..."

"You mustn't worry, Ahmad-aka," Lola took his hand, "You can't talk too much." "This is important. I saw her. Blonde hair."

"Who did you see?"

"The girl ... that night I did not sleep." The old man took a breath.

"Well, that's good," Lola said reassuringly, thinking he was raving. "When you dream of girls at night, that's good," she stroked his hand.

"Don't argue. She went out." The old man used his last energy. "From the workshop. with a shovel ... I thought she wanted to steal it but then she left in the car."

"Find her as she is that one ..." He could not finish this phrase. His breathing became intermittent and his eyes rolled up. Lola jumped up and ran out of the room.

"A doctor, quick, a doctor! He is dying!" She cried desperately.

There was a noise of running feet. While doctors fussed around Ahmad-aka, Lola sat in the hallway, covering her face and shaking her head.

"Ahmad-aka, Ahmad-aka, why did you keep silent before?" she whispered. "Lord, don't let him die ..."

When the doctors left the room, she immediately understood everything. She got up heavily, for some reason rummaged in her purse, then slowly went to the exit. She went outside, got into the car of the neighbour who was waiting for her. She turned to him and wanted to say something, but he was ahead of her.

"Do not, do not say anything. Older people have such a stupid habit - to die, and always at the wrong time." - Lola burst into tears and leaned against him. "Never mind, cry, girl, cry..."

Upon returning home, Lola mechanically took off her coat, looked at what the children were doing, and went into the kitchen. She also automatically poured water into the kettle and set it on the stove, forgetting to light a fire under it. She sank heavily into a chair and buried her face in her hands.

"What to do now?" she thought. "The man who knew the truth is gone. And now what?" The only people who could advise her were her friends. "So I need to call them," she decided. "With whom else can I share my grief?" Lola got up and went to the phone. Dialling Zarina's number, she asked her friend to come to her with Shahlo right now. Having finished the conversation, she sat down again in the kitchen and began to wait. After half an hour, both friends were with her.

"Well, tell me what happened to you, that we rushed to you like mad ones," Zarina demanded immediately. "I didn't understand anything on the phone. And you?" she turned to Shahlo.

"Me even more so," said Shahlo, "You told me even worse, and besides that I had to urgently come to Lola, I couldn't make out anything. Let's sit quietly," she suggested, "Lola will explain everything to us. Yes?" she turned to Lola.

"I'll try," said Lola. "Most importantly, my neighbour saw what was happening that night…"

"But why were you silent before?" Zarina could not stand. "Aziz is rotting in prison, and she is silent!"

"Can you not interrupt her?" Shahlo poked at her friend. "What kind of habit is that? Let Lola say something, and then ask your questions."

"I'm silent," Zarina encouragingly stroked Lola's hand, "Tell us more."

"I found out only today, in the hospital, he told me, Ahmad-aka," Lola sobbed, "About the girl and the car…"

"So why are you crying?" again Zarina could not stand. "He will write, the doctor will sign, and consider that your Aziz is already at home."

"He won't write … He will not write anything." Lola burst into tears. "He died… "What a twist!" Zarina gasped.

"Wait, huh!" Shahlo yanked and turned to Lola. "Were you alone with him in the room?"

"Yes, alone…" Lola nodded.

"So, no one else heard what he was saying?"

"Nobody…" Lola nodded again.

"Now, if you had a voice recorder…" Zarina began, but Shahlo cut her off.

"Stop fantasizing! If that, if this were … Can anyone but her confirm his words? No. So, no one will believe her words either. Nobody ever knows what she will come up with to save her husband."

"So, we must look for this girl," Zarina did not let up. "We'll find her and shake her properly."

"Who are you going to shake?" Shahlo asked, not hiding the ridicule. "Do you have her address? Number of the car?"

"But he named the signs," objected Zarina, "So we will search. Not sit back." "Good signs: maybe Zhiguli, or maybe not. The dark one. So at night they are all dark. Hair is blonde. That's all the signs. You never know how many blondes roll on different cars," Shahlo summed up.

"But not all of them are acquaintances of Alex!" exclaimed Zarina.

Shahlo looked at Zarina in surprise, wondering something.

"Oh, you are probably right," she said. "After all, you can think when you want." "Oh, shut it you." Zarina was offended, "You are making a fool of me."

"Girls, do not quarrel," Lola said.

"We don't quarrel," Shahlo reassured her friend. "The only bad thing is that we do not have the opportunity to delve into the

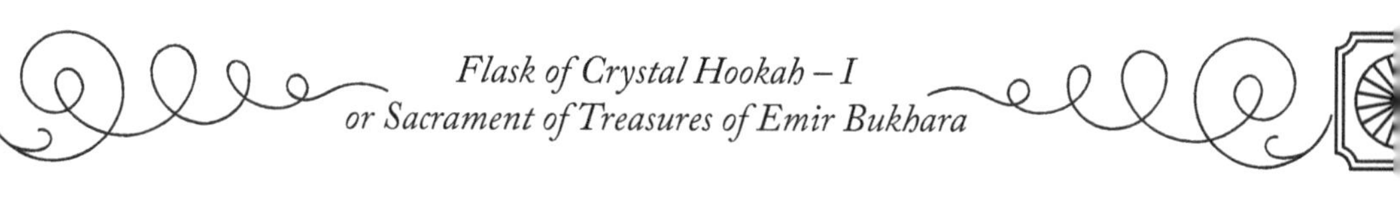

materials of the investigation. There, after all, all his friends are probably gone. However! We do not have someone?" she looked inquiringly at Zarina and poked her finger at her.

"A lawyer," Zarina muttered. "In a leather coat," she added expressively, showed Shahlo her tongue and turned away.

"Good girl," Shahlo praised her. "I'll talk to him. Then we'll see…"

35

The next day, Shahlo came to the lawyer for help. She told him everything she had heard from Lola and asked him to find the girl that Ahmad-aka had mentioned. All of the above was very interesting to Oleg Nikolayevich, which was Aziz's lawyer's name.

"So, you say that there was a girl there that night?" "Not me - Lola's neighbour," said Shahlo.

"And who, unfortunately, died." He scratched his chin with the tip of his pen. "Curious."

Oleg Nikolayevich got up from the table and began to pace around the office.

"Of course, I was sure that it could not have been done without a third person, and that was a girl... Although why not?" He shrugged. "Here is just one snag - knowing this fact gives us absolutely nothing."

"How nothing?" Shahlo was surprised. "This is a participant, and this completely removes all charges from Aziz."

"How? Yes, very simple. Even assuming you find her, and what next? asked Oleg Nikolayevich. "Who and what can show her in this case? No traces, no prints, no witnesses. Nothing, you understand?" he spread his hands. "So, from the point of view of the law, she does not seem to exist in relation to this murder. Even if you and I are sure that she hit Alex."

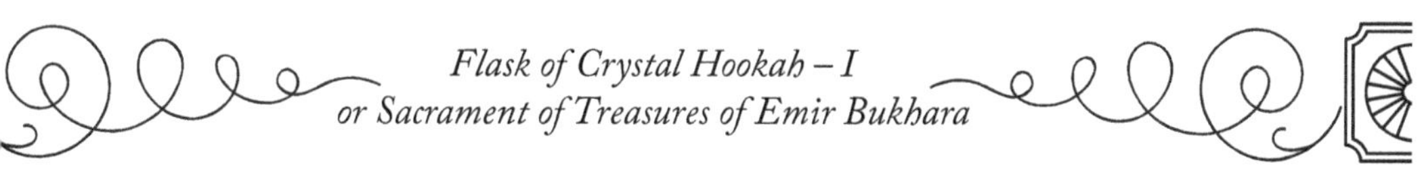

"But should there be a conscience?" Shahlo got excited. "After all, because of her, an innocent man was arrested and charged with murder."

"Dear Shahlo," Oleg Nikolayevich grinned. "I perfectly understand your feelings, but conscience, except for the fact that this is a very flexible and extensible thing, it is not a legal concept. Therefore, the conscience and the letter of the law very often exist in different planes. You yourself will confirm it now. Suppose while defending yourself against a rapist, you accidentally or intentionally killed him. No one saw that. In conscience, you should be thanked for saving society from such a – person. But according to the law, formally, you killed a person, exceeding the limits of necessary self-defence. Although," he shrugged, "No one can tell how to define such limits in similar situations. So, what do you prefer? Bravely go to trial, or quietly run away and try to forget everything? I think the second, and at the same time your conscience will feel great. Am I wrong?"

"Right," Shahlo quietly confirmed. "And what shall we do?"

"Firstly, do not lose heart. I will build my defence, keeping in mind your information, and I assure you that we have a very good chance. Secondly, I will once again look at the case file. Maybe there is something to help you find her." He thought for a moment, then carefully looked at Shahlo. "Perhaps I could give her a guarantee that I would get her out. But let's not get ahead of ourselves. As soon as I find out something, I'll call you. Have we agreed?"

36

Ten days later, with the help of the lawyer, the friends had managed to figure out who that girl could be who was with Alex on the night of the murder. Having given the address to the taxi driver, they drove up to her house and waited. About twenty minutes later, Zhiguli drove into a site near the house. Lika got out of the car, closed it and went to the house. Shahlo called to her:

"Lika?"

"Yes." Lika looked at Shahlo in surprise.

"Hello. My name is Shahlo, and this is my friend Zarina. We need to talk with you about one very important matter."

"About what?" asked Lika. "Unfortunately, I do not have much time. I'm waiting for guests. Maybe next time?"

"It is very important." Shahlo said this with such significance that Lika hesitated.

"Well, fine," she agreed. "Just excuse me, I can't invite you to my place."

"It's not necessary at all," said Shahlo. "Let's sit over there." She pointed to the square in front of the house where the benches were. Women went there and sat on one of them.

"I'm all ears." Lika looked at her watch.

"In short," Shahlo understood Lika's hint, "Our friend's husband has got into trouble. He was arrested and charged with what he did not do."

"That's a pity." Lika was surprised. "But how can I help you? I don't quite understand why you came to me."

"We know that you..." Zarina began, but Shahlo stopped her right there.

"Wait, do not interfere. I myself will explain everything in a nutshell. So, a certain person was trying to set fire to the house of our friend, but he was not alone. The second person, obviously defending their own life, accidentally killed the attacker. Leaving, this second person tried to destroy all traces of her presence there."

"Interesting story." Lika turned pale, but struggled to control herself.

"Because of this interesting story, an innocent person is in prison!" Zarina flared up.

"Wait a minute!" Shahlo interrupted again. "But one elderly man couldn't sleep that night," she continued, "and witnessed that moment. The dead man was called Alex

Kanaki. Did you know him?"

"That was before he went to prison." She clenched her car keys in her fist so hard that her knuckles turned white. Since then, I haven't seen him. He's already asked me about it. The investigator."

"Oh sure. But the second person whom the elderly man saw was a girl. We assumed that this was - one of your friends."

At these words, Zarina goggled in surprise and opened her mouth to say something, but Shahlo looked at her so that she immediately closed it and swallowed.

"Do you know who it could be?" Shahlo looked probingly at Lika. Lika took a cigarette from her purse and nervously lit it.

"I don't have many friends, and not one of them has been arrested yet. Maybe your witness-"

"He died," Shahlo interrupted Lika. "I managed to tell about this only to our friend. So formally, his words were never said. As you see, I'm being absolutely frank with you and I want you to understand that legally nothing threatens your girlfriend right now. Only one "but"."

"What?" Lika crumpled an unfinished cigarette and threw it aside.

"An innocent person is under investigation and is awaiting trial. A sentence that he did not deserve. And his children too. This is the "but.""

"What do you want from -" Lika hesitated, "my friend?"

"That she saves him." Shahlo looked into Lika's eyes.

"Testify?"

Lika's nerves were on edge and her voice was tense as she spoke. "She's already saved him and his children once. Now you want her to go to court instead of him for this? Have you thought about her?"

"I've spoken with our lawyer," Shahlo said. "He guarantees her an acquittal."

"What if he's mistaken?" Lika could not restrain herself. "If she met a man whom she loves and who loves her? And if they've already arranged their wedding?" A man appeared in front of the house with a bouquet of flowers. He saw Lika, smiled and waved his hand.

"I'm sorry, you ask too much from … her." Lika got up and went to the man. When she approached, he kissed her, and they entered the porch.

"What was all that about a friend?" Zarina exclaimed, annoyed that she had not been given anything to say. "What did you make up?"

"Easy easy, do not worry. Let's imagine such a situation." She jabbed her finger at Zarina. "If today a stranger comes to you and says that you stole a refrigerator from him and demands you return it, what will you tell him?"

"Well, yes, I would send him off with a flea in his ear," Zarina reacted, without thinking twice.

"Right," smiled Shahlo. "You know how to do that. Any questions?"

Zarina thought for a moment and realized the connection. She shrugged. "Now what? Do you think she'll do what we want after your conversation?"

"I don't know. Probably not. But we had to talk to her."

"And what have we achieved?"

"Nothing yet. But at least there is a little hope. We also have a lawyer, and a very good one. Therefore, we will hope and believe. Now let's go, friend, and take a walk. We've stayed here too long"

The day of the trial came. There were only twenty people in the courtroom and all three friends - Zarina, Lola and Shahlo - were sitting behind the lawyer.

"The floor is open to the accused's counsel," the judge announced.

"She hasn't come," Zarina whispered quietly into Shahlo's ear.

"If you were her, would you come?" Shahlo whispered in response.

"I don't know."

"Neither do I. Let's wait. Not all is lost yet."

"Respected court," began Oleg Nikolayevich. "I would like to call as a witness an expert who examined the scene of the incident and worked with the material evidence."

"Invite the witness," the judge ordered.

An expert was called and he entered the hall and took his place. Oleg Nikolayevich turned to him. "Tell me, where was the padlock from the front door to the workshop?"

"It was on the ground, near the door," the expert answered.

"How was it opened?"

"With some kind of metal object."

"Not the key?" said the lawyer.

"No, there were characteristic scratches inside."

"So, if the accused simply forgot to hang it on the door, there would be no such

scratches?"

"I think no."

"And more specifically?"

"There wouldn't be."

"So we can definitely say that on the night of the incident the door to the workshop

was locked, right?"

"We can."

"Good. I ask the court to register this important detail."

"Why is he making so much of this?" Zarina whispered in displeasure. "Wait," Shahlo told her. "He seems to have come up with something."

"I have no more questions for the witness," Oleg Nikolayevich said. "Next, I ask you to call a forensic expert if the prosecution has no objection."

"We have no objection," the prosecutor answered.

The judge gave the order and the second witness took the place of the first. Oleg Nikolayevich calmly set to work questioning the second expert.

"I want you to say once again what was the cause of the victim's death."

"Death occurred as a result of a fall on a sharp object, which damaged vital organs."

"The report states that the victim was hit on the head with a shovel," the lawyer

said. "Could this have caused the fall?"

"Yes."

"Did you find other traces of external influence?" "No, there were no other traces."

"Could this blow have caused death even before the victim fell on the sharp object?"

"No, it could not."

"Why?"

"The blow was too weak and could only have temporarily stunned the victim."

"Tell me, in your opinion, does the accused give the impression of a physically weak person?" Oleg Nikolayevich pointed to Aziz.

"I protest," the prosecutor intervened from his seat. He did not understand where the other lawyer was going and this worried him. "This question is not relevant." "I'm going to prove to the court that it is relevant."

"The protest is rejected," the judge said and turned to the witness. "You can answer the question."

"No, he doesn't," the forensic expert answered, looking at Aziz. "Thank you," Oleg Nikolayevich said. "What part of the head was hit?"

"The right occipital."

"With the permission of the court," Oleg Nikolayevich said, turning to the judge, "I would like to clarify these points with the help of an assistant."

"I will allow that," the judge confirmed - and the prosecutor became even more nervous. He opened the folder with documents lying in front of him and began to leaf through them. Oleg Nikolayevich put the assistant in front of the expert, and he stood behind. "Imagine," he said as went through the actions, "that my assistant is the victim, and I am the accused. I will strike." He made a motion with his hand and turned to the expert. "Where in this case will the body fall?"

"In the direction of the blow." The expert shrugged.

"That is, straight?" Oleg Nikolayevich did not stop.

"Yes."

"But according to the report that was compiled on the incident, the body fell on the pin, and that is quite far to the left. So, I had to hit swinging from the right and then the blow would have fallen on that part of the head that you pointed to. Then the body would fall in accordance with the report." He made a hand move from right to left. "Right?"

"That's right," the expert agreed, "So he was pushed in that direction."

"You are mistaken - he wasn't." Oleg Nikolayevich shocked the witness. "Because the accused couldn't strike either from behind, or with a swipe!"

They started whispering in the hall. Zarina and Shahlo looked at each other, then looked encouragingly at Lola, who was waiting.

"In the first case," the lawyer continued his attack, "A low lintel would not let him, and the head wound would have been in another place. And in the second case, the door itself, which opens to the right, would prevent him from swinging."

After these words, the prosecutor pulled out the corresponding sheet with the scheme and buried himself in it.

"In addition, the force of the blow does not match the physical abilities of the accused. Now - the most important question." Oleg Nikolayevich raised his hand. "Where must the person, who struck, be so that all the elements of the plan of the incident coincide: the location of the wound on the head, the direction of the blow and the direction of the fall? Only to the right of the victim, that is, behind the door, inside the workshop." Oleg Nikolayevich changed his position in relation to the assistant and reproduced the direction of the blow. "Have I correctly determined the position?"

"Perhaps yes."

"In your opinion, are other options possible?"

"If we take into account all the obstacles," he glanced at the prosecutor, who made some notes in his notebook with a grim look, "there are no other options."

"Thanks. I have no more questions for the witness."

The witness went into the hall and sat down. "Respected court," Oleg Nikolayevich turned to the judge. "We have discovered with certainty that, first, the accused at the time of the incident could not have been inside the workshop, since it was locked and the lock was opened with a foreign object. And, second, that the accused, even if he was behind the victim, couldn't, from the outside of the workshop, for reasons that have been shown, have struck him with a fatal outcome. The defence believes that this must have been done by a third person who was inside the workshop and entered there along with the victim.

The defence asks the court to declare my client innocent for lack of corpus delicti, and send the case for further investigation in order to establish the true culprit in this incident."

"The court will go into a meeting to decide the sentence." The judge stood up. "The court is adjourned until two o'clock"

... Oleg Nikolayevich turned to the friends sitting behind him: "Let's go outside for now."

They left the room. Oleg Nikolayevich lit a cigarette. Despite his outward calm, it was evident that he was exhausted.

"Will he be acquitted?" Lola asked hopefully.

"I hope so. The prosecution has no serious trump cards. All the evidence is indirect, just a stupid set of circumstances. So let them seek, this is their job."

"Thank you, you have done so much for us," Lola said with emotion.

"This is my job. Sorry, I must go. I need to gather my thoughts." Oleg Nikolayevich stepped aside.

Zarina, seeing that Lola was sobbing again, hugged her:

"What kind of woman are we with? If it's bad we weep, if good, then we weep too. Everything will be fine, friend."

"What if nothing happens?" sobbed Lola.

"Then we still seem to have one last chance," Shahlo said, unexpectedly. "Take a look." She looked at where a car was standing in the distance, beside which Lika stood. She was standing with her fiancé. It was evident that she was crying and the man was comforting her.

"Well – she's arrived," Zarina said in a whisper for some reason and grabbed Shahlo by the hand.

"You and Lola go to the hall, I will go and talk."

The secretary entered the room and announced:

"I ask everyone to get up - the judge is coming."

The judge went to her place and began to read out the verdict.

"Having listened to both sides of the process and carefully

considering all the circumstances of the case, the court has made a decision." At these words, Lola tensed and Shahlo took her hand. "The accused Umarov is declared not guilty due to the absence of corpus delicti and is to be released immediately. The case is sent for further investigation."

Relieved sighs and voices of approval sounded in the hall. Lola rushed to Aziz and pressed herself to him. Shahlo and Zarina came up to them and also hugged him. "Well, well, don't cry," Aziz began to reassure his wife, "All is well. I told you that everything would be fine. Let's go home, I miss the children. The girls will come with us, right?"

Zarina and Shahlo nodded happily. Together they left the courthouse and headed for the car. Shahlo turned and made a small sign with her hand. The man hugged Lika and shielded her from prying eyes. Standing on the steps, Oleg Nikolayevich noticed this scene and grinned quite a bit.

"Wow…"

He lit a cigarette and noticed the prosecutor coming down the steps. He went to the lawyer, asked him for a lighter and also lit a cigarette.

"Well, colleague, thank you for helping me," the other said.

"Not at all," Oleg Nikolayevich answered amiably, "I was glad to help."

"Well, what an assistant you are…" the prosecutor grunted.

"But you must admit it's still better to have a hanging than an innocent man behind bars. It seems to me so." Oleg Nikolayevich smiled.

"Who would argue? What did you hint at in your fiery speech? Weak blow …" The prosecutor looked suspiciously at the lawyer.

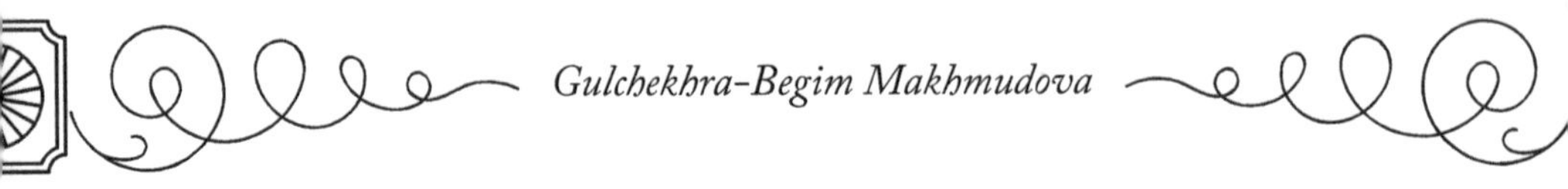

"Yes," Oleg Nikolayevich grinned. "A flight of fancy and nothing more."

"Just that?"

"Not much."

"Well, when we find your flight - we'll be counted ..." The prosecutor patted him on the shoulder and climbed the stairs to the building.

37

After Firuz-begim became the wife of Alimkhan and gave birth to a son, Alimkhan, in consultation with his mother, decided to rebuild their ancestral country residence. One day, walking around the large hall of the palace and discussing state affairs with his closest assistant, Ghafur-bek, he decided to discuss this issue with him.

"Dear Ghafur-bek, let us leave our state affairs for a short while and talk about something else."

"As you order, Your Highness." Ghafur-bek inclined his head.

"I decided to rebuild our country residence so that it had more light and beauty. So Firuz-begim and my son could feel they're in paradise. What do you say to that?" "Your father loved this place very much, but I don't think he would mind your plan." "Ah, Ghafur-bek." Alimkhan grinned. "Even in this case you remain a true diplomat and a skilled courtier. My father appreciated you for that, and I appreciate you too. Tell me, do we have skilled specialists who can realize my idea, or should I invite them from abroad?"

"Our land is full of talents, Your Highness, and foreign specialists. They have their own ideas and it is unlikely they will coincide with yours. They can create according to the finished project, and to come up with their own - this is unlikely to happen."

"It's logical. But I want the new residence, especially its interior design, to be unique."

"There is only one person who can do this."

"Who is it?" Alimkhan asked in surprise. "Usto Shuhrat, Your Highness."

"The father of Firuz-begim?" Alimkhan frowned.

"Yes, my lord."

"But he disappeared somewhere, didn't he?"

"No, he did not disappear, he simply left people so that no one would see his grief after losing his wife."

"Firuz-begim's mother is dead? How did it happen?"

"She didn't recover after losing her daughter, her mind became confused and once she left home and disappeared. A few days later she was accidentally found, but she was already dead…"

Shuhrat is sitting in the corner of the hut. Nearby is a faint lamp that illuminates the plaque on his lap. On the plate there is a piece of paper on which Shukhrat is drawing the faces of his wife and Firuz-begim. Portraits of both women are gradually clearly visible. Shuhrat stroked the sheet with his hand and tears appeared in his eyes.

"I know," he whispered, "That painting you is a sin, a great sin, and Allah will punish me. But how else can I see your faces, look into your eyes? Who else can I say how bad I feel without you? After all, you were the meaning of my whole life," he stroked the sheet again. "So I seem to be at your side for a few moments, but I must destroy you again and again so that no one sees it!"

He brought the sheet to the flame of the lamp, and lit it up. While it was burning, Shuhrat began to tremble. When his beloved face turned to ash, he rushed to the floor with sobs and began to beat him with his own hands.

"Damn my gift, damn it …"

"You think that in this state he is able to create something worthy?" Alimkhan asked doubtfully.

"Oh, you don't suspect, Your Highness, what true talent is capable of, and yet his talent remained with him. It is only necessary to give him a push, to bring him out of his stupor."

After a little thought, Alimkhan agreed:

"Well, let it be so. So far, I have never had to regret that I listened to your advice. What impetus will help him?"

"The news of the birth of a new life, his grandson. What could be more beautiful? But he still does not know about it."

"Yes, perhaps," Alimkhan agreed. "I do not ask you to do this personally. Pick someone who will find him and transmit this news. Then bring him to me, I want to talk to him."

"I'll do everything. May I, with your permission, send Iskander with this mission?" "Yes," Alimkhan nodded. "I will not need him yet. Now let's go to my study and solve some financial issues."

38

A noisy many-voiced Tashkent bazaar with its unique color, lazy and kind wrangles of traders with buyers who persuade them to sell their goods almost for nothing...

Shahob is sitting on the sidelines and watches what is happening. He has a cake in his hands, from which he breaks off pieces and slowly puts them into his mouth. A homeless dog is sitting next to him and looking at each piece - will he get one? Shahob glanced at the dog, broke off a piece of cake and threw it to him. The dog picked up a piece on the fly and swallowed it quickly. Near the Shahob, an old man with a bag stopped.

"Son," he turned to Shahob, "Help bring it home. I got old to drag such weights, my legs do not obey, eh-heh."

"Of course, father. Do you live far away?"

"No, it's here." The old man waved his hand. "My old wife was sick, so I'm doing the housework."

Shahob threw a bag on his shoulder, and they went. The old man minced ahead, showing the road. After a little glance between the houses, they stopped at one of them, surrounded by a dilapidated fence. The old man pushed a creaky gate, went to the front door and opened it.

"Thank you, son, you helped me out. You put the bag here, and come in, I'll give you tea to drink."

Seeing that Shahob was ready to refuse, he added:

"Do not offend the old man, come in."

"Good, father," Shahob agreed, looking around and not noticing anything that might alert him. "If tea then tea."

He put the bag at the door and entered. The old man rose after him.

"Come over here," he pointed to the door, "And I instantly will…"

Shahob opened the door and entered, opening the curtains. He stopped. In the room at the table there were two men. The old man at that moment nimbly grabbed the bag and quickly but silently slipped out of the yard. The men looked at Shahob curiously. One of them, of eastern appearance, pointed a hand at a chair. "Join in, Mr. Shahob. We want to talk with you."

Shahob pressed his hand to his chest and leaned slightly, not taking his eyes off the men.

"What can a poor dervish have to say to such educated people, who has nothing but a tattered robe and a piece …" he put his hand in the pocket of his robe, and Chambers, and it was he, immediately moved his hand on the table. The newspaper, which covered his hand, moved, and the barrel of a revolver appeared. Shahob shot a sharp look in that direction and slowly began to take his hand out of his pocket, ending the sentence, "Dry cakes."

His hand slowly pulled a piece of cake out of his pocket.

"Are you not going to take the last thing from the poor?" Shahob asked obsequiously.

Chambers chuckled mockingly and said in English:

"Not going to. Moreover, I already had lunch. I would like to know how old this stock stump is."

Shahob made a puzzled face and looked at Chambers' neighbor.

"Excuse me, friend, what did he say?"

The man looked at Chambers and he nodded his head just as mockingly. "He said that you may not worry about your food."

"Thank you, thank you," Shahob pressed his hand to his chest and bowed slightly again. "Then I will go; poor people always have a lot to do." He turned to leave the room.

"One question, dear pauper," Chambers said again in English. "Does Mr. Alimkhan know about your successful banking operations?"

Shahob stopped dead in his tracks, then slowly turned to Chambers and said in English:

"Perhaps we can continue our conversation, but only you and I." Shahob turned to the second man and apologised.

When the man stepped out into the courtyard and closed the door behind himself, Chambers showed Shahob to a chair opposite him. Shahob sat down, and for a few moments both carefully examined each other. Chambers was the first to break the silence.

"Of course, you have already guessed, dear dervish, that our meeting with you is by no means accidental. We have a mutual interest, and it's worth talking about."

"Are you sure that you were not mistaken in choosing an interlocutor? By the way, you know me, and I don't even know your name."

"Chambers, Major Chambers, from the British trade mission."

"I thought so," Shahob grinned. "And what is our mutual interest?"

"We have been watching you for quite some time, Mr. Shahob. You love money, you profitably invest it in stocks, for a rainy day, so to speak. It means that your loyalty to Mr. Alimkhan is not so unshakable that you refuse to increase your amount in your account with our help."

"Since the disinterested option on your part is ruled out," said Shahob, "Something will be required of me in return. Am I right?"

"Absolutely," Chambers agreed. "Not so much is required of you." "And if I do not agree, then you feed me to Mr. Alimkhan, right?"

"I am not considering this option," Chambers insinuated, "Because it is not beneficial to you nor me. Nobody will benefit from this, but we are smart people, right?"

"So, so," Shahob nodded. "Just don't flatter yourself too much on my account, Mr. Chambers, I do not have access to all the information that interests you. Do you really need this from me?"

"Do not worry, dear. The one to which you have access will quite suit us. You don't have to go to the bank yourself anymore and jeopardize your reputation as a poor beggar."

"Your concern is very touching, Major," Shahob grinned. "Perhaps I should

agree." "You see, Mr. Shahob, everything is not so complicated."

"Except one point. Your companion is a threat to me, and now for you too."

"Well, this problem will be easily solved," Chambers dismissed. "I will order that—"

"No," Shahob interrupted. "I prefer to personally resolve such issues. It's more reliable, you know."

"As you wish. Now let's agree on the connection..."

39

Iskander drove up to the hut where Shuhrat lived, got down from his horse and tied the reins to a nearby tree. He looked around the hut and shook his head.

"Such a master himself could live in the palace, but lives like a tramp. This is wrong."

He went to the door and knocked. No answer. He knocked again, but again no one answered. Suddenly, a voice came from behind him.

"Are you looking for someone, friend?"

Iskander looked around. In front of him there was standing a man with a bundle of brushwood on his shoulder. Well-worn clothing, painful appearance. He clearly did not look like the one Iskander was looking for.

"Yes, I'm looking for Usto Shuhrat!"

"No, I do not know where he is. Why?"

"He was needed not by me, but by our esteemed Emir. I also have news for him." "Why would the Emir need this hermit? Has he done something wrong?"

"No, the Emir needs his talent, his golden hands," Iskander had already guessed who was standing in front of him, but decided not to show it yet. "The Emir decided to rebuild the country residence and wanted the true master, who was considered and is considered Usto Shuhrat, to create a miracle there."

"What miracle can a tired and sick person do who has no one and nothing left in his life? What use will the Emir have from such a master? In vain you came for him." Shuhrat, and it was him, looked sadly at Iskander.

"But he still has his talent," Iskander said fervently. "This cannot be taken away or lost. It's needed not only for the Emir, but also his daughter, and even more - his grandson."

At these words, Shukhrat dropped the bundle and grabbed Iskander by the hand. "What did you say? Grandson?"

"Yes, Usto Shuhrat, grandson, your grandson. No matter how life offends you, you have someone to create for."

"Grandson," tears appeared in the eyes of Shukhrat. "I have a grandson, oh, Allah, if only my wife were alive! How happy she would be! I will go. Of course I will go!" Shuhrat fussed, not knowing what to do. Then he looked perplexedly at Iskander.

"But how ... I don't even have an old donkey, and my clothes... You can see for yourself."

"I'll take care of that," Iskander reassured him. "I'll be back soon, and you will collect everything you need for work."

"Yes, of course, I instantly will," Shuhrat rushed to the hut, and then turned to Iskander. "Thank you, and may Allah bless you for such a message, you brought me back to life."

Iskander bowed his head with a smile and jumped on his horse.

39

A security guard is leading Shahob to the study door, where Alimkhan is waiting for him. The doors open, Shahob enters his study and the doors slam behind him. Shahob bows in a deep bow.

"Forgive me, oh most gracious one, that an insignificant servant takes your precious time, and may your days last long."

"They don't bring insignificant servants to my study," Alimkhan grinned, "So let us leave these patterns for the public."

Shahob straightened up and sat in the chair Alimkhan had pointed him towards.

"As always, you have more bad news than good ones," Alimkhan continued. "The good news blurs your eyes and softens your mind. This is done by flatterers and traitors. The bad news should sober us up and impel us to act. Only loyal people bring that, even at the risk of incurring anger."

Shahob bowed his head and put his hands to his heart. Alimkhan looked at him carefully.

"So what's going on in our blessed Bukhara?"

Shahob finished his report and looked at Alimkhan. The latter felt that Shahob had did not finished everything and asked:

"Something else?"

"Yes. The last, but the most unpleasant news for you, my lord..." - Shahob hesitated.

"Well?"

"I'm afraid a British spy has appeared in your entourage."
"Who?" Alimkhan's face went dark.

"I don't know yet, my lord."

"Then where do you get such suspicions?"

"If their person had access to the information that interests them, why would they also try to recruit me?"

"Is that so?" Alimkhan raised an eyebrow in surprise. "It turns out that my faithful and loyal friend is now a British agent?"

"I didn't put up much resistance. It will be useful for you to know what these British dogs are up to and what they want, who sleep and see themselves as rulers of the East."

"What about them?"

"They will only get what you yourself deign to present."

Alimkhan thought, then with a hidden grin he asked:

"Maybe I should just chop off your head, and we will have one less agent?" "For all the will of Allah," Shahob respectfully bowed his head.

"And mine too. No, I still need your head, but others - " He paused and drummed his fingers on the arm of the chair. "You must find both of them. The one who weaves a plot against me, and the one who sold himself to the British." Then another thought suddenly occurred to him.

"Although... It is entirely possible that this is the same person."

Shahob first looked at Alimkhan in surprise, and then his face took on a usual expression.

"Your train of thought and foresight are truly amazing. I'll do everything." Alimkhan pulled out a drawer, pulled out a leather bag, and slid it toward Shahob. "Take it. You'll need it."

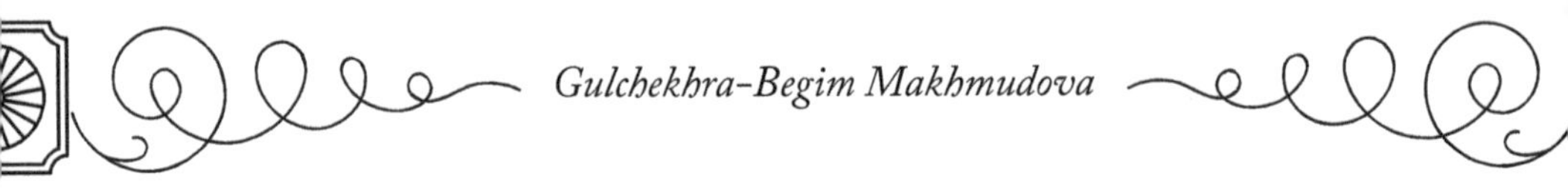

Shahob took the money, put it under his robe, stood up and bowed again. "Your generosity knows no bounds, my lord."

"That's true." Alimkhan grinned. "Now go." Shahob bowed and left the study.

40

Alimkhan was sitting at a table and writing something. Ghafur-bek entered, in his hands a narrow telegraph tape, his face strained. Before reaching the table, he stopped. Alimkhan looked up from his papers and looked at the kushbegi. "Something's happened?"

"Yes, my Emir, it has." Ghafur-bek went to the table and handed Alimkhan a ribbon. He took it and began to read.

"The revolution ... Abdicated the throne ..." Alimkhan hesitated, then looked up at Ghafur-bek. "This can't be so!"

He read the text again, then crumpled the tape in anger and threw it into a corner. He jumped up from the table and strode around the room.

"It is unthinkable! I suggested that he use our methods to clear the nest of vipers that was formed in his possessions. But no! They decided to play democracy in a European manner. He's done it! Oh my God!"

Alimkhan did not know what to do with his own hands, then he grabbed a vase and angrily threw it into a corner.

"Worthless man, worthless ruler! To give such an empire to a bunch of talkers and crooks! He wanted to avoid a little blood to strengthen his throne, so now he will get much more! So much that his whole empire will shudder!" Alimkhan yelled at Ghafur-bek:

"Well, why are you silent, my upper kushbegi?"

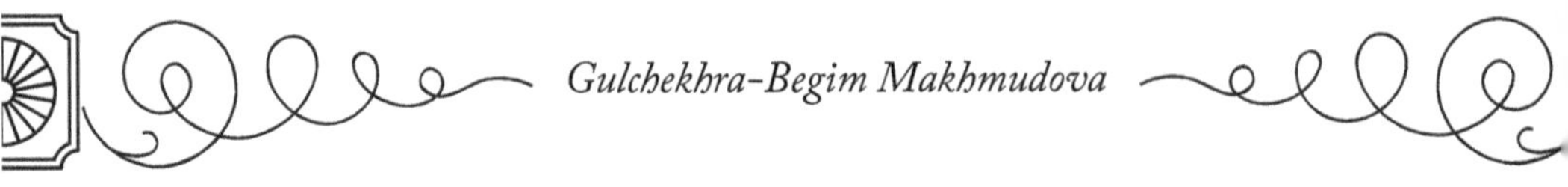

"You said everything, Your Highness, I have nothing to add to this."

"Is this infection creeping in here too? No, we cannot let it. Fire and sword, fire and sword! Or do you advise me to do the same, and let the mob have fun on the ruins of the great Bukhara?"

"No, I cannot advise that."

"Then think, kushbegi, think! Now leave me alone, I need to think too..." Ghafur-bek bowed to the Emir and left. Alimkhan tiredly sank into a chair and closed his eyes.

41

House of Kadyr-bek. He is sitting in an armchair and thinking intensely about something, nervously tapping on the arm of the chair. There was a soft knock on the door, then it opened, and a full man appeared on the threshold. It was Salimbay.

"You called me, venerable Kadyr-bek, and I am in front of you."

"Close the door tightly," Kadyr-bek ordered, "and come here." He did as ordered, and stood before him.

"Does it not surprise you that you are still alive, Salimbay?"

"Everything is in the hands of Allah!" Salimbay feignedly portrayed humility.

"But in mine too," Kadyr-bek added threateningly, "Do not forget about it. I should have tied you to horses three years ago and torn you to pieces, and it would really hurt. This is because of your mistake Firuz-begim is still alive, and even gave birth to an heir."

"Who knew," objected Salimbay, "that this old fool would want to try my dish?" "Then she died, you dog. After that, the Emir cut all servants and hired new ones. I don't even talk about security, you yourself know.

Okay, I already heard these excuses. I will give you another chance to correct my mistakes. Is your old witch still alive?"

"Alive? What will happen to her?"

"So let her try for you. Take care of Firuz-begim's father." "Shuhrat? - surprised Salimbay.

"Shuhrat," Kadyr-bek confirmed. "He performs miracles there in the new residence, the guarding is weak, it will be easier to get close to him. But no sudden deaths, Salimbay, do you understand me? Everything should look like a disease. It's better if he infects his daughter."

"Of course, of course, Kadyr-bek. The witch has this: burns from the inside, slowly, but surely. However," he hesitated, alluding to a fee.

"You can't continue," Kadyr-bek grimaced. He took a small bag from his pocket and threw it to Salimbay. "Hold it."

He grabbed it and quickly put it in his bosom.

"Now go and do your thing," Kadyr-bek added, "Just do not forget about the horses. The second mistake will be your last one."

42

The country residence of the Emir. Shuhrat went up to a table on which pieces of mirrors were laid out with a ganch pattern applied to them and tried to see if the pattern on glass was well held. But none of the samples stood the test. Shuhrat tiredly sat on a stool and began to languidly sort through pieces of paper with some notes. "Not that, again, all is wrong. Does not hold. What shall I do?"

Not far from Shuhrat, an old man, Saeed-aka, was sitting on the floor and stirring some mixture in a cup. He was carefully watching Shuhrat. Then he got up and approached him.

"Well, son, does your miracle not work?"

"It doesn't work, father. I've tried everything, but it does not hold. It seems that there will be no miracle of mine."

"How many years have I lived? I've seen everything but never anything like the beauty you've thought up. It's a pity to drop such a thing. Our Emir will be upset. Are you trying so hard for him?"

"Emir? You should not think so, father. I try for people, and not just for our Emir."

"But who will see this?" the old man asked.

"Who? You see. Others who work here will also see. They will tell the others. Oh, if I could only find the right glue, I would then create such a fairy tale!"

"True, son, you need to work for people. Then the memory of

you will be long. You say special glue is needed?"

"Yes, father. I've tried every type but with no luck."

"Well, then it means I'll be useful for you," Saeed said fairly. "I have one friend, a master - you will not find the same. True, he does not let anyone close to his secrets, not even his students. If you tell him your idea, he may want to help you." "Really?" Shukhrat was enthused. "Tell me, where does he live? I'll run to him and kneel down!"

"Why tell? I myself will take you to him, otherwise he alone may not let you over the threshold. But with me - is another matter."

"I agree, I agree! When will we go?"

"Right now. Collect your samples while I wash my hands..."

Alimkhan liked to spend time alone in the library and only the elite could disturb him. "Have a seat, dear Ghafur-bek. I've been looking at the reports that you've prepared and I am very concerned.

I need your analysis of the situation and the measures that we must take. The so-called "opposition" opens its mouth wider and requires of me to share power with them. Some Bolsheviks sow confusion and disrespect for the throne among the people. Where are we going?"

"Alas, Your Highness," said Ghafur-bek, "There is less and less pleasant news, and more and more reasons for concern. The consequences of the revolution in Russia begin to make themselves felt.

This infection has come here, but it's not the opposition that scares me. By itself, while it hides in the corners, it is not dangerous. It represents no one but itself, and no power stands behind it. We know everything at random and can reassure them at any time, either by throwing a piece to them, or by buying, or..." Ghafur-bek made an eloquent gesture with his hand.

"I suppose," Alimkhan agreed with him. "In this our opinions almost coincide. But what about the Bolsheviks?"

"But this," Ghafur-bek smoothed his beard, "can be a very serious problem. Their idée fixe is world revolution and therefore they are not limited to the borders of Russia, but begin to scatter their ideas everywhere, including here. They flirt with the mob and stir up the water in the canals."

"They also want power?"

"Not just power. Unlimited power, and only for themselves. The "people" they care about so much are just a tool. It is very easy to play on base instincts, and they use it. They are very dangerous, and we have no antidotes yet."

"So you need to chop off the hand that plays this instrument," Alimkhan said firmly. "If it were so easy to do, Your Highness. Throw a stone in the pond. The stone is already at the bottom, and the waves are still diverging in circles. Where to look for the stone?"

"What do you suggest? Sit and wait? Or immediately commit the same madness as Tsar Nicholas to appease the mob?"

"Oh no!" exclaimed Ghafur-bek. "That would really be madness! But we can play on their godlessness, and when they creep out into the light, we will declare the sacred jihad and set our fanatics against them. This is a task worthy of your mind and effort. "I suppose," Alimkhan paused, pondering what was said. "But fanatics will need weapons. Whose weapons will we supply them with? British?"

"If the stick helps to defeat the enemy," Ghafur-bek said with a thin smile, "What difference does it make, from what tree it is cut?"

"You are right as always, Ghafur-bek, I will think about it. You will be engaged in revealing our enemies. Do not wait until they breed like locusts."

"I'm already doing this, Your Highness."

"Good. Let's get a little distracted. How are things at our residence?"

43

Shuhrat and Saeed-aka came to the house of master Bakhram. Old Bakhram was sitting in the courtyard and mixing something in a clay bowl, pouring a pinch of powder from a bag lying nearby.

"Good morning, Bakhram," Saeed greeted him, "Doing your work as always? Receive the guests."

"Ah, it's you, Saeed," Bakhram gloomily looked at those who approached. "As always at the wrong time. I haven't waited for the guests."

"But whenever I come," Saeed grinned, "it is the wrong time. You mix something even in a dream. Your wife, I suppose, is already afraid of approaching you, huh? You constantly grumble, like an old stump."

"Yes, I am the old stump," Bakhram muttered, but it was noticeable that he was not dissatisfied with the arrival of an old friend. "Well, what have you come with?" Bakhram shook off his hands, wiped them on the apron and looked at the others.

"Not with what, but with whom," said Saeed. "Here's Usto Shuhrat."

"Really?" Bakhram also frowned, but looked appraisingly at Shuhrat. "Well, I have heard. And what does the noble master need from an old grumbler?"

"Your help is needed, dear Bakhram-ota," said Shuhrat.

"Help? I don't understand anything in your business, son, so

Saeed's brought you in vain."

"No, I need your art, and Saeed-aka has said that, apart from you, no one can do it."

"Uh, you never know what this old talker will say." However, it was evident that Bakhram was pleased with this assessment. "Okay, tell me what kind of help you need."

"Just a moment..." Shuhrat opened his bag and took out the packages. "Here, take a look."

From one bundle, he took out a fragment of an ornament and from another a piece of glass. He laid the ornament on the glass and showed Bakhram.

"I want to glue them together," he explained, "and I can't. I've tried everything, but nothing holds."

"What for?" Bakhram looked dismissively at the glass. "Who needs such nonsense?" "You are right," smiled Shuhrat. "Nobody needs this type of thing. But what about this?"

He took out a piece of the mirror and put the ornament on it and a ray of sunlight flashed across the surface of the mirror.

"And if it's a very large mirror?" continued Shuhrat, with enthusiasm. "If all the walls are covered with such mirrors and ornaments?"

"But this ..." Bakhram shook his head in surprise, took the mirror with the ornament in his hands and turned it this way and that. "How did it occur to you, son? Where will you get so many mirrors, and even very large ones?"

"We will get the mirrors," Shukhrat rejoiced at the fact that Bakhram did not remain indifferent to his idea. "Bakhram-ota, we will. But I need special glue and I can't do that. I've tried everything."

"Oh, he's tried everything!" said Bakhram meaningfully. "So, not all, since you cannot solve such a simple task."

"Simple?" taken aback Shuhrat.

"Dear ones," Saeed-aka interfered with the sly voice in his voice, "Do I interfere with you? Maybe I will go?"

"Go, go," Bakhram dismissed him, not looking back at him. "Anyway, there's no use in you. Tell your wife to let you out of the house less often, you only interfere with people's work. I have one composition."

"Ok, what kind of person are you, huh?" Saeed smiled, pleased that everything worked out as it had to. "We cannot hear good words from you!" Saeed-aka left the courtyard..

"I haven't tried it on glass," Bakhram continued. "I won't lie. So let's try. You sit, and I'll bring something now..."

He went to the house, leaving a smiling Shuhrat.

Several months passed. One day, Alimkhan, accompanied by Ghafur-bek and his entourage, drove up to the residence. Dismounting, he meticulously examined the exterior trim and was pleased. He turned to Ghafur-bek:

"If everything looks the same inside, it means that you were not mistaken in your choice."

"I am sure that you will have nothing to reproach with the master who created this beauty."

They walked to the doors into the great hall. At Ghafur-bek's signal, guards opened the doors in front of Alimkhan. He entered and stopped, amazed at what he saw. Large mirrors hung on the walls, decorated with exquisite ornaments.

"Incredible!" Alimkhan exclaimed. "I wouldn't have thought that this was possible! I've never seen anything like it anywhere else. How did he do it?

"I think that even he will not be able to explain how such ideas are born," Ghafur-bek answered. "This is a gift from above, and it is not accessible to our understanding. We can only delight our eyes with the embodiment of this gift."

"Yes, this is a master who really has no equal, and he is worthy of any award. Let him be brought to me."

"I am very sorry, my lord," Ghafur-bek said distressfully, "But for now it is impossible to do so."

"What does it mean - impossible? Why?"

"He is seriously ill and, I'm afraid, he may not get up."

"So, we need to send our best doctors to him," Alimkhan said irritably, "So that they put him on his feet. He deserved it."

"Please forgive my courage," Ghafur-bek responded to these words, "But I already did this as soon as I found out about his illness."

"You did the right thing, Ghafur-bek. What do they say?"

"Nothing, Your Highness, only shrug. This disease is unfamiliar to them."

"Bad," snapped Alimkhan. "We cannot lose such a gift. This is too wasteful. I want you to personally go to him. Take Dr. Serov with you, he came from St. Petersburg three days ago, he is going to open a hospital here. Maybe his knowledge is enough for treatment."

"I will do this today," Ghafur-bek bowed.

"For protection, take Iskander with you."

"Yes, your highness. Do you take a look at the garden?"

"Not today. I will when I come here with Firuz-begim and our son. They should see it." Once again he looked around the hall and headed for the exit.

Alimkhan entered the female half, where Firuz-begim was playing with her son. She saw Alimkhan and turned the child in his direction. "Look who's here! Run and meet him!"

The child quickly fluttered towards Alimkhan, spreading his arms and smiling. Alimkhan caught him and threw him up. The child screeched joyfully, then grabbed his father's beard.

"Look, do not tear it," Alimkhan smiled, "Otherwise they will expel me from the palace." He turned to Firuz-begim. "How is he today?"

"Good, my lord," Firuz-begim answered. "He slept normally and did not cry at all."

"A real warrior should not cry, right?"

He again threw up his son and he screeched again joyfully. Alimkhan lowered him to the floor and began to walk with him around the hall, holding his hand.

"Today I watched the decoration of our country residence and was simply amazed at its beauty. I think you and our son should definitely look at the miracle created by the hands of your father."

"Definitely," cried Firuz-begim. Her face brightened with joy. "I can't wait any longer. Will father be there?"

"No." Alimkhan frowned slightly. "Your father is seriously ill and will not be able to come."

"Oh!" Firuz-begim's face showed fear. "What is wrong with him?"

"I've sent the best doctors to him, but they still can't understand what's the matter. Today, Dr. Serov will go to him, maybe he will figure it out."

"Poor father..." Tears appeared in Firuz-begim's eyes. "Will you allow me to see him?"

Alimkhan thought for a moment, then answered:

"Yes, I'll let you and our son see him. But only after my conversation with Serov... I must be sure that his illness is not contagious. I can't risk you being ill."

He passed the child to Firuz-begim, and she firmly pressed him to her.

44

The doctor entered the room where Shuhrat was lying, and carefully looked at him. Gray, haggard face, sunken cheeks, blank eyes. Serov put his little bag near the bed and sat on a stool.

"Why are you so sick, my dear chap?" he asked sympathetically. "You have so much to do and you still need health. But you're wasting it." He took Shuhrat's hand and felt for a pulse. "This is not good."

"My business is over, doctor," said Shukhrat. "I managed to do the most important thing, and the rest is no longer important. It is only a pity that I won't be able to look after my grandson."

"So, your pulse is, of course, weak, and this is not surprising. Let's take a closer look at you and listen to you."

Serov began to get his devices from the bag.

"They've already watched and listened and taken blood," said Shuhrat. "But they just couldn't understand anything."

"Well, an extra look will not hurt," he lifted the eyelid of Shuhrat and looked at the pupil. "Blood, you say, was taken? A simple matter, they know how." He pressed the instrument to Shuhrat's chest and began to listen to his breathing. "Now don't breathe, please. So, now if you please, show me your tongue …" Shuhrat obediently opened his mouth. He put the tools in his bag. "Now tell me, dear Shuhrat, where does it still hurt and when did it start?"

"Nothing … Nothing hurts, doctor. Just …" Shuhrat hesitated.

"Well, well, go on."

"It's just that I feel like I am drying up and crumbling from the inside and that I am shrinking away. It was Allah who punished me for my sins."

"Uh, no, you're wrong here," the doctor objected. "I do not think that Allah would punish such a talent, even if there were some, so to speak, sins. You just got tired, worked, as they say, for wear and tear, and you overdid it."

"Yes, I'm tired, very tired. The pills haven't worked."

"What kind of pills?" Serov jumped up.

"I don't know, they brought some."

"This is when you worked at the residence?" "Yes, then."

Serov tried to give his face a calm expression so that Shuhrat did not notice his emotions.

"Well, okay. Now you need complete peace and to drink more milk. Better goat's milk. I'll come and talk with you again." Serov jokingly shook a finger. "And no bad thoughts, my dear chap."

The doctor said goodbye to Shuhrat and left the room, closing the door behind

him, leaving behind much doubt and intrigue.

Saeed, who was waiting for his appearance, looked at him questioningly, but Serov stopped his question with a gesture.

"Where can I wash my hands?"

"In the yard, doctor. I'll see you off."

They went out into the courtyard and Saeed began to pour water from the jug into Serov's hands.

"Tell me," Serov turned to Saeed, "Were you there when they took his blood?"

"I was. There was a doctor and he was holding a cup."

"Did you notice what color it was?"

"I don't know," Saeed shrugged. "Maybe my eyesight is getting worse but it seemed to me that it was not - " he hesitated, choosing the right word.

"Dark?" prompted the doctor.

"Yes, not so dark, and like I have seen it in my lifetime."

"But this is already bad," Serov frowned. "Not good at all." "Tell the truth - is he dying?"

"I don't know, dear chap, I don't know. First, we need to make an accurate diagnosis, and then we will draw conclusions. Do you know what pills he took?"

"I don't know, doctor. One kid ran to him, an apprentice, brought food, and then disappeared."

"How - disappeared?" The doctor was surprised.

"Yes, he did ... He just stopped coming and that's it, no one else saw him. And where he went - who knows..."

"Yes, indeed. Anything might happen. Well, thanks. I have to go. Try not to leave him alone with his thoughts. Talk with him and distract him."

"Ok, doctor. I will do all I can. Thank you." "Goodbye, I'll be back in a couple of days."

He went outside and got into the carriage, which was waiting for him. Alimkhan was slowly walking along the path through the garden. Dr. Serov, who had immediately been brought to the Emir's palace after his visit to Shuhrat, was sent to him. Before reaching Alimkhan, he stopped in confusion. Alimkhan noticed this.

"Please forgive me, Your Highness, but I have not yet managed to comprehend all the subtleties of oriental etiquette and ..."

Alimkhan stopped him with a gesture. "But I do not demand this from you, Doctor Serov. I am more interested in your medical knowledge."

"Well, yes, yes ..." Serov was embarrassed. "Do you want to hear my opinion about Mr. Shuhrat?"

"Unfortunately, I haven't heard anything intelligible from my doctors, except for general phrases about the frailty of being and the fragility of our body. What can you say about his condition?"

"I'll try to be brief. His condition makes me very anxious and, I'm afraid, this is a matter of several days, perhaps the end of the week."

"In other words," Alimkhan frowned, "It is impossible to cure him?"

"Alas, Your Highness, the matter has gone too far."

"Have you ascertained what is the cause of his illness?"

"I have only two theories, Your Highness. On the one hand, this person could be simply very tired of life, having given all his strength to his labours and thus his body simply refuses to work any more. Such cases, though infrequent, do occur. On the other hand..." He hesitated, not knowing how to correctly formulate his thoughts.

"Or - what?"

"Or someone has helped him shorten his days."

"In other words - poisoned?"

"Some symptoms indicate this," Serov confirmed.

"Again ..." Alimkhan's face darkened. Noticing the doctor's surprised look, he explained:

"Three years ago they tried to poison my wife. Fortunately, this attempt failed. Now here it is ... Which theory do you personally lean towards, doctor?"

"To the second, Your Highness. As I found out, he was taking some pills. In my practice there was a similar case."

"However, if there is poison, then there is an antidote."

"Yes, of course, but that assumes that we know what the poison is. We do not know this."

"My people will find out. Those who did this will regret that they were born into this world." He clapped his hands and the servant ran up. "Call Iskander to me." The servant sped away. "My wife wants to see her father and Shukhrat is her father. Can you guarantee that his illness is not contagious and will not harm her?"

"Yes, I can, Your Highness. I took the Hippocratic Oath and am responsible for my words."

"I hope so. Thank you Mr. Serov, you can go now."

The doctor bowed and was about to leave, but Alimkhan stopped him with a gesture. "Make a list of what is needed for your hospital. They will provide you with everything."

"Thank you, Your Highness, I will make such a list."

He bowed once more and left. On the way to the exit, he came in contact with Iskander, with whom he also exchanged bows.

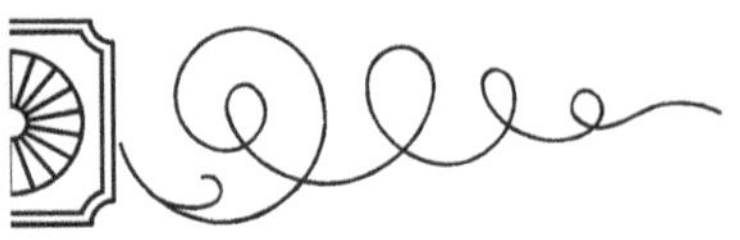

45

Iskander approached Alimkhan.

"I am at your service, my lord."

"Today you will accompany my wife and my son to her father. Strengthen the guarding so as not to let a single hair fall from their heads. After returning, you will immediately begin to find out who wanted to get rid of Shuhrat and why and what poison was given to him. Talk to Dr. Nikolsky, he knows something. These people have to speak."

"I will find them and they will speak, my lord. If they are still alive," he added.

Alimkhan carefully looked at Iskander.

"Yes you are right. If alive ... Then hurry up. You can go." Iskander bowed and left, leaving Alimkhan in a gloomy mood.

Firuz-begim entered the room, where the dying Shuhrat was lying, holding her son's hand. The condition in which she found her father made her put her hand to her mouth. The face turned gray, sunken cheeks, dried, skin-covered hands lying on top of the blanket. An absent gaze directed somewhere inward. Firuz-begim went to his bed, touched his hand.

"Father..."

The sound of her voice lifted Shukhrat out of his daze, he looked in her direction, and life in his eyes thawed.

"Firuz-begim, my girl! You have arrived ... Praise be to Allah! He sent me my angel before my death."

"Don't say that, father, you'll get better. Doctors will treat you, I believe."

"Doctors ... What do they understand of my illness ..." He began to peer eagerly at the features of his daughter, then he looked at the boy. "I never hoped to see you again. This is my grandson, huh?"

"Yes, father, this is your grandson. See how big he is already? He even fights with Iskander on sabers and loves to draw. Really, son?" The boy nodded importantly, looking at Shuhrat.

"That's good," Shuhrat made a feeble attempt to smile. "There will be someone to protect you ... It is a pity that your mother is not here now, how glad she would be." "I remember her," Firuz-begim's eyes went wet, "I never forgot about her, father." "Me too ... Never mind, soon I will see her and tell how grown up and beautiful you have become and what a wonderful grandson we have. She will be happy." "Don't say that, father, you cannot die." Firuz-begim was already unable to restrain her tears. "Have you done all your work on this earth? Or do you not want to transfer your knowledge to your grandson when he grows up? Who, besides you, will do this?"

"Don't cry, my girl, it hurts me to see your tears. Now it doesn't matter what I want or don't... Allah's will. All is right. My earthly affairs are over, it's time to relax. I'm very tired..."

"No no!" protested Firuz-begim. "You will definitely get better. Promise me that the next time I visit you, you will no longer lie in bed and say goodbye to life!"

"Good, daughter, I will try. Next time we'll talk with you a little longer, and now go, I need some rest."

"Good, father," she took the boy in her arms. "Next time he will show you what he has learned. She touched her father's hand again.

Do not forget, you promised." She wiped away her tears and went to the door. Shuhrat called to her.

"Wait a minute..."

Firuz-begim turned around.

"Yes, father?"

Shuhrat looked at Firuz-begim and his grandson for a long moment.

"There is nothing. Is Iskander with you?"

"Yes, he is here."

"Let him come to me. Now go."

He made a weak farewell hand motion and closed his eyes. Firuz-begim came out, barely restraining sobs.

Leaving the sobbing Firuz-begim to the care of the maid, Iskander went into the room to Shuhrat and stopped at the door. Shuhrat opened his eyes, looked at Iskander and made a sign to him to come closer. Iskander came up and stood near the bed.

"I'm here, Usto."

"I have a request for you, son. I can't do without your help."

"Everything, what is in my power, will be done, Usto." "Good ... Lift me up so I can sit."

Iskander easily lifted Shuhrat and leaned against the head of the bed, placing a pillow under his back.

"Yes, that will be good," said Shuhrat. "There on the shelf is a plank, paper and pencil, bring them to me. I have to do something in time..."

Iskander looked at the shelf, went up to it, took what Shukhrat requested, and placed it in front of him.

"That's what you asked."

Shukhrat put a sheet of paper on a small board, took a pencil, closed his eyes for a few seconds, then opened them and tried to draw several lines on paper. But the weakened hand did not obey him. He gritted his teeth and squeezed a pencil in his fingers so that his knuckles turned white, and again he did not succeed. He groaned from powerlessness.

"Damned hand ... Just when I need it the most, it refuses to serve me..."

"Don't torture yourself, Usto," Iskander said. "You can do it tomorrow if you feel better."

"Tomorrow?" Shuhrat shook his head. "I'm afraid this is too long for me. Bring me the lamp."

Iskander brought the lamp and brought it to the sheet so that the light fell on him. "No, not there. Closer..." - Iskander moved his hand with the lamp closer, as Shukhrat asked. "Now hold it tight."

Shuhrat released a pencil from his fingers, straightened his palm and slowly began to raise it to the tongue of flame, until the palm was directly above it. Iskander immediately took his hand with the lamp to the side.

"What are you doing, Usto?" he exclaimed.

"Hold it," Shuhrat said firmly. "When your last battle comes, will you hide your head cowardly too?"

"This is another matter."

"No, not another. For me this is the same final battle. Hold it, Iskander..." He hesitated, not daring to fulfill Shuhrat's request, so as not to harm him. "Well? You are a warrior!" Shuhrat said resolutely.

Iskander looked into Shuhrat's eyes, then slowly moved the lamp. The palm of Shuhrat was again above the tongue of flame. Iskander saw veins swell on Shuhrat's forehead, sweat came out, and a feverish glow appeared in his eyes. It smelled of burning flesh. Finally, Shuhrat removed his hand from the flame and again took the pencil.

"Now I'm ready..."

With quick and clear movements, he began to put strokes on a sheet of paper, and Iskander was amazed to see the familiar features of Firuz-begim, and then her son, appear on paper. When Shukhrat made the final touch, his hand dropped powerlessly onto the blanket, his head leaned back on the pillow. In the eyes of Iskander, besides amazement, fear also appeared.

"What is this?" whispered amazed Iskander.

"This?" Shuhrat looked Iskander in the eye. "This is my last sin, and I want it to go to the grave with me. You can do it?"

Iskander carefully picked up the paper and peered at the images. Tenderness appeared in his eyes, and Shuhrat noticed this. Then he carefully folded the sheet and hid it in his leather pouch.

"Yes, Usto, I will do as you wish. I bow to you. You deserve this sin." As a sign of respect, he bowed his head in front of Shuhrat.

"Thank you, son..." It was evident at what price he's done his last job, and that his strength was leaving him. "That was my first request..." He paused, panting.

"Further. Protect my daughter and grandson." Iskander looked at Shuhrat in surprise.

"But they are under the protection of the Emir! What can a simple warrior do?"

"Of the Emir? This may not be enough. Love can sometimes work miracles." Iskander could not restrain his surprise.

"How do you know that...?"

Shuhrat stopped him with a gesture.

"There is no time for unnecessary words, my time is running out ... I want to leave calm for their fate."

Iskander straightened up and laid his hand on his chest.

"You can be calm, Usto. My life belongs to them."

"Good ... Now go, I need to get ready. I'm very..." - and already in a whisper Shuhrat added, "...tired..."

Shuhrat closed his eyes, a spasm ran through his body, and he calmed down. Iskander bowed before the great master and left the room.

46

More than ten years have passed since the last events. Sitora, Shahlo's daughter, has grown up, and she is already seventeen.

Sherzod, the son of Zarina and Alibek, had graduated from high school, and he was sent to study abroad. Shahlo had long ago built her own business and was deeply occupied by her favourite job.

Sitora came into her office. Shahlo was talking to someone on the phone.

Seeing her daughter come in, she pointed her finger at her chair.

"Sit," Shahlo covered the phone with her hand, "I'm finishing."

Having heard the interlocutor's phrase, Shahlo changed her tone to a more decisive one:

"Sorry, but this option does not suit me. You promised to deliver samples by the 18th and today is the 20th and again you are postponing it. You disrupt my work and nobody will be interested in the excuse that your employee is ill. We will simply be deleted from the list, and I cannot allow this."

"It will be ready in a week," the interlocutor said, "you will receive everything, even on a larger scale. Is one week breaking your plans?"

"This is out of the question," Shahlo resolutely said. "We have an agreement with you and be so kind as to comply with it. Find a replacement for your specialist, but I should have samples in two, at most, three days later. Otherwise, I will be forced to look for another supplier."

"Good," the interlocutor surrendered, "I will do everything that's possible, do not worry."

"And the impossible too. All the best." Shahlo hung up and looked at her daughter. "I have a festival on the grapevine, and he is looking for good reasons for me!"

"In Paris?" Sitora asked.

"As always. How are your tests?"

"Fine," the daughter replied lightly, "Passed almost all of them."

"Why can't you do without this "almost"? Please, what is your stupid manner of slouching? Soon you will be curled up."

"Habit," Sitora smiled.

"Not the best one," Shahlo said mockingly angrily. "Do you want some coffee?" "No, thanks."

"I will drink." Shahlo got up, poured coffee into a cup and sipped. "That's what I thought. Should I take you with me?"

"Where to? To Paris?!" Sitora's eyes glittered joyfully, and she jumped up from her chair.

"No, to the village," Shahlo smiled, "Which is called Paris." "Yes, even now!" Sitora rubbed her hands.

"I have no doubt about that. There is only one problem," Shahlo added sadly.

"What?" Sitora was wary.

"Stooping and smacking ones," Shahlo jabbed a finger at Sitora, "are not allowed there."

Sitora immediately straightened up:

"When did I smack?"

"When a mouthful of bubble gum. So what? Will you fix your

flaws? You have such little time."

"Five seconds and there is not a single flaw!" She went to an empty place and made a pose. "It's alright?"

"Horror!" Shahlo grabbed her head. "Naturally, the girl with the Place Pigalle." "Really? And so?" Sitora changed her position.

"Already better, but not by much. You will have to work. Did you watch a movie that I brought from the last festival?"

"These hinged transformers?" Sitora portrayed a parody of a fashion model. "Normal people don't walk like that."

"They do walk. So?" Shahlo looked inquiringly at her daughter. "We will argue or what?"

"Of course, "or what!"" without hesitation, exclaimed Sitora. "When are we going?"

"In three weeks."

"Hurrah! Does dad know?"

"Not yet." Shahlo frowned.

"Again, he will swear that you are leaving, you are leaving the house, and you are taking me with you."

"It's strange," said Shahlo, "Why don't I swear when he goes on business trips?"

"Well, he's for work."

"And me?" asked Shahlo. "Am I doing foolishness from idleness, or what?" "Of course not. I think he's just jealous of you," Sitora said with the look of a connoisseur.

"Jealous?" asked Shahlo. "Of whom?"

"It doesn't matter. Men can be jealous."

"Wow! How did you know?"

"I read it in a book," Sitora smiled slyly.

"I know your books," Shahlo waved her hand. "That's all, as an expert on male jealousy, I have a lot of work. Finita la commedia, go and train.”

“Yes, ma'am!” Sitora took a visor in the American manner.

“Well, there you go..” Shahlo smiled and shook her head.

Arriving home, Shahlo decided to call Christian, with whom she had not talked for about two weeks, and to warn about her arrival. She dialled Christian's Paris apartment number. The receiver was picked up by his wife, Jacqueline.

“Hello.”

“Hello, Jacqueline. This is Shahlo. Sorry to bother you, but I'm going to go to your festival and would like to discuss something with Christian first. Could you call him?”

“Hello, Shahlo. I'm sorry, but Christian is no longer here.”

“Could you tell him ...” Shahlo suddenly faltered. “Excuse me, Jacqueline, maybe I misunderstood you. What does it mean - Christian is no longer here? Did you say that?”

“He died, Shahlo. A few days ago.”

“How - died?!” from this unexpected message, Shahlo's eyes widened. “He ... I don't

understand anything. Accident?”

“Not an accident. He himself-”

“Oh my God! Jacqueline, accept my most sincere condolences. You know how much Christian has done for me.”

“Thank you, Shahlo. When you are in Paris, call on me, I am always glad to see you. “Of course, Jacqueline. I promise that I will definitely come to see you. Try not to lose heart.”

“Thank you, Shahlo.”

“Goodbye, Jacqueline ...” Shahlo hung up.

Sitora came into the room and saw that her mother was very upset with something. “Did something happen?”

“Christian died ...” Shahlo's eyes were wet.

“What? Such horrible news!” gasped Sitora. “What happened to him?”

“Killed himself. Poor Jacqueline...”

47

The plane landed at a Paris airfield. Shahlo and Sitora entered the airport hall, through which passengers, employees, and servants scurried.

"Mum, how are we going to get to the place?" asked Sitora.

"By taxi, of course," Shahlo answered.

"By the way," a male voice sounded from behind, "there are other modes of transport."

Shahlo turned at the voice and exclaimed in surprise:

"Oh my, Janis! How did you end up here?"

"Is that instead of a hello?" Janis smiled.

"Well, of course hello!" exclaimed Shahlo. "I'm terribly glad to see you." Janis took her hand and kissed it.

"As I understand it, this charming mademoiselle is your daughter?" "She is. Her name is Sitora," Sitora and Janis greeted one another.

"And where is your curtsey?" Sitora jokingly portrayed this movement. "Now you look like a decent girl."

"Do not torture the child, Shahlo," Janis smiled. "Do you still want to take a taxi?" "Not any more." Shahlo smiled too.

"Mom, will I wander around until the luggage is brought?"

"Go for a wander, just not for long. Do not get lost."

"I will try."

Sitora walked away. Shahlo and Janis looked at each other.

"Hello," said Janis gently.

"Hello, Janis. I did not expect you to come to the airport."

"I wanted to see you as soon as possible. Sitting and waiting for your call, knowing that you are somewhere nearby, is unbearable." He took her hand and pressed it to his lips. Through the window, Sitora saw this and froze in surprise.

"You will laugh, but I rode here like a boy on a first date."

"I am not laughing." Shahlo ran her fingers along his cheek. "Any woman would be happy to hear that."

"You are not any woman - you are the only one. Even time does not change you. You are the same as the first time I saw you."

"Do you mean that pale, tattered person who crawled out of the plane? In that case, I was very well preserved."

"I mean - " he did not finish, because Sitora approached, who was very interested in this scene.

"I've not come too soon?" she asked with a naive expression. "I just could not stand it: there are so many interesting things but for some reason they only accept cash." "You're just in time. Firstly, they are about to bring your luggage, and secondly..." - he took a credit card from his pocket and handed it to Sitora.

"Here is just enough for a couple of these seedy boutiques. Shall I ask them to pack?"

Sitora's mouth opened in surprise.

"Janis, immediately hide this disgrace. And you," she turned to Sitora, "please close your mouth, this is indecent."

Sitora pointedly clapped her teeth.

"Do not spoil the child, Janis, otherwise she will grow up a lazy and tedious leech." "Well, mom ..." Sitora tried to free her ear.

"I have no words." Janis shook his head, hiding a grin. Then he crooked his elbow to Sitora and she pointedly took his arm. "It seems, mademoiselle, that you weren't very lucky with your mother."

"I am starting to think so, too," Sitora immediately agreed, looking slyly at her mother.

"You are traitors and betrayers! Conspirators and terrorists," Shahlo added. "Let's get the luggage…"

Shahlo, Sitora and Janis left the airport building and got into a car which was waiting for them. Janis's bodyguards followed the car.

"Janis," Shahlo asked, "what are your plans for tomorrow?"

"In general, except for a business meeting in the evening, none," replied Janis. "By the way, I would like you and Sitora to come with me. It will be interesting and useful too. What do you think of it, Shahlo?"

"I have no special objections, if it is ok to come without an invitation."

"Is my invitation enough?"

"Quite."

"Why did you ask about tomorrow?"

"I promised Jacqueline to visit her as soon as I arrive. Do you know about Christian?"

"I know, I was at his funeral."

"I don't understand," Shahlo said sadly, "How could he do this. He was always such a buoyant person, and he and Jacqueline were just such a lovely couple."

"She didn't tell you anything?" Janis asked. "No – and I found it uncomfortable to ask her."

"His sociable nature let him down. He loved life in all its manifestations and as a result - AIDS."

"Oh my God!" Shahlo exclaimed. "I can't imagine! But still,

this is not a reason to part with life. After all, many people live with it."

"But he couldn't. He did not want to torment himself, nor even Jacqueline. He really loved her. Do you want me to go with you?"

"Yes, that would be easier for me."

"Then I will call you in the morning, and we will arrange a time."

"What will I do?" Sitora interrupted the conversation, "Will you leave me to guard the room all day?"

"If your mother does not mind," suggested Janis, "Then you will have a car at your disposal that will take you across Paris."

"I agree!" Sitora clapped her hands.

"On one condition," objected Shahlo. "That the driver will not have your credit card, Janis, and broad powers to buy up a lot of Parisian temptations for this lady," she said, nodding towards Sitora.

Janis looked mischievously at Sitora and spread his hands in dismay:

"That's how all my well-laid plans collapse. Alas…"

48

Before going out in the evening, at the invitation of Janis, Shahlo and Sitora decided to choose a dress for Sitora. Sitora took the dress held out by her mother, put it on and then grimaced with displeasure.

"Mom, don't you think this dress ages me?"

"Of course. Twenty years."

"I'm serious."

"It's time to get used to dressing accordingly. Or are you going to spend your whole life in jeans?"

"They're convenient."

"Convenient. A walk like a surveyor's."

"Oh, poor me," Sitora falsely signed. "For men it's easier. Pull the trousers on –

and look like a person immediately." She straightened the dress yet again and looked at herself in the mirror. "How do I look?"

"Now, you look like a person."

"Ok. Fine. Mom, who is Janis, by the way?" Sitora tried to make the question sound completely harmless.

"My old and very good friend."

"What did he say about the shops? Could he really buy them or is it just boasting?" "Really," Shahlo confirmed and added in a couple of seconds, "Along with the airport."

"Come on!" Sitora was amazed. "Gosh!"

"Street expressions." Shahlo grimaced.

"Sorry, they slipped out." Sitora looked innocent and surveyed herself in the mirror while straightening her dress. "How did you meet him?"

Shahlo glanced suspiciously at her daughter:

"Do you remember the story of Lola's house?"

"Sure, I remember!"

"So, he helped to settle everything."

"How does he feel about you?"

"He's in love with me." She again carefully watched her daughter, who was pirouetting in the mirror.

"And you with him?" Sitora did not let up.

"So, Müller," Shahlo could not stand it, "Will you torture me for a long time? Let's better repeat our lesson..."

Fashion Week in Paris saw, as always, a large number of guests and participants. In one of the halls, tables were laid for a buffet and on the podium top models were showing off the latest creations of well-known designers.

Among those who were walking around the hall were Janis, Shahlo and Sitora. Janis noticed that Sitora was sceptical about the models and turned to Shahlo.

"As far as I can see, your daughter looks a bit unimpressed with all this. Doesn't she like it?"

"You can ask her yourself. True, having some idea of her manner of expression, I cannot vouch for the correctness of the answer. Despite all her upbringing." "Nonsense, the usual costs of youth. Since," he turned to Sitora, "Is it not inspiring?"

"Not really. As if they had been pre-flattened for a long time."

"I told you." Shahlo grinned at her daughter's remark.

"Here is the answer."

"Do you prefer more magnificent forms?" Janis smiled.

"For some reason, it seems to me that a woman should have normal female attributes." Sitora explained her position. "When the look slides over the figure, like a puck on a hockey rink, in my opinion, this is too much."

"You wanted to say - shortage?" Janis poked fun at her.

"Well, yes, exactly."

"Well, quite abruptly, but honestly."

"Mom warned you," Sitora answered.

In one of the groups of people, the focus was on a tall but stout man who was animatedly telling something to his interlocutors. A couple of times he cast a careful look at Sitora, then apologized to the interlocutors and headed towards Janis and Shahlo.

"Do not want to hear the opinion of the one who creates these beauties?" Janis asked.

"I saw him somewhere in the hall. (at that time the same man approached them).

Ah, here he is. I was just talking about you. Meet the director of the largest modelling agency Arno Breval, and these are my companions - Madame Shahlo and her daughter."

"I am very glad to meet you," Arno bowed, "All the more so as I specially approached you with selfish interest."

"Arno is in his stride, no introduction and immediately starts the battle," said Janis.

"Alas, he is right," Arno sighed. "That's how I work. May I ask what is mademoiselle going to do in Paris?"

"Mademoiselle is going to study as a designer," Shahlo answered for her daughter. "Great job," Arno agreed, "I have a counter-offer," he turned to Sitora, "Would you like to try the Paris podium as a model?"

"Me?" she was surprised at such an unexpected offer.

"Naturally. I watched you from the side and I want to note that you have all the qualities for this. Although you will have to sweat for sure."

"Actually, that was not my plan," Sitora said uncertainly.

"Who said that would violate your plans?" walked ahead Arno. "Until noon you burden your soul, and in the afternoon – the rest is yours. No contradictions and complete harmony. So?"

"Just like that?" Sitora did not know what to answer to such an onslaught. "I don't know, I'm not sure that I can handle both this and that at the same time."

She looked at her mother. Shahlo wanted to say something, but Janis was ahead of her.

"Madame Shahlo wants to say what they need to think about it." "I'm right?"

"Janis, you are a troublesome person!" Shahlo laughed.

"It's just that I remember this was your favourite phrase," Janis said meaningfully. "No problem! Arno exclaimed. "Here is my card," he handed Shahlo his business card, "You can contact me at any time, and we will continue the conversation in more detail. Unfortunately, I shall leave you, I have to finish one important thing, but I will not say goodbye."

Arno bowed and hurried into the hall.

"Did he seriously suggest this?" Sitora looked incredulously at her mother, who, in turn, looked at Janis.

"Absolutely," said Janis. "He never just says anything for no reason. If he himself came up, then this means something."

"I don't know, I never thought about it," Sitora said uncertainly. "Mom?" "What - mom? You have been made an offer – you decide."

"Do you think it will work out?"

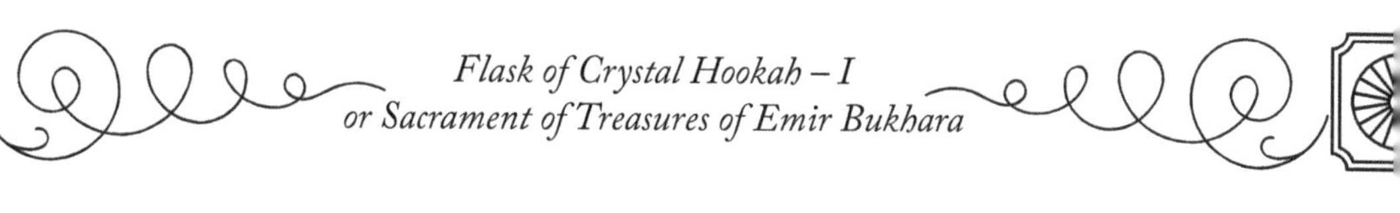

"But it will depend only on you. If you don't pull it, you can reverse it, that's all. What do you think, Janis?"

"I completely agree with you. I was thinking," he looked slyly at both of them. Maybe I could introduce you to Luc Besson, just in case?" Everyone laughed out loud...

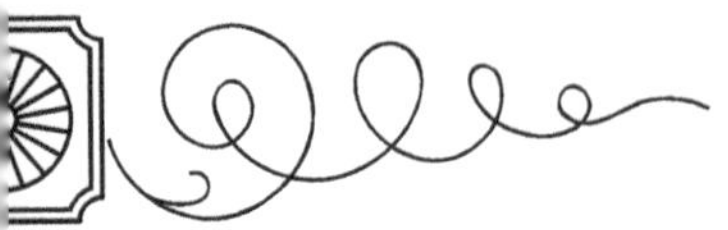

49

The courtyard of Salimbay's house is vast. At the fence in the far corner of the courtyard there is a heap of ground. From time to time, a young guy's head comes out of the pit, and another portion of the earth flies into the heap. Salimbay is sitting under a tree on a trestle bed and drinking tea, glancing sideways at the pit. His hands are shaking a little. Finally, the boy sticks his head out of the pit and turns to Salimbay.

"Master, the pit is ready. This will take a lot of garbage. Should I get out?"

"Wait, I'll see."

He set the bowl, stood up and headed for the pit. His face tightened, his eyes flashed, and he wiped his sweaty hands on the flap of his robe. He went to the pit and looked into it.

"Well done, Nuri, you have done a good job. Just what I need. Give me the shovel."

Nuri gave Salimbay the shovel and looked at him questioningly.

"So I get out?"

"Yes, get out," Salimbay nodded.

Nuri put his hands on the edge of the pit and pulled his body up. At that moment, Salimbay raised the shovel and with all his strength brought it down on Nuri's head. The latter, without making a sound, collapsed in a heap at the bottom of the pit. Salimbay peered into the pit.

Nuri was lying on his back, a trickle of blood oozing from his mouth, his eyes looked lifelessly into the sky. Salimbay staggered back and began to gasp for air to get rid of the nausea rising in his throat.

Recovering a little, he began to quickly pile the earth back into the pit.

"I hope there won't be much stench from such a thin one ..."

Iskander rode on horseback to a country residence, dismounted, looked around, and went to one of the workers.

"Have you been working here for a long time?" "Yes, from the very beginning. Why?"

"And you're familiar with Usto Shuhrat?"

"Certainly! Who does not know him. True, they say he is very sick."

"Yes, he's sick," agreed Iskander. "Who was most familiar with him, do you know?" "Oh, old Saeed. They were together all the time."

"Show me him."

"Why show? There he is, sitting under a tree." He waved his hand in the direction of the tree, under which Saeed was sitting and drinking tea. "Well, thank you."

He went in the indicated direction and went to the seated old man. He looked up at Iskander.

"Hello, father. Are you Saeed?"

"Yes, it's me."

"I need to talk with you about Usto Shuhrat."

"Well then, son, let's talk. How is he? He was transported from my house and now I can't even visit him."

"That's what I want to talk about with you," said Iskander. "He is bad, very bad. Death has come into his head and counts the last hours. I want to know who sent her to him ahead of time?" Seeing Saeed's surprised look, he added:

"Yes, the doctors say he was poisoned, and I have to find the jackal who did it. Will you help me?"

"Oh, what a disaster!" Saeed shook his head in dismay. "Who could he interfere with? Such a man, such a master!"

"Father, you won't help the case with lamentations. Have you been with him all the time?"

"Yes, all the time."

"Then think and tell me, who could give him poison?"

"I can't do it," Saeed thought. "He ate separately, they brought him food." "Who brought it?" roused Iskander.

"Oh, a boy, Nuri. He was identified as an apprentice in Shuhrat, so he carried food to him at the same time. But he couldn't do this, he was a good guy, sensible." "Why - was he?" - surprised Iskander.

"So many days and yet he does not appear. Just as Shuhrat fell, I did not see him."

"It's strange. I must find him and talk. Where does he live? Do you know?"

"No, son, I don't know. You should ask Salimbay. Nuri previously worked for him, and then Salimbay sent him as an apprentice to Shuhrat."

"That's it. Probably, he brought food from the house of Salimbay?"

"Probably, from where else?" Saeed looked puzzled at Iskander. "What does it mean?"

"I want to find out, I really do. I have to see this Salimbay, I know this name. Thank you, father, you helped me a lot."

Iskander said goodbye to the old man and left. Saeed thought deeply, then shook his head.

"Ah, poor Shuhrat. How could he prevent Salimbay?" Iskander drove quickly.

The door was opened by a servant.

"Is your master home?"

"My master is having lunch. Come back later, dear."

"Later it will be too late," snapped Iskander. "Go and say that Salimbay has arrived on a very urgent matter."

"If I disturb him," the servant objected, "He will cut off my ears."

"If you don't disturb him, I will cut them off!" Salimbay grabbed a dagger from his belt and moved to the servant. The latter shrieked in fear. "Alright, alright, I'll go and say it."

He slammed the door and ran into the house. With a guilty look, he approached Kadyr-bek, who was biting into a leg of mutton.

"Forgive me, master, for disturbing your peace, but Iskander is at the door in a great tizzy! He threatened me with a dagger!"

"Oh, yes? And what does he want?"

"He says it's very urgent. He's crazy!"

"Urgent?" Kadyr-bek burped and put his mutton leg on the dish. "Okay, take him to the living room and let him wait there."

"Thank you, master."

He sped off to the gate. Kadyr-bek looked with regret at the unfinished meat, burped again, then dipped his fingers in a bowl of water and slowly began to wipe them with a towel, weighing up the reasons for such an unexpected visit by this man. Then he called softly: "Mansour ..."

A gloomy-looking man with a scar on his cheek came out of the next room. "I'm here, master."

"When I'm talking to him, be around, but don't show up." "Yes, master. I understand."

Kadyr-bek got up, straightened his robe and went into the living room. He made a displeased face and turned sternly to Salimbay:

"You have disturbed my peace and for this you must have a very important reason, otherwise - "

"Nothing matters more, dear Kadyr-bek!" It was evident from Salimbay's expression that he was very scared. "They are looking for me."

"Who and why? Who needs you?"

"Iskander, Emir's bodyguard. He asked about me. And about that bastard Nuri. He sniffed something out."

"You said you dealt with this Nuri?" Kadyr-bek was also worried.

"Yes, he will not tell anyone. But if Iskander attacks me - Protect me, I beg you!" "Yes, if this loser clings to you, you will even recall how you robbed a caravanserai two hundred years ago."

"What should I do?" begged Salimbay. "Without your help, I will perish!"

"Firstly, stop whining," Kadyr-bek interrupted his lamentations. "Secondly, you need to immediately disappear from the city for a while." He rubbed his beard, thinking something. "But you yourself cannot get out of the city, do you understand this?"

"I understand, I understand," Salimbay nodded his head.

"So, listen and remember. My people will help you. Go home, prepare your family. Do not take unnecessary things, only the most valuable ones. As it gets dark, my horsemen will come for you and take you out of the city. Got it?"

"May Allah protect you, the venerable Kadyr-bek!" Salimbay fell to his knees, "I will not forget your kindness."

"Now go, you have little time."

"Yes, yes, I understood everything." Salimbay jumped from his knees, grabbed Kadyr-bek's hand and kissed him. "May your days last long."

Bowing on the move, he hurried to the exit. Kadyr-bek squeamishly rubbed his hand on the robe.

"Mine will last long, but yours ... There's no chance to let you out."

After the departure of Salimbay, Kadyr-bek called:

"Mansour!" He appeared from the next room. "Did you hear everything?" "I did, master."

"What do you think?"

"Long tongue - big problems. Frightened long tongue - very big problems, master."

"Right. If Iskander gets to him first, this tongue will spin like a mill. Meaning what?"

"We need to shorten it and as soon as possible, master."

"So do it. But at the root, got it?"

"Yes, master."

"You will go as it gets dark. All that he gathers there, bring here. I will not offend you - you will be satisfied."

"Thank you, master. I'll do everything right."

"Now go and get ready."

Mansour bowed and disappeared into the back of the house. Kadyr-bek muttered thoughtfully:

"You will do everything, but what am I to do with you then? Okay, we'll see."

50

In the house of Salimbay, there are frantic preparations for flight and everything is upside down. Salimbay puts in a small leather bag all the valuables that he has taken from various hiding places in the house. His wife takes out her clothes and throws them into a cloth spread out on the floor. Salimbay, unable to stand it, almost yells at her.

"What are you doing, you stupid chicken? Do you think a caravan will come for us? Throw away all that junk!"

"Why are you cursing?" she replied, offended. "You yourself said to take all the most valuable things."

"The most valuable thing is whatever you can carry and at the same time run fast!"

"But I can't carry it all by myself!"

"Do not anger me, otherwise you will run naked. Oh Allah! Why did you create women!"

"As if you don't know why," the wife said playfully.

"Shut up! Where is your mother? Conjuring over a magic carpet? Lead her quickly, they are about to come for us."

The woman snorted, pushed aside the drapery on the wall, behind which was a door, pushed it open and went inside. Salimbay tightened the neck of the bag and carried it closer to the door. He looked around the room again and kicked away a pile of clothes with anger. The voices that came muffled through the door died away. The drapery moved and Salimbay's confused wife came out, looking at her husband in dismay. He cried out in exasperation:

"What now?"

"She said that she would not go anywhere, and that we all would not go anywhere, and that we would pay for our sins."

"She's totally out of her mind, old hag! We will pay if we do not leave. If she's stubborn, I will bind her and shut her mouth so that she will not croak."

He started toward the door of the old woman's room, but a careful knock came from the yard. Salimbay turned and walked toward the door.

"That's all, they called for us," he told his wife. "Bring her here, otherwise I'll do it

myself." He went to the door and asked:

"Who's there?"

Ghafur-bek's study in the palace. Ghafur-bek is sitting at the table and carefully listening to Iskander's story, occasionally stroking his beard.

"And so I decided to get your advice first, and then report to our Emir. If Salimbay is one of Kadyr-bek's men, then ..."

"It still docs not mean anything," interrupted Ghafur-bek. "You did the right thing to come to me. You will go to the Emir when all the figures in this matter will stand in their places and when you will have answers to all questions. Do you have them?"

"Not yet, but I will find them."

"Do not rush. Everything will depend on what Salimbay says," Ghafur-bek paused a little. "If he says ..."

"To me - he will say," Iskander said sternly.

"Again, you are in a hurry. If you see someone's tail in the bushes, this does not mean that the owner of this tail is in the same place. First you need to get Salimbay."

"Tomorrow morning I will take it."

"Tomorrow?" Ghafur-bek sceptically shook his head. "I'm afraid that tomorrow you

will have no one to take."

"Then I'll go now."

"Yes, right now, and may Allah help you."

"Thank you, Honorable Ghafur-bek. You will be the first to know about everything." Iskander bowed and quickly left. Ghafur-bek got up from the table and walked around the study, pondering something. Then he said in thought:

"If Kadyr-bek really stands behind all this, then you had to go after Salimbay yesterday. I have a hunch that this Salimbay will not tell anyone. But Kadyr-bek knows, if anyone does, how to separate the tails from the body... But how could Shukhrat annoy him?"

He shook his head and returned to the table to his papers.

"Who's there?" asked Salimbay.

"Kadyr-bek sent me for you. It's time to go." Mansour's muffled voice came from behind the door.

Salimbay opened the door and let Mansour into the house.

"Finally." He turned to his wife, and Mansour was behind him. "Come on, quick..." he didn't finish, surprise was frozen in his eyes, and blood appeared from the corner of his mouth.

Mansour pulled the knife from Salimbay's back and wiped it on the latter's dressing gown as he crawled at Manour's feet.

"One has left," he said indifferently and looked at the woman. Horror froze in Salimbay's wife's eyes, her mouth began to open slowly. She let out a heart-rending cry of "Mo-o-m!" and rushed to the secret door. The blade thrown by Mansour stuck in her back and she, clutching the curtain in her hands, fell to the floor. The

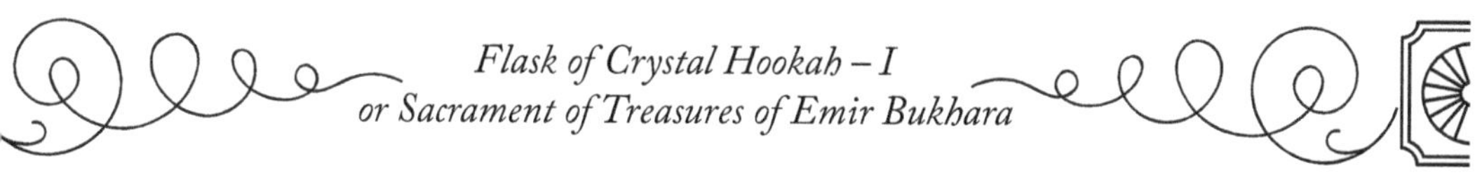

curtain fell down from the wall and covered the woman, exposing the door.

"The second left," Mansour added indifferently, "so that the husband did not get bored."

The door began to open slowly, and on the threshold an old woman with matted gray hair and crazy eyes appeared. She pressed a small leather wineskin to her chest.

"Ah, here is our witch with her treasures. Also going to leave? Come on, come here!" Mansour went to her, removing a saber from its scabbard as he walked. "You won't need it any more."

"You too! You won't get anything, Mansour the killer!" the old woman shouted. Shocked, Mansour froze, with his saber held above the old woman. "You will burn forever in the underworld!"

She squeezed the wineskin with her hands and, as Mansour brought the saber down on the old woman's head, a stream of some liquid spurted from it into his face.

The old woman fell, and Mansour, having dropped his saber, clasped his hands to his face. An animal cry escaped his chest and his face was transformed into a single mask of blood. Mansour blundered round the room, bumping into objects and waving his arms. Catching the lamp, he dropped it on the floor, and the flame immediately began to spread everywhere.

Mansour's clothes caught fire. Stumbling over one of the bodies, he fell, engulfed in flames. A moment later, Salimbay's whole house was ablaze.

Iskander, along with two soldiers, was speeding to Salimbay's house. From afar, he saw the glow of a fire and spurred his horse. As Iskander moved closer, the roof of the house collapsed, throwing millions of sparks into the sky.

The residents of neighboring houses were already crowding on the street, discussing what was happening. Iskander dismounted and went to one of them.

"Is that by any chance Salimbay's house?"

"It is."

"Where is he?"

"Who knows? I was one of the first here and no one has run out of the house. Not visible in the street, anyway."

"Why is no one putting out the fire?" asked Iskander.

"How to put it out from here? You will not come after all. May God forbid that neighbouring houses do not catch fire."

"It turns out that no one saw or heard anything?"

"My house is on the contrary, I first ran out. There was no one. True, my wife…" "Who noticed, was it your wife?" asked Iskander.

"Yes, it sounded to her as if someone was screaming. So, she pushed me to see what that was. As I came out – there was already a fire. And nothing more."

"That's clear. Alright, make sure that the fire does not spread to neighbouring houses. Stay here," Iskander addressed the soldiers. "You will observe, listen and remember. I will send more people."

Iskander walked up to his horse, grabbed the reins, and looked back at the conflagration.

"Yes, Ghafur-bek was right." He jumped on his horse and galloped back to the palace.

51

A year has passed. Shahlo was about to leave the office, but then the phone rings.

She picks up the phone.

"Hello."

"Mom, it's me, hello!" Sitora's voice could be heard.

"Sitora, my girl! Glad to hear from you. You haven't called for a long time. How are you?"

"It's bad, mom, that's why I call. I do not like to complain, but I have no one else to talk to."

"Tell me what's going on there," Shahlo said in alarm. "Hope nothing serious?" "Mom, I can't be here any more," Sitora complained. "I'm so sick of everything that I want to go home."

"What are you so sick of that caused such a panicky mood?" Shahlo felt relieved from the heart. "Everything turned out so wonderfully for you, such a success, and suddenly you say "I want to go home". Is it really that bad?"

"All this is beautiful on the catwalk, photographs and glossy covers. What is behind the facade is difficult to convey and difficult to withstand."

"Of course it's difficult, I understand. But Arno warned that there would be no sweet and easy life, and that he would have to work hard to gain recognition."

"Yes, I did not count on an easy life. If the whole thing was only physical activity, I would not complain. Of course, sometimes I want to howl, because everything hurts from these endless fitting and waddling along the catwalk, and Arno was right. But I am not stressed because of that."

"Explain, I do not know at all the kitchen in which you're cooked."

"Mom, I want a quiet life, but here everything and everyone are strange, though they smile, as if I am their close one." Shahlo felt her daughter's mood. "I'm tired of all these hints, half-hints, bores of all kinds and ages with their suggestions. I can't fight off all this anymore, I'm tired. I want a normal, calm life, at home, where everything is familiar and understandable. Do you understand me?"

"Sure I understand you," Shahlo sighed.

"I also want to have a family, a husband, and children. You probably did not expect me to say that?"

"No, I didn't expect it, but I'm glad about it. Here is what I will tell you. Once you

have decided so - spit on all this hype and vanity and come home. I love you very much and am proud that I have such an adult and smart daughter. When shall I wait for you?"

"I will try as quickly as possible. If I can, then at the end of next month. The old contract will end, and I'm not going to sign a new one. You won't be angry that I was kind of pissed off and didn't want to walk above the stars?"

"Don't talk nonsense," Shahlo reassured her. "Finish your business and go home."

Will you call again?"

"Of course!"

"Very well. I kiss you. Bye. And don't lose your heart..."

Without abandoning her intention to open her own business, Zarina carefully prepared the necessary documents and calculations. She understood that Alibek would never agree to support her, which means that he had to be convinced by a full set of arguments.

Zarina once again looked at the documents and put them in a folder. Then she went to the phone to call her husband. She picked up the phone, thought, and then hung up. "He will say again that he has a meeting. I'll do it without a call."

Zarina got dressed, left the house, took a taxi and gave the address. Arriving at the Ministry building where Alibek worked, she took the elevator to the desired floor and went down the corridor. There was no one in the waiting room. She opened the first door leading to her husband's office, grabbed the second handle and then she heard a woman's laugh coming from the office. She froze.

"Oh, Alibek, what are you doing? It tickles!" the woman laughed.

"I'm trying to nibble your pretty ear," Alibek said.

"What will I tell my husband? That I lost it?"

"You can say that a vampire attacked you. By the way, where is your husband?"

"On a business trip. You sent him yourself."

"Yes? Wow, right on time."

"What are you doing? What if your wife comes now?"

"She isn't coming. She will call first and before she arrives we will have time to crawl in different directions."

"Why crawl?" The woman laughed.

"Because my legs are weakening and my head is spinning when you are near. You are so sweet and so seductive, babe."

At this moment, the secretary entered the reception room and, seeing Zarina at the door to his office, unexpectedly slammed the

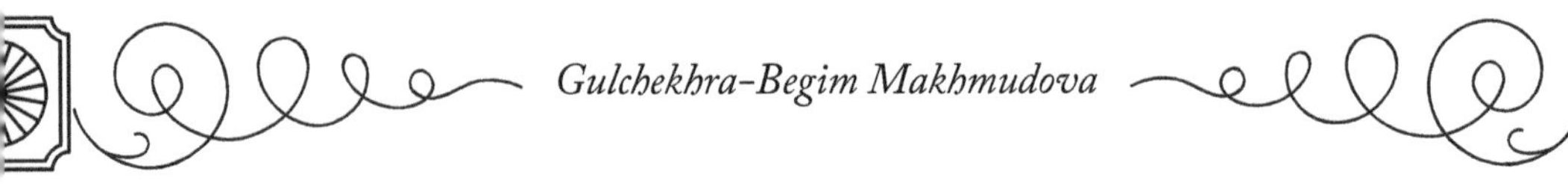

reception room door loudly. In the office, they were silent imme-diately.

"Oh!" the secretary cried softly.

Zarina looked at her, pressed an expressive finger to her lips, and carefully closed the door. Her face was pale; perspiration appeared on her forehead. While she was walking out of the reception room, the secretary, with a confused expression on her face, did not take her eyes off her. Having caught up with her, Zarina said quietly:

"I was not here. Do you hear?" the secretary nodded her head, but Zarina again repeated in syllables. "I was not here."

She went out into the corridor, closed the door behind herself and leaned against the wall.

"So, then - " she whispered, "We bite off ears at meetings? What a fool I have been!"

Zarina lowered her head and quickly went down the corridor to the elevator.

52

The only one with whom Zarina could openly talk about this ugly discovery was Shahlo. She could be trusted without the fear that the whole city would know about it tomorrow. Without delaying this conversation, Zarina dialled Shahlo's number. When she answered, Zarina said:

"Hello! It's me. Are you very busy?"

"Ah, Zarik, hello. As always, I work without stretching my back. Do you want to chat?"

"I need to talk to you," Zarina said seriously, which was not like her.

"Is this urgent?" Shahlo felt tension in her voice.

"Not as urgent as important," Zarina answered. "No, and urgent too." "Good," Shahlo agreed, "Let's talk. What happened to you?"

"I don't want to talk about this on the phone. Maybe we'll meet in the city?"

"Not now, and not in the city. I need to finish my work, and this is an hour and a half. After that I have to go to my grandmother, where we can talk. Suits?"

"Of course. Then in a couple of hours I will drive up."

"Agreed! So at two?"

"At two. Bye." Zarina hung up...

Zarina at the appointed time arrived at the house of Firuz-begim. Together with Shahlo, they sat in the yard.

"It's good here, calm," Zarina said a little sadly. How many times I've come here, and always felt in her house as in the most native place."

"Yes, she has an amazing aura. Everyone notices this, but cannot explain why this happens. So what is your important conversation?" asked Shahlo.

"I don't know where to start. So everything unexpectedly happened... Silly..."

She lowered her head. There was silence. Zarina's face showed that something was gnawing at her, but she couldn't get the courage to start a conversation.

"Well, what are you talking about?" Shahlo could not stand. "If you want to speak

out, then speak out - don't plague yourself."

"In short - I caught him."

"Whom?" surprised Shahlo.

"Alibek."

"Really? With whom?"

"I don't know, I didn't actually see."

"And was it definitely a woman?"

"Are you messing, yeah?" Zarina resented.

"Having fun, huh? You found out last."

"What do you mean? Zarina jumped on her. "So you knew?"

"Of course not."

"However, this did not surprise you very much, did it? I can read your face."

"Not really," Shahlo agreed. "Gossip sometimes came to me, but you understand that

gossip and facts are not the same things."

"You were silent?" Shahlo was indignant.

"What do you think I should have said? You know very well that I do not collect and do not spread gossip. If they reach me, then they die."

"I would like to know," Zarina flared up, "How many of them died next to you?"

"Aw, stop it. Is quantity so important to you?"

"It's just very disgusting to feel like a fool who is neglected."

"Didn't you notice and feel yourself?"

"What should I have noticed and felt? I believed him, you know? I believed..." she sobbed. "I am really a fool..."

"Fools do not know how to believe, so calm down: you're smart," Shahlo patted Zarina on the arm. "It's just that you didn't fully understand the male nature and therefore reacted so painfully."

"But what does male nature have to do with it?"

"Despite the fact that, by and large, men were like primitive animals, they remained so, although they learned to shave and wear pants. They have it in the genes - spawn as many offspring as possible so that their tribe does not die out."

"Thank you very much for the consolation," Zarina was offended. "You also justify him. Genes are to blame, so let them hang around with anyone and wherever. Maybe I should let him bring them home? If Kadyr were unfaithful to you, will you also be so calm?"

"No need to exaggerate, I do not justify him. There is simply no need to make universal tragedy out of this. As for Kadyr..." Approaching Firuz-begim interrupted her phrase.

"What are we arguing about, girls?"

"Ah, an old story," Shahlo waved his hand. "Man and woman."

"It's about that," Firuz-begim grinned, "How many ones

should he have - one or a dozen? Indeed, an old story. As much as he could feed or support. Someone may have two, someone 150, and to someone even one is tough. Read the story, it says it all. Especially in the East. So polygamy exists and exists. Everywhere, only with different sauces. The wife is single, and the rest - ... Well, you know. The structure of men is that their main function from the day of creation is to impregnate and so that the clan gets continued - otherwise the tribe will cease to exist ... it all began with the primitive system...

Do you want me to tell you about the order and rules in the harem... well, for example, Emir of Bukhara... after all, there is an opinion that Emir entered into intimate relations with all concubines and there was a special bed and there was perverse violence but in fact, it's not quite so...

Since ancient times, the Emirs and Sultans behaved proudly and with dignity - very rarely anyone stooped to overt debauchery and violence...

The concubines were really beautiful young girls - they were prepared and beautified by the wise doctors - tabibs, and as a result, under the Arkes of the harem, as a "house of happiness" a unique art of creating and maintaining beauty was born, which despite the high walls and strong locks significantly influenced on what is today called perfumes and cosmetics. Skin care with the help of essential oils and plant extracts, soap, perfumes penetrated through the walls of harems to Europe...

The makeup of the oriental beauties was bright and contrasting - especially the eyes, they should have hit the man's heart at first sight and for this they used antimony on sheep's fat and usma with basma on almond oil, adding ash ... Antimony and usma were believed to have healing properties and improve eyesight. So that the lips were red, women of the East chewed betel-paste made of betel pepper with the addition of lime and oil and cinnamon sticks tirelessly chewed all the inhabitants of the female half of the palace for the scent of breath...

According to legend, the Prophet himself refused to take a letter from a woman whose hands were not adorned with patterns of henna...

Well, if you remember ten secrets of beauty from Scheherazade - now this is face and body skin care from your famous French Brands of Luxury Perfumes and Cosmetics - right, Shahlosh?"

"Of course, you are right, as always, our honorable Begim and your educational program is useful to us," Shahlo laughed merrily, "But Glory be to Allah and our Government of Independent Uzbekistan, the world has changed and our civilized life is beautiful, without your harems and polygamy... I am happy to live in our free country, where I can fully realize myself as a simple and loyal subject not to Emir, but to our President and people and that's great!"

"But what should I do, be a husband's faithful wife? I can't pretend that nothing happened, that everything is likc before." Zarina lamented.

"Well, make a different appearance," Shahlo said decisively. "Stars are better visible through the sloping roof ... Finally, take care of your restaurant and go into it with your head. In the end, pretend that you have someone. Just don't go with your head bowed. To forget the bad means to let the good in. Don't forget it all depends on you - life changes only when we change ourselves..."

"Is that all? Do you think this will work?"

"I don't know about him, but for sure it will stay with you," Shahlo said confidently. Zarina was silent for a moment, thinking

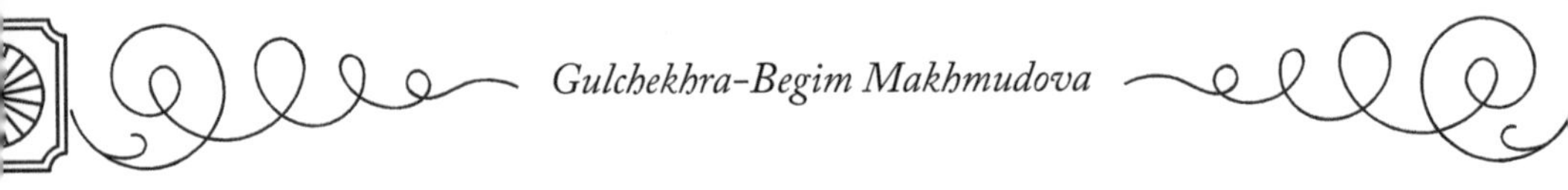

over what Shahlo said. Then she raised her head, and in her eyes there was no longer that resentment with which she had come. There was determination in them.

"Ok, I will try."

"Well, great," Firuz-begim summed up. "If you are finished with your problem, let's go have a meal. Everything is ready."

"Thank you, Firuz-begim but I do not want anything. There is no mood," Zarina began to refuse.

"Get up and let's go," Shahlo took her hand. "If you refuse - you will no longer be let in here. Grandma does not forgive such insults."

"Do not scare the girl, Shahlo. When didn't I let anyone in?" turned to Zarina. "You won't refuse tea, will you?"

"I won't refuse tea," Zarina nodded.

"The main thing is to start," Shahlo pulled her, "The rest will get itself. Get up, sufferer..."

53

However, Zarina's troubles did not end there, and fate sent her another difficult

test.

Literally a month later, Zarina, very worried, again came to Shahlo's home.

"Hello, friend. I came on business with you. Are you not very busy?" "Not really, come in," Shahlo invited her. "Why are you so concerned?"

"My heart is not in place. Here, look," she handed Shahlo an envelope, "Came from the States today. But this is not from Sherzod, there are no letters from him for a long time. This is some kind of official one. Can you translate? You know that I'm not very good at English."

"Let's try. Sit down. Do you want some tea?"

"Later," Zarina refused, "First this. Oh I really do not like such letters."

"Don't get worked up in advance, please. You never know what could be there. Let's see what we have?" She unfolded the form and began to translate. "Madam, such and such, the college management informs you ... your son ... a month and a half ... state police ..."

"What are you mumbling?" Zarina was worried. "Can you be clearer? What do the police have to do with it?"

"Wait," Shahlo frowned, "Let me finish reading."

While she was reading silently, Zarina looked at her intensely.

"I see ..." Shahlo laid the sheet on the table and looked at Zarina.

"What do you understand? Can you really say what's in the letter? What is happening there?"

"I'll say it now. Just do not start to panic ahead of time. In general, Sherzod is not in college."

"How is he not in college?" Zarina asked with fear in a voice.

"He and two others have disappeared from their course and have not been able to find them for a month and a half. They assume that they have left somewhere, or they were taken away, but where they are now - no one knows."

"Oh!" Zarina turned pale and grabbed her heart. "Son..."

Shahlo quickly jumped up, took a vial from the cupboard and dripped a little into the bowl.

"Here, have a drink," she handed Zarina the bowl. Zarina looked at her friend with unhappy eyes and averted her hand. "Drink, I said. That's good, you'll be better now."

"Sherzodik, my son." she muttered. "How so?"

"Please get your black thoughts out of your head," Shahlo began to reassure her friend. "If something bad happened to them, the police would be the first to know.

Maybe they really left somewhere."

"Where?"

"But who knows what is in their heads. Young, at least plenty of fantasies are in their heads. Maybe the treasure they rushed to look for, so they do not remember about relatives."

"What treasure?" exclaimed Zarina. "What are you saying?"

"Oh, it's just for example. We don't know what they really did."

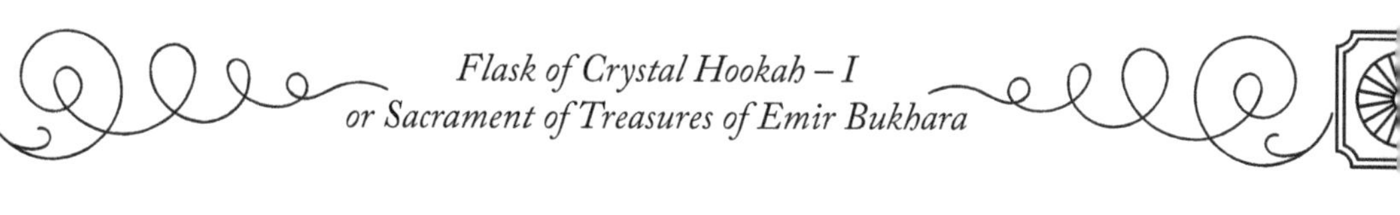

"And if they…" Zarina did not finish and burst into tears.

"Just let's not guess, okay? Then we ourselves will go crazy. Do you know how many of these "ifs" you can invent? You should always hope for the best, do you agree with me?" She looked at Zarina intensely who nodded through her tears.

"Is Alibek on a business trip? Course he is. Then you stay with me, under my supervision. It's better than walking home from corner to corner with your thoughts. Calm down a bit, and then think about what to do next. Come on, lie down…"

54

Since Marina had found out that Alibek, whom she loved and from whom she was expecting a child, was married, she lived alone and raised her son Alik.

A friend, businessman Andrei Nikolayevich, appeared in her life, who treated Alik as his own.

He repeatedly suggested that Marina marry him, but she refused, being afraid again to make a mistake. Despite all his business, Andrei Nikolayevich tried to give all his free time to Marina and her son. He understood that it was difficult for her to make a decision, which he sought from her. But he loved her and did not lose hope of convincing Marina to become his wife and to overcome the fear of a new mistake.

A difficult week was left behind, and he drove them out of town to relax a bit and, if possible, make another attempt. They settled on the shore of the lake. Alik sat on the shore with a fishing rod, and Andrei Nikolayevich made a small fire.

"Well, fisherman, are they biting?" he shouted to Alik.

"Not yet. They are still thinking," the boy said.

"Didn't you forget about the worm?"

"No, of course. I baited the hook with the fattest for them."

"Well, then wait. In fishing, it is the most important thing."

Andrei Nikolayevich went up to Marina, who was sitting on a spread blanket, leaning against a tree. He handed her a wild-flower:

"Can I join the vacationers?"

"You can, I left you a piece of the blanket," Marina showed to the place next to her. "Very kind of you, ma'am," he said, sitting next to her. "Do you like the air?"

"Wonderful!" Marina took a deep breath of clean air. "No matter how much you breathe, it's not enough."

"Do not be greedy, share with the others too?"

"With which others?"

"Well, with me, at least. To make it easier for words to come out."

"I didn't notice," Marina said mockingly, "That you have problems with this."

"It depends on what words. Can I ask a question?" Andrei Nikolayevich as a student raised his hand.

"Come on."

"Will you marry me?"

"Andryusha, you already asked this question."

"I have asked and I will ask again. But you stubbornly do not want to answer it."

"Tell me, what doesn't suit you?" Marina held out her hand and slightly ruffled his hair. "Do you definitely need a stamp in your passport?"

"No, I don't need a stamp," said Andrei Nikolayevich with annoyance, "But I need a wife. Legitimate, beloved, and only mine. And a son. Why do you not understand me?"

"Yes, I understand everything, Andryusha, but don't be angry, I'm afraid to change anything in my life. Why are you not afraid to lose your freedom? Take on other people's problems?"

"I scorn such freedom! What do you mean by saying other

people's problems? Caring of you and Alik? You yourself see what kind of relationship we have with him."

"Sorry, I speak nonsense. I don't understand myself. I must be glad that I have you, and agree without hesitation. Another would have done so, but I'm a stupid woman, right?"

"Absolutely," assented with a grin Andrei Nikolayevich. "Therefore, you need a stamp and a tough male hand. Will you marry me?"

Marina smiled, stroked his cheek:

"What a bore you are, Andrei Nikolayevich. After all, you will not leave me alone?"

"Rest assured."

"Give me some more time, okay?"

"But only a little, and only to prepare for the wedding." "Do not be greedy, let me breathe the air of freedom." "No, pipes. A month or two - and down the aisle."

"And he also asks why I do not agree. The dictator. Okay, I will be getting ready. Then do not complain."

"You will not get it! I see..."

Alik's voice came from the shore:

"Biting! Uncle Andrei, biting!"

"Sorry," he kissed Marina, "I have an urgent matter."

"Calm, calm," he prompted Alik in a half-whisper. He was also taken by the fisherman's excitement, "Take your time, let it swallow it properly... Come on!"

55

The wedding day of Marina and Andrei Nikolayevich was approaching, but the closer it got, the more uneasy Marina felt. She had a feeling that something was about to happen. With these misgivings she was walking around the room, pressing her fingers to her temples.

"But what is it? After all, everything is fine, everything is fine. Why am I nervous?"

She went to the cupboard in the kitchen, took out a bottle, shook out a couple of tablets from it and swallowed them. Then she went into the room, opened a large closet and took an envelope from the top shelf. She sat down at the table and began to browse the contents. It was a little - just a couple of photographs and two or three pieces of paper.

"Fifteen years," she said slowly. "Well, you never know what."

She took a blank sheet of paper and began to write:

"My dear son.

You often asked me about your father, who he is, and where. All the time I put off this conversation until later, persuading you to grow up a little at first so that you understand everything. So you have grown up. If you read this letter, then I didn't have time to tell you everything myself. So, something happened ... But it doesn't matter. It is important that you know who your father is. Then you will decide for yourself whether you need it or not. Maybe, I'll still marry Andrei Nikolayevich, and we will live together. Maybe... So. A year before your birth... "

... Marina wrote the letter and set it aside. Looking out the window, she thought for a long time. Then, as if she woke up, shook her head, took a sheet, re-read, crumpled nervously and threw it into the basket.

"I'm completely crazy," she said nervously, "Perhaps I should also order a memorial service ..." Marina put everything in an envelope, went to the cupboard to put it in its place, but, not reaching it, stopped. She returned to the basket, took out a crumpled piece, straightened it, folded it up and put it in an envelope. Then she put the envelope on the top shelf. She repeated again:" "You never know..."

... After Zarina received the news of her son's disappearance, her friends Lola and Shahlo tried to do everything to at least somehow reassure her. For the sake of this, Lola even decided to go to the fortune teller, the old acquaintance of Firuz-begim - Asya Fyodorovna.

Entering a quiet lane, Lola walks to the fence, looks at the piece of paper with the name of the fortune teller again and presses the call button. She stood. Without waiting for an answer, she pressed the button again. There was the sound of a door opening in the house, then shuffling steps along the path.

"I'm coming, I'm coming, why you ring for nothing," the fortune teller went to the gate and opened it. "Who do you want?"

"Sorry," said Lola, not quite surely, "Are you Asya Fyodorovna?" "Well, I'm Asya Fyodorovna. Who are you? From the clinic?" "No, I'm on a different matter," Lola hesitated.

"Oh, yes?" Asya Fyodorovna gave Lola an attentive look. "For what?" "I was told that you are very good at knowing things, so I came to you."

"I guess?" Asya Fyodorovna grinned, "Who told you such nonsense?"

"My friend's grandmother," Lola was confused, "Firuz-begim. Do you know her?" "How would I not know, we have been acquaintances for about fifty years. Well, come on in, if she sent you." She let Lola in, closed the gate, and they went to the house "For a long time I have not seen her. How is she?"

"Not bad, only rheumatism sometimes gets at her."

"Well, at our age, it's like a free supplement to all the other pleasures." They entered the house. "Come here," the fortune teller pointed to the room, "I'll be back, I'll just take the medicine."

Lola entered the room, looked around and sat down at the table. A minute later, Asya Fyodorovna entered the room and sat opposite.

"I guess, then?" she repeated the words with a slight grin. "The ones who guess, girl, they are forecasters, and I just retell what the cards tell me. Whether it is true or not is another question."

"Yes, she told me that you have some magical cards. Is it true?"

"Wow, she remembers. I don't know if they're magical or not, but sometimes they bring benefits." After these words, she carefully looked at Lola. "Why spread them on you? Everything is alright with you." Lola looked at her in surprise.

"Why are you so surprised?" Asya Fyodorovna asked, "Cards are pieces of paper, you need to work with them so that they speak."

"Actually, this is not for me," Lola said embarrassed, "This is for my friend. Her son..." Lola took out a photo of Sherzod and handed it to a fortune-teller. "Here he is."

Asya Fyodorovna took a photo, looked at the image, slowly ran her hand over the surface.

"A good boy, kind... He drifted far away..." Lola opened her mouth to say something, but Asya Fyodorovna stopped her, "Just tell me nothing. OK, let's see what the cards show us."

She went to the dresser, took out the cards and put them down.

"But why didn't she come?"

"Oh, she does not know, we ourselves decided to come."

"Well, if it was your own choice, do it," Asya Fyodorovna laid out the cards, did all the necessary manipulations and thought it over. Then she looked up at Lola. "All this is strange, but I'll tell you that, and you yourself decide whether to believe it or not. He is not free, but this is not a prison or a cell. An impact is exerted on him, but not physical. He is alive and well. Only so far he is under someone's bad influence. But it will break out and show up. When exactly - I do not know, I will not lie. Let his mother wait for him, nothing bad will happen to him." She folded the cards, "That's all I can say. Did you expect a long story with details from me?"

"I don't know, this is the first time..." "On the one hand, Lola was a little disappointed, but on the other, the cards showed that everything was not so bad. "Probably the most important thing is that he is alive and that he will return. After all, this is the most important thing for her, right?"

"True," agreed Asya Fyodorovna. "Let her believe, and everything will be fine. "Then I'll go," Lola got up from her chair, "Thank you," she reached into her purse and took out the money.

"But take it away," Asya Fyodorovna said sternly, "Or else I'll put an evil curse on you."

"Oh!" Lola exclaimed and quickly slipped the money back into her purse.

"Oh, are you scared?" Asya Fyodorovna smiled good-naturedly. "Do not be afraid, just this is what I do not know how to do. Tell

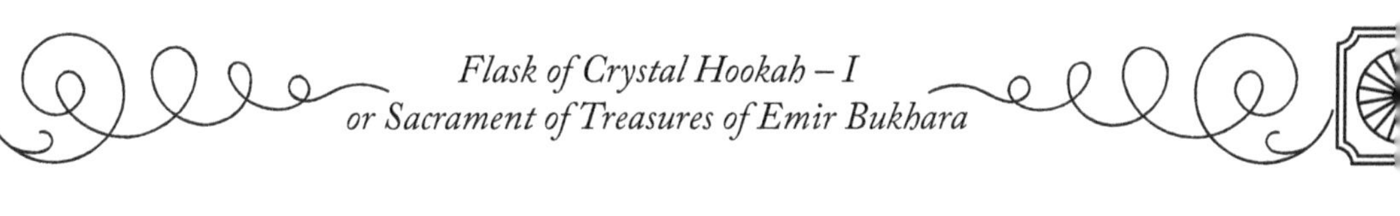

my friend a big howdy. May she take care of herself."

"I will definitely tell her," Lola sighed in relief, smiled at the fortune teller too and went to the door.

56

The day of the registry office came. Andrei Nikolayevich's car drove up to the house, and he opened the door.

When Marina came out, Andrei Nikolayevich hastened to meet her. Before reaching a couple of steps, Marina stumbled and almost fell, but Andrei Nikolayevich managed to catch her.

"Well, are your legs stumbling from fear?"

"Andryusha, this is a bad omen." Forebodings rolled over Marina with renewed vigor. "Let's put it off until tomorrow?"

"You are so big, but you still believe in different signs. Aren't you ashamed?"

"Andryush?" Marina looked at him questionably, her eyes were frightened. Andrei Nikolayevich kissed her and tried to calm her down.

"We only need to get there and submit documents. We'll be quick, and then to the restaurant. We will drown your fears in a glass of great champagne."

He led her to the car. Before sitting down, Marina cast a glance at her windows. Alik looked out from one and waved his hand. She waved back and sat down. Andrei Nikolayevich sat nearby, and the car started off.

"Are you unguarded today?" Marina asked uneasily.

"They are nearby, do not worry. In the registry offices, thank God, they still do not shoot."

While they were driving, Marina was silent and nervously tugging at her handbag.

"Are you nervous?" Andrei Nikolayevich took her hand.

"Something is wrong with me. May I smoke?" Marina asked.

"Yes, we've almost arrived."

"I will, a little."

She opened her purse and took out a pack of cigarettes. The car stopped at the intersection. Marina opened the window from her side, took a cigarette, took out a lighter, but it slipped out of her fingers and fell to the floor.

"Sit, I will take it." Andrei Nikolayevich leaned over, and at that moment shots rang out from a passing car. Marina leaned back. The driver stepped on the gas and the car screeched out of place.

"Let it rip, Nikita," shouted Andrei Nikolayevich. He straightened up and pressed Marina to himself. "That's all, everything is in order, do not be afraid, I'm here…" He stroked her head and started: his hand became wet. He took his hand away - the palm was dark red."

"Marina…" he said in shock, "Marina!"

The driver in the mirror saw blood on the hand of his boss. "You have blood, Andrei Nikolayevich, have you been injured?"

"This is not my … blood … To the hospital," he cried again, "Quick… This is hers… Come on, rip… Marina!!!"

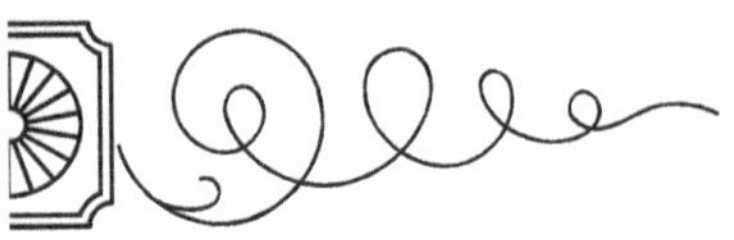

57

1920 has come. The hall in the palace Iskander was conducting a fencing lesson with Firuz-begim's son. Both have toy sabers in their hands. From behind the curtains, Firuz-begim is stealthily watching them.

"I attack - you defend!" commands Iskander. He lunges, the boy parries it with a learned movement.

"Good! And so?"

Iskander makes another attack and the boy again manages to fend off the blow. "Well done!" Iskander praises him, "Now so..."

He made several saber movements in a row. The last blow touches the boy's shoulder. He stumbles and falls to the floor. He grabs his shoulder and whimpers. "I'm hurt, I'm tired. It's not fair…"

Iskander squatted beside him and spoke to him in a serious tone:

"Imagine, brigands attacked your mother, and you were to protect her. Then you say: "Lord brigands, wait a little, I'm tired and I'm hurt. At first I will rest a bit, and then I will give you a nice shake-up, and you sit on the grass for a while".

From behind the curtains the muffled laughter of Firuz-begim came, but Iskander pretended not to notice this. The boy laughed too.

"A real warrior does not whimper or complain. He fights to the end, understand?" "But I don't cry," the boy objected. "It's just…

Now watch out, brigand!"

He jumped to his feet and began to strike. Iskander fought back, squatting, then lost his balance and fell on his back. The boy's saber rested on his chest, he was out of breath from fatigue, but terribly pleased.

"Ah! Give up! You won't attack anyone else!"

"I surrender, oh noble warrior!" Iskander begged mockingly. "You won!"

At that moment Alimkhan entered the hall. "What do I see?" he said, hiding a smile.

The boy rushed to his father, and Iskander rose to his feet and bowed.

"My son defeated Iskander himself?" Alimkhan picked up his son and held him in his arms. "Since he forgot how to use his saber, I will have to dismiss him. Let him now peel the potatoes in the kitchen."

"No, no, don't!" the boy protested ardently. "First, Iskander defeats me, and then he becomes a brigand, and I defeat him. Do not need him in the kitchen!"

"Well, that's another matter."

Alimkhan lowered the boy to the floor and patted his hair, then turned to Iskander:

"How are his successes in military affairs?"

"He is trying, Your Highness."

"Alright, continue the lesson." He pushed the boy forward and left the hall.

"Well? Have you had a rest?" Iskander asked the boy.

"I have."

"Then go ahead, djigit!.." Iskander stood in position.

Leaving the hall, Alimkhan went to his study and ordered that the main treasurer Hamrakul-bek be sent to him. After a while, he opened the door and entered the study.

"Greetings, O Most Serene!" he bowed and stood waiting,

"Greetings, dear Hamrakul-bek. Come in and sit down. I have an important question for you."

"You have my full attention, Your Highness."

"This is my question," Alimkhan began. "You are my chief treasurer, and who, if not you, should know about the conditions of our finances. What we own today, in what it is expressed, weight, quantity and, of course, the total cost. Can you give me a full report now?"

"Right now?" Hamrakul was confused by surprise. "No, Your Highness. I still have not received your instructions regarding weight and quantity, and therefore I can only talk about the total cost, excluding revenue from the treasury and expenses over the past two months. I'm working on it now."

"Bad," Alimkhan frowned deliberately. "Approximate data does not suit me. Consider that you have received such an order from me. How much time do you need to make a full audit of our treasury and pack everything in bags by name?" "To pack?" Hamrakul could not hide his surprise.

"You have it all lying on the floor or laid out in pots?" Alimkhan asked harshly. "No, but…"

"So how much time do you need?"

"Such a large amount of work…" Hamrakul was bewildered. "A month, Your Highness."

"I give you two weeks, dear Hamrakul-bek." "T-two weeks?" Hamrakul stared in shock.

"Yes. Two weeks later, the full list should be on this table. You will get as many people as you need. Everything you need will be brought right there, to our basement. So, a couple of weeks you have to do without your young wife. Proceed immediately, and until the work is completed, no one will stick the nose out of there, including you, dear Hamrakul-bek. A matter of national importance, you understand."

"I understand ... But what about ..."

"I will order it, and your family will be warned. You can go now. I'm waiting for your report in two weeks."

Hamrakul got up, bowed, and with a dejected look went to the door.

When Hamrakul left, Alimkhan rang the bell, and a servant entered the office with a bow.

"Call Rasulbay," he ordered.

"Yes, my lord."

After a few seconds, the door opened again, and a frightening-looking man entered the study and bowed silently in a bow.

"Listen and remember," Alimkhan told him without the preamble. "Take a dozen sturdy guys and go with them to the basements of the Treasury. They do what Hamrakul-bek orders them to, you - observe and restore order. Even the mouse should not leave the basement until the work is completed. Got it?"

"Yes my Lord. What should I do when they finish work?" a bloodthirsty grin appeared on his lips.

"Take your time, and don't scare them ahead of time. Then I will tell you what to do. Go now."

Rasulbek bowed and left the study. Frowning, Alimkhan said:

"The animal. If only to kill someone."

58

Firuz-begim put her son to bed, straightened his pillow, blanket and sat down next to her.

"What will you tell me before you sleep?" asked Firuz-begim.

"I want to be as strong as Iskander, and to handle a saber dexterously as him. In my opinion, he is the best warrior. Do you like him?" Firuz-begim was embarrassed by an unexpected question.

"Iskander is really a very good warrior."

"And my grandfather? Did he fight well?"

"No, son, he did not fight. He even had no saber." "Why?" the boy said disappointedly.

"He used other weapons, which are sometimes stronger than the one that kills." "But is this possible?" the boy asked incredulously.

"It is. This is a gift to create beauty with one's own hands. The weapon brings death and grief, and beauty brings joy to people, makes them kinder. Therefore, people always remember and honour those who created beauty for them, and very rarely remember those who were killed."

"How can I stop these brigands if they attack you?"

"Did I say," Firuz-begim said with a smile, "that we don't have to learn to fight and

be as brave and dexterous as Iskander?"

"No, you didn't."

"So, we need to learn both."

"Who will teach me another one?"

"Me. But not now, because you have to sleep. That's all, close your eyes," she kissed the boy, "Have only beautiful dreams. Sleep…"

Shahob opened the gate and entered a small house on the outskirts of Bukhara. Closing the door on the bolt, he took an envelope from his pocket, opened it and, going to the window, began to read a note from the envelope.

"You need to get consent from your friends to guard and escort the caravan to the border in two weeks."

At the end of the note was a personal symbol of Alimkhan. Shahob thought about it, re-read the note, then took out the matches and burned the note and envelope in the stove.

"I would like to know what this caravan will carry, and how to persuade the British to guard and accompany the cat in the bag. Hmm, a caravan …Who is our Emir going to export abroad? He walked thoughtfully around the room. Or what?" He stopped in the centre of the room.

"Who or what? What" he exclaimed. "It seems, I know what it will be. There is only one thing in the Ark that cannot be left if you are planning to leave far from the Bolsheviks, and they are all pushing and pushing. Treasury…Yes, exactly! But the British do not need to know about this. It is necessary to come up with a believable fairy tale for them. Believe it or not, it's not so important. Well, as they say, "No problem". Treasure. Treasury… Ah, how interesting."

The basement where the Emir's treasury is stored, Rasulbek sits on the top step of the stairs near the door and carefully watches the workers commanded by Hamrakul.

"Put the coins from the dish into this bag, the dish to the side. All the stones on this table."

He went to the table where the man was sitting and sorting precious stones. "Transparent - separately, pearls - separately, doodle!" he yelled at the guy who mixed pearls and diamonds in one pile. "Have you never seen pearls?" "I haven't seen, sir," the guy muttered in fright.

"Here, look," Hamrakul grabbed one pearl and stuck it under his nose. "Not transparent, round. Do you understand now?"

"Got it, sir," the guy nodded his head.

"Look!" Hamrakul warned him. "If you swallow at least one to get out of here for

your girl, here he is," Hamrakul pointed towards Rasulbek, who eloquently tapped his

knee with a dagger. "He will chop you up to make mincemeat of you, but he will get

it. Got it?"

"Yes, yes, sir."

"It concerns everyone! Work, look live. For three days now I have not hugged my young wife because of you loafers!"

Somewhere on the border with Afghanistan there was a large army tent. Several officers are sitting in the tent, Lt. Col. Chambers and Shahob. Colonel Mulligan enters the conversation.

"All that you said, Mr. Shahob, of course, is rather amusing, but I see no good reason why we should risk the lives of dozens of British soldiers in order to accompany the Emir's households, their belongings and it's still unknown what."

"I am only a messenger, and I transmit only what Emir deigned to entrust me. The rest will be only my guesses and assumptions."

"The Emir could have trusted his messengers more," Mulligan quipped. "Well, then share your guesses with us. Maybe this will help us make the decision that the Emir expects of us."

"As far as I can imagine, the caravan will transport valuables for a certain amount.

"How valuable?" the colonel asked quickly.

"I think not much."

"Why do you think so?"

"As far as I am aware, our Emir is going to teach the Bolsheviks a good lesson in order to discourage them from approaching Bukhara and return what they managed to capture. To do this, you need well-trained mercenaries, not sarbaz, who will flee with the first shot.

With a caravan, an Emir's confidant is sent to Afghanistan for negotiations. As an advance, he will have to carry something with him to encourage the Afghans to come to Bukhara and fight the Bolsheviks."

"Here is how?" surprised Mulligan. "We have no such information about the military plans of Mr. Alimkhan."

"Obviously, you draw your information from a very small source, Mr. Colonel." "You want to say," Mulligan contemptuously remarked, "that Kadyr-bek..." and then stopped short under the angry gaze of Chambers.

Mulligan coughed and tried to correct his mistake: "That Kadyr-bek, your minister of war, is not able to cope with the Bolsheviks on his own?"

Shahob pretended not to notice this mise-en-scène, although a slight smile flickered in the corner of his mouth.

"Excuse me, Colonel, but I'm not a military man, and I can't judge what I don't understand. I have set out to you the request of our Emir, and my powers are limited to this. When can I get your answer?"

"I think in two hours. We need to discuss and weigh everything."

"Then," Shahob rose from his seat, "if you don't mind, I'll go and have some rest. The road was very tiring, and I still have a way back." Chambers also got up from his seat.

"I will accompany you and show you where you can relax so that no one bothers you."

He let Shahob forward, and they left the tent.

When Chambers and Shahob walked far enough from the tent, Chambers began a conversation.

"I can tell you right now what their answer will be. Unfortunately, our brave colonel thinks more often with his ass, not his head."

"I also know the answer," Shahob grinned. "By the way, I had no chance to personally congratulate you on your promotion, Lieutenant Colonel."

"With your help, Mr. Niyazov. And your bank account has been significantly increased."

"There is a trifle left," Shahob grunted, "to have time to use it." "Do not be a pessimist, because great things wait for us." "What are you talking about?" Shahob said, deliberately surprised.

"About the caravan, what else? While our warriors listened with their ears to your fables, I used my brains. Answer me one question," they stopped on a hill, and Chambers lit a cigarette. "After all, the caravan will be sent regardless of their decision, right?" he nodded toward the tent.

"I think yes," Shahob carefully looked at Chambers. "What does that imply?"

"This implies that we both know what this caravan will actually carry."

"We know?"

"Well, alright, we guess, what a difference. Do you have any idea what the promise holds?"

"Can you imagine," Shahob frowned, "what are you going to get me into? Or do you think that I dream of being skinned alive, chopped into small pieces and fed to hungry dogs? This is not the most abominable option, you know."

"Brr!" Chambers winced. "Let's get by without the details. I just can't get used to your oriental quirks. Still. After all, you are an adventurer by nature, a player, otherwise you would not be here. Do not tell me that a living dog is better than a dead lion or something like that. Let's play once, but for the most part."

"You're in a hurry, Lieutenant Colonel. We will postpone the solution of this question until the moment when our guesses do not turn into something more real."

"Well then," Chambers agreed, "that makes sense."

"Then, if you do not mind, I still would like to relax a bit." "Of course. Please…"

59

Kadyr-bek rode a horse to a military garrison, from the gates of which a convoy of strong horses were led out. Ahead on horseback was a guardsman from the Emir's personal guard.

"Wait!" Kadyr-bek shouted.

"Who allowed this? Immediately back!"

"The Emir's order to select 20 horses for a commercial convoy."

He handed Kadyr-bek a document. He read, with a displeased look, returned the document and waved his hand, giving consent and Kadyr-bek drove into the garrison gate, stopped at the headquarters building, dismounted, throwing the reins to a soldier who had run up to him. The head of the garrison ran up to greet Kadyr-bek, but he waved him away, entered the building and went into the office. He sat down at the table, opened the folder with the papers, but after a few seconds irritably shut it.

"What kind of commercial convoy? We are sitting like on a powder keg, these red ragamuffins are just about to advance, each horse is worth its weight in gold, and he is going to trade. Well, the soldier still didn't demand for protection..." Kadyr-bek stopped at this thought: "Didn't demand ... Why?"

There was a careful knock on the door. Kadyr Bek yelled: "Get out!" After a short pause, he continued his thoughts:

"Why ... my horses, but not my guard? So that Kadyr-bek does not know where and with what load they will gallop? No, that won't do. My heart feels that it will not be a simple convoy... I will find out, I will certainly find out..."

In one of the studies of the suburban residence, Alimkhan is listening to Shahob's report on his negotiations with the British.

"So," Alimkhan summed up, "your friends refused. Why?"

"They don't want to risk their soldiers, not knowing exactly what and how much the caravan will carry."

"They are not supposed to know," Alimkhan said irritably. "What difference does it make if they are well paid for it?"

"Apparently, their greed expressed itself, they were afraid to cheapen. Or my version of what will be in the caravan did not suit them. I had to improvise, not having your exact instructions."

"I hope it was at least believable?"

"Quite. Yet -"

"Okay. Maybe it's for the best. Who knows what could have crossed their minds. But the caravan will go anyway, and you will accompany it," he paused, rubbing the bridge of his nose.

"The British are not so stupid and may try to start their own game. You know their habits and tricks, but my man, whom I sent with a caravan, is not. Therefore, your task will be to identify and suppress their attempts. I have very few people whom I can entrust to such a thing."

"Your trust," Shahob pressed his hand to his heart, "the highest praise."

"Therefore, be nearby, I will need you in a few days."

"Of course. And one more thing for you. It seems that I managed to find out from our British friends who from your surroundings works for them. Rather, they blurted it out."

"Yes? Who is it?"

"I am very sorry to inform you about this, Your Highness, but this is our respected lower kushbegi."

"Who?" In surprise, Alimkhan got up from his chair.

"Yes, this is Kadyr-bek."

"I hope," Alimkhan looked intently at Shahob, but he did not look away, "You understand what the price of your mistake can be?" Shahob stood up and bowed in response.

"Yes, Your Highness. I threw a fishing rod in a conversation, and the British man fell for it. The name of Kadyr-bek was named."

"Sit down." Alimkhan waved a dismissive hand. "I believe you and am not surprised at anything. Moreover, one thread was already reaching for him, but it broke off. Okay. Not in vain I kept this greedy and envious jackal away. He will pay me for everything. But not now, it's not time yet. Now the most important thing is the caravan. You have a few days to rest. Now go..."

Shahob entered his house, sat down at the table and bowed his head wearily. Then he began to massage his temples with his fingers. He got up, went to a basin of water, scooped up water with his hands and refreshed his face. He removed a towel from the tack on the wall and began to slowly wipe it.

"So, everything is clear with the caravan, I was right. What next?" He hung a towel on the tack and returned to the table. He sat down and sat back in a chair.

"Then you need to count. Does our Emir need extra eyes next to the treasury? No. This means that those who will accompany the caravan, are already deceased, just do not know about it yet. Two main characters remain: me and the second.

Someone must return and report to the Emir, where the treasury is. Whom will the Emir keep alive? Me or that second? Me or him?"

He stood up and walked from wall to wall, flexing his fingers.

"The answer is simple: no-bo-dy! Friendship is friendship, but the treasury is another matter. So, I simply have no choice. He grinned bitterly. "Well, you have to be friends with Chambers and try to stay alive."

He sat at the table, took out a piece of paper, and wrote a few words on it. Then he folded it several times, put it in the fold of the robe and went to the door. A messenger dashed into Chambers' tent and handed him a small bundle.

"An urgent message for you, sir."

"Good. Wait outside, corporal, get an answer now." "Yes, Mr. Lieutenant Colonel."

He also promptly left the tent. Chambers unfolded the bundle in which was a piece of flat cake. Chambers grinned.

"Our dervish in his role."

Breaking a cake, the edges of which were fastened with silk thread, he pulled out a note and read it.

"The game begins, I urgently need a connection."

Chambers took out the matches and burned the note. Then he smiled.

"Well then, I was not mistaken about you, Mr. Dervish. Play, we'll play." He sat down at a small table and quickly sketched an answer to Shahob. He also folded it several times and put it in a leather case. Then he called the messenger. "Corporal!"

The corporal dashed into the tent.

"I'm listening, Mr. Lieutenant Colonel."

"Send it immediately," he handed the case to Corporal, "And with all the precautions.

Is it clear to you?"

"Yes, Mr. Lt. Col.!"

He saluted and rushed out of the tent. Chambers sat down again at the table and thought...

60

Alimkhan pensively walked around the garden and recalled the Surah of Yusuf from the Holy Quran in verse 53: "And I do not acquit myself. Indeed, the soul is a persistent enjoiner of evil, except those upon which my Lord has mercy. Indeed, my Lord is Forgiving and Merciful."

Greed is an evil force and lures in various ways... one of them is gold ... and its magical radiance...

Bukhara residents have always considered the golden glow yellow and not red like many others have. For centuries, in the mines of the Bukhara oasis, gold has been yellow, the most valuable alloy...

"It doesn't matter what colour." Emir was pondering, "Gold always brought misfortune to the head of mankind... Neither the ancient Assyrians, nor the inhabitants of Babylon and Egypt, nor Alexander the Great, nor Amir Timur became happy from untold riches."

As the legend tells, Alexander the Great willed after his death to carry him to the cemetery with his right hand raised up and with his palm open, showing everyone around the world that the Great Leader and Lord of the World goes to another world without riches and treasures...

Alimkhan recalled how he had run into the female half as a child and heard his mother Eshonoy-begim telling Emir's concubines the parable about a madwoman who lived in ancient times in Bukhara, who was invited to a rich house and dressed in gold jewellery by the ones who, laughing, were allegedly preparing her for marriage...

When the mad woman saw herself in a sparkle of gold, she suddenly began to make quite reasonable speeches and those around decided that she was cured... but when the gold jewellery was removed from her, she again became crazy.

The approaching Iskander interrupted Alimkhan's thoughts about a transitory world.

"I'm waiting for your orders, Your Highness."

"Orders will come later, Iskander, but first I want to ask you something. I heard you telling my son about mountains, caves, secret passages along which brigands made their way with their prey. What of this is true, and why is this fairy tale for a child?" Iskander smiled:

"I only thought up the brigands, my lord. Everything else is true." "Now tell me about it, but without the brigands."

"I was born and raised in those places. My father always took me with him to look

for mummies and collect healing herbs, so I know every path in the mountains and

every cave that you can climb into."

"And the secret passages?"

"Once, my father and I went down into a cave and, due to my oversight, could no longer go back upstairs. We had to look for another way so as not to die. Several tunnels led from the cave, but only one could lead us to the light. We still found it, although there was almost no strength left, and despair crushed our throats and clouded our minds.

"Do you remember this place?"

"I will not forget it until my death, although many years have passed." "Can any of the outsiders find it?"

"This is impossible, Your Highness, if you do not know exactly where the entrance is."

"Good. How much cargo can fit there?"

"Much, very much."

"Even cargo of a caravan, twenty carts?"

"Even out of twenty, my lord."

"Does it not surprise you that I ask you this in detail?"

"So, these are your plans. My business is to comply with your orders, and not discuss their necessity."

"The order will be like that. You will lead the caravan to this place, you will hide the cargo in this cave and you alone will know what kind of cargo it is."

"I will do it without even knowing."

"No! You should know, because ignorance often leads to silly oversights, which should occur. When the caravan is ready, you will receive detailed instructions from me. You have a few days to prepare and rest."

"Yes, my Lord. I swear by my life that you will not have to regret that you have entrusted me."

"I know, Iskander. Now go..."

Settling down under a branchy tree and making sure that there was nobody nearby, Shahob imperceptibly pulled out a leather case, which he had just received from a messenger, from the folds of his robe. Taking a note from there, he unfolded it, quickly ran his eyes over and hid it again in the case. He shook his head and muttered; "Very original, Chambers. Dervish with a red patch on his left sleeve."

With the same success, he could wave the British flag or sing Rule, Britannia. Maybe spit on them and try to play my own game? OK, the road will be long, there will be time to decide everything..."

61

Iskander walked around the hall, where he usually trained with Firuz-begim's son. Firuz-begim entered the hall and headed toward him. Thinking about the matter that the Emir instructed him, he did not hear her easy steps. "Hello, Iskander."

Iskander flinched in surprise, turned and bowed with an embarrassed look:

"I greet you, my Mistress."

"Iskander, don't call me "Mistress", I don't like this word."

"Good, my…" Iskander hesitated, and Firuz-begim laughed. Iskander was even more embarrassed. "Forgive me."

"Alright, forget it. Unfortunately, there will be no lesson today, the boy got a little sick, and the doctor left him in bed."

"What is wrong with him?" Iskander asked with concern."

"No need to worry, ordinary cold. But he needs to lie down."

"What a pity. I had to leave the other day and was hoping to spend a couple more lessons with him before leaving."

"To leave?" an alarm sounded in Firuz-begim's voice. "For a long time?"

"I do not know. It will not depend on me."

"But will you be back?"

"Yes," said Iskander with meaning, "I will definitely be back. Maybe I can at least talk to him a little?"

"I think it won't harm him. Lying in bed all the time is not too much fun for the boy." They went into the room where Firuz-begim's son was lying in bed. Seeing Iskander, the boy was delighted.

"How nice of you to come! So you will show me your secret blow, as promised?" "Right in bed? No, first you have to get better, and then, when I arrive, I will definitely teach you this blow."

"Are you leaving?" The boy was upset.

"Yes, I have a very important business."

"With whom will I fight when I recover?"

"I think it would be nice for you to learn how to fight your illnesses while you lie."

"How is this?" The boy was surprised. "I don't see them!"

"But you feel them. So, you must constantly repeat for that nasty disease to go away, I'm not afraid of you. I am stronger than you, and if you do not back down, I will kick your ears. The disease will get scared and will creep away from you slowly."

"Is that true??"

"True. I checked on myself. It works very well." "Then I will scare it, let it creep away."

"Well done! When I pass the holy spring, I will ask for a magical talisman for you that will protect you from troubles and diseases."

"Great!" exclaimed the boy.

"Come back soon! I..." he thought,

"I will give you a magic handkerchief that drives away evil spirits. My mother gave it to me." He pulled a white silk handkerchief from under the pillow and handed it to Iskander. He glanced at Firuz-begim, and she nodded her head in agreement.

"Thanks," Iskander carefully folded the handkerchief and put it in his bosom.

"You really helped me out. They say that along the road that

I will go, many evil spirits dangle from boredom, and just wait for someone to play mean tricks on. Now I'm not afraid, and they will not delay me on the road. That means I'll be back soon. Get well."

He exchanged with the boy their conditional gestures of warriors, looked into Firuz-begim's eyes, bowed and quickly left. Firuz-begim followed him with her eyes, then said:

"May Allah protect him…"

62

Kadyr-bek, accompanied by the head of the garrison, is walking around the territory, looking at the soldiers involved in military training.

A group of soldiers try their hands at fighting. One of them, of medium height, but sinewy, easily laid his rivals one by one under the thunderous exclamations of those gathered. Kadyr-bek showed him to his companion.

"Bring him to my office."

"Yes, master."

Kadyr-bek is sitting in his office, considering his actions in relation to the caravan.

There is a knock on the door.

"Come in."

The door opened and the garrison commander entered the office.

"I brought him," he reported.

"Let him in."

"Yes," he darted out of the office and pushed the soldier to the door: "Go and watch out!"

The garrison commander waved a finger at him. The soldier nodded his head and entered the office. The door closed behind him. The soldier bowed to Kadyr-bek:

"Command, my lord."

"What's your name?"

"Ghafur, my lord."

"How many years have you been serving?" "Eleven, my lord."

"Do you know who I am?"

"I know. You are Kushbegi, the chief of all the chiefs."

"Of them all!" Kadyr-bek muttered under his breath.

"Right. One word of mine, and they will let you go home, forever. Do you want to go home?"

"I want, Lord Kushbegi." his eyes sparkled.

"You will do as I say - you will go, you will also receive a reward."

"I will do whatever you command, Lord Kushbegi. I swear on my life."

"Then listen and remember. After three to four days, a commercial convoy will leave the city. They will need drivers, and you must be among them. They will pick from the rabble that hangs out in the square in front of the palace in search of work," Kadyr-bek threw a few coins on the table. "Find some rags so as not to differ from them, and today begin to hang out with them. Don't let any tattered man overtake you."

"Nobody will overtake me," Ghafur said decisively.

"Listen further. You must remember everything: where does the caravan go, what road and, most importantly, what does the caravan take. If it stops and unloads, you must remember every stone, every bush, so that later you can find this place with your eyes closed. You'll come back and report everything to me exactly. From today, you should look and behave like those in the square, and not like a soldier. If they get to the bottom of you, you can pay with your life. Got it?"

"Everything will be, as you said, Lord Kushbegi," Ghafur reached out. "How will I inform you that they took me to a caravan?"

"I will find out, it's not your concern. That's all, go and get ready. Remember - your fate is in your hands. And the last thing. No one should know that I sent you. Clear?"

"I would rather bite my tongue, Lord Kushbegi." "Go to work," Kadyr-bek waved his hand

Ghafur, bowing, backing away, left the office and closed the door behind him.

"He will bite off his tongue..." muttered Kadyr-bek. "May it even be... only bring information..."

In his study, Alimkhan gives the last instructions to Iskander.

"Very few people know about this caravan, and no one except me knows what it will transport. For too curious ones, this can cause unnecessary and dangerous interest. You must be constantly on the alert, notice any trifle, notice any outsider who tries to get closer to the caravan."

"What should I do in such cases?"

"Ruthlessly nip. But first, finding out from whom the interest comes. Just do it so that no one notices anything in the caravan."

"Forgive my courage, sir," said Iskander. "Do you think that a traitor can accompany the caravan?"

"I have to consider any probability, even that. No one, you hear, no one should interfere with our plans. The future of great Bukhara depends on this. You will pick up the drivers from the scum that hangs about in the square. My guards will guard the caravan on the way. Check them out yourself." "What should I do with the drivers then?"

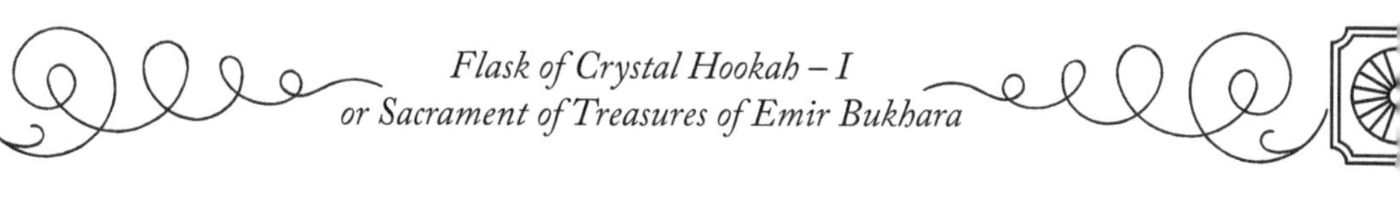

"They will be left with the load, forever. But this is not your concern. Shahob will do this."

"Shahob?" Iskander asked in surprise. "Who is it?"

"Dervish, my man on special missions. He will ride with you." Alimkhan noticed Iskander's restless gaze. "Do you want to ask something?" "If you allow me, my Lord."

"Ask. You will not have another opportunity." "Forgive my insolence, but should I trust this person?"

"No, you shouldn't. I send him with a caravan so that he is in sight, and to find out if he is so faithful to me, as he says. If you have even the slightest doubt about his loyalty, he should stay there, along with the drivers. But be careful. He is not a simple dervish. That's all you need to know for now. You will know the rest from me before departure. Now get ready. You can go…"

63

A few months later, the daughter of Shahlo Sitora returned from France, leaving the career of a top model, and is now preparing for the wedding. She really wanted to live a normal life, have her own family, children, and now all her desires should be realized.

Mom and daughter were just discussing issues related to the upcoming wedding of Sitora, when the doorbell rang.

Shahlo opened the door and saw on the threshold a man with a small oblong box in his hands and a folder under his arm.

"Hello," the messenger said. "Is your name Shahlo?"

"Yes, it's me," Shahlo was surprised, but she didn't show it. - Hello.

"You have a package. I should have passed it on to you personally. Here it is," he opened the folder and took out a sheet of paper and a pen from it. "Sign here, please." "Who is it from?" Shahlo took the sheet and put her signature.

"From Greece. Sorry, but that's all I know. Thank you, goodbye," he handed the box to Shahlo.

"Goodbye," Shahlo took the package and returned to the room to Sitora, her face was joyful. "I recognize Janis. He, as always, cannot do without surprises." Shahlo carefully opened the box, took out a crystal decanter from there and shook her head with a smile.

"How many years have passed, but he remembers."

"Mom, what is this?" Sitora asked with interest, pointing to the decanter.

"This? It was once drunk by the gods on Olympus." "Oh, really?" Sitora asked incredulously.

Shahlo thought. A memory returned her to that very evening on a yacht, and she felt very warm at heart and a little sad. It was worth the effort to bring herself back from the past to the question that her daughter had asked her.

"Really," Shahlo put her hand into the box and took out a beautifully packed bundle, turned it around, laid it on the table, deciding not to open it for now.

"This is probably what the gods ate," Sitora joked unsuccessfully.

"Don't joke like that," Shahlo looked seriously at her daughter, and she understood her mistake.

"Sorry, mom, I blurted out without thinking."

"Okay. There must be a note," she put her hand back in and felt for the envelope. "Yeah, there it is. Now we will know everything."

With a smile she opened an envelope, took out a folded sheet of paper, unfolded it and began to read.

As she read, her face changed expression: bewilderment, fear, pain. Tears appeared in her eyes. Sitora watched her mother warily. Having read, Shahlo put the sheet on the edge of the table, slowly left the room and closed the door behind her. The sheet fell to the floor.

Sitora carefully walked to the door and listened. From there muffled sobs were coming. Sitora picked up the sheet from the floor, sat down at the table and began to read.

"My dear and only beloved woman. This letter seems to be the last thing I can do in my life. And although the doctors say that I still have a lot of time, for some reason I don't believe them. It's a pity that it all ends; you and I will never see each other again.

You will find a ring in the box, this is our ancient heirloom. Until recently, I hoped that I could put it on your hand myself. It didn't work out ... Let this be your daughter's wedding present from me. It should bring her happiness, which was not enough for me.

The only thing that comforts me is the memory of you, which will not go anywhere and which will leave with me. This is sometimes more important than anything else. Do not be discouraged and regret nothing. Everything was right. Goodbye. And be happy ..."

Shahlo entered the room, her eyes were tearful. She sat down, took a letter from Sitora's hands, folded it and put it in an envelope. Gently ran a hand over it.

"A liar. Stubborn, stubborn liar," Shahlo said in a trembling voice, barely restraining herself so as not to cry again. "But I felt that something was happening to him, and he only laughed it off and weaved fables to me."

"But you could not do anything, even if you knew." "I could be there, at least for the last days..."

"Or maybe he..."

"No," Shahlo shook her head sadly, "he couldn't let me see him like this. Weak.

This time he did everything... right.

Janis, Janis ... She closed her eyes for a few seconds, having gone into the past. Then she opened the package, took out a case from there, opened it, held it in her palms, then extended it to Sitora.

"This is for you. To the wedding."

Sitora saw the ring and her eyes opened with surprise. "I can't ... You must have it, this is the memory of him."

"He wanted so. The memory... It will not go anywhere from me either. We will both remember him."

"Then ... you yourself will put it on my hand at the wedding. So will it be right?" Shahlo silently nodded in response and hugged her daughter...

A month after this conversation, Sitora's wedding took place. It was a grand event, presented in the way that they can do in the East. Hundreds of invited guests, festive fireworks, artists, musicians and dancers. And a huge wedding cake.

Firuz-begim sat at the place of honor, who was proudly looking at her great-granddaughter, Sitora. She looked like a shah-queen in her bride's outfit.

Shahlo, although she tried not to show it, was worried as if it was her own wedding. Choosing the right moment, she went to Sitora, took her hand and put a ring sent by Janis on her finger, then kissed her daughter. They looked at each other, and each without a word understood what they could say to each other.

64

After the death of Marina, Andrei Nikolayevich convinced Alik that they should now live together.

Alik was the only one left to remind him of his beloved woman.

Once, when they two were sorting through things in an old apartment, Andrei Nikolayevich found the letter that Marina left to her son. He read the letter and became gloomy. Holding the letter in his hand, he had ambivalent feelings: if he gives the letter to Alik, he may lose the person close to him, and if he does not give it, it means he will deceive this person, and he may also lose him.

For the first time in his life, he did not know what to do. Alik noticed a change in his face and went up to him.

"What is the matter with you, Uncle Andrei? Something happened?"

"So far, nothing," Andrei Nikolayevich answered with uncertainty, "but it can... You know what, let's sit down and discuss something," Andrei Nikolayevich made a difficult decision for himself.

When they sat down, Andrei Nikolayevich handed a letter to Alik:

"There is such a thing..." he hesitated. "In general, you better read it yourself, and then you will tell me your opinion. I will smoke in the meantime."

Andrei Nikolayevich got up, went to the window and lit a cigarette nervously. Alik opened the letter and began to read. Having finished reading, he laid the sheet aside, then looked at Andrei Nikolayevich who was standing at the window. He seemed to feel his eyes and hoarsely asked:

"Well, brother, are we going to do something?"

"I don't know, Uncle Andrei. It seems that I should be glad that my father was found, but somehow I do not care ...Is it possible to be so?"

"Oh, Alik," Andrei Nikolayevich sighed and turned to him. "Whatever can happen in life, and even this is possible. I'm not your father, but you're like my own, and no one is closer..."

"You are another thing altogether, you were always with us, all the time, and you loved my mother very much, I know. And he? He left us and forgot. He had another family. He doesn't need us."

"That's how it is," Andrei Nikolayevich nodded, "but maybe he didn't know that you had appeared?"

"Maybe he didn't know about me, but he still left my mother. Is that fair?" resentment appeared in Alik's eyes.

"No, brother, it isn't, you're right here," Andrei Nikolayevich again went to the window and lit a cigarette. "So what shall we do? To tear the letter and pretend that it never existed, or..." He did not finish.

"Or - what?" Alik asked. "You want to offer something, don't you? You are afraid to say, I see.

"Yes, Alik, I'm afraid, so afraid. Most of all I am afraid to lose you, and yet I will say something. What do you think?" He took a deep breath, coughed, "Maybe you should go to Tashkent, look at, Well, you understand..."

"Are you not afraid that I will stay there?" Alik looked at Andrei Nikolayevich searchingly.

"I already told you what I'm most afraid of, but I have no right to influence your decisions. You are already grown-up enough to decide for yourself what to do and what not."

"Good," Alik said resolutely. "I'll go to Tashkent, but first only with you."

"And secondly?" Andrei Nikolayevich looked at Alik.

"Secondly, just to see, do you understand me, Uncle Andrei?" "What if..." - Andrei Nikolayevich stopped half a word.

"No, Uncle Andrei. I already have a father, and I don't need a second one..." Andrei Nikolayevich turned to the window to hide his moistened eyes.

"Thank you ... son," his voice trembled, and he had to make an effort to make it sound even. "So, let's go to Tashkent..."

A car is slowly driving along one of Tashkent streets. At the wheel - Andrei Nikolayevich, Alik is next to him. Both have tense faces.

"Here, Number twenty-one, then the next one after that." Andrei Nikolayevich nodded.

He stopped the car, not reaching the desired house a bit, turned off the engine. Silence fell in the cabin, both looked at the plate with the number twenty-three. Andrei Nikolayevich could not get out of the car first.

"Are you afraid?" he asked Alik.

"Not much. Only somehow not at ease. As if I'm going to be imposed on him. In vain I started it. He does not know who I am? Well, let him not know further."

"Do not say that. Sometimes a lot depends on what you find out. After all, I once did not know you either, but now I can't imagine what will happen if you leave my life, even though I am not your father. You see how it happens ..." he turned away in the other direction to hide his feelings.

"Yes, I won't go anywhere, Uncle Andrei," Alik laid his hand on him, "Come on, Uncle Andrei, really. After all, I also have nobody left except you. I will just come in and go out."

"Well, then go, don't flog a dead horse. If you decide, bring it to the end. Do not

forget that you also have a brother."

"I remember. So shall I go?"

"Come on, move..."

Alik took a deep breath, opened the door and slowly went outside. At this time, Zarina was sitting in the kitchen and looking thoughtfully out the window. In front of her was a photograph of Sherzod on the table. She saw how close the car stopped, in which there were two: a man and a boy. After a while, the boy went out and began to look at her house number. Then hesitantly moved in her direction. Something in the boy's face seemed to Zarina painfully familiar, and her heart ached. The boy looked back at the car, then took the last step and reached for the button. A bell rang in Zarina's apartment. She started feeling some weakness in her legs, went to the door and opened it.

"Hello," Alik addressed her.

"Hello," Zarina answered with a shaky voice. "Who did you come to see?"

"Does Uncle Alibek live here?"

"Yes, here." Zarina could not look away from the mole at his temple.

"Can I talk to him?"

"He's at work now, but he should be here soon. Do you have any business with him?" "Yes ... No ... I'll probably go. Sorry." Alik already turned to leave, but Zarina stopped him.

"Wait, that won't be good. Since you have come, I think it will be ugly if you leave like that. I suggest you drop by. We will sit and talk. For some reason, it seems to me that we have something to talk about. Do you agree?"

"I agree. Only…"

"What - only?" asked Zarina.

"Nobody invited me."

"So I invite you then. Come in." Zarina let Alik and closed the door. "Let's settle in the kitchen, it will be convenient there. Come on in, sit here." She took sweets from the cupboard, set it on the table and sat opposite. "Help yourself." Alik broke a piece, chewed.

"Tasty, I've never eaten this before. Are you his wife?"

"Alibek's? Yes."

"And you have a son?"

"I have." Inside her, everything contracted with a hunch that something was about to happen. "Here is his picture," she handed Alik a photo. Alik took the photo and began to examine it.

"He also…" Alik stopped short. He looked at Zarina. She looked at him intensely.

"What also?" She did not know where to put her trembling hands.

"No…" Alik was embarrassed. "I just …" he lowered his eyes, not knowing what to say. He moved the photo to Zarina.

"Probably you wanted to say that he also has a mole on his temple, right?" Alik nodded without raising his eyes. "You know what his name is?" Alik nodded again "What happened to him?" Zarina hardly pronounced these words. "Do you know what happened to him?" in her voice were both hope and despair at the same time.

"No, I do not know. Sorry…"

After these words, Zarina somehow went limp, her shoulders dropped. She covered her face with her hands and said aloofly:

"Nobody knows... Nobody knows anything..." "Sorry," Alik touched her hand, "I really don't know."

"Sherzod is gone," Zarina removed her hands from her face and looked tiredly at Alik. "For a long time. And here you are. You know my husband, you know my son's name, and I thought..." she paused. "Who are you, Alik? You didn't just come for nothing, did you?"

"I ..." he hesitated, then pulled an envelope from his pocket and handed it to Zarina. "Here."

Zarina looked at the envelope for several seconds, not daring to take it. Then she took out the contents. It was a letter from Marina and a couple of photographs. She unfolded the sheet and began to read. As she read, pain appeared in her eyes. After reading and looking at the photographs, she closed her eyes and leaned back in her chair. After a few seconds, she got up heavily, went to the window, tried to light a cigarette, but her hands were trembling, and she crumpled it in an ashtray.

In the window she saw Andrei Nikolayevich, who nervously walked around the car, occasionally glancing at her house...

"I don't know what to say, Alik... All this is so..." she pressed her hands to her temples and shook her head.

"Don't worry, I don't need anything from him. He didn't know. I just wanted to see him before leaving..."

"Ah, Alik, Alik. He knew or he didn't... Does it really matter?" At that time a telephone rang. "Sorry."

She went into another room and picked up the phone.

"Yes."

"It's me," Alibek's voice came in the receiver. "Don't wait for me for dinner; I will linger. There is too much work."

"It's a pity. They are waiting for you here."

"Who can wait for me?"

"Alik."

"Who? Which Alik?"

"Alik, your son."

"What?!" Alibek lost his temper. "What are you talking about? Which son?"

"Oh yes. You do not know that you have a son. Do you also know Marina from Moscow?"

"What Marina, what Alik? Are you completely crazy? Damn you with your jealousy..." he dropped the phone and nervously walked around the office. "Fool...

Tomorrow some Zeynab from Turkey will appear, should I also make excuses? Where did she dig this Marina..." Alibek stopped short. The memory gave him a picture of him walking with his arms round Marina in the park, and then the scene when he saw her from a bus with a boy. He sank heavily into a chair.

"No... It can't be…" he got up, went to the secretaire, poured a full glass and dusted it. "Nonsense..."

The secretary looked into the office:

"Alibek Ghafurovich, they ask you on the phone." "I am not here," he barked. "They say that is urgent..."

"I'm not here," Alibek shouted, "I left, flew away, died. Clear?"

A frightened secretary darted out of the office as a bullet. Alibek went to the mirror hanging on the wall, loosened his tie, and peered into his reflection.

"Nonsense..." he repeated again, as if coaxing himself. "She would immediately seize me."

He said, and he did not believe what he said.

"Not?" he turned to his reflection. "Wouldn't she seize?" He walked away, poured another glass, drank, sat down at the table and put his head in his hands. Then he said bitterly: "She wouldn't. She did it right. Who needs this?" He raised his head, then with all his might struck his fist on the table. The glass on the table cracked…

65

Zarina slowly hung up the phone, ran her hand over her forehead, then went into the kitchen. Stopped at the door. Alik looked at her.

"He won't come, right?"

Zarina shook her head in the negative:

"I'm afraid he will arrive late. Some important affairs he has…" "I understand. He did not believe, huh?"

"Sometimes people commit such acts for which they are ashamed of long, long years, only they are afraid to admit this, even to themselves. Can you come to us tomorrow?"

"We are leaving tomorrow, with Andrei Nikolayevich." "Is that the man waiting for you outside?" "Yes." "Who is he?"

"A very close friend of my mother. And mine." "Did your mom come with you too?"

"She was killed …" Alik lowered his head. Zarina gasped. "By chance … They were going to get married, and now … Now we are left alone, and I have nobody except him."

"Do not say that. I will always be glad to see you. If Sherzod was here…" She became silent.

"He will be found, he will certainly be found," said Alik, "you only believe." "You would be friends, I know," Zarina said sadly.

"Let me leave you my address?" suggested Alik. "He will come and write to me. Then you will come to visit us. Good?"

"Of course. We will definitely come," Zarina gratefully looked at this unfamiliar little boy who had suddenly become so dear to her.

"Alibek …" she paused. "Don't judge him. He was not ready for your appearance today. To realize this, a man needs a different look at his whole life. It takes a lot of courage. Sometimes it may not be enough."

"I understand…" Alik agreed in a very adult way. "Probably, I'll go, Andrei Nikolayevich is worried. Will I take it?" He pointed to the letter and photographs. Zarina folded everything and handed the envelope to Alik.

"This is part of your memory of her. Take care of it." "Thank you." Alik got up. "I will see you off."

They left the house together. Zarina stroked Alik's hair.

"I wish you to be happy…"

Alik nodded silently, touched her hand and went to the car. Andrei Nikolayevich had already got behind the wheel and turned on the engine. Alik got into the car, and it slowly started off. Having caught up with Zarina, Andrei Nikolayevich slowed down, and they exchanged a long attentive look. When the car left, Zarina remained standing below and looked in the direction where they had left…

Alibek arrived in ten minutes. He got out of the car and walked unsteadily to Zarina.

"Well, where is he?" he asked defiantly.

Zarina did not even look in his direction and spoke only one word:

"Get out…"

"Why do you talk to me like that?" Alibek was indignant.

Zarina abruptly turned in his direction and again spoke only one word:

"Get-out…"

But what Alibek saw in her gaze, and the tone with which she said it, made him hang his head and he slowly walked into the house…

The morning after Alik's visit, Alibek, battered and exhausted on a sleepless night, entered the kitchen. Zarina was standing by the window and looking at the street. Alibek took a couple of steps in her direction and stopped. Without turning to his side, Zarina said:

"Everything is on the table. You can have breakfast."

Alibek indifferently glanced over the table, stepped closer and slightly touched her shoulder. Zarina started and moved away from him.

"I want to talk to you," he said quietly.

"About what?"

"About everything. I wanted to…" He was silent for a moment.

"Forgive me…" Zarina turned around with tears in her eyes, there was bitterness in her voice:

"For what exactly?"

"For …" he hesitated, lowered his eyes, then looked directly at her.

"For me."

"Just like that?"

"Not. I need time, some time."

"Do we still have it?" Zarina asked bitterly.

"We do. We must have it. It's impossible not to have it. Also… Where did he stay?"

"Already nowhere. He flies away today."

"How - flies away?"

"Like this. He came to meet, to look a…" she did not finish talking. "Nothing else."

Alibek looked at his watch:

"I still have time," he said, and went to the door.

"Do you want to catch up with the past?" Zarina asked quietly.

Alibek stopped abruptly, turned around and firmly said:

"No, I want to fix the present, our present. Our future…"

He left the kitchen, took a purse with keys and documents and left the apartment. Alibek got into the car, turned on the ignition, looked at his watch

again. "I have to catch it…"

He got the car onto the road and rushed towards the airport. At the intersection,

a traffic policeman blocked the traffic. Alibek jumped out of the car and went up to him. "What happened?"

"The delegation is coming."

"Listen, brother, I urgently need to go to the airport. Maybe I'll slip in?"

"Everyone needs it." He showed with his rod to the intersection, which was already blocked from two sides by cars. "I cannot do anything. Order, you understand." "Is this for a long time?"

"Who knows?" responded the traffic policeman. "Maybe 10 minutes, maybe half an hour."

"I see," Alibek slowly went to his car, got into it and put his head on the steering wheel…

66

Bukhara, the square in front of the Ark Palace. At the edge of the square, a small space has been cleared, in front of which there are three dozens of vagrants crowding.

Among them is Ghafur. From scratch is a bag of sand. Iskander points his finger at the next candidate for the drivers. He had already taken three, and they stood aloof with a pleased look.

"You."

The tramp went out, went to the bag, grabbed it, threw it on his back and immediately sat down on the ground with it. There was laughter in the crowd of onlookers. "Not good. Now you," he pointed with his finger at the big man.

He went to the bag, spat on the palm of his hand, grabbed the bag, but could only lift it. Laughter rang out again. Ghafur separated from the group and went to the fat man. "Uh, there is a lot of meat, but little use. Get out..."

He grabbed the bag and freely picked it up, lowered it and picked it up again. The onlookers hummed approvingly. Ghafur made a movement as if he wanted to return to the group of tramps, but Iskander stopped him.

"Wait, you're quite good. Go there," he pointed at a group of lucky ones. "Thank you, master, I really need a job."

Ghafur pressed his hand to his chest and stepped aside. Iskander continued the selection. A man separated from the crowd of onlookers, who carefully watched what was happening, and without hurry went from the square.

Ark Palace, a repository of valuables where inventory and packing of treasures are carried out.

Hamrakul, the chief treasurer, sealed the last bag and put a tick in his sheet. He rolled up the paper into a tube, tied it with a ribbon and sealed it with his seal too. He turned to Jumabay.

"That's it, my work is finished, and so is theirs," he nodded to the workers. "Can I go to my young wife now?"

"Of course, respected one. But first, the Emir ordered everyone to be treated properly and generously awarded." He opened the door and made a sign with his hand. A huge tray with pilaf was brought into the room and put on the table. There were teapots with tea and bowls. "Eat, drink, and the reward will come later."

All the workers immediately crowded around the tray and began to eat with their hands.

Hamrakul winced, but also took a few handfuls of pilaf and sent them to his mouth. He poured tea into the bowl and drank. Workers did the same. Suddenly, one of them grabbed his stomach with his hands, wheezed and fell to the floor. After him the second, third. Hamrakul's eyes were horrified. He also grabbed his stomach with his hands and wheezed with difficulty:

"What is this…?"

"This?" mockingly, Rasulbek responded. "This is a reward I promised. You see, everyone is already happy!" He pointed to writhing bodies and laughed outrageously. Hamrakul swayed, his knees bent, and he fell to the floor next to the others. Rasulbek took Hamrakul's papers and put them in his bosom.

"You won't need them anymore …"

The garrison of Bukhara, Kadyr-bek is watching what is happening on the parade ground. He was approached by the same man who was in the square and watched the selection of drivers and bowed.

"Well?" Kadyr-bek asked impatiently.

"All is well, master. He was taken as a driver." "You saw it yourself?"

"Yes, master, with my own eyes."

"Then it's really good." He smiled contentedly and threw a coin at him. "This will work. Go now..."

One of the rooms of the palace is where Alimkhan's mother Eshonoy-begim and Firuz-begim were sitting, they were talking about something intently. Alimkhan entered. Both fell silent and looked at him. Alimkhan went into the room and sat down.

"It's good that you are both here. We need to talk." "Something happened?" Eshonoy-begim asked with concern. "Not yet." He turned to Firuz-begim. "How is our son?" "Already better, glory to Allah."

"This is good ..." Alimkhan nodded and paused. "In Bukhara, it is becoming restless. We have to leave the city. We are departing."

"Far away?" Eshonoy-begim asked. "Far away. Possibly, for a long time. I want you to start preparing for departure today."

"What should we take with us?"

"Only that which cannot be dispensed with on a long and difficult road."

"But what about the boy, my lord?" asked Firuz-begim. "He's not so healthy yet." "We have time, and I hope that he will recover by the return of Iskander. On the same day we will leave Bukhara. I think that 8-10 days is enough for Iskander." "Is everything really so serious?" Eshonoy-begim asked.

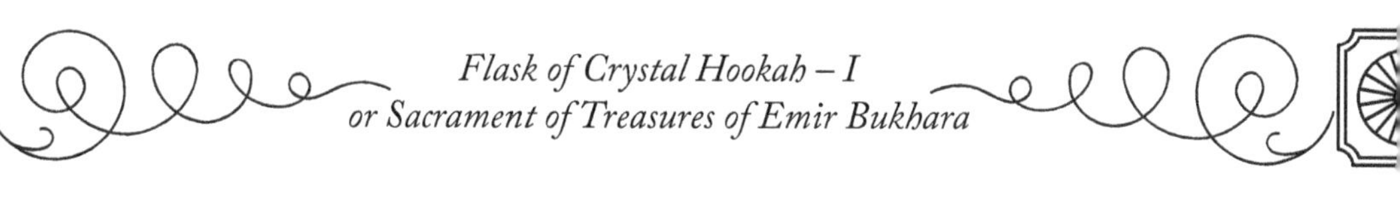

"I'm afraid it is. Therefore, you must be prepared." He got up tiredly. "That's all, affairs wait."

Alimkhan headed for the exit. Eshonoy-begim and Firuz-begim exchanged anxious looks and watched the departing Emir.

67

Ark Palace and the head of the Emir's personal guard shows Iskander a detachment of guards who were selected to guard the caravan. Iskander walks along the line of guards, meticulously examining each one. In one of the guards, he recognized his childhood friend Khamid. He also recognized Iskander, but both refrained from showing their acquaintance. Iskander turned to the chief.

"Good. I am sure that such a detachment will cope with the task. Send everyone to the barracks, so that no one leaves before my order. They should be ready to set out at any moment. You can take them away. This one," he pointed at Khamid, "I need him. He will go with me."

The commander gave the command, and the detachment headed for the barracks. Khamid and Iskander went towards the palace. When they hid from prying eyes, Iskander joyfully said:

"Khamid, my friend! How glad I am to see you again!" "Me too, so many years have passed!" They hugged.

"We have a difficult job ahead of us, and what can be more reliable than the shoulder of a friend!"

"You became such a great boss," said Khamid slyly,

"Me too..."

"Ay, stop it! For you, I'm the same Iskander and nothing has changed. Although others do not need to know about us. By the way, do you still shoot a bow accurately, as before?"

"Did you forget about the eagle that I knocked out?"

"I did not forget."

"Yes, it was a good shot. I think that now I am not worse. But why? Can it come in handy?"

"I don't know yet, but whatever can happen in life. Let's do it so. I'll call you in the evening, and we'll chat somewhere in a secluded place, okay?" "Of course! I'll wait." "Agreed. Now go back to the rest. See you in the evening…"

Somewhere on the border with Afghanistan a messenger entered Chambers' tent, handed him a small sealed case and immediately went out. Chambers unsealed the case and pulled out a note. There was a date and only a few words:

"The parcel is dispatched in two days."

"Two days later," Chambers estimated, "that means - today, if it's on its way in two days. Wonderful. It's time to send a liaison." He turned the map around and ran a finger along the route, jabbed a finger at one point. "Here he will be waiting for our travelers. Sergeant!" He shouted.

A sergeant appeared in the tent.

"This is urgent, now listen to me, Lieutenant Alistair!"

The sergeant saluted and darted out the tent.

Another alarming night came in Bukhara.

The city gates opened, and a caravan slowly moved forward from the city, which looked like an ordinary merchant one - with bales and carpets.

Ahead of the caravan was Iskander. When the caravan left, the gate closed behind it. About fifty meters from the city wall, a detachment of guardsmen was already waiting for them to guard.

Iskander made a sign with his hand, the guards took their places around the caravan and continued to go on.

Old Saeed-aka worked in the inner garden of the Ark Palace, making minor repairs to the garden buildings. Firuz-begim with her son, who felt better after illness, entered the garden. They walked along the path and stopped not far from where Saeed-aka was working. "Mom, is Iskander coming soon?" the boy asked. "I don't know, son." "But will anything not happen to him?"

"I don't know that either." At these words, Firuz-begim's face became gloomy, and Saeed-aka noticed it. "May Allah keep him on the road."

"But he said that he would definitely come back and show me his hold. We will fight again."

"If he said so, then it would be so," Saeed-aka confirmed to the boy. "Forgive me, my mistress, for interfering in your conversation."

"Do you know Iskander, father?"

"I know, my mistress, I know. I also knew your father, may his soul abide in paradise. I lived a lot and learned a little to figure out who is a good person and who is not."

"Is Iskander good?" the boy asked.

"Yes, my little master, very good," said Saeed. "He has a very good reason to return here safe and sound. So he will be back."

"Reason?" Firuz-begim said, surprised. "What reason?"

"Forgive the old man, my mistress, but I can't say this, this is not my secret. Your father entrusted it to me before dying, and I cannot break the word I gave him. Forgive the old man again."

"I understand. I can't make you reveal it. But maybe this is related to..." She was embarrassed and blushed slightly.

"He, who has ears, will hear but he, who has intelligence, will know. Why do you need my words, my mistress, if you yourself know the answer?"

"I also want to know the secret!" said the boy, who was listening attentively to their conversation.

"I'll tell you later, before going to bed, OK?"

"Well, just do not forget!"

"I will not forget. Thank you, father," she turned to Saeed. "You brought peace to my soul."

"If you need anything, my mistress, I will do everything I can for you."

"Good. Come on son, it's time to take medicine, you must be healthy by the arrival of Iskander."

She took the boy's hand, looked at Saeed carefully again, and left.

Following the path planned by Iskander, the caravan approached the sacred spring. The guards dismounted to draw water.

Iskander went to the source, scooped up crystal clear water in his palm and pressed it to his face. Then he straightened up and looked around. Not far from the source, he noticed an old woman in well-worn clothes who was staring at him intently. He went to her.

"Hello. Do you live here?"

"Yes. Here too..." the woman answered strangely.

"You looked at me like... Do you know me?" asked Iskander.

"I know. I see..." she fell silent.

"What?"

"What kind of man you are. Brave, strong ... Only lie and betrayal are near you.

Death walks near you." At these words, Iskander shuddered.

"But don't be afraid, go straight ahead." She put her hand in the bag, which was hanging on the side, took out a thing from it and handed it to Iskander. "Here it is, take this." "What for? What should I do with this?" Iskander, puzzled by the words of the woman, looked at the object handed over to him.

"This is a talisman. It will protect you from troubles and diseases and protect you from enemies. Do not take it off. Not everyone is given the opportunity to have such protection; do not part with it. You deserve it..."

The woman turned and walked away, somehow quietly disappearing among the trees. Iskander turned the little thing in his hand. It was a shabby leather pouch with some kind of pattern on the surface, with a thin leather cord to carry around his neck. He hesitated a little, then hung it around his neck and hid it under his shirt.

Once again looking in the direction where the woman disappeared, he returned to the detachment.

"Who was this woman?" Shahob asked. "Who knows her... It seems she lives here..." "Did she want something from you?"

"She asked us not to desecrate anything here. Have you drawn the water?" Iskander changed the subject.

"We have."

"Then on horseback and forth..."

Everyone took their places, and the caravan moved on.

68

Firuz-begim is sitting with her son in his room and teaching him how to make a toy himself.

"Now you take this piece, you do it like that, now you stretch its ears … What does it look like?"

"The head!" the boy clapped his hands in joy.

"Whose head?"

"Horses or burros."

"That's right, horse's. Now we do like this … Now we attach legs, like this … Have you made a tail for a horse?"

"I have, here it is…" he handed his mother the tail he had prepared.

"Great tai … doing so… done. What have we made?"

"Hooray, the horse!" the boy clapped his hands again.

"And who will ride it?"

"Iskander!"

"Why Iskander?" Firuz-begim said, surprised, who was expecting another answer. "He is the bravest and the strongest, therefore the first horse is for him."

"OK, you persuaded me," Firuz-begim smiled. "Now let's make some more horses, put them in a row, and what will we do?"

"We can do it …" he hesitated, and then asked uncertainly. "Caravan?" "That's right, caravan. Will we make a caravan?" "Of course we will!" "Then you do tails and legs for horses, and I do the rest."

"Aha! The hardest thing I got!"

"But you are a man! Is a man afraid of difficulties?"

"Who said that I'm afraid? I just said that my work is the most difficult, which means that I will do it."

"Agreed. Here is your piece of clay, come on, sculpt..."

After spending all day on the road, the caravan stopped to rest.

Everyone settled down for a snack - the drivers separately, the guards - separately.

Iskander sat next to Khamid. Shahob, as always, settled alone at a distance.

A beggar appeared on the road in tattered clothes, with a dirty face, hair in different directions. He went to Shahob and held out his hand, asking for alms. Shahob pulled out a piece of cake from his bosom and threw the tramp. He grabbed it and began humiliatingly thanking Shahob, but he only waved away the tramp and he hastened away to the nearby village visible. This scene was closely watched by Iskander.

"Does this tramp seem familiar to you?" he asked Khamid.

"What? A tramp like a tramp," Khamid replied nonchalantly. "Are there few of them hanging around? We have seen so many along the road."

"And what, all of them had patches on their left sleeves and a torn earlobe?" Iskander pointedly asked his question.

"You mean that..."

"I want to say that this tramp is not spinning around the caravan without a reason, and I don't like it at all. Can I entrust you with one important thing?" "Of course!"

"Then find this tramp and talk to him. Let him tell you why he is spinning around the caravan and who sent him. Will you do it?"

"You can have no doubt," Khamid assured his friend. "If

everything is so serious, then he will tell me everything he knows."

"Good. But do it so that no one notices or finds out anything. Come up with a reason to go to the village and address me officially so that no one suspects anything."

"Got it."

Khamid got up and went to the carts, and Iskander sprawled on the ground, showing that he intended to rest.

As the sun began to rise, the detachment began to gather on the road. Iskander prepared to wash himself and asked Khamid, who was nearby, to pour water from a wineskin. Khamid came up, took a wineskin and began to pour water little by little onto Iskander's hands. Unbeknownst to the rest, Iskander quietly asked Khamid: "Well? Have you talked?"

"I have. He was in such a hurry to tell me everything that he could not stand it and died in my arms."

"Poor one. What did he manage to tell?"

"That the British hired him. If I let him go, they will make me rich, all the pockets will be full."

"Why didn't you agree?"

"My pockets are full of holes, I still can't sew it up. I had to refuse."

"Thank you, Khamid," Iskander expressed his gratitude. "I knew I could trust you. I don't promise to make you rich, but I'll sew your pockets myself, with my own hands."

"What else," said Khamid. "What will my wife do when I get married? Doesn't it interest you whom he has been visiting?"

"To our dervish, to whom else. Am I right?"

"Right." Khamid was surprised by Iskander's ingenuity but tried not to show it. "And what now?"

"Nothing, everything is as usual," answered Iskander. "We'll

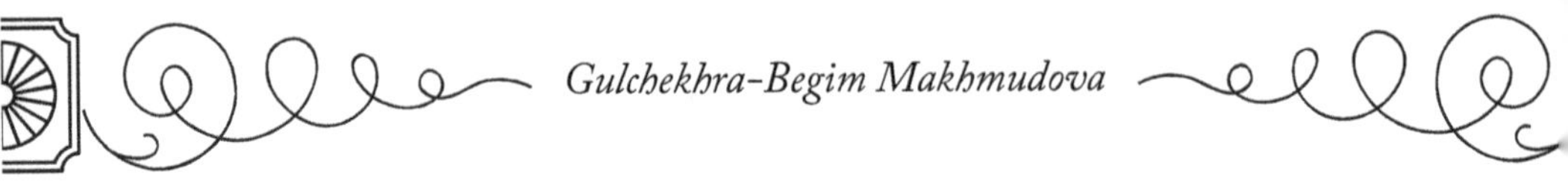

see there. In the meantime, he should not suspect anything, you get me?"

"Of course."

"Well, thanks for the water. How much can I wash myself."

Iskander took a towel and began to wipe himself. Khamid laid a waterskin on the ground, made a stand in front of Iskander and went into the squad.

69

... Another year has passed. Sitora gave birth to a child, and this event was decided to be celebrated among all relatives and friends with families.

The main part of the celebration was already over, and now all the guests were divided into small groups to exchange impressions and news.

Zarina retired and sat in the distance. Her face became sad, and her eyes began to get wet. She thought about how wonderful it would be if her Sherzod was here now, along with everyone.

Shahlo saw a lonely sitting friend and went up to her. Zarina was about to say something to Shahlo, but she was ahead of her:

"No, do not say anything. I know everything and understand everything. What

you are thinking and who you are thinking about. I know that you're tired of the

phrases "be patient" and "everything will be fine," and yet I believe that everything

will really be fine, you just have to wait."

"Do you really believe this fortune teller?"

"Not as much to her as to my grandmother's forebodings, and she also said that nothing bad had happened to him.

You may not believe me, but her visions have never failed her. Therefore..." she did not finish, because one of the guests shouted that she was being asked for on the phone. "Wait, I will accept another congratulations and will be back. In the meantime, get your charming but swollen eyes wet." She kissed her friend and headed for the phone. She picked up the phone:

"Hello!"

"Aunt Shahlo?"

"Yes. Who is it?" Zarina is looking in her direction, but Shahlo's shrugged. "Aunt Shahlo, you did not recognize me? It's me, Sherzod."

"Who ?!" her breath was caught, she put a hand to her mouth. Zarina saw this and tensed.

"Yes, I am, Sherzod. I called home, but nobody answered there. Do you know where my mom is?"

"Oh, God, you're found," Shahlo breathed out. "Mother? Yes, I have your mother, I have. You're found."

"Of course I am found, where I am to go. Can I talk to her?"

"Not just can, but you must, and immediately, you little rascal!" Tears welled up in her eyes from joy for her friend. She beckoned to Zarina with her hand. She got up and began to slowly approach. Seeing Shahlo's tears, she stopped dead in her tracks. "What? What happened?"

"Pick up the phone."

"No..." Zarina began to shake her head, "No..."

"Don't make me angry, friend," Shahlo smiled happily through tears, "Don't be afraid. Pick up the phone quickly."

Zarina hesitantly picked up the phone, her hand was trembling, looking at Shahlo's face, she tried to determine what was awaiting her. "Y-yes..." "Mother?"

"Oh!" The phone slipped out of her hand, but Shahlo managed to catch it, and she grabbed Zarina with her other hand, whose legs suddenly weakened. One of those standing nearby quickly set up a chair, and she sank down on it. From the phone came: "Mother? Why are you silent? It's me, Sherzod. Mother?"

But Zarina only repeated in a weak voice through her tears, looking around those standing nearby: "Sherzod! Sherzod…"

Firuz-begim from her place was watching them all with an understanding look, nodded her head contentedly and said in an undertone:

"Everything will be fine, everything will definitely be fine…"

A few days after Sherzod's call, Zarina decided to fly to Germany to meet him there and return home with him. She put one more thing in her bag, sat down and thought. Alibek came up and sat in front of her:

"Have you already put everything together?"

"Most likely. I just can't get my thoughts together, all the time I imagine how I'll with meet him…"

"We could meet him here, all together. Maybe you shouldn't go?" "Do you want to dissuade me?"

"To be honest, yes. I don't want to let you go alone."

"I can't. I have been waiting for him so much that every extra day is torture for me. Do you understand me?"

"Of course I understand. I also cannot wait for his arrival. And the fact that he will soon be at home, alive and healthy, is for me as a gift of fate. But…" he shook his

head, "I don't want you to leave now."

"Why?"

"I don't know, I can't explain. Some kind of vague state of anxiety I have for you, for us. It probably sounds silly, but without you I will be sad and lonely."

"You never told me that before."

"Before..." he stood up and strode around the room. "Before, I didn't tell you much that I should have. I didn't do... I want all this to remain in the past. Can we start all over again?"

Zarina looked at Alibek warmly.

"We can, Alibek. Just let me bring our son home and we'll start. OK?"

"Well, let it be the way you want. What if I fly with you?"

"You better be here. What if he doesn't manage to fly through Germany? He comes home - and then there is nobody. No, you better stay, just in case. Don't worry about me. What can happen to me?"

"I don't know, maybe you're right. Can I help you?" He nodded at the bag.

"If only to throw away the excess... I'm leaving for a few days, but packing so much..."

"Well, then let me do all this and ..." he pointed to the window.

"Again, for yours?" Zarina smiled. "But we agreed. Or not?"

"Okay. If you change your mind," he jabbed the bag with his finger, "I'm near." Alibek and Zarina arrived at the airport, went into the departure hall. Alibek

put the bag on the floor. Zarina took the documents and a ticket from her purse. "Well, I go. They won't let you go farther. Don't worry about me; I'll get to the place and call." She took the bag and turned to go to the checkpoint, but Alibek stopped her.

"Wait."

Zarina turned around. "Have you forgotten anything?" "Yes.. I need..."

"What?"

"I wanted to say. I will feel bad without you ..." He lowered his eyes. Zarina slowly turned to him, peering at his face. "I want you

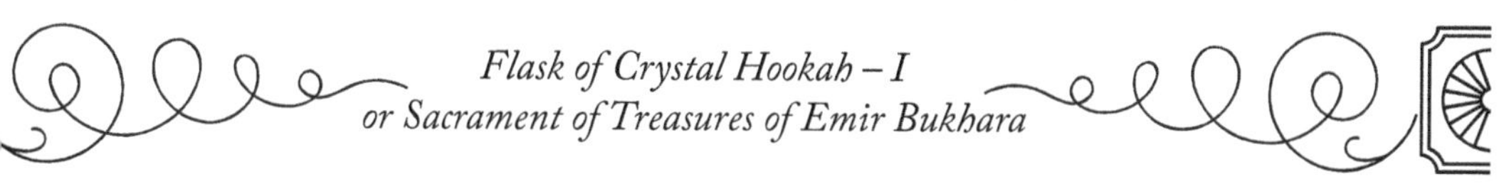

to know that. Come back soon."

Zarina went up to him.

"You have no idea what a gift you just gave me."

"This is not a gift," Alibek impulsively hugged her shoulders. "Please stay, it's not too late. I have so much to tell you.

"I cannot." Zarina kissed him. "I'll be back, and you will tell me everything. We will tell each other everything. Yes?" she pressed her hand to his cheek.

"Yes." Alibek took her palm and kissed. "Then go quickly, I will wait for you…"

He turned her and pushed her slightly. Zarina went to the registration, gave the documents and the ticket, looked back at Alibek, who was watching her intensely, made a sign with his hand. Alibek nodded, turned sharply and quickly went down.

70

A small house in the suburbs of Frankfurt. Several people are sitting in the room. The Senior is a short, solid man, his face is quite good-natured, glasses in a gold frame. But the look is prickly and hard, from which the interlocutor becomes uneasy...

"So, this is the basic scheme." He turned to sit on the right: "Moussa, are people ready?"

"Ready. Three, coming from different ends, everyone will have transit." "Documents?"

"Already tested," Moussa confirmed, "You will not cavil. But there is one problem."

"What?"

"Fatima. Here, I have not been able to do anything yet."

"Why do I get to know this just now?" he looked at Moussa so that he cringed. "She is the main link. I hope you understand well that there can be no mistake?"

"Of course, of course," said Moussa. "Therefore, I am looking for a suitable option with a legend and documents that will not cause any questions during verification." "Where are you looking? At the stashes?"

Moussa pulled out a handkerchief and wiped his sweaty forehead. "Everywhere, I try."

"You try poorly, and slowly." He addressed the sitting ones: "Any suggestions?" Mehmed, a young man of about thirty with a thin smart face, immediately responded from his place:

"It is necessary to use the airport itself."

"Explain," the Senior raised an eyebrow.

"Tracking the flows from different directions, it is easier to find what you want. In addition, if the right person is quickly intercepted, then he will not have time to leave too many connections for which he will then be pulled."

"You are making progress, my boy," the Senior looked carefully at Mehmed. "I was not mistaken about you. Now you are dealing with this issue. Moussa will help. Moussa looked hostilely at Mehmed, and the Senior noticed this. "I will not tolerate any personal grievances and showdowns, is that clear?" he looked at Moussa. He nodded. "So, it is. The main focus is on the eastern areas: Egypt, Syria, Turkey, well, and so on."

"Central Asia," added Mehmed.

"What?" the Senior asked.

"And Central Asia," Mehmed repeated. "That would be an ideal option."

The Senior was silent for a while, looking at Mehmed and wondering something in his mind.

"Perhaps you are right. Central Asia. You will elaborate the details with Moussa. Nobody has cancelled his experience yet." Moussa smiled pretty. "Report results immediately to me. That's it for today, work..."

Frankfurt Airport building and two young guys are sitting at a cafe table, apparently students of European appearance. They are carefully looking at the arrivals, from time to time checking with the photograph that lies on the table under the list of flights.

"Well, one more flight for nothing," one said, and ticked the list.

"How else will we be here?"

"They pay us money for this," another said, "And it has not yet fallen from the sky. Just think, work. Sit and watch. Get paid for it. More coffee?"

"Enough, it's not getting anymore. What if today it will not?"

"Are you going to become a journalist or not? You have to track your luck, wait. Told you - a movie star arrives incognito. So, we will catch our exclusive on the front page."

"What if she's made up?"

"Well, not as the old woman? We'll find that out. Our eyes are sharp."

At this time, the arrival of the flight Tashkent - Moscow - Frankfurt was announced. "Today it is the last from that side. Are we lucky?"

"So, are we not lucky? Come on, hawk eye, get to work." They began to peer intently at the group of arrivals, looking for a similar face. "Look, there!"

"Where?"

"Right, near the counter. Is that her?"

His friend peered, out of the corner of his eye he looked at the photo.

"Well, you are strong. Looks like she is. I will not say that it is a copy, but it is very good." "What shall we do?"

"What to do? Make a call. Work with your camera." He took out his cell phone, checked with a piece of paper, and dialled a number. "Hello? This is Karl. It seems our star has arrived ... Yes, one meets her, some guy.... With a case... Yes: with

glasses, a tie, some kind of card on his chest... No, it's not visible... She? The bag on wheels, on the shoulder she has a small, brown... Yes, I understand." He turned off the cell: "Well, colleague, our mission seems to have come to an end. It remains to receive money and a piece of fame. Now we pass by her, take a bigger picture." "No problems."

They got up from the table and went towards Zarina, who was standing near the counter and waiting for her documents to be checked...

71

Zarina passed passport control, went into the hall and began to look around, looking through the eyes of the person meeting. A guy with glasses came up to her, a small case in his hand, a Peace Corps card pinned to his shirt. He turned to her. "Excuse me, are you Mrs. Zarina?"

"Yes it's me."

"Hello, my name is Franz, Franz Meinhof. I am from the Peace Corps and I was asked to meet and get you to the hotel."

"And Sherzod?" the first thing Zarina asked. "Do you know when he will arrive?" "They told me," Franz smiled, "That everything is fine with him, and they will inform me of his arrival. You are the first to know about it, so don't worry. You need to rest from the road and have patience. Come, I'll take you there."

The guys, who were watching them till that moment, walked past them and headed for the exit from the airport. Mehmed was sitting in the parking lot in the car. It was him who Karl had just talked to. Mehmed took out his cell phone and dialled a number.

"Ali, all attention to the exit. I need an address where they will go. See for yourself if this is the option we need. Call me right away." "Got it, I'm on the spot," Ali answered.

Franz and Zarina left the airport building. Franz waved his hand, and a taxi pulled up.

"Hotel "Inter"." He opened the door for Zarina, they sat down, and the car started off.

Standing nearby Ali dialled a number.

"It's me. Hotel Inter... Very similar. What we need... Yes, I'm going."

Mehmed dialled another number:

"Moussa? Our client is going to the Inter Hotel... Yes, it does. Your task is the maximum of information, I'm not supposed to teach you with your experience. After that - as agreed... Yes, in the same place. That's all."

He turned off his cell phone and leaned back in his seat, tapping his fingers on his knee and considering further steps.

Taxi drove up to the hotel. Franz helped Zarina to get out, and they went inside.

They approached the reception desk, near which Moussa was already spinning.

"A room was ordered in the name of Mrs. Khasanova."

"I'll see now," the manager snapped the keyboard keys and looked at the display. "Yes, that's right. Please, your documents."

Zarina took out documents from her purse and handed it to the girl. She handed her the form and asked to fill it out. Having done this, Zarina returned the form. The girl looked at it and smiled politely.

"Sorry, but here, you filled in incorrectly." Seeing that Zarina was embarrassed, she added " Don't worry, I will give you another."

She gave Zarina a new form, and Zarina turned it over, crumpled it, and threw it into the nearby can. She filled out a new form and gave it away. The girl looked over and smiled friendly again.

"Did I mess up again?" asked Zarina.

"No, now everything is in order. Here are your documents. Are you here for a long time?"

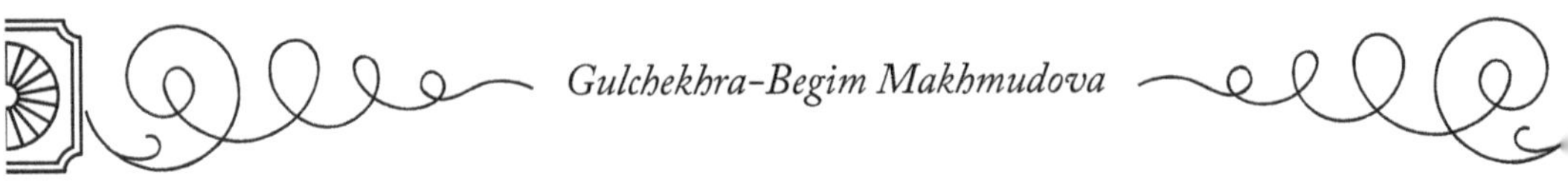

"I don't know, I have to wait for my son."

I think 5-6 days. Not more," said Franz.

"Good," the girl said. "In any case, you have nothing to worry about. Have a nice rest. Here is your key, number 302."

"Thank you," Zarina took the key and turned to Franz. "Will you accompany me?" "Certainly. Please," he showed a direction with his hand, and they moved away from the counter. Moussa, who was constantly spinning nearby, pretended to drop something, bent over and imperceptibly pulled out a crumpled form from the can, and just quietly put it in his pocket. He straightened up, smoothed his hair and went to the exit of the hotel. Going out into the street, he took out his cell phone and dialled Mehmed's number.

"Everything is good. Option - you can't imagine a better one ... Yes, all that is needed. Okay, I'm going."

He made a sign with his hand, a taxi pulled up, his man, Yusuf, was driving, got into the car and they drove away from the hotel.

72

Moussa drove up to the house where the Senior and Mehmed were already waiting for him. When he entered the room, the Senior immediately got down to business. "Let's go in order, that's the main thing."

"The necessary object was found," said Mehmed. "It is not difficult to make a replacement, the similarity allows. Moussa collected all the necessary information." "Yes," Moussa nodded his head, "We have everything we need." She arrived alone, no connections. Met a certain Franz from the Peace Corps. She is going to wait for the arrival of her son. We will neutralize Franz, to lure her out of the hotel is a couple of trifles. The rest is a matter of technology."

"But isn't it all just working out for you?" the Senior looked intently at Moussa. "A mistake can cost us a lot," he said, looking from Moussa to Mehmed.

"Moussa and I worked out all the details, so there will be no mistakes. Tomorrow we will shoot it, Ali and Yusuf will do this. The day after tomorrow Fatima will enter the role. So, after two days you can proceed."

"So," the Senior tapped his fingers on the table. "It means, in two days? Are you sure

Mehmed?"

"Yes."

"Good. After two days, we'll begin the operation. Work."

Mehmed and Moussa got up, bowed and left the room. The Senior quietly repeated:

"So, two more days? May Allah help us…"

In the morning, Yusuf's car stopped near the hotel. In the back seat is Ali with a video camera. An hour had passed before they took their position, but Zarina did not go out. Yusuf grunted impatiently:

"How long will they mess about? We cannot be here all day."

"So, we'll move to another place or we will walk there by turns until she leaves. She is a woman, so she will feel like going to the shops instead of hanging around in the room." Ali exclaimed patronisgly.

A car drove up to the hotel, from which Franz got out. Yusuf nodded in his direction:

"Isn't that the one who met her?"

Ali looked at the photo.

"He is. Now he will call her, she will dart out and he will drag her back and forth." "That's great, a good movie will turn out,' he patted the camera.

Another twenty minutes passed before Franz and Zarina left the hotel, consulted about something, and walked along the street.

"Well, are you going to catch them up or should I give you a lift?" asked Yusuf.

"Come on to the next intersection and squeeze somewhere. I will go out there and keep watch. It will be seen further. Move it." Yusuf started the car and they drove off…

Having followed Zarina for half a day and having shot the necessary material, they returned to the safe house, where Fatima was waiting for them. They gave her the tapes, and she sat down to look at them.

In the evening, Mehmed came to Fatima to her apartment. He found her watching the footage. Seated next to her and asked:

"What do you say?"

"Very well," Fatima answered, stopping the recording.

"Where did you find one?"

"Middle Asia."

"Will anybody notice her absence during the operation?" "There is no one. So you can feel completely calm." "Perfectly. Is there a version of her urgent departure?" "The son has health problems, and she rushes to him."

"Decided to play on maternal feelings?" grinned Fatima.

"There is nothing sacred inside your heart."

"We'll talk about the soul after the operation, but for now, transform yourself." "And the documents?"

"You will get them on the way to the airport. You will have time to work them out. Do you need anything else? Makeup, rags?"

"No, I have enough of this trash."

"Then all. Get ready and wait for the signal."

"When?"

"If nothing out of the ordinary happens, then the day after tomorrow." The cell phone rang, Mehmed pressed a button: "Yes ... It's all right ... Okay, I'm going."

"Chef?" Fatima looked at him questioningly.

"Yes. Waiting for a report." He got up, took a folder with documents from the table and went to the exit. Fatima called to him:

"Will you come after the report?"

Mehmed looked at her carefully.

"I'll call…"

A phone rings in Zarina's room. She picks up the phone.

"Hello!"

"Is that Mrs. Khasanova?"

"Yes it's me."

"My surname is Genscher," the male voice came in the receiver, which belonged to

Moussa. "The fact is that my colleague Franz urgently left on business and asked me

to call you about your son."

"Sherzod? What happened?"

"Don't worry, he's okay," Moussa reassured her. "He just got a little sick and therefore cannot fly to you yet."

"Can I somehow contact him and talk?"

"I think no. He is in the hospital now."

"How is he in the hospital? You said that he's okay! You're lying to me. What is wrong with him?"

"I beg you, do not worry. All I know is that he has a minor nervous breakdown after everything he has experienced, and now he needs to undergo rehabilitation."

"I have to be by his side, you hear, Mr. Genscher?"

"That's why I am calling you. Our organization can arrange for you to fly to Madrid

for the next flight, if you do not mind."

"You're asking? What should I do?"

"Just pack your things and go downstairs. Do not forget about your documents. I will be waiting for you at the exit and I will take you to the airport. Just hurry up."

"Yes, yes, wait for me - I won't be long. How will I recognize you?"

"I'll be carrying a namecard. The name is Genscher."

"Yes, of course, I'm sorry... I won't be long..."

She hung up the phone, helplessly looked around at the room, then opened her bag and began to randomly stuff all her things in there. She threw cosmetics into her purse and checked the documents. She took the bag, looked around the room again and went out.

After talking with Zarina, Moussa dialed a number on his cell phone:

"Yusuf, get ready, she will be out now."

"Got it."

Moussa dialed Mehmed's number:

"We're starting now. Make the appointment."

"I see. I'll wait."

By phone, Mehmed ordered Ali and Fatima to go to the highway, and informed the boss that the operation had begun.

Zarina quickly walked through the hall to the exit. The female administrator called out to her.

"Are you leaving?"

"Yes. I am going to my son. I'm sorry."

She went outside, and Moussa immediately approached her:

"I called you," he said, pointing at the card on his chest. He then made a sign with his hand and a taxi with Yusuf at the wheel drove up. Moussa opened the front door. "Sit down, please, the driver will put your bag in the boot."

Jumping out, Yusuf grabbed Zarina's bag and put it in. Moussa sat in the back seat directly behind Zarina.

"To the airport," Moussa commanded. Yusuf nodded and started off.

Having left the city, the car drove onto the highway. Yusuf and Moussa occasionally looked at each other through the rearview mirror.

"Are you sure there is nothing seriously wrong with my son?"

Zarina asked uneasily. "Absolutely," Moussa said as convincingly as possible. "What is the point of them deceiving me or mine of deceiving you? Be so kind, give me your documents, for now I will fill in the papers."

Zarina took the documents from her purse and passed them to Moussa over her shoulder.

"Thank you. There will be less fuss at the airport."

He opened the folder and put Zarina's documents inside. Then he took out a form and pretended to fill it in. His cellphone rang. Moussa pulled it out of his pocket.

"Yes? Of course, everything is in order, we are already on the move... Yes, everything is as agreed... I will tell you."

He turned off his cell phone. "Franz called, he's worried. He asked me to say hello and bon voyage." He and Yusuf exchanged glances in the mirror and both grinned.

"Thank you. He did a lot for me."

"Yes, he is a very kind person."

A car drove out of the side road on which Fatima and Ali were driving. Keeping its distance, it followed the taxi. A bridge across the river appeared ahead and the rear car signalled with its headlights. Yusuf slowed down and began to pull over. In front of the bridge, the taxi stopped. Zarina looked at Yusuf in surprise. "Why have we stopped?"

"A brief break."

"Why?" Zarina asked, surprised. "We are late!" Moussa pulled out a small club from under the seat.

"Not any more." He hit Zarina hard on the head. She lost consciousness, her head falling back in the chair. Moussa hit her again. "It's never too late there."

Fatima and Ali got out of the car that drove up behind. Ali

quickly took out Zarina's bag and threw it into his car. Moussa gave Fatima the folder with the documents. "Remember the contents of the bag and tidy up if necessary. Then the documents. That's all. Go. Mehmed will meet you."

"What about this?" Fatima pointed at Zarina.

"She'll learn to swim without surfacing." Moussa grinned. "Drive! Do not waste time."

Fatima once again looked at Zarina, shrugged and went to the car that Ali had already started. She got in and the car rushed off. Yusuf and Moussa dragged Zarina out of the car and leaned her against the door. Moussa began to remove her jewellery.

"Quickly! Give me a weight and then into the water, while it's quiet," he ordered and Yusuf darted to the boot to prepare the weight and a rope. Suddenly, in the distance, a howling of a police siren was heard. Yusuf and Moussa looked at each other in dismay.

"What?"

"Close the boot and start!"

"And this?"

"She will die herself," Moussa spat aside.

He jerked Zarina upright and pushed her from the slope into the river, jumped into the car and rushed away.

Zarina's body slid down and was half in the water. She showed no signs of life. A convoy of cars drove across the bridge, in front of which a policeman was riding a motorcycle with a siren on.

73

Bukhara, the palace of Ark. The study of Alimkhan.

There are two in the study: Alimkhan and the upper kushbegi Ghafur-bek.

"How much longer do you think our Great Bukhara will hold

out?" Alimkhan asked. "It is regrettable to report this, Your Highness, but, according to my calculations, everything will be decided in the next two weeks. The mob sticks to these Bolsheviks, like flies to honey, and this wave is becoming increasingly heavier, but there is nothing to restrain it. We underestimated them and are paying for it. I think that you, Your Highness, will have to leave Bukhara for a while."

"For a while?"

"I'm afraid to make mistakes in the predictions, Your Highness. If the Bolsheviks give nothing but promises to which they are so skilful, the crowd will go against them. Then they will not last long."

"What if they give?" Alimkhan asked.

"What can they give? They themselves have nothing. In any case, you better wait out these events at a fairly large distance. I would really not want you to repeat the fate of Tsar Nicholas."

"Well, perhaps this is the only reasonable way out of this situation," Alimkhan agreed with his courtier. "I believe that you should also prepare for your departure, Kushbegi. You have a week. Is it enough for you?"

"Of course, Your Highness. What should I collect?"

"Obviously," Alimkhan smiled, "that you have collected enough for all the time of faithful service to our house."

Ghafur-bek also smiled and bowed his head.

Chambers is walking irritably around his tent. In front of him Lieutenant Alistair is standing.

"What is the matter, Alistair, can you explain? For three days there has been no news from your messenger. What happened?"

"I don't know, Mr. Lieutenant Colonel. Our person is constantly on duty at the appointed place, but no one appeared."

"Has our dervish made a mistake? No, it cannot be. So that a person with his work experience gets caught in rubbish... Or is he not our dervish anymore? Why are you standing, Alistair? Go, work, think how to fix the situation. Do not remove our person from duty." The lieutenant saluted Chambers and left the tent. "Or maybe he started his game? No, it's unlikely... He alone will not shoulder such a burden... I will have to go to the general and ask him for a biplane..."

Entering the mountainous area, the caravan began to rise into one of the gorges. Iskander made a sign to stop, and the caravan froze. The drivers got out of their carts, the guards dismounted. Shahob was looking around worriedly.

"That's all, horses will not go further," said Iskander. "We will carry it in our hands."

"Why here?" Shahob was worried. "We did not reach the border, did we?"

"Plans have changed. Unload here, and then we'll see." Iskander got off his horse and went to the drivers.

"Do you see the cave a little higher?" he showed a hand on the slope. "Transfer everything there. But carefully, in bags there is dynamite, and I do not want everyone to tear into pieces."

The drivers were frightened and backed away from the carts, but Iskander hastened to reassure them.

"Don't be afraid, it won't just explode, but don't pound the bags against the rocks, all right?" Everyone nodded. "Good, get down to work. Unload the first wagon. I will go upwards and show what needs to be done. Shahob and you three," he pointed at the guards, "come with me. You," he turned to Khamid, "you'll be in charge here. Let's go..."

Iskander began to climb upwards, holding his saber with his hand so that it would not hit the stones. The rest followed him...

"You're crazy, Chambers!" the general attacked him. "Do you even understand what you are asking for?"

"I understand, Mr. General. We were left without communication, so now we are blind and deaf, and we have no idea where the caravan is and where it is moving. The only way to find out is to look from above. Without your biplane we cannot do that.

"Not a single caravan is worth the risk of losing this car with the pilot, Chambers," the general categorically said.

"This one is worth, Mr. General," Chambers objected to him.

"Do you mean a bunch of trash and a dozen damsels of the Emir? We have already discussed this."

"This is outdated information. In fact, the caravan is carrying something else, and this other is worth the risk."

"And what, according to your latest information, does the Emir actually transport?" "Until I can say this, Mr. General," Chambers declined to give a direct answer, "but when we find the caravan, you will be the first to know about this cargo, I promise. You will not have to regret that you agreed to my request."

"I'm fed up with your secrets, Chambers," the general snapped. "If you were not supported there, you would not have been here for a long time. OK, I'll think about your proposal. But one thing I can tell you very definitely. If anything happens to the car because of your adventure, I will give you to the tribunal and shoot you. Are you willing to take such a risk, Chambers? Or think more?"

"Ready, Mr. General. Because I don't have time to think. When can I get your answer?"

"Wait at your place, I will send an officer to you. Come on, Chambers..."

74

In the cave, pointed to by Iskander, there were Shahob and three drivers who brought the bags to the passage which leads to another, lower cave. There were other drivers downward who were taking the load.

Among the drivers upwards is Ghafur. Iskander leaned against the exit from the upper cave, carefully examining the surroundings. One of the last bags slipped out of the driver's hands and fell on a sharp stone.

The bag was torn, and gold coins poured out of it. The drivers were dumbfounded by what they saw, then looked at each other. Shahob tensed, estimating the situation. "Well, what are you staring at?" He shouted at the drivers. "Have you never seen gold? Quickly collect everything and down. Get five gold, and five more if you shut your mouths."

"Why don't we take everything and we'll give you ten gold so that you shut your mouth?" one of the drivers offered.

He moved toward Shahob, followed by two others, trying to take Shahob into the ring.

"Try, if you're so brave," Shahob suggested to him.

He grabbed two knives from the sleeves of his robe and threw them at the drivers, both of them fell. Ghafur jumped on Shahob at the moment, when he pulled out a third knife, and ran upon it.

But, falling, Shahob hit the back of his head against the same sharp stone.

Iskander rushed into the noise, who quickly estimated everything that happened when he saw Ghafur, who crawled away from Shahob and leaned against the wall, holding the knife that was sticking out of his chest.

A pool of blood was creeping out from under Shahob's head, but he was still alive. Iskander leaned over him.

"How silly ..." he whispered. "So close..."

"Why, Shahob? Why are the British?" Iskander removed the waist scarf from the lying driver and put it under the head of Shahob.

"It doesn't matter anymore... There is no time..." Life was leaving Shahob's body. "Don't come back ... He will be well rid of everyone... and you..."

"Who?"

"You know..." Shahob whispered with all his strength. "So silly."

"You also wanted gold?" Iskander turned to Ghafur. "Here it is, take it." He nodded toward the bag.

"Don't kill me, help me..." a wheeze burst from Ghafur's throat. "They will thank you, very well..."

"Who will thank?" Iskander asked. "Why should I believe you?"

"Kadyr-bek, he is a very big man, and he will not be stingy. But only I have to return help."

"Kadyr-bek, you say?" grinned Iskander. "I know. This one really is not stingy..." "You see... help me... he promised me freedom..."

"Freedom? Let me see your wound, take your hand away."

Ghafur removed his hand from the knife. Iskander grabbed the handle and pulled out the knife sharply. Blood gushed out of the wound and Ghafur went limp.

"I will give you freedom myself."

Iskander got up tiredly, wiped the knife, put it under the boot-leg, looked at the heap of gold on the cave floor, at the corpses, and shook his head.

"How many more lives do you need to take?" Screams came from the lower cave. "Apart from these…"

Iskander threw the gold down and pushed the corpses there. Cries of horror came from below. He went to the stone, which used to close the passage to the lower cave, tensed and closed the passage with it. The screams became almost inaudible. Iskander turned, left the cave and began to go down to the guards.

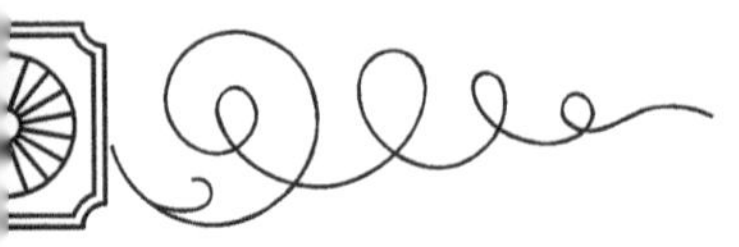

75

Alimkhan called the chief of the palace guard to him and began to give him instructions on further actions in relation to the caravan and those people who accompanied it.

"Listen and remember," Alimkhan began. "What you have to do is a matter of national importance. A detachment of my soldiers returns to Bukhara without fulfilling my order. They must be punished."

"What should I do, my lord?" The head of the guard pulled himself up to attention.

"Take people, set an ambush at the entrance to Bukhara and shoot them down like traitors."

"Everyone, my lord?"

"No, one must stay alive. This is Iskander. First, he must report to me why my order has not been executed. Do you understand? Iskander should not suffer."

"Got it, my lord. Not a single hair will fall from his head."

"Take him to the palace, then he knows the way. Say that I'm waiting for him with a report."

"Everything will be done as you ordered, my lord."

Firuz-begim accidentally heard this conversation, clutching her mouth with her hand, then slowly and carefully began to leave her husband's study.

When Iskander came down, Khamid looked at him questioningly.

"They will remain there to guard the cargo until they come after him."

"What about Shahob?"

"He too. It's getting dark. We will spend the night here, and in the morning we will go back. Rest everyone."

He went into the tent, lay down, but Shahob's warning, which he had made before his death, did not go out of his head. Iskander could not disregard him, before death people do not lie, and it was too much like the truth.

Iskander lit a lamp, took out a kerchief from his pocket, which Firuz-begim's son gave him, spread it and began to put on it a plan of the burial of the Emir's treasures. To do this, he had to make a small incision in his palm and apply the plan with his blood.

Having finished this work, he bandaged his hand with a rag, made sure that the blood on the kerchief had dried up, folded the kerchief and hid it in the leather amulet that the old woman had given him at the sacred spring. Then he turned off the lamp and tried to sleep.

76

Firuz-begim approached Saeed-aka, who was working in the garden, she looked very alarmed, and, looking at her, the old man became worried.

"You look so scared, my mistress. Something happened?" "It happened, Saeed-aka. Could you help me?"

"Of course, my mistress. Everything in my power. What should I do?"

"You must warn Iskander, he is in danger, but he still does not know about it. He must not return to the palace."

"How can I find him? I don't know where he went. Where can I find him?"

"He does not have to be looked for. He himself will drive up to Bukhara, only an ambush will wait for him, and you need to get ahead of them, to meet him earlier. Can you?"

"I'll try. But how do I get there? Walking is difficult for me, and I don't even have a donkey."

"You can buy it. Here, take it." Firuz-begim took a gold bracelet from her hand and handed it to Saeed.

"This is a very expensive thing, my mistress," Saeed hesitated.

"And the life of Iskander?"

"You're right, madam. No gold can pay for the life of one good person." He took the bracelet and put it in his bosom. "Don't worry, my mistress. I'll do everything." "Thank you, Saeed-aka. Allah will reward you for your kindness. Please hurry up…"

In the morning, Iskander's detachment took off and headed back to Bukhara.

Iskander rode ahead of the squad gloomy, lost in thought. Bad forebodings seized him more and more. He began to realize that he did not expect anything good in Bukhara, because he had been involved in the secret of the treasury of the Emir of Bukhara, and such witnesses were not left alive.

Shahob was absolutely right.

But he also had to return to Bukhara. There were Firuz-begim and her son, and he remembered the promise made to Shuhrat before his death. And he loved her, too. Khamid saw his condition and several times tried to talk with Iskander, but he only waved off, and Khamid abandoned his attempts, deciding that Iskander himself would figure it out.

When they drove past the sacred spring, Iskander once again wanted to talk to the strange woman who gave him the amulet, but that one was nowhere to be seen. Having a little rest, the detachment again continued on its way home. Bukhara was already nearby.

77

In the early morning, Saeed-aka appeared in the bazaar, looked around. A fat man with running eyes rolled up to him.

"What are you looking for at such an early time, father? Gift for wife? New Chinese silk robe?"

"I'm looking for a donkey," said Saeed.

"What?" the fat man said, surprised.

"Donkey, didn';t you hear me? Which I can ride, do you understand?" "Ah, donkey!" the man laughed, "you should've immediately said so!" "I said so. So, do you have a donkey or not?"

"Yes, yes, how not to have. Good, strong. But expensive, probably you don't have that much money, father."

"I have. First show me the donkey, and I will decide if it costs as much as you say or not."

"You're right, father. Come on, I'll show you." "Is it far?"

"No, very close. Over there, around the corner," he waved his hand to the side, "it's standing in the courtyard."

"Well, let's go, show it," agreed the unsuspecting Saeed.

"Of course, of course," the man quietly looked around and made a sign to someone with his hand. "Well, almost come."

They turned a corner and stopped.

"Where is the courtyard?" Saeed asked perplexedly. "Where's the donkey? You decided to make a joke with me?"

He grabbed the seller by the chest and at that moment a knife was thrust into his back. The old man gasped and crawled to the ground.

"There is no courtyard, but there is a donkey." The man said, glancing around. "Here he is. Old and stupid. Hide your knife." He turned to his accomplice. "And look around while I rummage."

His accomplice leaned against the corner and began to look around, while the fat man rummaged in the old man's robe. Feeling the bracelet, he took it out and turned it in surprise.

"Wow, but the old man was not simple. Where did he get such an expensive thing? Okay, we're going in different directions. Meet me where as usual..."

They quickly dispersed in different directions, leaving a dead old man with frozen surprise in his eyes...

Iskander's detachment was approaching Bukhara. Ahead is Iskander, his hand is inflamed from a cut and he feels weak, his head is spinning. Suddenly he sees the head of the palace guard in front of him. He makes a sign to stop. He is approaching Iskander.

"I have the Emir's order to escort you to the palace. He is waiting for you with a report."

"And my detachment?" Iskander asked.

"They will be taken care of. Hurry up, the Emir is waiting for you with a report." They drove forward, leaving the detachment behind them. After a few seconds Iskander heard shots. He turned sharply.

"What is it?"

Iskander saw the guardsmen lying on the ground. His detachment, with whom he had made such a difficult and dangerous journey, was no longer there, like his friend Khamid. Iskander looked at the chief of the guard "For what?"

"The order of the Emir," the chief of the guard replied calmly, "and I executed it."

"I see," Iskander bowed his head. "Well, let's go to the palace..."

Iskander is going through the palace. Passing by the hall, he saw Firuz-begim's son.

He also saw Iskander and rushed to him.

"Iskander, you have arrived! That's great! Mom was worried!" "Is it True?"

"True, the word of a warrior!"

"I also gave the word of the warrior that I would be back, and I also kept my word. But I'm in a hurry now. I have an important business for you." Iskander quickly removed the amulet from his neck, put it on the boy and hid it under his shirt. "This is a magical amulet that keeps from troubles and diseases, remember, I said I would bring it?"

"Of course I remember!"

"Then wear it, but don't show it to anyone, otherwise it will lose its magic power."

"Even to mom?"

"Yes, to mom you can. But no one else. Will you do it?" "Of course."

"The word of a warrior?

The boy made their symbol:

"The word of a warrior!"

"That's good. Now I need to go. Later we'll talk..."

78

Not far from the study where the Emir was waiting for him, Iskander saw Rasulbek. He bowed to him, but he could not hide the crooked smile that was so familiar to Iskander. Iskander shuddered inwardly and finally realized that Shahob was right. Iskander gave his saber to the guard standing at the door, opened the door and entered the study...

The boy entered the room, approached his mother and looked at her slyly. She is smiling.

"Did you come up with something again, sly little one?" "No, I didn't think of it. I saw it."

"What did you see?"

"Not what, but whom."

"Well, and whom?"

"Iskander, that's who!"

"Who?!" Firuz-begim's expression quickly changed.

"I said - Iskander!"

"But how did he..." Then she understood everything, tears appeared in her eyes. "Poor Saeed-aka, forgive me. It's my entire fault..."

"What happened to him? Why are you crying?"

"No, no, nothing happened to him, he just got a little sick. I'm not crying anymore, you see?" She tried to smile, but she did not succeed. "Have you not forgotten that we are going on a trip today?"

"Did not forget."

"That's good. Then go and get some rest, the road will be difficult..."

"I must inform you, my lord." Iskander began his report. "There were two traitors in the detachment. One of them is a driver, a man of Kadyr-bek."

"Again, Kadyr-bek! I hope this driver does not come to him with a report on the caravan?"

"No, my lord. He also stayed to guard."

"And who is the second?"

"Shahob. He tried to contact the British, and I had to stop these attempts."

"You did the right thing, Iskander. I was not mistaken about you. I hope you drew a plan for the place where our cargo rests?"

"No, my lord. I did not want to risk your confidence due to any accident. Everything is in my head."

"Again you did the right thing. I see you're hurt?" "Nothing serious, my lord."

"Good. Then sit down at this table and draw a detailed map of the place where everything is hidden. After this, you will rest, and I will send you the best doctor."

"Yes, my lord." Iskander bowed his head.

He wanted to add that he had already seen this doctor by the name of Rasulbek but decided that it still would not change anything in his fate. He sat at the table and began to draw a map of the area, but this map had nothing to do with the one he gave to his son. Having finished the drawing, he got up and bowed. "I'm done, my lord. Here is all that you have entrusted to me."

"Good, Iskander, I will not forget what you did." he handed

Iskander a heavy bag, "for you for your faithful service. You can go."

Iskander bowed and left the study, took his saber from the guard and went around the palace.

"It's a pity," Alimkhan said, "It's a pity to lose such devoted people, but, unfortunately, his head is too valuable to go anywhere. It's a pity…"

Passing through one of the dark galleries of the palace, Iskander felt something was amiss and inwardly get up all his courage. He had to get out of the palace alive, and he was not going to become an easy victim. Nevertheless, the attack of Rasulbay was unexpected. He appeared from nowhere and attacked Iskander from behind.

Grabbing him by the throat, Rasulbek threw him to the floor, but for Iskander's physical strength, their fight would immediately end.

But by some incredible effort, already losing consciousness, Iskander managed to get a knife and stick it into Rasulbek's neck. He wheezed and loosened his grip. Iskander opened his hands, clutching his throat, and rolled to the side, breathing heavily. Rasulbek wheezed, pouring blood, and powerlessly scratched the floor with his hands.

Iskander cautiously approached, pulled a knife from Rasulbek's throat and thrust it into the heart with a sweep. Rasulbek twitched and fell silent. It was the same knife that Iskander took from Ghafur's chest and which belonged to Shahob.

Having dragged Rasulbek's body to a far corner so that he would not be immediately discovered, Iskander quietly left the palace.

79

The same night, turmoil reigned in the palace. Servants packed in the carts the things of the Emir's family, food for the journey, all the necessities.

Eshonoy-begim - the mother of Alimkhan, Firuz-begim and her son are already ready to board the carriage. Eshonoy-begim is wrapped in a shawl, she was shivering, it was clear that she was very ill.

"You are trembling, are you ill?" Firuz-begim begim worried. "Never mind, girl, this is probably from excitement."

"Let me call the doctor?"

"No," said Eshonoy-begim. "We will go now, and I do not want to detain everyone. I'll lie down on the way, and everything will be alright."

Alimkhan gives his last orders before leaving. Before him is the head of the Sarbaz, forcibly drafted into the army of the poor.

"The Bolsheviks should not get anything. Let your Sarbaz do what they want - rob, burn. The city is theirs. But first, let them visit the house of Kadyr-bek, there is something to profit from there. His house is to burn."

"What to do with Kadyr-bek himself and his family?"

"Let them burn with their house. He deserved it for his betrayal."

"It will be done, my lord."

"Do it..."

A small caravan, accompanied by Afghan mercenaries, is leaving the gates of the city, in which cries are already heard, flames are visible. Alimkhan looked back at the city.

"This is how the great Bukhara collapses. I don't see Ghafurbek in the caravan." Alimkhan asked the detachment commander. "Where is he?"

"I don't know, my lord."

Alimkhan grinned bitterly.

"So, the faithful servants disappear...The old fox."

Iskander understood that he urgently needed medical help, and therefore he first tried to get to Dr. Serov's hospital.

One glance at Iskander's inflamed hand was enough for him to begin the operation right away.

Having finished his manipulations and cleansing the wound, he bandaged his hand and put Iskander to the couch.

"What is happening in the city..." Serov shook his head, "What is happening. People seemed to be crazy and ceased to be people."

"Not all, doctor," answered Iskander. "You didn't cease, and I didn't cease..."

"Yes, of course... It's just from a lack of understanding of what is going on ... How do you feel?"

"Bearable, doctor."

"I don't know how it can be bearable, but you have complete exhaustion, young man. I don't know what you were doing there, but you don't have as much strength as you are trying to convince me. You need complete peace for at least two or three days. Will you stay here?"

"Thank you, doctor, I can't." Iskander hardly rose from the couch. "I still have to do something. I want to leave Bukhara."

"Where do you go in this state? Your uniform is not for walking at such a time." "You are right here, doctor, I really need to change clothes. Could you find something?"

"There. Old but clean. Come on, I will show. Choose something for yourself..."

80

The Emir's detachment is moving away from Bukhara, it is already dawning. Alimkhan drove up to the carriage in which Firuz-begim, Eshonoy-begim and a boy were. He saw that Firuz-begim was not sleeping. She is holding his mother's hand and from time to time wipes perspiration on her forehead. "How is she?"

"Bad, my lord," Firuz-begim said wearily. "She has a fever, and something is

wheezing in her chest. I do not know what to do. Why did she refuse the doctor?"

"Are you giving her the medicine?"

"Yes, but it seems it is not helping her."

"All the same, let her take it. I'll think about what can be done."

Having once again cast a glance at his mother, Alimkhan left the carriage...

By some unthinkable back streets and avoiding crowded places, Iskander managed to get out of the troubled city. He is wearing an old robe, a hat is on his head, and it is almost impossible to recognize him.

He's slowly walking along the road, in his hand is a staff on which he leans. It can be seen that he was very weak and the movement was given to him with difficulty.

Having reached the outskirts of a small village, the Emir's detachment stopped to rest. Firuz-begim jumped out of the carriage and ran to Alimkhan. Seeing her, he

immediately hurried towards her.

"What happened?"

"My lord, it seems that Eshonoy-begim is dying..." There were tears in Firuz-begim's eyes.

They quickly returned to the carriage. Eshonoy-begim was already taken out of it and laid on a spread blanket. She was breathing heavily but was conscious.

"Alimkhan..." She called in a weak voice.

"Yes, mom, I'm here. A doctor will come soon, he will help you."

"No! My time has come. You'll go on without me. Do not forget your mother, Alimkhan..."

"Don't say that! I can't leave without you!" said Alimkhan.

"Do not argue. I know..." Alimkhan leaned over to hug his mother, but she pushed him away with her hand. "No... you can get infected. Go, order everything to be as it should be. Do not waste time, go Alimkhan, my boy."

Alimkhan touched her hand as a sign of farewell and quickly left, glancing back at last at his lying mother. Eshonoy-begim gave Firuz-begim the sign with her hand, and she came.

"Girl, take care of yourself... and son... he must continue our family. Yet, I want to take my hookah and save it." she tensed in the last effort, "remembrance..." That was her last word. Firuz-begim was sitting motionless near mother and crying when Alimkhan ran up with the doctor. Seeing the crying Firuz-begim, he understood everything and compressed his lips.

"Your help is no longer needed, doctor. You were riding here too long."

The old man turned pale and began to back away from the Emir in fear, but he no longer noticed him, he was looking at his mother. Then Firuz-begim coughed.

Alimkhan sharply turned in her direction.

"And you…"

"No, no, my lord, I just choked, everything is fine with me. What are we going to do?"

"We will go further. After we take care of my mother for the last time…"

Iskander staggering reached the edge of a village and fell unconscious. This was accidentally seen by a shepherd boy, who immediately ran home for help. Running to the house, he shouted:

"Grandfather, grandfather, outside some man fell."

81

A car was driving along the road, and there was a married couple inside it. At the wheel is a husband with his wife sitting nearby. A large insect struck against the windshield and left an unpleasant mark on it.

"Was it really impossible to wait until I passed? Will leave droppings on the glass." The man said angrily.

"Well, wash it off, what's the problem?" his wife smiled. "The problem is the tank, in which again there is no water." "Of course, it is my fault again."

The man smiled.

"Naturally, someone should be left holding the baby."

"You are the most evil and nasty husband of all that I know," His wife said, playing along with him.

"I warned you before the wedding that I have many shortcomings."

"You purposely said this quietly and illegibly, so that I would not have time to come to my senses. There, the river is ahead. While you are drawing the water, I will think about how I can fix this major mistake of my life."

"No, let's go together," her husband shook his head. "You cannot be left unattended." He stopped the car on the side of the road behind the bridge. Slyly looked at the wife. "Will you go voluntarily?"

"I have to, you won't manage without me anyway."

They got out of the car, the man took out a canteen from the boot and they went to the shore.

"Uh, no, we won't come down here," he said disappointedly. "Let's look from the other side." They crossed the road and were in the place from where Zarina was dumped. "Quite another." He stopped, seeing Zarina's body lying below.

"What?" His wife looked at him in surprise.

"Look," he waved a hand in the direction of Zarina.

"Oh my, who is it?"

"I don't know," he was about to go downward, but his wife did not let him go. "Where are you going?"

"Down, we need to see what's wrong with her. It is unlikely that she herself has

slipped there, maybe she is still alive."

"Let's call the police," his wife asked.

"If she is alive, then help is needed now.

"Then I'm with you."

They both began to carefully go down. The man crouched near Zarina, took her hand and began to feel the pulse.

"Alive, but her head is smashed, you see, blood? She must be turned over and pulled out of the water."

They carefully pulled Zarina out of the water and turned her over onto her back. She moaned weakly.

"She urgently needs to go to the hospital," the man handed his flask to his wife. "Draw up the water, and we will carefully lift her up."

His wife took water and handed it to her husband. He took a handkerchief from his pocket, dipped it and carefully wiped the

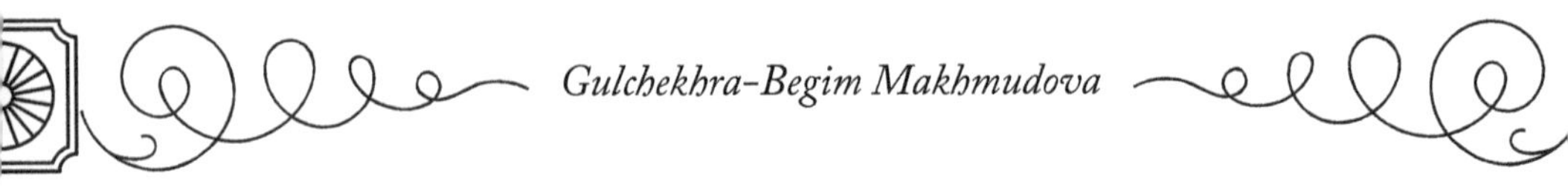

blood from Zarina's face.

"Now let's take her to the car."

"Where will we take her?"

"To Dietrich. This is his own ground. I will call him to be ready." "And the police?" Asked his wife anxiously.

"Then we'll figure it out. The main thing is to get her medical help. Come on…"

82

After the story of what happened, Mehmed was just beside himself. He yelled at

Moussa:

"So what? You just left her there and that's it? If she is alive?"

"What did I have time for?" Moussa justified himself. "The police came running behind, we barely managed to come away."

"If she remains alive and the police question her, then you won't tear yourself away from her, you get it? Do you even understand that you have endangered all of us and the operation? What should I report to the boss? That you are too lazy to let her go to the bottom and left to sunbathe on the coast? Do you know what will happen to you after that?"

"Wait," Moussa turned pale. "Do not report. I'll be right back there and finish it all, I swear."

"You have exactly one hour," Mehmed threatened. "After that, I can do nothing for you. Then you have to go to the bottom instead of her."

"I'll do everything, Mehmed, I won't let you down..." He was shaking with fear. He jumped out of Mehmed's car, rushed to Yusuf's taxi, flopped into the seat. "Drive faster to where we left her, otherwise we're goners, got it?"

"Got it, got it," Yusuf started the car and they rushed back to the place where they had thrown Zarina...

The couple's car drove up to the clinic, Dietrich was already waiting on the street. He greeted the arrivals, opened the back door and began to examine Zarina's head. When he touched her, she moaned weakly again.

"We need to take a picture urgently," he said. "I'm afraid her injuries are bad."

He waved, and a gurney was rolled out of the clinic, and Zarina was carefully placed on it.

"Urgent fluoroscopy," he ordered, "I'll be right there. Thank you, Henry. Hilda, did I tell you that your husband is a wonderful person?"

"I don't remember," Hilda smiled.

"Then write it down on a piece of paper," Dietrich smiled back. "And always carry it

with you. Thank you both, I have to go."

"Should I call the police?" asked Henry.

"No, I'll do everything myself."

Dietrich made a farewell hand gesture and walked quickly to the clinic. Heinrich and Hilda looked at each other. He took her by the shoulders and kissed her. "Let's go home, dear," he said exaggeratedly carefully. "I am simply compelled to treat your memory. Then there is just a confusion with these pieces of paper..."

Yusuf's car drove up to the bridge. Moussa jumped out of the car and ran to the

slope. There was no one downward. Yusuf came up. "What, she's not there?"

"Not." He felt uneasy about the possible explanations with the boss. "Damn both her

and the police."

"So she slid into the water," Yusuf suggested.

"Let's go down, let's fumble," Moussa could not offer anything else. They went down to the water. On the shore near the water Zarina's shoe lay, which fell from her feet, when Henry and Hilda pulled her out. "Look," Moussa showed, "this is hers. So she's still there," he nodded at the water.

"What if she got out?" Yusuf said uncertainly.

"Of course!" Moussa could not stand it. "She went along the highway with a broken head and with one shoe... Ugh, it doesn't matter. In short, she isn't here, drowned. So we'll report back."

"You shouldn't be mistaken, because with our heads we will answer, if that. What if someone suddenly found her?"

"If they had found her, now the police would have licked everything here. So no

mistake. Let's go upwards."

"And the shoe?"

Moussa tucked the shoe in and threw it into the water.

"Swam to look for the mistress."

They went upwards, Moussa took out his cell phone, dialled Mehmed's number: "It's me. Everything is in order, she's at the bottom... Of course, I'm sure... No, neither the police, nor outsiders, everything is clean... Okay, let's go." He turned off the cell, looked at Yusuf. "Well, why are you staring at me? Come on, start, we have to go."

"Well, if we have to, then we will." Yusuf shook his head and started the car...

83

"Is the picture ready?" Dietrich turned to the assistant.

"Yes, I'll bring it now." She went out and returned a minute later with a picture:

"Here you are."

Dietrich took a picture, attached it to a transparent stand, and carefully examined it. "Yes, someone tried hard so that she no longer needed a head. The bone is fragmented, you see?" He pointed a finger at the characteristic outline in the picture. "We must urgently operate on her. Get her ready..."

A police car drove up to the clinic, and an inspector got out of it. Dietrich left the clinic and went to meet.

"Hello, Inspector, I called about the victim." "Where is she?"

"In the ward, I just finished the operation."

"Can I talk to her?"

"This is impossible, she is still unconscious."

"Do you have her documents?"

"There was nothing with her - neither things, nor documents. Therefore, neither who she is, nor where, nor how she ended up at the crime scene, we will not know until she wakes up."

"How soon will this happen?"

"Hard to say. It's a miracle that she survived at all." "Well, as soon as she wakes up, call me right away." "Of course."

"Waiting for your call." The inspector shook Dietrich's hand and went to his car.

Dietrich watched him and returned to the clinic...

Zarina with her head bandaged is lying in the room. Dietrich is sitting next to her. He has a tired look and reddened eyes from tension. He is staring at Zarina's beautiful face for a long time. Then he took her hand.

"Who are you and where are you from? Why do I have the feeling that I have known you for a long time, but found you only now?" He held out his hand to touch her cheek but did not. "Sleep, the worst is over. We will still have time to talk." He got up and left the room. He went to the doctor on duty:

"If you notice that something is going wrong, immediately call me home. Do you understand?"

"Yes, of course, I'll definitely call you."

When Dietrich walked away, the doctor followed him in surprise with his eyes.

Franz entered the hall and went to the administrator.

"Could you check, please, if Madame Khasanova is at her place?" "She left, don't you know?" the administrator was surprised. "How - left? Where to?" it's the turn to be surprised at Franz.

"This morning, in a hurry. She just said that she was flying away urgently to her son."

"I don't understand anything. Why would she fly somewhere if he arrives in two

days? Have you noticed anything else?"

"No," the girl shook her head.

"It's strange somehow. She could call me. Okay, I'll try to find out where she went so fast. All the best."

"Goodbye, Mr. Meinhof."

Franz left the hotel, thought, then shrugged and went to his car. From another car, standing at a distance, Ali watched him...

In the safe house, the same three – the Senior, Mehmed and Moussa, who was very worried and often wipes his forehead with a handkerchief.

"Once again I want to hear about the degree of readiness for the operation," the Senior said harshly. "There should be no errors, not one. Mehmed, what about the airport?"

"The whole chain is working, people have arrived, everyone has transit, Fatima is ready."

"Let us suppose," he nodded, then looked at Moussa with a prickly look. "Moussa, you surprise me. What a wacky story was with that woman? Mehmed reported that there are no problems. But he knows this from your words. Therefore, I want to listen to you myself."

"There was a small mess-up," Moussa wiped his forehead again, "The police frightened us. But Yusuf and I returned and completed everything. She is where she must be."

"Can you give a guarantee that she will not come up in the near future at any police station and will not tell about its caring companions?"

"I can, of course I can," Moussa began to fuss. "If she does come up, it will not be very soon, and certainly not at the police station."

"Then why are you so twitchy and nervous?" The Senior looked suspiciously at Moussa.

"How not to be twitchy when the police are pushing from the tail," he wiped his forehead again and looked ingenuously at the Senior.

"Allah save you if you make a mistake. Mehmed, tell everyone

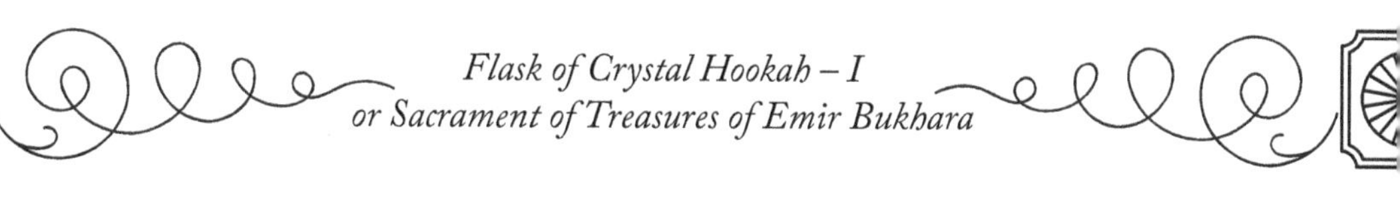

that the operation is going according to plan and tomorrow everyone is acting as scheduled. Report to me constantly. Tomorrow is a hard day. But the goal is close, and we will go to the end. Go ahead."

Both left the room.

"Phew," Moussa panted." When he looks like that, all my insides fall."

"You do not make mistakes, then they will not fall out completely. Do you understand my idea? Or remember about Hazrat?"

"Ah, no, I'm so sick. I Found what to remind me ."

"It's just not to let you relax. Let's go…"

84

A plane to Madrid took off, and the flight attendants began to deliver drinks. One of the cabin attendants, finding the right person, handed him a foil-covered plastic package with the words "Your order, sir," and went on. Having taken weapons from the received boxes, the terrorists began to seize the aircraft.

Fatima opened her box and pulled out a remote control with a red button. The man next to him looked at her in surprise.

"Is it your breakfast instead?" he joked.

She laid her finger on the red button and looked at the joker:

"If I press this button, there will be no one to have breakfast on this plane, do you understand?"

The man turned pale and shook his head in shock. A glass of drink in his hand froze in the air.

"Now," Fatima commanded him, "go to another place, quick." The man, cautiously looking at the remote control, clumsily got out of his chair and, backing away, sat down in the chair opposite through the passage...

At this time on the ground, a headquarters was urgently set up to resolve the situation with the seizure of the aircraft. A tall, thick man entered the room and took his place at the head of the table. He turned to those sitting at the table. "Outline the details to me," he looked at the head of the airport.

"Let's start with you."

"The board was heading to Spain," the airport chief began. "Half an hour ago, we

received an alarm from the pilots. After that, the terrorists got in touch and gave

their demands."

"What do they want?"

"To release their leader and give out $50 Million."

"What if we don't?"

"They will begin to kill the hostages. On board there are 132 people, not including the crew."

"Where are they directing the plane?"

"They demand a landing in Tripoli."

"Excluded," the Chief categorically rejected such an option, "we won't get them there. Thanks, sit down. What is known about the terrorists?" he turned to the next participant in the meeting.

"Nothing so far," he answered. "We check the passenger lists, check with the file cabinet. There are three suspicious people at the moment."

"Check everyone, find out how weapons could get on board. Track possible links here. Is the capture team ready?"

"Completely," the special forces chief confirmed. "Ready to ship at any time. Only the destination is needed."

"We must convince them to sit in Ankara," the Chief set the task. "Who will negotiate?"

"Me." a short, stout man rose from his seat.

"Good. Do you understand your task?"

"Completely."

"Then proceed. Say that they will receive the money in Ankara, and let their leader be exchanged for hostages. They don't need to know the rest. When will they make contact?"

"After 7 minutes," said the negotiator, looking at his watch.

"Everyone get down to work. Information should come to me immediately," he put his hands on the table, making it clear that the meeting was over...

Fatima is sitting in her chair. She covered her hand with the remote control with a kerchief. One of the terrorists approached her. "Transferred our conditions?" "Yes. They agree, but the plane should land in Ankara. They say that we will not reach Tripoli."

"You never know what they say!" Fatima said angrily. "No Ankara, only where it is said."

"What if they disagree?"

"So we won't reach Ankara either," Fatima said ominously.

"What do you mean?" the terrorist asked.

"This." Fatima removed the handkerchief from the remote control.

"You are crazy!" her interlocutor was seriously scared and stepped back a step. "We didn't agree! (he became agitated) Our task is to take the money, our man, and leave. That's all. I am not going to turn into fertilizer ahead of schedule."

"But I don't care what you are going to and what not," Fatima snapped and tapped the button lightly. "You have your own task, I have my own. It will be as I said. You understand me?"

"Good, good, I understand, just don't play with this," he nodded to the console. "I'll go tell the rest."

He quickly left, and Fatima again covered the remote with a handkerchief and closed her eyes. Passengers stared at her from the seats opposite. One of them crossed himself.

The senior negotiator entered the room. He looked grim.

"Is something going wrong?" The Chief asked.

"The situation has worsened. They said they agreed on Ankara, but their accomplice threatened to blow up the plane if they landed there."

"An accomplice?" This message put the Chief off balance.

"I was only told about men. Where did the explosives come from? God knows what!" "Apparently, the one who planned everything decided to hedge this way," the negotiator explained.

"Just a second. If I understand you correctly, do they have disagreements on board? Could you take advantage of that?

"I think yes. They can tell her that the plane will land in Tripoli and distract her during landing. She won't be able to check anyway. In Ankara, while there will be a transfer of money and hostages, the group will be able to check the luggage compartment. Then - according to plan."

"Proceed." agreed the Chief.

The negotiator nodded and left. The head massaged the temples, took a sip from the glass and muttered: "Ah, how much I dislike it..."

"Is she crazy?" one of the invaders of the plane, who was talking with Fatima, asked in fright.

"You should have seen her eyes! She seemed to have buried everyone. She docs not remove her finger from the button."

"What will we do?" Another terrorist intervened in the conversation. "It turns out that we played blindly. It is necessary to neutralize her, I did not subscribe to such an end."

"They gave advice from the ground: to distract her when landing, so that she doesn't guess about Ankara. Then we have a chance."

"Only a hole in the head can distract her."

"Then you do it. You are our master in such matters."

"What if she has time?"

"Then you will have nothing to worry about. Try to talk her

round and press first. "Okay, I'll try..."

The ship commander makes an announcement on the internal radio.

"Our plane will make an emergency landing in Tripoli. Please fasten your seat belts. Fatima looked at her watch and shook her head in disbelief. When the plane had already lowered before landing, she looked out the window. She recognized the contours of this city, and it was not Tripoli. A contemptuous grin appeared on her lips:

"Ah, jackal spawn..."

The airplane landing gear touched the concrete strip, her accomplice was walking down the aisle towards him, he held his right hand in his jacket pocket, clutching a gun.

"That's Tripoli, as agreed. Would you like something to calm down?" Their eyes met, and the terrorist understood everything.

"You won't have time," Fatima grinned contemptuously. The terrorist shot through his jacket, but Fatima managed to press the button. A terrible explosion rang out on a concrete strip...

The senior of the capture group reports to the chief by telephone from Ankara: "We do not know. It was already going along the strip, and here - an explosion. Everything was blown to pieces, something terrible is happening on the field... No, it was simply impossible to survive there. Yes. To return the group." At the other end, the chef slowly hung up the red telephone.

"That's all," he said wearily. "Nearly one hundred and fifty people ... Damned fanatics..."

85

Alibek is standing at the window and looking thoughtfully at the street. From the working TV comes the voice of the speaker.

"... A terrible tragedy. During the landing, the plane exploded, committing...Alibek shuddered and turned sharply to the TV from Frankfurt. The plane was captured by terrorists and changed course. Everyone is killed on the plane. The police had discovered..." Alibek did not listen further. He turned off the TV and strode nervously around the room, not understanding why he was so excited about this message.

Sherzod is walking around the hall of Frankfurt Airport. Without waiting for the person he was to meet, he left the building, took a taxi and showed the driver a business card with the address. He nodded his head and drove the car.

The taxi stopped at the Peace Corps building. Sherzod got out of the car and stepped inside. Finding the right door, he opened it. The woman at the table looked inquiringly at him.

"How can I help you, young man?"

"I need Mr. Meinhof, Franz Meinhof."

"Sorry, but he is not here. We have not been able to contact him for several days. It isn't like him to leave without warning. Do you have business with him?"

"Yes. My mother flew to Frankfurt and he met her. I thought

I would see them at the airport but did not wait and came here."

"Yes, yes, I remember," the woman confirmed. "He was telling me something about this incident. You haven't seen your mother for several years, right?"

"Yes."

"Moreover, it is not clear why he did not meet you." She was at a loss. "Wait a minute. She flipped through a register and found the necessary note.

"Here, he took her to the Inter Hotel. Now I'll call there and you can talk with your mother. Probably, Franz had to urgently leave, and he did not have time to warn anyone." She found the hotel room in the directory, dialled it and smiled encouragingly at Sherzod. When answered at that end, she asked:

"Good afternoon, can I find out what room Mrs. Khasanova lives in?"

"This woman does not appear to be in our hotel," the administrator answered after a moment's pause.

"But our employee took her to your hotel himself. Check again, please."

"Wait a second, I'll check ... Yes, she was at our hotel, but she left urgently a few days ago."

"Where to?"

"Sorry, but I don't know, she didn't leave an address."

"Thanks." The woman hung up and looked puzzled at Sherzod.

"It's strange, she left several days ago. Where - no one knows."

"But she can't have left!" Sherzod didn't understand anything. "She came here after me!"

"So something serious has happened. Maybe at home? Haven't you called home?"

"Not yet."

"Well, call!" She pushed the phone to Sherzod.

Alibek already opened the door to leave, when the frequent rings of a long-distance phone call were heard. Alibek rushed to the phone and grabbed the receiver.

"Hello, Zarina? At last…"

"Dad, it's me, Sherzod, hello."

"Hello, son, I'm glad to hear from you. Thank God it's all over and Mom is next to you again. When will you arrive?"

"Dad, mom is not here, she did not meet me."

"How - no?" Alibek was alarmed. "What are you saying? So, they did not have time to warn her, and she is sitting in her hotel and waiting for news from you."

"We called the hotel, she is not there either. We were told that she had left somewhere urgently a few days ago. I thought something happened at home, so I'm calling."

"Left?" Alibek's hand trembled with excitement. "I don't understand anything. She could not leave without you. The one who met her, what was his name? How is Franz?"

"He does not say anything. This is strange, but he has also been gone for several days, and no one knows where he is. Dad, what should I do?"

"Now, son, now, I'm trying to figure out …" fear began to seize Alibek, but he could not show it to his son. "Maybe she persuaded Franz to fly to you and you missed each other? Can you find out?"

"I'll try. Or maybe contact the police?"

"Do not need the police, what does the police have to do with it… As soon as you find out something, call me right away, I'll be near the phone. Come on, son…" "Good, dad…"

Alibek hung up and looked at his hands. They were trembling. For some reason, an episode with the plane from the news surfaced in his memory. Alibek shook his head to drive away this thought...

Sherzod hung up. The woman looked at him sympathetically.

"What did father say?"

"He doesn't understand anything either. Maybe they and Franz really flew towards me?"

"Well, it's easy to check. If they flew somewhere, then we will find out." She picked up the phone and dialled the number. "Good afternoon. May I know that Mr. Meinhof and Mrs. Khasanova have not left Frankfurt in the last 5 days? ... Yes ... No, Franz Meinhof... Didn't fly out? And Madame ... Khasanova," she repeated the surname by letter. "Where to? To Spain? ... What? That one? ... Are you sure? ... Her son ... Yes, I'll tell..."

She hung up and dropped her head. Sherzod looked at her intensely. When she raised her head, tears stood in her eyes:

"She... She was on that plane..."

In the inspector's office, a telephone rang. He picked up the phone:

"Inspector Jurgens?" the voice of Dietrich came.

"Yes, hello."

"Hello, this is Dr. Gruber, regarding the woman with the trauma found." "Yes, I remember. Did she come to her senses?"

"She came, but another problem arose. She does not remember anything: not a single detail from what happened to her, nor who she is or where she came from. Complete amnesia."

"Unfortunate. So, the one who did this calmly walks free, and we don't even know who and where to look for. What is the probability that her memory will return?" asked Jurgens.

"There is always such a probability, the only question is when." "But you are a doctor? What is your practice saying?"

"I can't say anything definite yet, but my practice says that there can be as many options as you like," said Dietrich. "I understand your desire to interrogate her as soon as possible, but now your conversation with her will not yield anything."

"This is clear. Do you think something can speed up this process?"

"All she needs now is peace, care, attention. And no stress."

"What if we transfer her to a special clinic?" Jurgens inquired.

"That's just what I would not do. In my clinic, the conditions are as close to home conditions as possible, and if the situation changes dramatically now, this can give a negative result and worsen its condition.

"What are you offering?"

"I suggest leaving her in my clinic under my personal responsibility. Naturally, you will be aware of the results of her treatment."

"Well, I will report to my superiors, and I will inform you of the decision. Although I personally would also prefer to relax at home."

"So, what's the matter, Inspector?" Dietrich smiled.

"Come and I will provide you with complete comfort."

"Of course. As soon as they break my skull, I'll go straight to you. I'll call you in a

couple of days. Good luck."

"Goodbye, Inspector..."

Zarina is sitting on the bed in her room, on her head is still a light bandage. She took a pill from her nightstand, grimaced, then swallowed it and washed it down with water. Dietrich entered the room.

"Good morning, you look charming today."

"Are you laughing at me again, doctor?" "Why - again?" Dietrich said feignedly. "Yesterday you said the same thing."

"Yeah, you remember that, fine. Then why - the doctor, and not by name? Did you forget my name?"

"No, I didn't forget. Dietrich. But I'm not comfortable calling you that." "Nonsense," Dietrich dismissed. "It's a lot better than a dry doctor." While they were talking, Dietrich checked her pulse and reaction. "Well, not bad at all. It remains to repair your memory, and everything will be in order. Did you not fail to remember anything? Or someone else? What is your name?"

To all these questions, Zarina shook her head negatively.

"There is nothing. As if I had no past at all." She frowned and lowered her head. "Well, this is not a reason to despair," Dietrich objected. "Of the three components, you have two more, you just need to be patient and hope that a third appears." "What did you mean by the two that I have?"

"I meant the present and the future. How is your head? Does it hurt?"

"Not so much."

"If you change the hospital setting to home, everything will go much faster." "You know, Dietrich, that I have nowhere to go if they expel me from the hospital," tears appeared in her eyes. "Only the police and letting them find out who I am and where I'm from."

"That's what I wanted to talk about with you. Nobody is going to drive you anywhere. In the police, your condition is all the more unlikely to improve. I want to offer you help, just take your time with the answer. I have a big house, and you will be much more comfortable and calm there. Elsa will help you get comfortable."

"Is Elsa your wife?" Zarina asked.

"This is my housekeeper."

"Do you think this is convenient? You do not know me. What if I'm some escaped criminal, a thief, or someone else, God knows who? And when my memory returns..."

"Then," Dietrich smiled, "I will buy Elsa a gun, and she will run after you all over the house and search you before going to bed."

"Better immediately to the chain and in the booth in front of the house. At least some use."

"This is a fallback. In the evening I'll drop in and you promise me not to hide the spoons from the service under the pillow."

He got up and headed for the door. When he had already opened it, Zarina called out to him:

"Dietrich..."

"Yes?" Dietrich turned.

"Do you really think this is needed?"

"Yes, I really think so."

He smiled encouragingly at her and left the room. Satisfied with the conversation, he went into the hall and headed for the exit from the clinic. The head nurse called him. "Are you leaving, doctor?"

"Yes, I have business until evening."

"Will there be any special orders for today?"

Dietrich grabbed the handle of the exit door and thought for a second. "Yes. Today, all cncmas are cancelled..."

He went out, and the nurse's jaw dropped. The secretary sitting at the counter laughed out loud. The nurse compressed her lips, looked sternly at her, shook her head disapprovingly and went to her room...

86

After Sherzod called his father and said that his mother was in that crashed plane, Alibek lost his peace. He turned pale, haggard and lost interest in everything that was happening around. When Shahlo or Lola came to him, so as not to leave him alone, they had to force him to eat something almost by force. He did not want to believe that he had lost Zarina and clung to the slightest opportunity to convince himself that this was not so. Remembering his friend Farkhad, who worked at the Foreign Ministry, Alibek came to him. Farkhad again tried to describe what happened as gently as possible, but this had no effect on Alibek.

"No, I can't believe it," he said with desperate stubbornness. "She could not board this plane. Why would she fly to Spain? For several years she had not seen her son, and he was about to fly to Frankfurt himself. Can you explain this to me?"

"No, I can't," Farkhad shrugged. "Can you explain how her name appeared on the passenger list? At our request, we were sent this list, and there is all its data."

"She could not get on this plane, change her mind, someone could steal her documents! Yes, you never know what else!" insisted Alibek.

"Alibek, wake up, what are you saying? If she had not sat down, she would have been with her son now."

"Sorry, friend, I myself sometimes don't understand what I'm saying," Alibek said frantically. "But still, I don't believe it. If such a misfortune happened to her, I would feel. To lose her now, when everything began to improve, when the son was found - this is unbearable, I do not want to believe it."

"I understand you, but ..." Farkhad hesitated. "I didn't want to tell you... They have cameras everywhere... In general, we received a copy of the footage from registration and boarding. I copied something from it..."

At these words, Alibek tensed, and glared at his friend.

"Would you like me to show you?" Farkhad asked uncertainly, seeing the condition of his friend.

Alibek's throat constricted, and he only nodded his head.

"Good." Farkhad inserted a cassette and pressed a button. The screen lit up, people showed up in the airport building. A woman in black glasses went to the reception and held out documents, then turned to the hall, put her hand on the counter. Alibek glared at the image. The woman took away her documents, smiled at the girl, and walked away from the counter. Alibek recognized Zarina as this woman. The recording ended, and Farkhad turned off the TV. He looked sympathetically at his friend. "These are the things, brother..." He pulled out a cassette and handed it to Alibek. "I wrote this for you. I'm sorry…"

Alibek looked out at Farkhad with dull eyes, took the disc, for some reason he ran his hand along its surface, stood up, and, without saying a word, went to the exit...

A month has passed. As always recently, Dietrich did not stay in the clinic longer than usual. He came home, went into the kitchen where Zarina was busy, went up to her and kissed her on the cheek.

"It smells charming. Exotic."

"An absolutely banal dish."

"From which gluttonous doctors get fat and cannot squeeze into the ward to even get to the patient. But to refuse is beyond my strength. Who only taught you all this?" The question sounded completely natural, but it was one of those unobtrusive leading questions that Dietrich tried to somehow stir up Zarina's memory.

"You'll have to," Dietrich's question again passed by. "You came ahead of time and the final is still far away."

"Never mind. Until this moment, I can safely keep my diet."

He stepped back a couple of steps and began to look at Zarina. She felt his eyes and was embarrassed.

"What?" she turned.

"Just admire it. You know, before you, I came up with different things and tricks to stay at home as little as possible. Now I come up with tricks to get away from business and come early."

"You want to say that I have a bad influence on you?"

"Oh yeah! And how! You know, I absolutely do not mind. Therefore, the thought of leaving me just unbalances me."

"Of leaving? You are leaving?" Zarina was clearly upset.

"I have to. I was invited to a symposium with a report, and I can't refuse."

"Where to?" asked Zarina.

"To Tashkent."

"Where is that?" Zarina frowned.

"Central Asia. I'll bring you something exotic, something specific from there." "Is this for a long time? I will feel uneasy here alone."

"A week maximum. You will have the opportunity to calmly

consider my proposal. I just won't bother you."

"You said nonsense. It was me who intervened in your life with all my problems. Then..." she lowered her head, "I have already thought it over."

"And...?"

Zarina felt that with impatience Dietrich was waiting for her answer, but decided to tease him a little and made an innocent look.

"Maybe we better wait for your return, and I still think?"

"I'll prescribe castor," Dietrich jokingly threatened with his finger.

"I thought that I would still teach you how to tie a tie."

"Ah well? Don't you like the way I tie my ties? Well then, don't complain!"

He put his hand in his pocket and moved to Zarina. She curiously watched his actions, playfully assuming a defensive posture.

Dietrich came up, took a box from his pocket and handed it to Zarina. She took it and opened it. There was a ring.

"Dietrich, you're crazy!" she exclaimed.

"Yes, and for a long time." He took out the ring and put it on Zarina's finger. "Here is its place."

"I just have no words, Dietrich. It..."

"It is not necessary. For this you will help me pack my things. Otherwise, I will definitely forget something."

"Well, I knew that it won't be for nothing..."

Instead of answering, Dietrich hugged Zarina and pressed to himself... But she carefully turned away...

87

At the Tashkent Publishing House, the chief editor is sitting in his office and looking at the materials sent. Then he presses the selector button.

"Kadyr, come to me, please ..." he selected one sheet from a stack of papers and set it aside. Kadyr entered the office, and the Chief pointed to the opposite place. "Sit down." Kadyr sat down.

"Listen,." the Chief began, "I have an important business for you. The other day we will have an international symposium on neurosurgery here, the luminaries will come. I need a series of interviews, great interviews."

"I have such a person," Kadyr said. "He specializes in medicine." "No," the Chief rejected the offer, "I want you to do it yourself."

"You know that medicine is not my specialization, and young people also need to gain experience."

"It's not about the specialization. You have a grip, your own approach, and nobody will do better than you. The question is very serious and should be submitted accordingly. The young also find work, do not worry. They will be at your grab, internship. Well, so how? Have you agreed?"

"If necessary, then I will," Kadyr did not argue. "It is only necessary to get acquainted with the topic in order not to ask stupid questions."

"Here," the Chief handed Kadyr a folder, "Here is everything that can be useful to you. I rely on you."

"Sly you, however!" Kadyr could not resist. "They provided for everything in advance, and it seems to me that there's nowhere to go, right?"

"My work is like that, I'm sorry," he smiled and spread his hands. Kadyr opened the folder and felt a pack of sheets.

"Wow! And when will it begin?"

"The day after tomorrow."

"Clear. So, all-out effort and I will not be up to sleep. You are owed a can of coffee," Kadyr said jokingly.

The chief put his hand into the desk cupboard and put a can of coffee on the table:

"Is that fine, demander?"

"Yes, I, it seems, missed. What about..." but the Chief did not let him continue the thought.

"Do you remember a fairy tale about a goldfish?"

"That's it, I understood the hint." He took the can, twisted it in his hand. "Then I went to study."

"Go, dear. Good luck." Kadyr smiled and left the office...

After the next day of the symposium, at an evening reception, Kadyr went to the table at which Dietrich was sitting.

"Good evening, Dietrich. May I?" he pointed at a place at the table.

"Of course, take a seat. Do you have additional questions?"

"You see, Dietrich, I guess I asked the wrong ones. Some kind of dry interview I did. Figures, calculations - it's all good, but lifeless. But in each case we are talking about a specific, living person, his fate, loved ones. Do you understand me?"

"Of course. Figures are one thing, and real life is completely different, and sometimes it presents such occasions that do not fit into any statistical column."

"Well, that's what I had in mind," Kadyr said with interest. "When you talked about people who have lost their memory, I felt uneasy. I imagined that I did not remember anything and anyone, and I was scared. Is it really impossible to restore what has been erased?"

"Nothing is erased," Dietrich said. "These areas are simply blocked. It can be the events of a couple of hours, several weeks or even half of life. Our intervention, alas, does not always help and is not always justified."

"Well, let's say you can't remove the lock. What should such a person do?"

"The scalpel is not a panacea, Kadyr. A single recipe does not exist. Sometimes a trifle, an association, a trinket can solve everything. What should such a person do? Hope, wait, learn to live in new conditions, as if anew. You know, Kadyr, one such person has already changed my life. It turned out that I helped him not so much as he did to me. Are you interested?"

"Rather!" Kadyr felt that this was exactly what he lacked for his interview.

"A few years ago, I lost my wife and thought that with her demise my life finally lost its attractiveness. There was only work left, and I was sure that no one could replace it," he paused, once again reliving the past. "I made a mistake. A few months ago, a woman with a severe head injury was brought to my clinic. I did the operation, but her memory begins from the moment she regained consciousness. Neither who she is, nor what her name is, nor where she is from - nothing, you understand? Big white sheet.

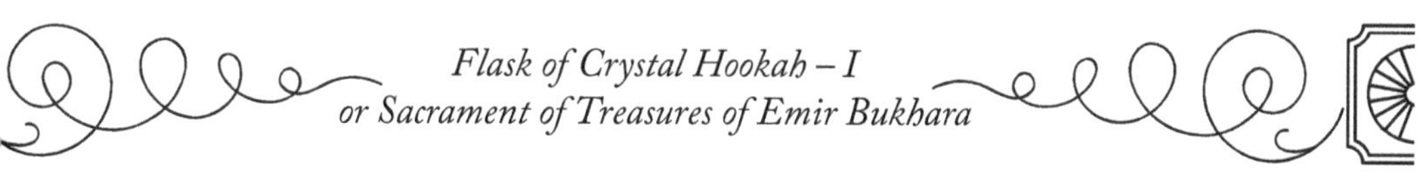

Now I cannot imagine my life without her."

"Have you tried to find her loved ones?" Kadyr asked interestedly.

"How? There were no documents with her. All I could do was look at the requests for the missing, even interpolating. Nobody is looking for her."

"So, she was lucky that you were there." With a sixth sense, Kadyr felt that he had touched something very important.

"We were both lucky. I count the days when I get home and see her. I promised to bring her something exotic for memory. Would you advise where to look?"

"No need to look. I will pick up something myself, it's easier for me to do it. Let there be memories from me too. Do you have her photo?"

"Of course I do, I took it before leaving." He reached into his jacket pocket, took out his wallet. At that moment he was called in to work. "Sorry, I'll be back in a moment, but for now, look." He took a photograph from his wallet and handed it to Kadyr. "Here," Dietrich stepped back, Kadyr looked at the photograph and was petrified. From the picture Zarina looked alive and unharmed...

88

Kadyr returned home in a state of utter confusion. He kissed Shahlo, who left the room to meet him, went into the kitchen, took a bottle of cognac from the sideboard, poured it into a glass and drank it in one gulp. Shahlo looked reproachfully at him. "Kadyr..."

"No, no, that's not what you think. Sit down, please, I need to tell you something.

Shahlo sat up and looked anxiously at her husband:

"Something has happened?"

"Happened..." He sat opposite, got up courage. "You just try not to worry, okay?"

"You scare me, Kadyr," Shahlo worried.

"Can you finally tell me what happened?" Kadyr took in air and said slowly:

"Zarina is alive."

"What?" Shahlo grabbed her heart. "Do you understand what you're saying?" "Understand. I saw her. Rather, not her, but a photo with her, a week ago."

"But that cannot be!" Shahlo shook her head. "She died! You took somebody for her, there was someone similar!"

"Could you not recognize her in the photo after so many years of friendship?" "Of course not!"

"And me too. Now listen to what I tell you, and then we will decide what to do next. So..."

Dietrich returned to the hotel and first of all called to Frankfurt to hear Zarina's

voice.

"No, everything is very good. True, a little tired, but this is nonsense. I want to go home… Yes, it ends. Two days later I fly out… No, you don't, you will meet me at home. I really missed you… For sure. I will kiss you, see you later." He hung up and went over the number, content.

"But shall we have a coffee with something?" Dietrich asked himself. Then he picked up the phone again and made an order…

"Do you believe it now?" he took Shahlo's hand.

"Oh my God!" Shahlo shook her head. "Incredible. But I'm extremely glad that she is still alive. What did they do to her? Does she not remember anything at all?"

"If she at least remembered something, she would be here now, not there." "Then who was on the tape?" Shahlo asked, perplexed.

"Now it doesn't matter. The most important thing is what should we do with Alibek?"

"We have to tell him everything! Can you imagine how happy he will be? He still

does not believe that Zarina died."

"He will rush right there."

"Naturally, how else?" Shahlo remarked.

"You think? Now imagine that you are her. A man comes to you and assures her

that he is your husband. What will you do? Run away with joy to pack your bags or will you call the police?"

"But he can prove it!"

"So what? Another shock? Are you sure this will help her, and not harm her even more?"

"No," Shahlo thought, "not sure, they're not joking with such things." "Even more so, she cannot be pulled out of a calm atmosphere now." "But something needs to be done?"

"Be patient and wait," he said.

"He said that sometimes a little push can be enough, right?"

"Yes," Kadyr agreed.

"What did he mean?"

"He said that this could be any trifle that we usually do not pay attention to like a smell, a picture, a bauble."

"A picture, a bauble." Shahlo repeated in thought, and then it dawned on her.

"A bauble. Here! She needs to get something from us, something that she knows very well, and, it seems, I even know what it is. Can you find a reason to give it to this doctor?"

"Why do I need a reason? I myself promised to find something exotic as a gift." "Good, that's very good." Shahlo's joy knew no bounds. "Let's go to Alibek. I'll come in and take something."

"It's already late, maybe tomorrow?" objected Kadyr.

"He is not sleeping yet, I know..." Suddenly she reached across the table and kissed Kadyr on the nose. He was taken aback by surprise and stared at his wife. "Alive, alive, our Zarinka! This is the most important thing. Let's go..."

Alibek is sitting in a dark room, in his hand is a remote control. He again and again looks at the tape Farkhad gave him. Sherzod came up behind and put his hands on his shoulders.

"Dad, it's too late already, you almost do not sleep."

"Go, son, rest, I will go soon too. I'll watch it again and go." The doorbell rang, Alibek started, jumped up, but Sherzod tried to stop him: "I will open it, dad."

"No, I myself." Alibek quickly went to the door and opened it. On the threshold Shahlo was standing. Alibek drooped. "Ah, Shahlo, come in." Shahlo entered and carefully looked at Alibek.

"Unshaven, rumpled, bags under the eyes. What are you doing with yourself, Alibek?"

"I forgot to shave," Alibek ran a hand over his cheek, "I'm sorry."

"Do you forget to sleep too?" Shahlo asked reproachfully. "Sometimes I eat. I can't sleep. Come, let's talk."

They went into the room, Shahlo saw the TV on and shook her head disapprovingly. "You watch it again. How many times have you watched it? Hundred? Thousand?" "I don't know, I didn't think … The more I watch, the more I cannot get rid of one thought. Maybe I'm losing my mind? Here, look…" he pressed a button on the remote control, and a familiar scene at the airport arose on the screen. "Here she comes, turns around, takes documents, leaves. That's her?" He looked inquiringly at Shahlo. That startled from an unexpected question:

"Why do you ask?"

"Because it's her, and at the same time, not her. I can't get rid of this thought, and it drives me crazy. I don't know where this feeling comes from, contrary to all the obvious facts. You understand me?"

"Of course, I understand, because I also can't believe it in any way…" To hide her excitement, she walked around the room, as if by chance stopped near a shelf with various trinkets. She took one of them. It was a small copper jug made as the magic lamp of Aladdin. "Wow, her beloved! How many years have passed when we girls rubbed it with all our might so that a genie with gifts would come to us."

"Take it to yourself, let it be a keepsake."

"Really? Can I?"

"Can."

Shahlo went to Alibek and kissed his cheek:

"Thanks, Alibek. You know, Kadyr and I will try to do something else. Since there are doubts, then you should not give up."

"Do you also think that some ridiculous mistake has occurred?" Alibek asked hopefully.

"Maybe. Now take some sleeping pills and go to bed, you need to rest. Don't forget to shave tomorrow and tidy yourself up. Do you promise?"

"I promise. Thank you."

"Then I go." She put the jug in her bag and went to the door. "I'll check tomorrow. Bye." She went out and closed the door behind herself...

Kadyr entered the hotel lobby, looked for Dietrich through his eyes and went to him. Dietrich also noticed Kadyr and rose to meet him.

"Good afternoon, Dietrich. By the look of things, you are already mentally flying home on the plane."

"Hello, Kadyr. Actually, mentally I am already at home, but my flesh is waiting to be sent to the airport."

"Never mind, they will soon unite," Kadyr laughed. "As I promised," he took out the transparent packaging tied with a ribbon from the bag, "I found something for you." He handed the gift to Dietrich. He took it and began to examine it with interest.

"As I understand it, this is not just a souvenir. Does this have any hidden meaning?" he asked Kadyr.

"Yes. This is a miniature magic lamp. In the folk tale, when they rubbed it with their palm, a huge genie appeared from the lamp and fulfilled all the wishes of the lamp owner." "So, in this little lamp a genie lives who fulfills modest desires?"

"I don't know," Kadyr smiled, "I did not dare to check. Who knows how his character has changed over the past couple of thousand years."

"Actually," Dietrich smiled too, "It seems to be called to play a dirty trick. Okay, I'll take a chance, at home of course. Thank you, Kadyr, I am glad to meet you. If you are in Frankfurt, be sure to let me know."

"By all means," Kadyr held out his hand. "Bon voyage, Dietrich. Good luck to you." "Thank you," Dietrich answered with a handshake. "Good luck to you too…"

89

Yusuf left the cafe, picking his teeth with a toothpick, and idly headed for his taxi. A woman with a package came out of the store across the road and went along the street. When Yusuf saw her face, he froze in surprise.

This was the woman they thought was dead. He quickly turned away and pretended to brush off his trousers.

When Zarina left, he quickly got into the car and followed her. He took out his cell phone and dialled the number.

"Mehmed? We urgently need to see you, something happened… It doesn't matter. Well, in about 15 minutes I'll come…"

He turned off his cell phone and wiped his sweaty forehead. The resurrection of this woman threatened him, and not only him, with major troubles. Having led Zarina to the house, he turned around the car and rushed to Mehmed…

Gloomy Mehmed and scared Yusuf are sitting at a cafe table.

"Could you have made a mistake?" he asked again.

"No, I could not. This is exactly her."

"How can you explain that she is alive and well? You and Moussa vowed that she drowned, remember?"

"So, Moussa said he was doing it. When we arrived there a second time, she was not there, only one shoe on the coast. So, Moussa said that..."

"Moussa, Moussa ..." Mehmed snapped. "Do you have your head on your shoulders? Or is it already bothering you? Do you even understand how this threatens you?"

"Mehmed," Yusuf begged. "I beg you, just don't tell the Senior. He will kill me, but for what?"

"And it'll be right. There is only one answer for such errors, and you know well which one. I'm not going to risk it because of you."

"I will fix it, I will fix it all," Yusuf fussed, "I know where she lives, and myself, with my own hands..."

"So, what is next? What if she managed to describe Moussa and you to the police?"

"Only Moussa, she could not remember me."

"What's the difference!" barked Mehmed. "If they take him, he won't last half an hour."

"So, we need him..." Yusuf stopped short and looked ingratiatingly at Mehmed.

"What - why do you need him? Come on, say."

"Well, it's... for security..."

"Yes? Without the order of the Senior?"

Mehmed thought. He rose in the eyes of the Senior, but Moussa remained the main obstacle to moving up. This case should have been taken.

"So..." Mehmed stared hard at Yusuf. "Now listen and remember. If you squeak about her to someone else, you're done. Further. Follow her and find out when and where she goes. I'll deal with

Moussa myself. Got it?" "I'll do everything, do not hesitate. Follow, and…"

"No "and" without my order," Mehmed interrupted. "If you do something wrong - do not expect protection from me. That's all, go, I need to think."

"Thank you, Mehmed, thank you. I owe you. Whatever you say, I'll do it." "Do not forget these words. Go on…"

Mehmed went into the room. The Senior was sitting at the table and working on a computer. When Mehmed entered, he pressed a button and the screen went blank. Then he looked inquiringly at Mehmed.

"Are you sure your business is worth such urgency and my time?"

"Yes, yes, sure. This is very urgent and very important. One of my friends in the police got this out for me," he handed the Senior a sheet of paper. "And so I asked for a meeting."

The Senior took the sheet and peered. On the sheet was a very similar image-mask of Moussa and several lines of text. The Senior swung the sheet down onto the table: "So they somehow unearthed it. Where could this fat peacock light up?"

"I don't know, but you can call him here and gut him," suggested Mehmed.

"So that he would lead a company of tails with machine guns? I already know what he will say. Take care of this, and as quickly as possible."

"You want me to…" began Mehmed, but the Senior immediately interrupted him. "You perfectly understand what I want, do not take my time."

"Yes," Mehmed bowed. "Do not worry, there will be no tails."

He bowed once more and left. The Senior took out a lighter and set fire to the sheet. While the paper was burning, he scornfully looked at the image of Moussa...

90

A taxi drove Dietrich to his house. Zarina came out to meet him. Dietrich hugged her, kissed her, and they went into the house. Dietrich threw off his jacket, loosened his tie and flopped into a chair. Zarina sat opposite. Dietrich was in such a good mood that she involuntarily laughed.

"You have such a pleased appearance as a cat who ate all the sour cream and is glad that he didn't get caught."

"No," said Dietrich with a smile, "I have the appearance of a man who has finally got home and is in the company of a charming woman whom he missed terribly. How do you feel?"

"Fine. Headaches subsided, I go to the store and I'm not afraid to get lost anymore. True, Elsa swears that I am taking away her duties. Today I took your favorite beer. Should I bring you some?"

"I have not deserved such a gift."

"Never mind, I will trust you…"

She went out for a beer, and Dietrich got up, opened the case and took out a gift from Kadyr. Zarina returned and handed him a beer. In response, he offered her a present. "This is for you, as I promised, from a distant Asian country."

Zarina took a souvenir from the package.

"Oh, what a delight!" She exclaimed, looking at it from all sides.

"Do you know what this little thing is for?" Dietrich mysteriously asked.

"Of course!" Zarina responded immediately. "It needs to be rubbed thoroughly with your palm and then - a genie will come out of it that will fulfil your every desire!" While she was saying this, the expression on Dietrich's face had changed

from playful to serious.

"How did you know that?" In his question there was not so much surprise as wariness.

"Well, then! In my childhood I had..." Zarina looked at Dietrich and stopped halfway through her sentence, seeing how serious his face had become.

"You remember that in your childhood you had the same thing?" Dietrich carefully looked at her.

Zarina stiffened, trying to remember something, but she did not succeed.

"No, I do not remember. I don't even know why I said that." Her face again assumed a serene look. "It doesn't matter, it's charming, thank you." She kissed Dietrich on the cheek: "Why do you look so serious?"

"I thought ..." He made an effort and smiled. "That the genie will have to work hard to fulfil my wishes."

"Uh, no," Zarina put her hand with the souvenir behind her back. "We will coordinate our desires so that he has an easier time of it."

"I agree. So, I have a desire to go with you to the restaurant in the evening." "I do not mind," Zarina readily agreed. "Will we rub?"

"No, he'll manage," Zarina waved her hand, "let him rest after the road..."

Moussa's Antique Store. The buyer paid for the purchase and went to the exit of the store.

"Come again!" Moussa said after her. "Soon there will be new items."

He counted the money and rubbed his hands contentedly. The doorbell rang and Ali entered the store and went to the counter.

"Senior calls, immediately."

"Why such a rush?" Moussa was worried.

"Ask me harder," Ali answered indifferently. "They told me - I informed."

"Okay, I'll just close the store."

"Come on, just be quick."

Ali went to the door and turned the plate so that the inscription "Closed" was visible from the outside. Moussa closed the safe, put the keys in his pocket and went to the window to lower the blinds. When Moussa leaned over, Ali stuck a syringe in the back of his neck. Moussa twitched and went limp. Ali lowered him to the floor, took the keys from his pocket, opened the safe and put all the contents in a bag. Then he opened the cash register and took the money from there. He looked at the recumbent Moussa.

"You won't need it any more."

He took a handkerchief from his pocket, grabbed the door handle, opened it and went outside. He closed the door with the key and headed for the taxi standing nearby, in which Yusuf was sitting...

91

Shahlo's office. A phone rang. She picked up the phone.
"Hello."
Alibek's excited voice was heard over the receiver:
"Shahlo, it's not her! You must come to me urgently!" "Who is not her?" not immediately Shahlo realized.
"Zarina! It was not she who boarded the plane!" Alibek could not restrain his excitement. "I need your help, will you come?"
"Of course I'll come," Shahlo responded immediately.
"Wait." She hung up and smiled pretty.
Ah, yes Alibek, clever one! Still, he looked out for something in this film! She took her purse and left the office...
Alibek opened the door and let Shahlo. He looked excited, there was no trace of past apathy.
"I understand," he grabbed Shahlo by the shoulders, "I realized that I was haunted! It wasn't her!"
"Are you going to shake me like a punchbag for a long time?" Shahlo pleaded. "Sorry, I'm just crazy. Let's go, you'll see yourself."
He led her into a room and sat in front of the TV, pressed a button on the remote control. "Just watch carefully." Shahlo was watching the recording and she hardly managed to keep a worried look. "Well?" she said perplexedly. "I've already seen that – it's nothing new. Explain where to look?"
"Not where, but at what. Look again." He turned on the re-

cording again and in the place where Fatima put her hand on the counter, he took a freeze-frame. "You see?"

"No." Shahlo was sorry to torment Alibek, but she had no choice.

"Well, I didn't see it either, but today I was putting myself in order, and it hit me like

an electric shock. Now tell me: have you ever seen Zarina have such short nails?" He

triumphantly jabbed a finger at the screen.

Shahlo leaned forward and peered at the image.

"No, I haven't," she had to agree.

"Right! The hand is not hers, and that's not her!" He lifted Shahlo from his chair and began circling the room, screaming with joy. "Alive, alive, alive!"

"Let me go, madman," Shahlo laughed, trying to free herself, "you will drop me." Out of breath and joyful, Alibek released Shahlo, and she began to set herself to rights. Sherzod stood at the door of the room and smiled too. "Aunt Shahlo, should I help you fight back?"

"It's useless," Shahlo dismissed, looking at Alibek's happy face. "He's worse than the terminator now."

"Now do you believe that she is alive?" Alibek's eyes shone.

"You will strangle me if I say no. It is clear that she was not at the airport. Only..." she stopped.

"What - only? Today I'll go to draw up documents and fly to look for her," blurted Alibek.

"This is exactly what you should not do now," Shahlo said in a serious tone.

"What are you saying?" Alibek could not believe his ears.

"Alibek, calm down your emotions for a while and listen to me carefully. I'm also very glad that Zarina was not on that plane. But then tell me: if Zarina is alive, then why hasn't she yet appeared?"

"I don't know," Alibek said perplexedly, he somehow did not have time to think about it.

"I don't know either and no one knows yet," continued Shahlo. "So she was in such a serious situation that she could not do this. Do you agree?"

"But ..." Alibek tried to object to her, but Shahlo did not give him such an opportunity.

"Agree or not?"

"Yes, I agree," Alibek reluctantly agreed.

"Therefore, until it becomes clear what kind of situation this is, we cannot rush headlong into search of her without risking harming her. This should be done by professionals. Our business is to give them a task and wait." "How can I harm her?" such a turn unsettled Alibek.

"What if she is held hostage, and then you make a noise?" "Do you suggest that I sit and calmly wait?" he said grimly.

"Yes, sit and wait. Do not interfere with special organs," Shahlo resolutely said...

In the police department, the commissioner was holding an urgent meeting.

"Let's compare all the facts. From the Bureau we were sent a list of people who are being elaborated for the explosion of an airplane. This Moussa also appears on the list. Before we caught hold of him, they killed him. An accident? Inspector, repeat the testimony of that woman."

"She forgot her umbrella in the store, and when she returned to pick it up, she saw that a man had left the store, he closed the store with a key, got into a taxi and drove away. She knew the owner of this store a little, because sometimes she went to him to buy something unusual. The stranger closed the door. It seemed strange to her, and she thought of writing down the number of the car. Then she saw someone's legs through the blinds that were not completely lowered and called us."

"Have you established who the taxi owner is?" the commissar asked.

"Yes," the inspector peered into his notebook. "This is a certain Yusuf Mehdi. He's not on our files."

"This does not mean that it cannot be a link in the chain." The commissioner looked at the inspector. "If they sensed something and began to remove the excess, then it could well become the next one. Immediately place him under surveillance and make sure that he is not perforated ahead of time."

"I will instruct my people, Mr.
Commissioner." "Every step and contact."
"I got it, Mr. Commissioner. Can I go?"
"Go..."

92

Zarina is sitting in the room, holding a gift in her palms. She looks thoughtful, as if she is trying to resurrect something in her memory. From this state, Dietrich's voice brought her out.

"Honey, are you ready?"

"I'm coming." She put the lamp on the shelf and went to Dietrich. He admired her. "Is there some kind of compliment I haven't given you yet?"

"Should I have a special register?" Zarina smiled.

"Later. Let's have dinner first. Taxi is waiting."

They left the house and got into a taxi waiting for them. When they drove away from the house, Zarina saw through the glass a man who was rubbing the glass of his car. It was Yusuf. For a moment, their eyes met. Zarina frowned, and Dietrich noticed this.

"Something is wrong?" he asked.

"I do not know. That man by the car." She hesitated. "For a second it seemed to me that I had already seen him somewhere, and my goose bumps ran wild and all this nonsense is creeping into my head. Do not pay attention."

"Maybe we'll be back, and I'll deal with him?" "And because of this get no desert? Never!"

The inspector got in touch with the observation team.

"How is our ward?"

"A little strange, Mr. Inspector," the observer answered. "He seems to be doing surveillance himself."

"Find out who interests him so much."

"One is Dr. Gruber," the observer explained, "but we could not find out who his companion was. Appearance is eastern."

"But this is already interesting. Keep an eye on him, report constantly..."

Dinner was already drawing to a close when Zarina once again massaged her temple.

"Headache?" Dietrich asked sympathetically and took Zarina by the hand.

"No, but today I've not been at ease all day. Sometimes pictures slip through my eyes, but I do not have time to catch them. This taxi driver for some reason does not get out of my head, but I don't know him?" either asking or asserting, said Zarina. "Sorry, I'm spoiling the dinner."

"Nonsense, you can't spoil anything. It's just that you are no longer used to the hustle and bustle, I have kept you locked up for too long. Do you want to go and just walk the streets?"

"I think, yes." They got up and went to the exit...

Dietrich and Zarina left the restaurant and slowly walked along the street. A noisy group of punks passed by and Zarina turned after them and again saw Yusuf on the other side of the street. Their eyes met. She grabbed Dietrich by the hand.

"It's him again, Dietrich. What does he want?" she said ,startled.

"Who?" He stroked her hand.

"That taxi driver I saw near the house. I'm scared. Let's get out of here fast."

"Why on earth should we run from someone?" Dietrich was

indignant. "Now I'll go and find out what he wants from us."

"No, Dietrich, don't go to hell with him," Zarina prayed.

"I'm sorry, but I won't let anyone scare you."

He resolutely pushed Zarina away and moved towards Yusuf.

He fussed, got into the car and started the engine to leave. Dietrich, who came up through the window, grabbed Yusuf, trying to stop him.

Yusuf grabbed his gun, shot Dietrich and sped off. Zarina heard the shot and, rushing towards it, almost fell under the wheels. Dietrich was still standing, pressing his hand to his left side, blood flowing out from under his hand. He began slowly to sink to the ground.

Zarina screamed. People began to run there and someone called an ambulance.

Zarina sank to the ground next to Dietrich, and raised his head. He was still conscious.

Zarina burst into tears.

"Dietrich ... Dietrich ... don't dare to die..."

"How ... unsuccessful ... it turned out ..." His lips hardly moved.

"An ambulance is coming, I beg you, just don't die ..." "Ask... genie..." whispered Dietrich.

His head leaned back lifelessly.

"Dietrich!" cried Zarina. Doctors ran up from the ambulance that arrived, put it on a stretcher and carried it into a car. Zarina lost consciousness...

Zarina is sitting in one of the offices of the police station, next to her a doctor is giving her an injection. She has a tormented and indifferent look. An inspector entered the office.

"How are you feeling?"

"It seems to me that I already feel nothing..." "Can you answer some questions?"

"Now, it seems, yes..." Zarina's gaze became somehow tense.

"Sorry, I don't quite understand," the inspector was puzzled by this answer. "Why now?"

"Memory... memory is returning to me... Oh my God," Zarina clasped her head in her hands, "They lost me, they went crazy, and I'm here... I need to call, say I'm alive... Give me the phone, then questions, please ..."

"Well, come with me..." Said the inspector who did not understand anything from these incoherent phrases, but decided not to rush things with an immediate interrogation.

After Zarina's call home, the inspector led her into his office. He poured a glass of water and handed it to her.

"Drink, you will feel better."

"Thank you," Zarina took a sip, "It's already easier for me but is Dietrich alive?" She asked hopefully in her voice.

"They couldn't save Dr. Gruber. I'm sorry."

Zarina closed her eyes with force, tears appeared in the corners.

"He still gave back. Ask, Inspector..."

Zarina went to the stove with the name of Dietrich, laid flowers, stood, took out a small copper jug from her bag and wanted to put it, but stopped. Then gently rubbed its surface and whispered:

"Tell him that I will remember him."

She carefully put the jug on the stove, straightened. Tears appeared in her eyes. She took a handkerchief from her purse, put it to her eyes, then turned and walked slowly...

93

When Emir's squad reached the sacred spring, it became clear that Firuz-begim was also seriously ill, while caring for Emir's mother. She was put in a small decrepit house of an old woman, the same one that Iskander had recently met and who had given him an amulet. Alimkhan is sitting by the bed of Firuz-begim.

"First mother, now you... Why do I have such trials?" "Don't say that, my lord. So, Allah wishes so."

"To take away my closest people?"

"No, to save the life of our son. You must go."

"And leave you?"

At this time, the door opened and the squad leader looked into the room.

"What else?" Alimkhan angrily attacked him.

"Sorry, my lord, the messenger has arrived, something very urgent." "Let him go to the door."

He stood up and blocked the doorway. A messenger came up from that side.

"They're coming, my lord ..." he began the report loudly.

"Speak quietly ..." interrupted Alimkhan.

"They're coming..." the messenger repeated already in an undertone. "Two days' journey..."

"Are there many of them?"

"Many, my lord..."

Alimkhan frowned.

"Alright. Go."

He returned to Firuz-begim's bed.

"Are they chasing us, my lord?" Firuz-begim asked, who heard the beginning of the conversation.

"That should not bother you. You need to get better, and then we will go further." "No, this must not be done…" protested Firuz-begim. "You must not risk yourself and our son." She coughed, tears appeared in her eyes. "Leave, I beg you. For the sake of our son. Please… Just let me say goodbye to him…"

Alimkhan took Firuz-begim's hand and pressed it to his lips. Then, without saying a word, he got up and quickly left the room. After a few seconds, a boy entered the room.

"Father told me that we were leaving without you. Why?"

"That's right, son. I'll get better and catch up with you. Will you wait for your mom?" "Of course I will. I know that will help you. Here…" He took off the amulet from his neck and put it on Firuz-begim's neck. "It will protect you from troubles and diseases, I know."

"Where did you get it from?"

"Iskander gave it to me and told me not to show it to anyone except you. Now he will protect you too."

"Thank you, son, now I'm calm. Go, I need to relax. Do not forget your mother…" She closed her eyes, sweat appeared on her forehead. The boy kissed her cheek and quietly left the room. Alimkhan stood near the house and talked with the old woman. "Take care of her and do everything as it's required." He handed her a bag of money: "That should be enough for you."

"What do I need money for in the wilderness? What will I do,

look at them?" "They'll come in handy for something. We have to go." He took the boy's hand and they went to the squad.

Iskander woke up, looked around in surprise at the room in which he was lying.

An old man came up to him.

"Woke up, son?"

"Where am I?" Iskander asked.

"At my place. My grandson saw you and brought you."

"How long have I been here?"

"It is the second day since. Like a dead man you were lying, I began to worry." "Second day?" Iskander tried to jump out of bed, but his legs did not obey him and he lay down again. "I have to go…"

"But where do you have to go in this state? Your legs don't hold you. Here, have a drink."

"What is this?"

"This? This will make your legs run faster. Its taste is, of course, nasty, but the benefits of it - wow!"

Iskander took the extended mug and drank it in one gulp. Then he wrinkled. "Really nasty. What are you preparing this poison from, father?"

"You better not know, son. Drink and be good. Soon you will feel better, then you will move where you need to."

"Are you sure?"

"Sure, sure," the old man grinned. "I doubt you are the first."

"Something is driving me to sleep again…"

"It should be so. Sleep a little more, you will be very healthy."

"Okay. It's just not for long…"

His eyes closed and he leaned back on the pillow.

The old woman entered the room where Firuz-begim was lying, and leaned over her.

She saw an amulet that was hanging around Firuz-begim's neck.

"So, after all, he gave up his defense. So, she is dearer to him than life. What am I to do with you, girl? Okay, let's try one remedy. You must be young. You look and get better. What will I tell him when he comes for you? He will come, he will certainly come..."

Iskander is walking along the road, leaning on a staff, approaching a hut at a sacred spring. An old woman came out to meet him.

"Well, finally appeared. How long have you been looking for her..."

"So is she here?!" a smile shone on Iskander's face.

"Here, here, where else can she be? Everyone left her, they did not hope that she

would survive. Here you are alone."

"What do you mean by "will she survive?""

"She was ill, very ill. I myself began to doubt whether I could heal her up. However, it turned out, I could, you can come in and say hello. Or were you just walking by?"

"Yes, I came for her, her!"

Iskander ran to the hut, opened the door and froze on the threshold...

94

The plane landed at Tashkent airport.

Zarina went down the ramp. On the field there are all her loved ones. She stepped to the ground, bags fell out of her hands, and she rushed to meet them.

After a few days, all three friends, their children, husbands scurry around in the yard, they set tables, and music plays.

Firuz-begim is reclining in her favorite chair, occasionally sipping a hookah and watching with gratification this joyous bustle.

"Praise to the Creator, for the Blessedness and Love given to Man, for the wisdom and the reason for man, using his strength in good intentions. Amen." She said quietly...

At that moment she was hugged from the back by Shahlo and she brought a bottle of perfume straight to her face...

"My beloved and dear, the wisest of the wisest - I present you the world's first Begim branded perfume called "Bukhara Spirit", produced in France based on very rare essential oils that you told us so often about - musk and ambergris, saffron and jasmine, cinnamon and vanilla. The scent of the Wise and Great woman who follows the Great and Wise man... The spirit of Sacred Bukhara...

Firuz-begim plunged into the scent of a new perfume and tears of happiness and joy, love and pride came out in her eyes for her people and the country where she lives her long, beautiful life...

Grandchildren and great-grandchildren rush and sit down near Firuz-begim and

Sitora slyly asked her:

"My mother told me. Is it true that you were the last wife of the Emir of Bukhara?" "True," she grinned.

"Only a long time ago, oh, how long..." "How did you live then? Tell me, huh?" Sitora cried.

"How?" Firuz-begim's eyes clouded, rushing into the distant past, a hand reached for a hookah ... "But didn't I tell you in childhood, my girl...?"

Firuz-begim reclined on gilded Bukhara sewing pillows with the invariable Crystal hookah of the mother of the last Emir of Bukhara, which at one time smelled a mist of scents in the Arjuman-begim's treasury in the Taj Mahal palace and this is

another story, a fairy tale or perhaps a true story.

Firuz-begim through the prism of a crystal hookah quietly and carefully removed an amulet from the bottom of the bottle with the burial plan of the Treasures of the Emirate of Bukhara...

She managed to save this piece of history and maybe her children will find their grandfather's treasure or maybe they will have other values and maybe they will have many more children and they will feel their own peculiarity without treasures and without hoard...

But no one will know about it...

So it was decided... Maktub...

Such is Fate... Matlub...

The last Emir of Bukhara, Said Alim Khan, was buried in Afghanistan in 1944 in the Kabul cemetery "Shukhadoi Solikhin" - "Cemetery of the Holy Martyrs". He bequeathed to cut out the following lines on the gravestone:

"Amiri Bevatan Zoruhakirast
Gadogar Dar Vatanmirad - Amirast"
"The Emir without a homeland is miserable and insignificant,
A beggar who died in his homeland is verily the Emir."

Parable:
A long string of caravans was stretching from faraway Persia to the kingdom of Emir of Bukhara.

Camels, laden with bales with luxurious fabrics, carpets and chests with jewels, slowly moved through the Karakum desert. Merchants, accompanying their wealth, were impatiently waiting for the appearance of the city outlines.

Among them was the young Saeed-Yahyo, the son of Mahmoud, the owner of Tehran's jewelry workshops.

Years passed, the goods had long been sold out, and most compatriots of Saeed-Yahyo returned to their homeland. But, the young man really loved the fertile land of Bukhara and its benevolent people. He bought a house in Zirabad (near Bukhara), where many merchants from Iran had already settled, and married his compatriot, the Persian Khadycha.

Having bought land nearby, he, along with hired workers, began to grow cotton. The last treasure chest that remained with him promised a well-off life for his family. And the future seemed beautiful to him, but the revolution that took place in Russia turned everything upside down. The remaining Iranians, including their relatives, began to hastily move abroad, but Saeed-Yahyo again decided to stay.

Children appeared in their family: they named their first-born Saeed-Meri, after him the sons Saeed-Ahmad, Saeed-Jalol and daughter Sadyka-begim were born. Later, their father will explain the meaning of the prefixes to their names:

"They mean belonging to our family - the descendants of the Great

Prophet Muhammad. It is extended along the male line, and all his sons are Seyyids, and their daughters are Begim. On the seventh day after Eid, Seyyid Day is celebrated. They say that everyone, who was able to visit and congratulate the seven descendants of the Prophet that day, is considered to have performed a charitable deed. Allah helps the Seyyids in all endeavors, remember this and live. After the birth of the daughter Khadycha-begim became seriously ill and soon died. Being left alone, Saeed-Yahyo continues to work and take care of very young children. In the future, they will often recall how in the evenings the father would gather all the children near the fire and tell them an amazing story about the adventures of Amir Arslan. In the mid-80s, an elderly Saeed-Jalol would find this book, entitled "Amir Arslan - the Persian Dastan," and immediately buy three copies: for himself, his brother and sister. This fascinating tale will give them a few more hours of a very short childhood.

1937 came. Armed men in uniform burst into the courtyard, bind Saeed-Yahyo and took him away, not even allowing him to say goodbye to the children. He only manages to give barely noticeable signs to his youngest son, who was barely ten years old. With the onset of twilight, adults - distant relatives and neighbors - began to come up to their homes. Little naive Jalol began to tell them all the details of the day's incident, not forgetting to mention that his father repeatedly pointed his eyes to the dog kennel. It became clear to everyone that exactly there a treasure chest was buried, the existence of which many of them knew.

But the time was already late, and therefore it was decided to postpone the search for treasure to the next day. Waking up in the morning, the children found that the whole yard was dug up. But, despite this, they dug up all over again, and all those who came yesterday zealously helped them. Of course, they did not find anything. The chest, together *with hope for the future of orphaned children, was mercilessly stolen that night.*

And this did not end there. Soon the land was taken from them, and the children were left without any ways and means of existence. Nothing was known about the father. Only in 1986, after countless requests from the brothers Ahmad and Jalol to the authorities, a response will be received in which it will be said that Said-Yahyo, repressed in 1937, was shot in 1939 for espionage. But also documents will be found relating to the case, refuting the accusation and confirming his heroic deed, which saved the whole village from the Basmatch raid. He would be rehabilitated posthumously. In Zirabad, they will call the street by the name of Said-Yahyo Makhmudov and give his sons his military ID, so they will have the first and only photograph of his father.

Let's go back to the past. The boys, left alone, undertook any work to feed themselves. The eight-year-old Sadyka took over the entire house- hold in the house. Probably, it was then that they rallied together and carried their friendship and love through their whole lives, caring for each other until the last day.

1941 year. Nineteen-year-old Saeed-Meri was taken to the front. At first, the relatives received news from him, but in 1942 they received a notice that Saeed-Meri was missing. Until now no one knows what happened to him and how he died.

During the war, all the boys wanted to seem much older and more adult, and that is probably why Said-Jalol and his friends decided to get their own tattoos.

It is very strange that Jalol, who has not yet turned 14, asks to depict a heart pierced by an arrow on his left hand, and under it write a woman's name – Lyuba. "Who is Lyuba," the guys were surprised. "I don't know, but I like that name," Jalol replied. The fact that this tattoo was crucial, he would understand much later. In the meantime, the war was on, and he and Saeed-Ahmad were working from morning till night, however, they barely had enough money to earn a living.

After the war, it got worse. Men returning from the front occupy their jobs, and the brothers are left without work. Hoping for luck, they moved to Bukhara. Having asserted that their documents were lost during the war, they received passports where the brothers state "Uzbek" in the "nationality" column. Knowledgeable people suggested that it would be easier for them to find a job. But this did not help Saeed-Jalol, and he continued to beat down the doors in the city.

He was noticed, however, not by those who were needed. After the war, the growth of banditry reached its peak. So the people of one of these groups saw a nimble assistant in the young kid. They invited him to be on the watch when they robbed a grocery store. For this, they promised him several cans of stew and loaves of bread. Jalol's doubts immediately dissipated, as he imagined his sister, rejoicing at such abundance. Everything went smoothly, and the bandits kept their word. Happily, he ran home with a bag of groceries, but there he was disappointed: the stern look of his brother and desperate eyes of his sister. He was forced to tell them everything. In the morning they went to the district police officer, where he wrote a sincere acknowledgement.

The gang was taken on hot scent, and all goods were returned. Given the assistance in capturing the bandits, the court was lenient to Saeed-Jalol and sent to a labor camp in the town of Chirchik.

Jalol remained grateful to his elder brother for life that he did not allow him to take the wrong path, despite even the deprivation of his freedom, during which the most important and main meeting in his life would occur.

***

The head of the Yakubovs family was the laconic, seemingly stern, Ghafur. His wife, Mahbuba, tall, with proud posture, spent all day in the kitchen. To feed her large family, she baked cakes every morning and cooked several times a day. Three daughters and four sons, the eldest of whom recently returned from the front - that's all the wealth that remained after her war. But she was the daughter of a noble merchant from Fergana and used to live in luxury.

Her dad, Olim-khuja, being a nine-year-old boy, fled home and went in search of his missing father, who several years ago went to Mecca with pilgrims and did not return.

Little Olim joined the caravan to Saudi Arabia, and returned home only nine years later. The servant, who opened the door to him, ran to report to the owners that some stranger in a white robe had come to them. Hearing about this, Olim's elder brother immediately realized that it was their brother who returned, and he was not mistaken. Soon Olim-khuja married, and he had 5 daughters, one of whom was Mahbuba. He continued the trading business of his father and managed numerous stores located in Fergana, Kokand and Tashkent. Traveling to different countries, he brought goods from Russia, India, France. And his daughters always had exquisite outfits and French perfumes.

Olim-khuja was a deeply religious and respectable man, and he always helped poor people. By his order, huge cauldrons were placed in the streets at every Eid, and they distributed the festive pilaf to all the hungry and destitute ones. And anyone in need could always find support and help from him.

For charitable activities and a generous heart, the Gates of Fergana were named after him, through which he entered the city, returning from Mecca.

After the revolution, in order to avoid complete confiscation, Olim-khuja decided to give the youngest daughters away in marriage and

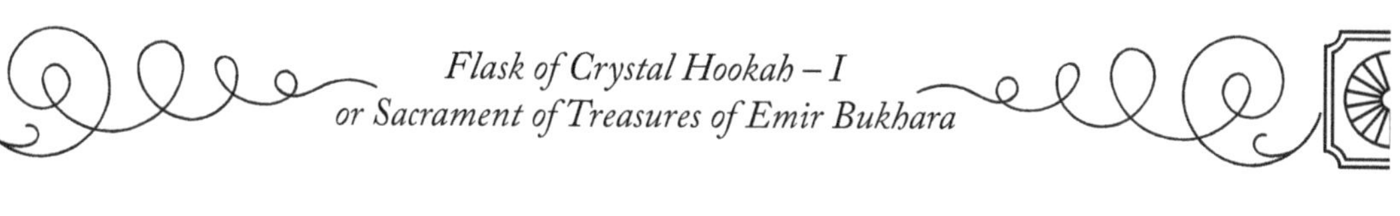

share all the gold and jewelry between them. Mahbuba was to marry Ghafur, the son of Yakub, the owner of huge vineyards in Tashkent. True, this was not included into young Ghafur's plans at all. Imbued with revolutionary ideas with all his heart, he traveled around the cities and villages with the propaganda brigade, and his marriage hindered his active revolutionary life. To avoid this fate, he ran away from his wedding three times, jumping over the fence. But each time he was caught and returned back.

Years passed. Their children grew up: Fattah, Sattar, Matlyuba, Vahed, Maksuda, Rano and Gavkhar. With their noble blood, the parents passed them the love and desire for knowledge, a deep decency, which will forever remain as the hallmark of the whole Yakubovs family.

When the war began, Ghafur worked as the head of the Chirchik trade base, and he was responsible for sending wagons with bread to the front. But in 1942, a major shortage was discovered at the base. The culprit was found and shot, but Ghafur, as the head of the base, could not avoid the punishment. He was convicted of negligence and sentenced to three years in prison. It was hard for Mahbuba, she was left alone with her children, to survive the war years. She had to sell gold and jewelry that she received as a dowry. For the proceeds, she bought food, cooked for children, and sent parcels to her husband.

The eleven-year-old daughter Matlyuba saddled herself with all the household management and care for her brothers and younger sisters. She bathed them, dressed, fed, washed and cleaned the house. During these years, she was not only an elder sister for them, but also a mother.

After his release, Ghafur could not find a job for a long time and eventually got a job as a seller in a grocery store in Akhangaran. The eldest daughter Matluba often came to him and on a fateful day, as always, was nearby.

On the day of the Great Victory, Ghafur closed the store in the evening. But here a group of drunken soldiers came who had just returned from the war. Feeling like heroes, they demanded to open a shop and treat them with vodka. Upon Ghafur's refusal, they began to beat him right in front of his daughter. Ghafur fell backwards, and they were kicking him with their boots everywhere. It is not known how this would end if people hadn't run to the cries of Matluba.

After the beating, Ghafur's blind eye forever remained half-covered by the eyelid. In general, he survived only thanks to the miraculous potions of Mahbuba, who prepared her powders and tinctures from various plants, and sometimes even used dried snakes. She determined their healing properties by smell, taste, and intuition, putting deep faith in the preparation of the medicine, which strengthened its healing effect a hundredfold.

Educated, fluent in Russian and Arabic, Mahbuba was a real poet, philosophically reflecting the reality of life in her poems.

Despite her husband's devotion to the Soviet regime, she never accepted this

*authority and was always proud of her "blue blood". Having stepped into the 21st century, she will tell her grandchildren and great-grandchildren the real story of the entire 20th century, seen with her own eyes and distorted by communist chroniclers. ****

Chirchik is a small town, and every day, going to school, Matlyuba walked along the fences of the forced labor colony. She had a red coat, given by her elder brother, slightly encircling her graceful figure.

Once, returning home, she heard a voice calling to her: "Hey, girl in red! Give a cigarette to the unfortunate!" Turning, through a metal fence, she saw a young guy with starry eyes and black curly hair.

One glance was enough, and his image was indelibly engraved on

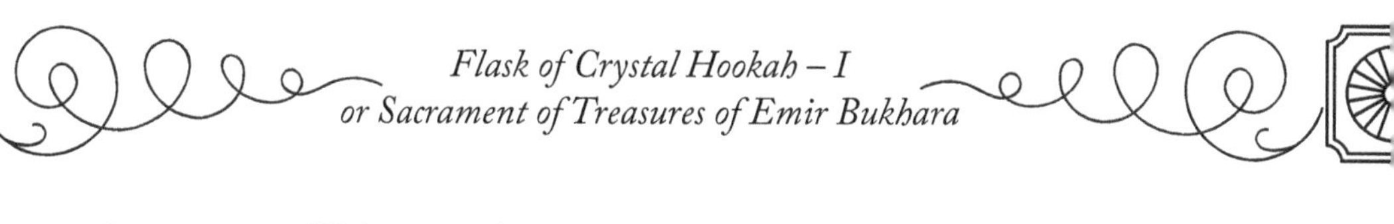

her memory. Waking up from a daze, she rushed home. For a long time he could not take his eyes off the runaway figure of a girl looking like the eastern peri.

The next day, Said-Jalol, and this, of course, was him, was already waiting for his beautiful stranger at the same time. Again, running past the colony, Matluba heard the familiar phrase: "Hey, girl in red! Give a cigarette to the unfortunate!" Arriving home, Matlyuba firmly decided to save on a school lunch and buy him cigarettes. So, she did, and, passing the colony, threw a pack of cigarettes through the bars right at the feet of Jalol.

Many days passed of their silent conversation. Flushed feelings in the soul of a young girl struggled with her good manners, which did not allow her to talk with unfamiliar guys, especially a prisoner.

Then one day she still slowed down her steps, allowing him to speak to herself. So they met. Short conversations through the bars brought the young people closer, and each time they parted, they continued to mentally communicate with each other.

During his imprisonment, Jalol graduated from high school and improved his Russian language. Thinking in Tajik, he was also fluent in Azerbaijani, which he knew thanks to his friends from Zirabad. Jalol began to study the native language of his beloved – Uzbek, and with his amazing memory it was not at all difficult.

Meanwhile, his imprisonment was drawing to a close, and the young people dreamed of meeting at large. But "kind" people informed Matluba to her mother. Mahbuba, beside herself with anger and shame, beat her and forbade even to pass the colony. But, despite this, the meetings of the young continued, however, much less often and with greater caution. The day of Jalol's liberation was approaching, and with good intentions he was preparing to get married to Matluba. He was dressed by all the "honest people" - his friends gave him the best. And the colony overseer Rakhmonbek volunteered to accompany him, who grew fond of Jalol as his son.

Opening the treasured gate, they saw a huge courtyard, two large houses located perpendicular to each other, and a beautiful garden with blooming roses and numerous trees. At the end of the path a woman was standing in a long dress and white shawl, famously tied to one side, from which two neatly braided plaits came down. From afar, Mahbuba tried to make out the faces of the people who entered, but then she noticed a screaming Matluba, who ran to hide in a closet, and understood everything. Outraged, she called her husband and was ready to drive away uninvited guests who had the audacity to come to their house, but Ghafur stopped her. In the doorway of the open door of the closet, he saw the eyes of his eldest daughter, full of tears and cries for help. "It's not customary for us to drive away guests, even uninvited ones," with these words he invited those who came to sit on the summer terrace on the aivan.

After listening to Rakhmonbek and Jalol, who told him the whole story of his life, he turned to the young guy: "Son, you are still very young, although you had to go through a lot. You have no specialty, no job. Our daughter is used to living in abundance, but what are you going to support your family for? You must first continue your education, find a decent job, so that we can entrust our daughter to you, and then we'll talk."

With these words, he saw Jalol off, who firmly set himself the goal of doing everything exactly as the father of his beloved said.

*Matlyuba's parents did not expect that he would enter this gate again soon, in just three years, but Makhmudov Jalol Yahyayevich they would call him. ****

In a year and a half, Jalol externally graduates from the Kokand

Automobile College and begins to work as a teacher in the Bukhara Driving School. A year later, he was transferred to the city of Denau, where he soon became the director of the Surkhandarya Driving School. He had no end of his students, and he was rolling in money.

Having accumulated a large amount, he went to Bukhara to his brother, who by that time was already working as an engineer of the Bukhara construction trust.

Jalol asked Ahmad to go with him to Chirchik to marry Matluba, whose thoughts about her did not leave him for a minute. Of course, the elder brother agreed, and they hit the road.

And two Iranians turned to the street leading to the Yakubovs' house. In fashionable clothes, polished shoes and a bag of money, they proudly walked past neighbors who opened their mouths.

Saeed-Ahmad was a very handsome man: tall, broad-shouldered, white-skinned, with regular features. Seeing him, all the women shouted in joy at the sight.

"Look, look, an angel has come down from heaven." It was really impossible to take the eyes off them, they were completely different and unlike anyone. Who are they? Where are they going?

The answer to this question was not long in coming...

Matlyuba's father kept his word and agreed.

On December 16, 1952, Said-Jalol and Matlyuba were married.

The wedding was modest, and the very next day they went to Bukhara...

Bukhoroi-Sharif... Sacred Bukhara...

Reviews

REVIEWS

Gulchekhra-begim Makhmudova's The Flask of the Crystal Hookah is an evocative and intricately woven novel that transports readers into the heart of Central Asia's rich historical landscape. Blending elements of adventure, mysticism, and philosophy, the novel sheds light on the overlooked experiences of Eastern women, positioning them at the forefront of history rather than relegating them to the shadows.

At its core, the novel is a meditation on time, memory, and destiny, centered around the symbolic Crystal Hookah, which serves as a bridge between generations. Through this mystical lens, the reader experiences the grandeur and tragedy of the Bukhara Emirate's final days, the rise of Soviet rule, and the evolving roles of women in a world shaped by power and upheaval. The prose is layered with Sufi wisdom, Persian poetic influences, and vivid descriptions of a world both real and dreamlike, offering a reading experience that is at once philosophical and deeply human.

One of the book's greatest strengths is its depiction of women as the quiet architects of history - whether through resilience, intellect, or sheer survival. Figures like Firuz-begim, the last wife of the Emir, and Matlyuba, a young woman caught between tradition and change, offer a nuanced perspective on the sacrifices and strength of Central Asian women throughout history. This is particularly significant given the historical tendency to reduce these women to passive figures, when in reality, they played crucial roles as advisors, poets, healers, and guardians of cultural identity.

While the novel is richly atmospheric and deeply researched, it demands patience. Its non-linear structure, shifting timelines, and philosophical interludes require careful reading.

FINAL THOUGHTS

Makhmudova's novel is a compelling contribution to Central Asian literature, offering a poignant exploration of history, power, and the endurance of the human spirit. It stands out for its lyrical prose, historical depth, and its unique focus on the lived experiences of women in a region often examined through the lens of war and empire.

For readers drawn to historical fiction infused with mysticism and poetic depth, this book is a rewarding, albeit demanding, read. It is especially valuable for those interested in the cultural history of Central Asia, feminist perspectives in literature, and the philosophy of fate and memory.

Strengths: Poetic language, historical richness, unique female perspectives.

A deeply reflective and thought-provoking novel that lingers long after the final page.

— Anar Umurzak,
founder of Innova Portfolio, LLC, USA based education and business partner across Central Asia, UK and USA, Business Development Director of Kazakhstan Cultural Business Association of North America, author of the business methodology book: "Magic of S.C.A.L.E.: AI's Deep Dive into Entrepreneurial Wisdom"

The book opens with a vivid depiction of the ancient city of Bukhara, where the author seeks to highlight its grandeur and unique character, infused with the aromas of the East. Then, almost imperceptibly, the reader's imagination paints the portrait of a little girl - the main heroine of the story. A tragic episode from her childhood abruptly cuts off, and like swirling clouds of hookah smoke, scenes from her life begin to emerge.

Suddenly, the reader is immersed in a new atmosphere - this time, the harem of the Emir of Bukhara - where fresh strokes further shape the heroine's portrait. But just as before, this episode intriguingly dissipates like hookah smoke, dissolving into the magical ambiance of the ancient city. With the same ease, the author moves through time, portraying the heroine in her old age. Through her memories, new characters appear, shifting the reader's focus to the life of her granddaughter.

The author employs a fascinating technique, allowing the reader to explore the heroine's character from multiple perspectives, gradually revealing her identity through her connection with her granddaughter. However, as the story approaches the modern era, the lives of the characters lose the distinct aroma of the East, blending more with European culture. Borders fade, and the characters, now almost indistinguishable from Europeans, move effortlessly from one country to another.

The book captivates with its rich characters, relationships, emotions, and conflicts. The author delves into profound themes such as friendship, love, human dignity, betrayal, and loyalty. Suddenly, within the framework of a family saga, mysteries from the legendary past of the East emerge, igniting the reader's imagination and creating an intricate puzzle that demands unraveling.

The novel presents two contrasting worlds - one, authentic and filled with intrigue and treachery under the absolute power of the Emir of Bukhara, and the other, post-revolutionary, striving for European values and equality. Only the main heroine, Firuz-begim, belongs to both worlds, serving as the delicate thread where they intertwine.

It is worth noting that the book is written in a fluid and engaging style, making it a compelling read from start to finish. The author vividly and realistically portrays each episode, with every character's story strong enough to form the basis of an entire novel. These stories interweave, like beads strung onto the thread of history, connecting different eras. Through the lives, struggles, and joys of individual people, the reader witnesses the unfolding of history - not as something distant and abstract but as a vivid, mosaic-like picture where each piece holds significance.

And in the epilogue, Firuz-begim, surrounded by family and friends, remains the guardian of both history and treasures, seated in her favorite chair, enveloped in the fragrance of a new perfume. Tears shimmer in her eyes - tears born from memories rising through the prism of the Crystal Hookah, dissolving into the air and leaving behind only a faint trace of the enchanting East.

— Tatiana Zamyatkina,
art historian and observer, Moscow State University,
artist, English and Italian teacher

For book lovers eager to embark on an intriguing journey across multiple historical epochs, diverse geographical landscapes, and the full spectrum of human emotions, The Flask of the Crystal Hookah – Part I: The Sacraments of the Treasures of the Emir of Bukhara by Uzbek author Gulchekhra-begim Makhmudova is a captivating choice.

Reading this novel feels like setting out on an adventure, encountering a vast array of characters, each with their own unique role in the unfolding story. While the central intrigue revolves around the life, destiny, and hidden mysteries of the Emir of Bukhara, the true key figures of the novel are the women of Central Asia - bound by blood and spirit yet divided by generations.

I was particularly drawn to the life stories of three friends - Lola, Marina, and Shohul - and the way the author portrays their relationships, interactions, and emotional experiences, whether joyful or sorrowful. Through their eyes, events in Central Asia and beyond are brought to life, giving the reader an intimate perspective on both personal and historical narratives.

Some chapters delve into contemporary times, offering reflections on recent experiences that may resonate with many readers. The novel's plot is full of twists and turns, keeping me engaged and constantly guessing what would happen next. The blend of reality and fiction is masterfully handled, making many of the described events feel strikingly real.

Among the book's most compelling aspects are the historical references to times long past - eras I have never experienced personally, yet found fascinating. These elements add depth to the novel, enriching its themes and providing a solid historical foundation for the author's ideas. I particularly admired the portrayal of Firuz-begim, Shohul's grandmother. As a bridge between Uzbekistan's past and present, she embodies wisdom, resilience, and cultural continuity. The narrative reveres her, presenting her as a guardian of history, traditions, and untold secrets. Some of her scenes are steeped in realism, whether depicting personal, everyday events or pivotal historical moments. Others, by contrast, feel almost ethereal, like fragments of an ancient fairy tale.

And therein lies the magic of this novel - the seamless interplay between reality and imagination. A skilled author, Makhmudova invites readers into a world where thoughts, memories, and inspirations intertwine, creating an immersive and enchanting experience.

The novel's rich tapestry of events and emotions - melancholy, mystery, suspense, joy - captivates from the first page. The intricate balance between logical developments and unexpected plot twists keeps each chapter dynamic and engaging. Some episodes evoke fear, others awe, and at times, the narrative demands careful attention to unravel its full meaning. Yet, this deliberate ambiguity enhances the story, allowing space for the reader's own imagination to fill the gaps. The book compelled me to turn the pages eagerly, fully immersed in its world.

I would highly recommend this novel to women of all ages and backgrounds, as it offers something for everyone - whether through its personal narratives, historical depth, or detective-adventure elements. Despite the title's reference to the Emir of Bukhara - undeniably a powerful male presence - the novel ultimately centers on Eastern women as the true guardians of his secrets, the custodians of cultural heritage and traditions.

Reading The Flask of the Crystal Hookah – Part I felt like listening to a modern-day Scheherazade, a gifted storyteller who weaves wisdom into every tale. It is a novel that inspires curiosity, encourages a thirst for knowledge, and reminds us of the power of storytelling itself.

— Oga Igumnova,
The ECG Guardians Council Member,
Coventry, UK

Gulchekhra-Begim Makhmudova's novel is a historical-philosophical melodrama, where past and present, reality and fiction, seamlessly intertwine. The author weaves a multi-layered narrative spanning several eras, unveiling the complex destinies of people whose lives are deeply intertwined with historical events.

At the heart of the book is Firuz-begim, the last wife of the last Emir of Bukhara. It is through her memories that the main storyline unfolds. Firuz-begim has lived a long life, witnessing changes in power, political upheavals, and the transformation of traditional Eastern society. Her perspective on the past is filled not only with personal experiences but also with profound wisdom. The author vividly portrays the clash of two worlds—the old East, governed by its own customs and traditions, and a new era where those traditions are gradually fading away.

A key symbol of the novel is the Crystal Hookah. It is more than just an object; it serves as a bridge between different times. The fates of the characters revolve around it, and it imbues the narrative with themes of memory, nostalgia, and philosophical reflections on the inevitability of time. This detail enhances the novel's atmosphere, making it both poetic and deeply meaningful.

Structurally, the novel consists of multiple interwoven stories. This enriches the narrative but also demands the reader's full attention. The author incorporates numerous references to Eastern culture, Sufi philosophy, and classical poetry. Quotes from poets and sages, as well as descriptions of rituals and traditions, add depth and historical authenticity to the work. However, this approach also makes the text more complex—it requires focus and thoughtful reading.

One of the novel's greatest strengths is its language and attention to detail. The author vividly and respectfully portrays everyday life, customs, and human relationships in Eastern society. Bukhara is not just a setting but a living city with a rich history, becoming a character in its own right. The reader can almost hear the rustling of silk, the melodies of traditional music, and the measured conversations of the townspeople.

However, for those accustomed to fast-paced plots, the novel may seem too slow. The author prioritizes introspection, internal conflicts, and historical context, which slows down the action. Readers seeking suspenseful twists or intense intrigue may find it harder to stay engaged throughout the book.

Overall, The Flask of the Crystal Hookah – 1 is a work for those who appreciate contemplative, philosophical literature. It will appeal to readers interested in Eastern culture, history, and traditions, as well as those who value rich literary language and atmospheric storytelling. The novel requires a certain mindset and a reflective approach, but for those willing to immerse themselves in its world, it offers a truly enriching literary experience.

— Zlata Klabukova,
writer, photographer, book and photo
exhibitions organiser, speaker

www.ingramcontent.com/pod-product-compliance
Lightning Source LLC
Chambersburg PA
CBHW040802010826

48981CB00029B/154